Edge of Pathos

The Conjurors Series

By

Kristen Pham

Chapter I

Valerie and Henry walked together to Babylon, not saying a word. She carried an urn with the ashes of the fallen flowers from her father's garden, since they couldn't bury his body.

Henry's mind had been shut tightly against her in the three weeks since Oberon had died, but now, for the first time, some of his emotions leaked out. At the taste of his grief, Valerie couldn't repress a little sob. Henry gripped her hand.

"He's with Mom, in the ether," Valerie said when she was sure her voice wouldn't shake.

"If you believe in that stuff," Henry said.

Valerie didn't reply, but she did believe. She had been at her father's side when a burst of power had been released into the universe at his death. He was somewhere, or everywhere, and that thought was the only thing that kept her grief from crippling her on some days.

Henry pulled aside a screen of vines, and they stepped into the most stunning spot in the universe. But its beauty was the painful kind, a reminder of times too sweet to last, like when their father had locked this place away from the world so it could be his private Eden with their mother.

They walked up the tiers of flowers and stopped at the top, where the view overlooked a huge lake. Valerie opened the urn, and the ashes drifted out.

"He might not have been perfect, but he was ours. He tried," Henry said, pressing his lips together as if that would stop a deep, unnamed emotion within him from escaping.

"Goodbye, Daddy," Valerie whispered, not bothering to wipe her tears.

Then she let herself sob for the first time since Oberon's death a few days ago. Henry held her as her body curled in on itself. He shook with tears of his own, and through their connection, Valerie knew that he was reliving the loss of his dad on Earth, Joe.

Finally, their tears dried up. Valerie was hollowed out, but drained of the poisonous grief that sucked all of the joy out of her soul.

"We'll have time to grieve again," Henry said. "When all this is over."

Valerie couldn't meet his eyes as she replied. "Maybe, if we survive. But for now, back to war."

❦   ❦   ❦

Valerie's life was barely recognizable from what it had looked like even a month before, when she'd been strategizing and preparing for battle. Now, there was no time for planning, only fighting. Not that she was complaining.

Fighting was easy, numbing, even with Earth's rules binding her magic. Lucky for her, there was no shortage of opportunities to wear herself out hitting and slashing through the legions of Fractus who had emerged like cockroaches since the barrier between Earth and the Globe had been shattered, and travel between the two worlds was as easy as breathing, for those who knew how.

4

Today, she was in a remote town in Chile, leading a small team of soldiers from her army, the Fist, in a standoff with about a dozen Fractus. Cyrus was by her side, as well, and they fought back-to-back.

Valerie punched a Fractus in the gut with the speed and grace of a leopard. He fell, smacking his head into the hard asphalt of the road on which they fought, but as he did, he slashed at her leg with a broken piece of glass, and blood ran down her shin. Before he could get another thrust in, she jammed her heel into a sensitive spot in his neck, and he was instantly unconscious.

Blood ran down her leg into her shoe, and the pain was too sharp to ignore. She could keep going, but she wouldn't bet her soldiers' lives on it.

"Fall back!" she called, struggling to her feet.

The four soldiers who fought with her today, all ex-Knights who had chosen not to follow Reaper, began to retreat.

"No, keep fighting! We got this," Cyrus said, ducking as a tall man slashed at him with a pair of knives. The only reason he didn't hit his mark was because Cyrus was blinding him by bending light.

Her soldiers shot her glances, their confusion evident.

"What's the call here?" Alex, one of her Knights, asked.

Before Valerie could answer, one of the Fractus leaped at Alex. With the accuracy born of a thousand throws, Valerie hurled her sword, Pathos, at Alex's attacker, pinning his shirt to a nearby tree.

"Fall back!" Valerie commanded.

She expertly kicked Cyrus's attacker in the head. As the Fractus fell, she turned to Cyrus. "Not another word from you."

5

"Your mistake," Cyrus said, his face red, but he followed as Valerie and her soldiers moved together.

Valerie's whole body felt like lead now that the adrenaline of the fight was subsiding. Being on Earth brought back her old sickness every time she returned, but with so many Fractus attacks on Earth, she couldn't afford to stay on the Globe full time.

Valerie, Cyrus, and the rest of her soldiers were close enough to grip hands. She squeezed a rock in her pocket, and a sensation passed over her like stepping through a bubble.

When she opened her eyes, she was in the garden outside of her house on the Globe with Cyrus and the Knights. She dropped her rock into the flowerbed next to the door, which was where it had come from in the first place. Now that the Byways had been destroyed, all anyone needed to travel between worlds was something from the planet they were traveling to. It didn't need to be charmed with magic or even be a special object—any old rock would do.

Which was why Reaper was having no trouble sending his army to Earth in droves.

"Good work," Valerie said to her soldiers. "They won't be attacking that city again today. I'll have Chisisi send a team back tonight to make sure."

"But we don't know what those Fractus were there for! We should have captured one and made him talk," Cyrus insisted.

"You can go home," Valerie said to the Knights, choosing not to respond to Cyrus's words.

Alex raised an eyebrow before following her fellow Knights into the woods. When they were out of earshot,

Valerie turned to Cyrus, forcing herself to suck in a calming breath so she didn't start yelling at him.

"Never do that again," Valerie said.

"Admit it, you made the wrong call," Cyrus said.

"Alex could have been killed! You confused my soldiers. Don't make me pull you off of active fighting duty."

"Fine, maybe I shouldn't have disagreed with you right on the field," Cyrus huffed. "But we could have taken those guys. I think they were out in the middle of nowhere for a reason."

"Do you think the charm that binds magic on Earth was nearby?" Valerie asked, unable to keep the disbelief out of her voice. "Wouldn't it be somewhere a little more impressive, like the Great Wall of China?"

"It makes more sense for it to be somewhere out of the way," Cyrus argued, his tone defensive.

Henry's mind connected with hers, and he burst out the front door.

"You're hurt!" Henry said, his eyes roving over her, looking for an injury.

Cyrus stepped back, scanning her until he saw her bleeding leg. "You never said—I didn't know!"

"It's nothing," Valerie said, pulling up her pant leg.

Cyrus knelt beside her, and his touch was gentle as he probed the wound.

"At least it wasn't made using one of the Fractus's new black weapons," he said. He looked up, and all of the arrogance was wiped from his expression. "This was why you had us fall back. You did make the right call."

Valerie nodded. "It was a piece of glass. It'll be fine."

"It can still get infected," Henry said.

Valerie fought the urge to snap at them both that their attention was making her claustrophobic, but she bit the inside of her cheek. Her father would have told her that she needed to behave like a leader at all times, and leaders don't whine.

"I'm going to go clean it," she said, shrugging off their attention as subtly as she could.

"I know you're tired, but Skye wants to see you tonight. He says it's important," Henry said, and his worry for her seeped through their mental connection.

She nodded, shutting her mind to his anxiety. She'd been doing that a lot lately, because adding Henry's stress and grief to her own was overpowering.

ço   ço   ço

An hour later, Valerie left her house and began walking to The Horseshoe, mercifully alone. Cyrus had returned home to shower and rest.

The woods around her, once lush, were now brittle and brown. The closer she got to The Horseshoe, the worse it became. Al, the Grand Master of the Stewardship Guild and a member of the Fractus, had used his Guild's power to send a massive drought to Silva, the capital city in Arden.

The result was that everything that had once been alive and green was dying. Water was hard to come by, as lakes that had once glittered now receded. It was an effective attack, because for the first time, Conjurors across the country were forced to make sacrifices.

It had always been a land of plenty—magic made accessing food, water, and every kind of necessity a given. No one knew what it was to go without, but they were discovering it now. Every person in Arden had a daily water ration, enough for a shower and drinking water. And if they didn't find a way to make it rain soon, even those rations would have to be cut back.

Going without something that most people considered a requirement for survival wasn't new to Valerie, but it hurt to see the cracked lips of the kids playing in the dusty streets. If she'd done a better job of convincing the Grand Masters not to follow Reaper, none of this would be happening.

She was distracted from her guilt as a tall centaur trotted out of the Relations Guild in her direction. Skye's mane looked like it needed a good wash, but his bearing was as regal as ever. Her friend and mentor, Gideon, jogged beside him.

"We're losing ground to the Fractus in the fringes of Silva," Skye said, skipping the pleasantries and getting straight to the point. "What's slowing us down is your policy of avoiding kill attacks. I'm not saying we should unnecessarily slaughter the Fractus, but we can't always take them prisoner."

"I know that," Valerie said, her mind spinning as she remembered the faces of the soldiers in her army who had died in the recent battles. "I wouldn't ask anyone to die rather than fight back."

"Sometimes, we must be willing to kill our enemies even when it is not in immediate self-defense," Skye said.

"That's not the policy that we agreed on when we formed the Fist," Gideon said, naming Valerie's army of supporters from around the Globe. Valerie could see from the stiffness of his stance that this was an argument he'd had with Skye before.

"You have to look at the broader perspective," Skye said, ignoring Gideon and speaking directly to Valerie. "They're shooting lightning at us from a mile away and people are dying. We need to combat them with an equally effective weapon."

"We don't have anything like that, even if I were willing to use it," Valerie said.

"That's what I wanted to talk to you about. Leo and Cyrus have an idea for a weapon that could send bursts of magic at the speed of light that would kill enemies instantly," Skye said.

"They said it was possible when you asked, not that they recommended using such a weapon," Gideon added, his lips forming a hard line.

Cyrus had been working with the Weapons Guild on creating weapons infused with light, but he hadn't mentioned anything about new ways to kill Fractus at a distance. Was that why he'd vanished instead of accompanying her to meet with Skye? He had to know what her reaction would be.

Valerie's face hardened as she met Skye's eyes. "We're not changing our policy. We take prisoners when possible and kill only when absolutely necessary. Otherwise, what makes us different from Reaper? He thinks he's doing the right thing, too, sacrificing a few to save the many."

Gideon's eyes connected with hers, and he gave her a small nod of approval. The tension in Valerie's shoulders eased a notch.

"Don't compare me to that madman," Skye snapped, and Valerie could see that his nerves were as frayed as her own.

She took a breath and shook her head. "Of course not. Excuse the insult. But there must be a better way. What if Cyrus and the lightweavers create arrows of light that can be shot into enemy lines? That wouldn't be fatal, but it might weaken their weapons."

Skye nodded slowly. "That would be something."

"And how about the work that the Glamour Guild is doing to disguise our army?" Valerie continued.

Skye launched into an overview of the effectiveness of various tactics they were employing, and Valerie nearly sighed with relief that the argument over new weapons to kill the Fractus was over—for now.

Chapter 2

It was night by the time that Valerie and Gideon turned their steps homeward. In the moonlight, everything seemed less like a wasteland and more like the city that she'd fallen in love with when she'd first come to the Globe.

"Oberon would be proud of how you are leading this war," Gideon said after they had walked silently for a ways. There was no bitterness in his voice, even though Gideon and her father had not been friends.

Valerie released a laugh that was also a sob. "He'd probably tell me to listen to Skye and kill as many Fractus as I can."

Gideon flashed her a brief smile. "You might be right. But he'd support you when you told him no."

They reached the garden in front of her house, and Valerie shut her eyes, letting herself remember her father—the taste of his awful pancakes, the effortless grace of his movements when he fought in battle, and, best of all, the pride in his stormy eyes whenever he looked at her.

Gideon's sharp breath brought her back to reality, and she opened her eyes and saw why he'd been startled. In the waning light, in the middle of a drought, her father's garden had bloomed. He had filled it with hundreds of white poppies. It was the flower that he said symbolized her, and it was the only kind he'd planted in his garden, apparently.

Had he somehow known that he would die, and had left this as a gift to her? It didn't matter. As the delicate scent of the flowers reached her, she laughed. Beside her, Gideon was smiling, too.

"I'm starting to see why your mother loved him," he admitted.

Valerie asked him the question she'd never had the guts to before. "You loved her, too, didn't you?"

He nodded once, and then squeezed her shoulder.

"And like Oberon, I am proud of you," he said. "I see her in you, next to the best parts of your father."

The lump in Valerie's throat made it impossible to speak, so she gave Gideon a hug instead. Finally, she cleared her throat.

"I promised someone the first bloom from my garden," she said. "I'll be back before dawn."

ço   ço   ço

Valerie raced through the forest to one of the trees that led up to Arbor Aurum, the capital city for the People of the Woods, and also the location where Elden, their former leader, was healing.

She climbed the tree effortlessly, because she'd had a lot of practice. The People were on the front lines of the fight with the Fractus, with a contingent on Earth and another on the Globe. They fought the Fractus guerrilla-style, hiding in the trees and leaping out to attack the army when they tried to advance into Silva. Valerie talked battle tactics with them several times a week.

When she reached the platform, it was full dark, but the stars were brighter up there. The wounded were all located in an enormous hollow tree deep in the city, where they could be protected.

Elden's alcove was usually attended by his wife, daughter, or one of his many friends, but at this time of night, he was alone. He slept fitfully, his fingers obsessively twining and untwining. He hadn't regained consciousness since he'd been almost fatally attacked with one of the black weapons wielded by the Fractus.

"I brought you a poppy, the first bloom of my garden, like I promised," Valerie said, speaking quietly so as not to awaken the other patients.

Elden's hands stilled at the sound of her voice.

"I wish you'd wake up," she continued, and let her body slump a little. For the first time in a while, she wasn't thinking like a leader, wishing that one of her most trusted generals would get back into the action. She was just a girl who missed her friend.

"Valerie, you're back," Cara said.

She turned and gave Cyrus's sister a smile. "You're still helping give the sick light treatments?"

Cara had fully embraced her potential as a lightweaver, and Cyrus was helping her develop her magic.

"My parents are horrified, even though I'm using my magic to save lives, not take them."

"You're doing the right thing," Valerie said.

"I know. Someday they will, too, I hope," Cara said. "In the meantime, I'm enjoying the fact that Arbor Aurum doesn't have cell phone service. The only means to contact me are magical, so I haven't heard from them since I left."

Valerie turned back to Elden. "Any change in him?"

Cara put her hand against Elden's chest, and Valerie watched light pulse from her hand into her patient, giving him a temporary glow. She wasn't sure if it was her imagination, but he seemed to breathe a little easier.

"Some days, he seems stronger," Cara said. "Other days, it seems like his recovery has plateaued. We don't know what the long-term effects of the Fractus's weapons are. And Elden had a very strong exposure."

Valerie was grateful that Cara didn't try to hide her doubts. She barely recognized the girl she'd met three years ago. That angry kid had been replaced by someone who seemed to know her purpose better than Valerie did.

"How's Cyrus?" Cara asked.

Valerie knew that she'd seen her brother earlier in the week, so she suspected that Cara was really asking how she and Cyrus were doing.

"There's not a lot of time for romance in the middle of a war," Valerie hedged.

"He loves you. If you don't feel the same, you need to let him know," Cara said, eyeing her critically.

"I love Cyrus!"

"You know what I mean," Cara said, her tone brooking no nonsense.

Valerie deflated a little. "I would never string him along."

Cara cocked her eyebrow at Valerie's Earth expression, but she nodded. "No one dies of a broken heart in real life. People move on."

"Okay," Valerie said, since Cara was still staring at her.

Cara broke the tension with a smile and a welcome change of subject. "Tell Ceru to come visit me."

Ceru was a journeyman at Cyrus's old guild, The Society of Imaginary Friends. He was one of Cyrus's good friends, and Valerie suspected that Cara had a crush on him.

"I'm not going to tell Cyrus you said that," Valerie teased.

15

"Thanks. Ceru never sees me as anything other than a child, though," Cara said, and her earlier maturity slipped away. "But I'm not!"

Valerie couldn't help being reminded of when she'd first met Thai. She remembered his bossy attitude with bemused affection.

"Why are you grinning like that?" Cara asked.

"Thank you, Cara," Valerie said.

"For what?"

"For giving me the first somewhat normal night I've had in a really, really long time."

Chapter 3

Valerie didn't need an alarm or a wakeup call to be up with the sun every morning. Her body seemed to know that it could only take the minimum amount of sleep it needed before sending her back to the endless string of tasks that awaited her every day.

As usual, she checked in with Chisisi first. She opened a drawer that had an ancient, handheld tape recorder and concentrated. Instantly, she was inside the outdated electronics shop in Japan where Chisisi was currently running the operations of the Guardians of the Boundary on Earth.

Thai was bent over a laptop with Chisisi, and the two were deep in discussion. Valerie cursed her traitorous heart for leaping at the sight of Thai's broad shoulders.

"Any attacks over the night?" Valerie asked, deciding to get in and out as fast as possible.

Thai turned and flashed her a smile that made her cheeks heat up in spite of herself.

"It was calm, for a change," Thai said.

Chisisi was still staring at the screen. "Your Thai has developed an interesting program to analyze the locations of the Fractus's attacks. It is proving most helpful in identifying where they will strike next."

"They're searching for something pretty systematically," Thai explained. "I think we can all guess what."

"The charm that's repressing magic on Earth, right?" Valerie asked.

"Young miss has the right of it," Chisisi said, turning at last. His eyes were shadowed from fatigue. He'd been working tirelessly to stop the Fractus since the death of his brother, and it was taking a toll.

"It's not going to be easy for us to find it before the Fractus do. There's way more of them than us," Thai said.

Valerie unconsciously rubbed her temples, where a headache was already forming. "At least when they're searching, they're less likely to be attacking humans."

Chisisi's phone rang, and he answered it.

"Yes," he said, his tone clipped. He listened, his body absolutely still. "I am on hand to help if you need it."

Chisisi hung up. "I'm going to Dubai. A battle is brewing there between the Fractus and my people."

"Send me instead," Valerie said.

"Send us," Thai corrected. "You need sleep, Chisisi."

He briefly touched the older man on his back, and Valerie could see the gentle affection in the gesture. Before Chisisi could respond, Valerie was blasted with a wave of pure panic from Henry's mind. Henry so rarely completely opened himself to her anymore that Valerie stumbled, and would have fallen if Thai hadn't caught her elbow.

"Henry needs help!" she said. Her vision cleared. "I'm sorry, Chisisi, but I have to go to him."

"Go, young ones. I will see to the Fractus in Dubai."

Thai gripped her hand, and they were back in Valerie's garden.

"Not here. The Society of Imaginary Friends. I'll meet you there," Valerie said, and took off at full speed, letting her magic power her legs.

18

But Thai was still holding her hand, and somehow he kept up, even though she was running so fast that the trees were a blur in her peripheral vision.

They didn't stop until they burst through the doors of the Guild. Standing in the middle of the playful, colorful center of the room was Zunya, surrounded by two-dozen of the boys from Jack's old gang of friends whom he'd given the ability to absorb magic.

The boys' white eyes and the black stitching on their throats were terrifying, and the Conjurors of the Guild, many of who were children, cowered away from the spectacle.

"I thought this would get your attention," Zunya's voice boomed across the room as his yellow eyes connected with Valerie's. "You're a difficult person to get ahold of now that people foolishly think you matter."

"What do you want?" Valerie asked, keeping her voice steady. Zunya fed on fear, and he already had a feast. She wouldn't add her own to the mix.

"I'm here to propose a treaty," Zunya said.

"Sure you are," she said, analyzing the possibility of getting to his side before he hurt someone.

"Reaper's idea, not mine. I recommended slaughtering you all," Zunya said. "Starting with these kids."

The high-pitched screams that followed his words only made him smile wider, but Valerie saw that he wasn't directing his power at anyone yet. He was here for something else, she suspected.

Her eyes flicked around the room to assess her advantages. Through her connection with Henry, she knew that he was watching from a platform thirty floors above with Dulcea. They were waiting for her signal to join in the fray.

19

A flash of light in a corner caught her attention, but she was careful not to direct her gaze in that direction. Cyrus was sending her a message that he was on hand, too. That was when she remembered what was happening in the Guild today. It was Dulcea's inauguration ceremony as the new Grand Master of the Society of Imaginary Friends.

"What is your master proposing?" Valerie asked, knowing that her choice of words would irk Zunya.

His expression darkened. Score.

"I'm my own master. But Reaper wants to declare a peace so we can tend to our wounded for ten days."

"He doesn't care about his wounded. You're all expendable to him. What's this really about?"

"You're right. We don't have any wounded that we care to nurse to health. But you do. You can have this time for a small price."

"I figured as much. What do you want?"

Valerie's mind whirred, imagining the possibilities if she had ten whole days of peace. Aside from giving their wounded a few days of uninterrupted care, they could port in water and fresh food from neighboring cities; restock their weapons, which were running dangerously low; and sleep. What was all that worth to her?

"We want access to the tunnels in Plymouth for those ten days," Zunya said, naming the underground city that was sealed against everyone aboveground.

"No way," Valerie shot back. "I'm not letting you slaughter more people for whatever sick reasons you have."

"No one in Plymouth will be harmed. We are using the tunnels for transportation of materials we need," Zunya said.

"Like we'd ever trust your word!" Dulcea shouted down at him. Henry yanked her back before Zunya could see who'd spoken.

"I know you're here, Henry," Zunya said.

Henry's mind was open to her, and Zunya's words registered like a poisonous snake slithering up his spine. Goosebumps broke out on her arms from the volume of Henry's terror.

But none of that fear was evident in his voice or stance when he jumped onto a platform that shot him to the ground. He stepped off and moved next to Valerie and Thai.

"Why doesn't he bend space and create a portal? He can go wherever he wants," Henry said.

"He has his reasons for wanting to go through Plymouth. But he promises that the people there will not be contacted or harmed in any way. And you of all people should know that Reaper keeps his word," Zunya said. "Didn't your daddy's end prove that?"

Valerie wasn't ready for the immensity of Henry's power when he unleashed it. A blast of psychic power knocked Zunya off his feet and slammed him into the far wall so hard that it cracked.

The room exploded in movement as all of the Conjurors surged toward the exits at the windows and doors.

"It didn't have to be this way. The offer was made in good faith. But Reaper's wishes or not, now you all have to die," Zunya said, rising to his feet.

The boys Zunya brought with him opened their mouths. The yawning caverns in their faces were like a void, and Valerie's power started slipping away from her.

"Cyrus, get over here!" she shouted, and then turned to Henry and Thai. "We fight back to back."

Pathos was already in her hand, and together, they moved as a pack toward the boys. The closer they got, the more her power was torn away, but she knew that they couldn't run. There were too many children at risk if they didn't eject Zunya and his gang right away.

They made it to the first boy, and Valerie had enough of her power left to knock him in the head with a spin kick. He fell to the ground, and the immensity of the attack on her magic ebbed by a tiny fraction.

At the same time, Cyrus reached them and sent a beam of light out of his hands. He was nearly knocked over by three kids aiming for an exit behind them, and Thai gripped his shoulder so he didn't fall. The beam of light turned into a fireball that shot straight at Zunya.

Zunya released a yelp of pain as the flames engulfed him. But the fire set off some kind of magical sprinkler system, and soon water was shooting everywhere, soaking everyone and putting out the fire Cyrus had started. In the resulting chaos, Valerie, Henry, Thai, and Cyrus pressed their advantage, knocking two more boys out as they raced toward Zunya, who was charred and crumpled on the floor, but still breathing.

A heady excitement filled Valerie, seeing Zunya injured for the first time in her life. But before she could rejoice, he slammed his fist into the ground, and black veins of magic shot through the floor, spreading to the points around the room where each of the boys in his little army stood.

Before Valerie could react, she saw all of Zunya's boys fall to the ground when the black line reached them. As one, they convulsed, and the lines in the ground swelled, pumping magic to Zunya.

Zunya inhaled deeply and stood. His eyes flicked from Valerie to Thai to Cyrus to Henry. Then he pulled a black dagger from his boot and threw it. There was a flash of darkness as it whipped through the air, and then embedded itself in the heart of a young Conjuror who was frozen against a wall, watching the scene.

Screams erupted as Valerie ran to the boy's side. Zunya used the distraction to leap through the window with superhuman speed.

For Valerie, nothing mattered but the boy. She shoved her way to his side, pushed back his sweaty mass of dark curls, and unleashed her vivicus power into his little body. Her power flooded her with its pain and potential. This time, she seemed to know when his little spark of life blazed up. He'd live.

Valerie struggled to pull back her power, and Henry helped her lock it up inside of her again before it consumed her.

Dulcea had scooped the boy up, though he looked more scared than weak.

Valerie saw blackness at the edges of her vision, but she pushed it back.

"I'm going after Zunya. I can stop him, I know it," Cyrus said, kneeling beside her.

"No," Valerie said.

Cyrus started to go anyway, and Valerie held him back by his arm.

"As the leader of the Fist, I'm telling you that you're too valuable to go after Zunya alone, and we can't all go until we secure this location," Valerie said.

She could see the struggle on his face. His eyes flicked toward the window Zunya had jumped out of, his body tense, and Valerie prepared herself to knock him out if she had to. But then, his eyes connected with hers, and she knew they were both remembering the last time he'd gone against her orders.

Cyrus jerked his arm away, but he nodded. "Fine, I'll stay."

Valerie summoned her strength, and Henry helped her stand. She put as much authority into her tone as she could to help calm the terrified children.

"Thai, go find Jack. These boys are his friends, and he might know whether they need a jail or a healer. Henry, help me get them somewhere secure in the meantime. Cyrus, get the kids out of here. They know you and trust you, and we don't know whether or not the threat is over."

Cyrus nodded, only a little grudgingly, but before he moved away, he paused and knelt by one of Zunya's boys. He touched him and released a gentle pulse of light.

The boy gasped and sat up. His eyes were normal, brown, and full of life. He reached for his throat, touching the black stitches there.

"Are you okay?" Cyrus asked him.

The boy tried to speak, but no sound came out. But he also didn't move to run or attack. Instead, he took a shuddering gulp of air, and his eyes filled with tears.

"I think you fixed him," Valerie said to Cyrus, staring at him with awe.

The boy nodded.

"Score one for the good guys," Thai said, and everyone, even Cyrus, grinned.

Chapter 4

After a long day of getting the Society of Imaginary Friends back in order, Henry forced Valerie to rest in Dulcea's office, and she didn't protest too much. She was used to the exhaustion that followed the release of her vivicus power, but this time, there was something else. As she turned the incident with Zunya over in her mind, the details kept escaping her. It was like her memory of what happened had eroded.

The thought made her shudder. Was her mind beginning to disintegrate, like Darling's?

The day was almost over before the Guild was back in some sort of order, though almost everyone had been sent home. Valerie's friends joined her in Dulcea's office after Zunya's boys had been transported to the Healer's Guild and all of the apprentices of the Guild were safely in the dorm.

Not for the first time, Valerie wished that Kanti was with them. According to Henry and Kanti's sister, Isabella, Kanti was busy with her duties as a princess in Elsinore. Aside from the fact that they could use her practical advice right now, Valerie missed the support of one of her closest friends. But they were all doing what they had to, and Kanti was hopefully raising an army in her home country that would give them an advantage against the Fractus.

"This guild is in one piece thanks to all of you," Dulcea said, passing around a tray of her famous chocolates. "I've been Grand Master for five minutes, and already, it was nearly destroyed."

"Strictly coincidence," Jack said, kissing her cheek. "You're the best thing that ever happened to this guild."

Dulcea smiled as Cyrus, Valerie, Thai, and Henry all chimed in with their agreement.

"I know we've got business to talk about, but first, I want to toast Dulcea," Valerie said. "In the middle of an awful time, you becoming Grand Master of this guild is a bright spark."

"Now I'll have a vote when the Grand Masters convene," Dulcea said. "And you can bet I'll be harassing the ones who are working with the Fractus to see the light and join the Fist."

"I pity them, trying to resist your sweetness," Jack said.

His exuberance was unmistakable, and Valerie could see that having his friends safely in Arden, away from Zunya at last and being treated by the Fist's healers, had removed any dark clouds hanging over him. Now, he could enjoy being young and in love, even if they were in the middle of a war.

"Enough already," Thai teased. "I'm on sugar overload watching you two."

"I'm shocked that I have to be the voice of reason here, but can we talk about Zunya? I think I should go and finish him off once and for all. Did you see how I almost killed him?" Cyrus couldn't keep the pride out of his voice.

"Whoa there, Super Mario. He's not going to make that mistake twice," Thai said.

Valerie and Henry released a surprised laugh at Thai's reference, but everyone else looked puzzled.

26

"It's an Earth-thing, from a video game," Henry said. "Mario is this little plumber who can throw fireballs..."

Henry trailed off as Dulcea, Jack, and Cyrus stared at them in obvious bewilderment.

Valerie found herself really laughing for the first time in weeks. She and Henry gripped each other, unable to stop giggling. She suspected that they were both a little hysterical.

Dulcea, Jack, and Thai smiled at them, but then Valerie met Cyrus's gaze and her humor vanished. He was staring at her with something unfathomable in his gaze, but it wasn't amusement.

              ઝ   ઝ   ઝ

After the meeting ended, Cyrus and Valerie left the Guild together, their hands loosely linked, while Henry walked next to them, his expression distracted.

"It was good to see you laugh tonight," Cyrus said, letting go of her hand. "But I thought I'd be the one to finally make you do it."

Valerie didn't know what to say, so she changed the subject. "Thank you for not running after Zunya today. I know you wanted to."

"But you are planning to send me after him, right? Once we form a good plan?" Cyrus asked.

"Cy, maybe you should practice your new power first. Are you sure you can even do it again?" Valerie asked.

"Stop talking to me like I'm a kid! I've been fighting this war as long as you have, even if I'm not the almighty leader of the Fist," he said. Then, under his breath, he added, "But maybe if I were the one leading, Zunya would be dead and we'd be a lot closer to winning this war."

Valerie could tell from the scowl on Henry's face that he'd heard Cyrus.

"Watch it," Henry said. "She's the one in charge for a lot of reasons, one of which is that she doesn't have a giant ego."

Cyrus's jaw clenched, but then, his eyes met Valerie's and he looked down. "Sorry, Val. I didn't mean it. I came so close to doing something important today, something heroic, and it's killing me that, in the end, I failed."

"Zunya will get what's coming to him," Henry said with more conviction than Valerie had heard in his voice for weeks.

Cyrus nodded and then split away from them, heading to his dorm while Valerie and Henry continued home.

"Can you imagine if we really could have ten days of peace?" Valerie asked her brother. "It's probably not leader-like to admit, but I'd love one day of doing something fun."

"I wanted to talk to you about that. I believe Zunya. I think Reaper's offer is genuine," Henry said.

Valerie turned to him in surprise, trying to read his expression in the moonlight, since his mind was completely closed to her.

"Are you sure enough to put the people of Plymouth at risk?" she asked.

Henry nodded. "It's not easy transporting things across the Globe, especially big things or people, fast."

"Even if his offer is genuine, it must be pretty important stuff he wants to move around if he's willing to give us a break," Valerie argued.

"Maybe he wants a break, too. We've got him on the defensive, at least on Earth, with that program Thai created. They're not making the progress finding the charm binding Earth's magic they thought they would. I mean, I'm guessing."

Valerie considered his words. "All right. I'll talk to a few people first, and if no one has strong objections, I'll accept Reaper's offer."

Henry stopped walking and turned to her. "Just like that?"

"I trust your judgment, Henry. Every single one of us needs a break from the constant battles. Even if it's for a little while."

Henry winced at her words.

"What is it?" she asked.

"You have so much faith in me. I don't deserve it," he said.

"You're my brother, my only family. I love you more than anyone in the universe," she said.

"Me, too," Henry said, his voice a little wobbly.

The rest of their walk home was quiet. Valerie thought about how grateful she was that even though she'd lost her father, she still had a family. She wasn't alone.

But what Henry thought about that put such a deep, worried frown on his face she couldn't guess.

Chapter 5

"This is an insult. They know the leader of the Fist has come to meet with them, so where are they?" Sanguina's voice rang out in the grove of trees, sending a cluster of birds fluttering into the sky.

"It's okay. I can wait," Valerie said.

She, Sanguina, and Chisisi had arranged to meet with the contingent of the People of the Woods who had returned to Earth, but they were an hour late.

"I see a flicker in the trees," Chisisi said, his voice calm as ever.

"Finally!" Sanguina huffed. "If I were still a vampyre, I'd leave them shaking with fear for days!"

"Probably best that you're not, then," Valerie muttered. "Now keep your voice down. They have amazing hearing."

She'd forgiven Sanguina for the years she'd spent terrorizing Henry and herself, but hearing her mention her prior life so carelessly made her shudder.

Sanguina was contrite. "I'm joking, of course."

Before Valerie could reply, two People stepped from the trees. She recognized them as elders who led the contingent of People on Earth, Oak and Meadow.

"How fare you, vivicus?" Oak asked her, nodding his head. His skin glinted with a touch of gold in the sun. He didn't acknowledge Chisisi or Sanguina.

"The attacks on Earth and the Globe have only gotten worse," Valerie said. "Have you had any luck following the leads that Chisisi sent your way?"

"This human didn't understand, but you will," Meadow said, her passion evident in the defiant thrust of her chin. "We have been occupied cleansing the rivers of the pollution that humans have dumped into the waters. Without pure water, we cannot help the animals that depend on it for survival."

"I know how important it is to help the plants and animals on Earth thrive," Valerie began carefully. "But if we don't stop the Fractus now, who knows what kind of destruction they could visit on the land?"

"Did you visit the lake in Armenia I spoke to you about, to see if there were any traces of ancient magic?" Chisisi asked.

Oak finally turned to Chisisi. "We did visit the site. There was once a great power there, but it is gone."

"What do you mean, gone?" Sanguina demanded.

"The object that is binding magic on Earth may once have resided there, but it was moved," Meadow explained, as if she were speaking to a small child.

"Could the Fractus have beaten us there, and they already have it?" Valerie asked, her heart beating faster.

"Not unless they did it many centuries ago," Meadow said.

"Are there any traces you can follow to see where it might have gone?" Valerie asked.

"We do not have the ability to follow magic trails, so there is no more we can do for you," Oak said. "We will leave you now for more important work."

31

"We wanted to ask—" Valerie began, but Oak and Meadow had turned and were already vanishing through the trees.

"Say the word, and I'll drag them back by their hair," Sanguina seethed.

Chisisi sighed. "Forcing them to help is more difficult than finding another way. Especially when we have a willing Conjuror on hand who is an expert at tracing magic trails."

"Chrome," Valerie said with a smile. The wolf was an old friend, and she would welcome the chance to see him.

"He's been following up a lead in Brazil, but it appears to be a dead end," Chisisi said.

"He's restless," Sanguina said. "He needs something to do, or he's going to search out more Fractus to fight again."

"Again?" Valerie asked.

Chisisi and Sanguina exchanged glances.

"The wolf Knight has been volatile," Chisisi said diplomatically.

"He attacked a Fractus crossing his path without being provoked," Sanguina explained. "The man would have surrendered, but Chrome was out for blood."

"Was the man killed?" Valerie braced herself for the worst. Gideon had warned her of Chrome's bloodlust.

Chisisi shook his head. "The man is safe, and a captive. But I thought it best to keep Chrome in remote areas where he is less likely to encounter his enemies."

"That's a temporary solution," Sanguina said.

"I'll talk to him," Valerie said. "I'm sure he's still grieving for Jet."

"As you command," Chisisi replied in his formal way.

"There's something else I wanted to talk to you about," Valerie said, and she launched into the story of her encounter with Zunya and Reaper's offer of a temporary truce.

"Do you think I can trust him?" Valerie asked Sanguina.

"In all the years I was with him, he never broke his word that I saw," Sanguina said. "It was a matter of pride. But it's a big risk."

"I'm planning to accept, unless either of you gives me a good reason not to," Valerie said.

"It would be a gift from the gods to have some time to regroup," Chisisi said.

"Thank you both," Valerie said, and returned to the Globe.

ॐ ॐ ॐ

Valerie knew when she smelled lilies that Azra and her foal were waiting for her near her house.

She saw a flash of silver fluttering in the wind. Azra was trotting from the trees, searching the area carefully before turning back and nodding to Clarabelle that it was safe to emerge.

The presence of the baby unicorn was almost as all-consuming as the first time Valerie had met her. Peace enveloped her like a glow, and everything seemed possible— even defeating the Fractus and ending this horrible war.

"You're here!" Valerie burst out joyfully. "Welcome! Is it safe?"

Safe or not, we had to come. Clarabelle is drawn to you. I could not keep her away. Azra gently nudged her baby with her nose, and Valerie heard her gentle cooing response in her mind.

33

Valerie knelt before the little foal, who left her mother to nuzzle Valerie's shoulder.

"It's so good to see you, little one," Valerie said.

Clarabelle made little noises in Valerie's mind. They weren't fully-formed thoughts, like Azra's, but Valerie understood the essence of what she was communicating. Connection, joy, a kinship of spirit.

Unicorns have always been drawn to the pure of heart.

Azra's words made Valerie unaccountably self-conscious.

The youngest unicorns are also the most powerful. To deny her instinct to find you would be like depriving her of food.

"But it's dangerous near me," Valerie said, looking up at Azra's eyes and seeing her own worry mirrored in them.

Unicorns are also drawn to war, with an overpowering drive to bring peace. It may be why our race is nearly extinct. I cannot fight Clarabelle's impulses, especially since they echo my own, so here we are.

Despite her worry for Azra and Clarabelle's safety, Valerie was also relieved to have someone to help guide her down the road ahead.

Summer, an ancient centaur who had helped Azra give birth to Clarabelle, emerged from the trees.

"The woods are clear," Summer said.

Summer has decided to act as our guard. Azra answered Valerie's unspoken question.

"This is my life's new purpose. I never thought I'd have one again," Summer said.

Despite her age and the painful way she moved after being tortured by Reaper, Valerie knew she would be a formidable foe if anyone tried to hurt the unicorns.

We are here now to tell you that we will be hidden in a protected grove in your woods. If you reach out with your mind, Clarabelle and I will hear you.

The tiny unicorn then poked her mother gently with her sky-blue horn.

Azra's eyes clouded. *She is trying to tell me something. That there is an offer of peace, a truce?*

Valerie couldn't hide her surprise. "How did she know that? Reaper offered us ten days of peace in exchange for access to Plymouth."

I have only dim memories of my own days as a foal, but when unicorns are young, they sense the possibilities of the universe like you would smell a scent on the wind. This offer is pleasing to her.

"It would be safe to accept?"

Clarabelle's certainty overpowered her mind, a sensation so sweet that she could almost taste it on her tongue.

"It confirms what I was already planning to do. I think I have a visit to make," Valerie said.

ɢ   ɢ   ɢ

When Valerie told Henry that she was planning to accept Reaper's offer on his own turf, she was expecting resistance. But Henry embraced her idea.

"If he isn't willing to honor my visit under a flag of truce, then he can't be trusted in Plymouth," Valerie explained.

"Agreed. But I'm coming with you," Henry said, and she knew he was deliberately opening his mind to her so she would see that he wouldn't change it on this point.

"I don't want it to look like it's an attack, so it can't be anyone other than you and me, at the most," she said.

35

"Then let's not tell the others. Cyrus, in particular, would never agree," Henry said.

"They'll only worry, and we have to do this," Valerie agreed.

Without any more verbal discussion, they turned their steps toward the woods behind The Horseshoe. The Fractus had made camp a couple of miles away, and Valerie knew from the People of the Woods that Reaper had been living there for the past few weeks as the Fractus had stepped up their attacks on Silva.

Valerie knew the instant they had been spotted. The branch of a tree moved slightly, and she saw a little rainbow on the ground as light reflected through something almost transparent. One of the invisible Fractus was the lookout.

The leaves rustled in the breeze, and adrenaline pumped through her system. She guessed that the wind carried the news of who was entering camp.

Her suspicion was confirmed when three Fractus appeared in front of them, as if they had stepped out of thin air. Which they might have, Valerie realized, thinking about Reaper's ability to bend space.

The Fractus could be from Elsinore—they were tall men dressed in elaborate armor that was as fashionable as it was functional. They all carried swords that looked as if they had been dipped in black ink.

Henry's fear swept through her before he closed his mind. She stared at him, confused. They knew that they would have to fight before their message to Reaper became clear. Why was Henry so frightened?

"We've faced these weapons before," she reminded him. "They won't be able to steal our powers. Pathos and your machete were both created by the People of the Woods and imbued with light by Cyrus. They're stronger than what the Fractus are wielding."

"That won't be enough this time," he replied, his face grim.

Before Valerie could ask him what he meant, the men attacked. She let her magic rush through her, and Pathos was a blaze of light, flashing as she parried with two of the Fractus who attacked her at the same time.

"She really isn't bad," one of the Fractus said with a sneer, though Valerie could see that he was breathing hard.

Next to her, Henry blasted the third man with his telekinetic power, sending him skidding across the ground.

In a move so fast that her attacker didn't notice, Valerie cut his armor in six key places, and it dropped to the ground with a clatter, leaving him clad only in his underwear.

"My next attack won't leave you unscathed," Valerie said with a smirk of her own.

She ducked as her second attacker swung wildly at her head. He became unbalanced by his move, and she expertly knocked him in the head with her elbow without even bothering to watch.

She kept eye contact with the first man the entire time.

"Tell Reaper we're here to discuss his truce."

Valerie was so confident of her victory that she didn't see that the man was smiling, in spite of looking ridiculous. She stumbled backward when his eyes turned black. She was so transfixed that she didn't notice at first that Pathos was no longer glowing. In fact, the area around them seemed dimmer, as though it was quickly becoming twilight.

"What's happening?" she asked, sparing a glance at Henry.

It was a mistake. Henry was grappling with his attacker on the ground, and Valerie could see that he was gritting his teeth to avoid making a sound of pain. His attacker's eyes were black, too.

Her distraction cost her, as her attacker knocked Pathos, which was now devoid of light and ice-cold, out of her hands. The black weapon of her attacker sucked away her powers. She fought the urge to drop to her knees.

It was so dark now that it was difficult to see. She tried to summon the energy to leap at her attacker before her powers vanished entirely.

"Truce! Tell Reaper truce!" she called desperately, considering for the first time that this might be a fight she and Henry wouldn't win.

Beside her, Henry managed to head-butt his attacker, and she swept her foot in front of her. Her attacker stumbled, but didn't fall. He must already be channeling her magic, which had been absorbed by his black weapon.

"Stand down," Reaper said, and the two Fractus who were still conscious dropped their weapons and stepped back, their eyes returning to normal. Abruptly, light returned to the woods.

"Good puppies," Valerie said, struggling to keep fear from entering her voice. Reaper couldn't know how close he'd come to defeating her, or he might decide that having her dead or captive was more important than having access to Plymouth.

The men scowled at her, and she was glad that her words had found their mark.

"Enough," Reaper said. "You are here to accept my truce?"

"Yes," Valerie said.

As her heart rate reached a more normal pace, her loathing for the monster in front of her surfaced. It would be so easy, so tempting to kill him in one move.

But that was what he wanted. He'd done everything he could to provoke her into killing him, and he must have a powerful reason for doing so.

"Tell me how to gain entrance to Plymouth," Reaper commanded.

"No. I will allow you to enter on my terms, or not at all," Valerie said. "Gideon will let you in, and he will monitor your movements while you are in Plymouth."

Reaper considered her words. "He may watch from the ground. I won't let you see what we are doing, or this truce is worthless."

"Agreed. If anyone in Plymouth is so much as contacted by the Fractus, never mind hurt, the deal is off. The Fist will attack you full force."

"I do not break my word," Reaper said, his eyes flashing.

"We have allies among the people of Plymouth who know secrets of that land you can't imagine," Valerie bluffed. "We're almost hoping you attack us down there, because you will be decimated."

Reaper looked thrown by her words, and Valerie gloated inwardly. He didn't have to know that she was lying.

"After ten days, you're out of there. You never learn the secrets required to enter. Gideon will let you in and out," Valerie said.

Reaper was glowering at her now, but he nodded. "Truce begins now."

"Good. Henry, let's go," Valerie said, glad that Reaper's power wasn't being a mind reader, which would have allowed him to sense her profound relief that the truce started now

39

and she wouldn't have to fight her way back to the relative safety of Silva.

Because with Reaper's powerful new weapons, she wasn't sure she'd make it back.

Chapter 6

As soon as Valerie was confident that they were out of earshot, she turned to her brother.

"Who were those guys? I've never heard of powers like theirs. Do you think that's common in Elsinore?" she asked, stunned.

Henry shook his head. "No. Those powers are new."

"This changes everything. Our weapons are useless once their power drains them of light," Valerie said. "We'll have no protection against their black weapons."

"I know," Henry said miserably.

But he didn't look surprised.

"Did you know about this?" Valerie asked.

Henry's jaw worked, as if he was trying to choke back the words. "Yes."

Before she could question Henry further, he turned and fled. Valerie could have followed but enough of his pain seeped through the defenses that he'd built around his mind to let her know that he couldn't handle any more contact with her. But why?

ᡐ   ᡐ   ᡐ

When Valerie visited Chisisi that night, he looked more rested than she'd seen him in a long time. He was at a safe

41

house in India, deep in conversation with a man who had his back to her. His eyes crinkled in a real smile when he saw her.

"Young miss must have sensed that we were speaking of her from across the universe," Chisisi said.

The man turned. It was her former physician, Dr. Freeman.

Without thinking, she gave him a hug, and he returned it without hesitation.

"Is it Commander Diaz now?" he teased her, his dark brown eyes twinkling.

"Whatever you like, as long as you do what I say," she joked back, surprised at how much the sight of her friends lifted her spirits.

"We won't waste these ten days of peace," Dr. Freeman said. "I've been working on a rather clever way to identify other children who might be sick from the rules of this world binding their magic. I am a bit of an expert on the symptoms."

"That's a great idea," Valerie said. "Maybe we can find a way to bring them to the Globe."

"Perhaps," he said. "But most of these children only suffer mild discomfort, not life-threatening illnesses like you did. Ripping them away from everything they know might not be the best solution."

"What are you thinking, then?" she asked, curious.

"I told you that young miss doesn't mind having her ideas overturned for better ones," Chisisi said, his pride in her unmistakable.

"What if they're our backup plan? Hopefully, we'll be able to protect the charm binding magic on Earth until the Fractus have been driven out. But if we fail, we would know the human children who have magic that will be set free."

"You can't be suggesting that we'd ask these kids to help us fight the Fractus in a worst-case scenario?" Valerie asked, her back stiff.

Dr. Freeman gave her a stern look that she recognized from her years as his patient when she didn't take all of her medicine. "Of course not. But if magic is tied to genetics, then their families may have more magical potential than average. We can reach out to their parents and ask them to form a kind of reserve militia as a last line of defense against attacks."

"That's brilliant," she acknowledged. Dr. Freeman flashed her a smile. "But it's terrifying to imagine the Fractus destroying enough of the Fist for those people to be needed."

"Hope for the best, prepare for the worst," Chisisi said.

"Dr. Freeman, will you lead a campaign to educate and train the families you identify as having magical potential?" Valerie asked. "You already know how to lead a team, and you've faced tougher problems than this one."

She could almost swear that he stood a little straighter at her words.

"I won't let you down."

"You never have before. I doubt you ever could," she said.

༄ ༄ ༄

Her kitchen was still command central on the Globe, even though there were bigger offices in the various guilds in Silva. Somehow, working there tricked a part of her mind into thinking that her father was watching over her as she made plans, lending her his strength.

"Cerise sent a contingent of the People of the Woods to Silva today with a new supply of water," Gideon said. "But even with this stopgap, if we don't find a way to win back the Stewardship Guild, we will lose the city."

Valerie's mind worked through the possibilities.

"Can you get me a meeting with Al?" Valerie asked. The Grand Master of the Stewardship Guild had sworn loyalty to Reaper, but Valerie hoped it was more from fear than from embracing his ideals.

"Skye sent him a note, but there has been no reply," Gideon said.

"Then it's time for me to visit him personally. Do we know where he's located these days?"

"You must not challenge fate too often. Reaper let you go when you went to his camp last time, but next time, he may decide to capture you instead," Gideon cautioned.

"What's the alternative?"

Gideon paused for a few heartbeats before replying. "Send an emissary he trusts."

"Who? He isn't talking to Skye."

"Track down his friends, family," Gideon said. "Perhaps they might be easier to convince."

Valerie considered his logic. "Okay. I'll try that first."

The door opened and then slammed shut loudly, and Claremont stomped into the kitchen.

"You're not a queen. Do I always have to come visit you at your castle? It's a great way to get me marked as a traitor and killed," she grumbled, searching through Valerie's pantry for food as if it were her own.

"Make yourself at home," Valerie said.

"It's the least you can do," Claremont shot back, stuffing her mouth with chocolates that Dulcea had sent over.

"Maybe you're right," Valerie said, barely able to hide her grin at the chocolate smeared all over her ex-enemy's face.

"You're gonna love me soon, anyway. Guess who I convinced to see the light? Mira. He's been on the fence a while, but thanks to me, he finally sees that Reaper is too nuts to follow," Claremont said triumphantly.

"Well done!" Valerie admitted. Mira was an influential Master Knight, and his power of shapeshifting would be invaluable. Her mind already raced through the possibilities.

"Before you get any brilliant ideas, Mira can't trick Reaper. His power has to do with affecting the mind, and Mira says Reaper has the best-protected mind he's ever encountered," Claremont said, guessing Valerie's train of thought.

"He could not penetrate my mind, either, to my knowledge. His power will be useful, but what is more valuable is his ability to rally others," Gideon added.

"And we're going to need the help, because the rest of my news isn't good," Claremont continued. "A ton of soldiers from Elsinore showed up to support the Fractus."

Valerie nodded. Kanti's negotiations must not be going well. She wished that she could speak to her friend about what was going on in her country. Could Reaper be transporting soldiers from Elsinore through Plymouth? She wished that she'd asked Kanti for her advice before accepting this truce.

Cyrus burst through her door then, out of breath and flushed.

"Come now!" he said, out of breath. "There's going to be a riot!"

Without waiting for details, Valerie took off after Cyrus with Gideon on her heels. She was still half a mile from The Horseshoe when she heard the shouting.

She cleared the trees and saw that a crowd of Conjurors was swarming two People of the Woods who had arrived with giant casks of water. They had both drawn their weapons, and were back to back, barely keeping the mob at bay.

"What's going on?" Valerie shouted, pushing her way through the crowd. "Are we allies or are we Fractus?"

"They brought half the water they promised!" A man standing several feet taller than her shouted.

"And they want to ration it out to us like we're children," screeched a woman.

Valerie reached the center of the group and made eye contact with the People, who lowered their weapons at her approach.

"I'm sorry," she said to them. Then she turned back to the crowd. "The People of the Woods are our allies, and they're doing us a favor. If they hadn't agreed to cart water from the far reaches of Arden, we would all be forced to move. We owe these people our thanks."

"Barbarians. No more than I'd expect," Valerie heard one of the People mutter beneath his breath.

She decided not to try to change his opinion right then.

"We thank you for your help," Valerie said through clenched teeth. "Please leave with our gratitude."

The People of the Woods scowled, and the one who had spoken spat on the ground in front of the crowd before they turned and left.

At the insult, the mob started to surge forward. Valerie, Gideon, and Cyrus shoved anyone back who tried to follow the People, forming a kind of human wall. The tall man pushed his way to the front of the crowd and shoved Valerie hard—or tried to.

But on the Globe, with nothing binding her magic, he wasn't a threat. Before Cyrus could overreact, Valerie pushed the man back, sending him reeling like a bowling ball into the people behind him, knocking them down.

Valerie had to stop herself from wincing at her overly enthusiastic display of strength. Instead, she glanced behind her and saw that the People of the Woods had disappeared into the dry, brown forest.

Robbed of its initial target, the mob turned its anger on her.

"This is what comes of allowing a child to lead us," the giant man said. "We should make our own rules."

"Maybe the Fractus are the better option. At least they aren't thirsty," said a centaur, pawing the ground and stirring up the dust.

"And perhaps Reaper would send you to be slaughtered on Earth, fighting to consolidate power for him," Gideon said. "In your dying breath, you may wish that your worst problem was having to bathe every other day instead of every day."

"Valerie and the Fist are devoting every ounce of their energy to save all of you!" Cyrus shouted, his eyes blazing. "Do you want to live under a dictator who decides that those with the most power should rule over those with the least?"

The crowd began to disperse, and a few Conjurors even hung their heads. Cyrus squeezed her hand.

"They don't understand what you've sacrificed for them. But they will," he said.

"They are unused to hardship," Gideon said. "This will not be the last of the unrest. Peace is a beautiful thing, but it makes the realities of war unfathomable for those who are distanced from it."

Valerie nodded. "They aren't wrong. We've won some battles, but I'm failing to win this war. How many fewer soldiers will we have the next time we fight the Fractus on a grand scale? So many people are losing faith in the Fist—and in me."

"We have to rally them," Gideon said. "We need a way to release their energy in a positive way."

"Are you talking about a party?" Cyrus said, a glimmer of humor sparking in his eyes. "Please tell me you're talking about a party, Gid, because I am your man."

Gideon laughed. "Cyrus, I do indeed mean a party."

"You've got your mission, soldier," Valerie said. "Let's remind the Conjurors about the way of life we're fighting to save."

Chapter 7

Henry and Thai burst into Valerie's bedroom the next morning. Luckily, she was dressed, and she drew Pathos from her sheath, ready to fight.

"What's wrong?" she said, her mind snapping into alert focus. "Did you find out what Reaper's doing during this truce? Is it too late to stop him?"

"Sorry, Val," Henry said. "Everything's okay."

"Better than okay! I've figured out my power!" Thai said, smiling like a kid on Christmas morning. "I can amplify other Conjurors' powers!"

"What do you mean?" Valerie asked, sitting down as her blood pressure returned to normal.

"I was mentally searching for contacts in Arden who might know Al, the Grand Master of the Stewardship Guild," Henry explained.

"Good thinking," Valerie interrupted, surprised. Henry rarely participated in the war effort, instead vanishing for hours at a time only to come home exhausted and sleep for days.

"That's not the important part. Thai came and slapped me on the back, and suddenly my mind became more focused than it ever had," Henry explained. "It was like skimming a book, except that I was touching different minds, quickly looking to see if there was a connection to Al. I did it in minutes, and I thought it would take days."

"No offense, but are you sure it had to do with Thai? Maybe the effect is in your mind, and you imagined that Thai was helping."

Henry huffed impatiently. "I know what it's like to tap into others' powers. Remember when the whole Empathy Collective helped me search for my dad? We all joined minds. And you and I have shared magic before, too."

"It's not only Henry," Thai continued, speaking fast from his excitement. "Remember when Cyrus shot that fireball out of his hand? I was touching him."

"We ran super-fast together when we were holding hands, racing to the Society of Imaginary Friends, too," Valerie remembered. Her joy and amazement at Thai's power filled her up. "Thai, this is incredible!"

"I know! I thought maybe my only power would be that I cloned myself and made Tan. But there's more to my magic than that. Think how much I'll be able to help defeat the Fractus now," he said.

"Your eyes are huge right now," Henry said to her with a rare smile.

"Thai's right. This could change the game," she said.

Thai picked her up and swung her around, still exuberant. "Those Fractus are toast!"

Even Henry was laughing now, and Valerie let herself be carried away in the moment, because who knew when they'd have another one?

๛   ๛   ๛

Still riding the high from Thai's news, Valerie, Henry, and Thai went to track down the person Henry had found who was connected to Al.

"So who is this friend of Al's that you think we can convince to help us?" Valerie asked Henry as they walked to The Horseshoe.

"Her name is Willa, and she's a master in the Literary Guild," Henry said.

"Is she Al's daughter? Friend?" Thai probed.

"The only family of Al's that I could find when I reached out with my mind was a sister in the Guardians of the Boundary who is firmly aligned with the Fractus. Other than her, Al knows a lot of other Grand Masters and, of course, Conjurors in his guild, but no one who I sensed had any power over him."

"I'm really curious now," Valerie said. "How come you think he might listen to Willa?"

Henry reddened a little. "I didn't want to probe through her mind like a complete creep, but I think Al has been trying to date her for a long time. And she finally accepted before everything went down with the Fractus."

"Love. No more powerful reason to change your mind," Thai said.

Valerie couldn't miss the intensity in Thai's gaze, and she forced herself to look away. "Is Willa sympathetic to the Fist?"

"That's the best part. Reaper imprisoned her dad for years, and the poor guy died in a cell in the Black Castle," Henry said.

"That's awful," Valerie whispered, remembering the bleak jail in the castle's basement.

"She may hate the Fractus as much as we do," Henry said.

51

They'd reached the building that housed the Literary Guild. It was white, like all of the buildings that formed The Horseshoe, but it had tall windows that rose a hundred feet high.

Inside was a library with soaring bookshelves. Valerie moved to the center of the room and turned in a circle, taking in the millions of books that seemed to go on forever.

"She's up there," Henry said, pointing up at a short woman on a floating platform.

Willa selected a book from a dusty shelf and turned, riding her platform to the ground, where she stepped off. She was a little plump, and her face had deep wrinkles by her eyes and mouth.

Willa was already reading the book in her hands, so absorbed that she didn't see Valerie, Henry, and Thai watching her.

"Excuse me?" Valerie said.

Willa looked up, and her eyes widened before she turned and ran. Unprepared for her reaction, Valerie didn't immediately start chasing Willa until Thai took off after her.

Willa was agile, and she leaped on a platform and was zooming out the doors before Valerie had even reached a full sprint. She was shooting across The Horseshoe so fast that Valerie was sure they'd lose her, when Thai gripped her hand.

How could she have missed it before? Her power surged in her, easy to access and pumping through her like the blood in her veins. She moved faster than she ever had, running with her hand in Thai's.

She spared Thai a glance, and his smile was wide as they sprinted together.

"I wondered how I'd ever keep up with you. Guess I can after all," he said, barely breathing heavily.

"Focus," she ordered, unable to keep a smile off her face.

Henry flashed an image of Willa racing past the Empathy Collective, heading toward the woods. With the image came a feeling—fear. Henry sensed that Willa was running for her life. Valerie saw her dress blowing, and she and Thai raced toward her.

"Willa, wait! We only want to talk!" Valerie shouted.

Willa turned, but she didn't slow down.

"We've got to get to the bottom of this," Thai said, and they surged forward, gaining on Willa.

Quickly, they overtook her, and Valerie tackled her to the ground, making sure to shield her so that she didn't fall too hard.

Willa backed away, shaking. But when she spoke, her voice was steady.

"Killing me won't accomplish anything," Willa said. "It will be a stain on your conscience for the rest of your life."

"I'm not going to hurt you," Valerie said, releasing Willa once she stopped wriggling. "Why would you think that? I'm here to ask you for a favor, not to take your life."

"Then what did you bring him for?" Willa said, her eyes flicking to Thai. "I know he does Reaper's dirty work. When I visited Elsinore, I saw him taking away innocent Conjurors who refused to support the Fractus in chains to Dunsinane."

Thai's mouth turned in a sharp frown. Willa had mistaken Thai for Tan, his clone.

"This isn't who you think," Valerie said, and explained Thai's identity.

Willa's posture relaxed, but she continued to eye Thai suspiciously.

"Why are you searching for me, then? I don't have my father's power to detect sources of deep magic, if that's what you're hoping. My magic allows me to help things grow, like flowers. Not very useful during wartime."

"We're here because of your connection to Al, the Grand Master of the Stewardship Guild," Valerie quickly interjected.

Willa scowled. "That traitor?"

"We're hoping you can convince him to leave the Fractus," Thai said.

"Why would you think that I would have any influence over him?" she asked, her brows lowering in suspicion.

"We discovered that you two had a...connection. That he cares about you," Valerie said.

"How? No one knows about that. We never even had our first date. I cut him off as soon as he put his resources behind that monster, Reaper."

"My brother, Henry, has the power to touch minds, to see inside–"

"He invaded my mind? Then he's no better than the Fractus you're fighting!" Willa said. "How could you allow that?"

Valerie was filled with shame. She'd never considered that breaking into someone's mind, reading their most private thoughts, was no better than what Kellen had done to her when he'd controlled her actions with fairy dust. In some ways, it was worse.

Thai's hand briefly touched her back in support, and she straightened. She had to face her mistake head on.

"I'm sorry," she said, not allowing her voice to waver. "I try to be a good leader, but in some ways I'm still a kid. It was a stupid mistake. I didn't think. I apologize for our invasion, and I understand if you don't want to help us."

"I didn't say that," Willa said with a reluctant smile. "I can see why the Conjurors follow you. And I would do anything to see Reaper suffer after what he did to my father. But I don't see how I can help."

"Do you think Al is a bad man, at heart?" Thai asked.

Willa shook her head.

"Then talk to him. You might be the only one he'll listen to right now. If we can't find a way to end this drought, we'll lose Silva," Valerie said.

"I know if it were me, I'd listen to the woman I love and try to see things her way," Thai added.

"It is rather a dream of mine to be called upon to change the tide of a war, like a hero of old," Willa said, her voice dreamy. "I'll talk to the fool."

"Thank you," Valerie said. "I will not forget your noble service."

Willa grinned at Valerie's flourish with words.

"I like you, little vivicus. So I'll solve this problem, one way or another. You have my word."

క్తు   క్తు   క్తు

After a long meeting with Skye and Calibro about the progress the Fist's Grand Masters were making in their inroads into Dunsinane, Valerie walked home alone for the first time in a long while.

She breathed in the still night air as she slipped between the buildings that formed The Horseshoe. She was always on the lookout for attacks, but right now her instincts were quiet.

Which was why she never saw the hand that reached from behind to grab her and tackle her to the ground coming. Fortunately, her magic surged within her without hesitation, and she grabbed the creature by his wrist and hurtled him over her shoulder. He landed hard on the ground.

"You'd think I'd have learned by now," Mira said.

Valerie saw Mira's small brown form in the moonlight and gave him a hand to stand.

"I'd apologize, but as a Master Knight, you really should have known not to sneak up on the Fractus's biggest enemy in the dead of night," Valerie said, but not without a little smile. "I hear you've joined the Fist?"

"Perhaps foolishly, I trusted Kellen. He was the best leader of the Knights that we'd had in a long while. I believe Reaper tortured him, changed his brain, like he did to Rastelli. He is not the fairy I once knew," Mira said.

"I'm glad you're on our side now."

"As am I. I spoke with your friend, Claremont, and have identified a group of Knights who are considering leaving the Fractus. What holds them back is not that they believe in Reaper's cause, but they fear the consequences if they leave. You have to prove that you can protect them and their families."

"I don't know if I can," Valerie admitted. "Reaper's reach is far, and there will be those who fall, no matter how many I try to save."

"You'll have to think of a better story when you talk to them tonight," Mira said with a wry smile.

"Tonight?"

"I've gathered a group at the Guild," Mira said. "Kellen is at the Black Castle with Reaper. There will be no better time to win their hearts."

Valerie nodded. Passing up the chance to secure such powerful supporters would be a mistake, no matter how unprepared she was.

When she passed beneath the arches of her guild, it strangely reminded her of when she'd walked into the launch chamber in the Great Pyramid, which had sent her to the Globe for the first time. Power and possibility rippled through her.

As her eyes adjusted to the darkness in the courtyard, she saw dozens of her fellow Knights waiting for her. They were murmuring to each other, but quieted when she passed beneath the arches.

"She's here," someone whispered.

The awe in the voice took Valerie aback. Not because it was the first time she'd heard it, but because it was the first time that it hadn't surprised her, or embarrassed her. Leading the Fist was part of who she was now.

"Thank you for taking the risk to be here," Valerie said, and her voice carried, echoing around the courtyard.

"Valerie doesn't ask you to follow her blindly," Mira said. "She will hear your concerns, but for now, listen to her."

There was utter silence after his words, and Valerie took it as her invitation to speak.

"I don't know why you chose to follow Fractus. Maybe you believed in his cause, or feared for yourselves or your families. Whatever your reason, I don't judge it. I am grateful you might be ready to leave.

"There is no way that I can promise absolute safety to your or your families, or that our side will win every battle. But someone once told me that having right on your side is important. I didn't believe him then, but I do now. The Fist doesn't seek vengeance against the Fractus, but to end the bloodshed."

"The wish in all of our hearts!" someone shouted, and Valerie squinted into the crowd. She recognized the face of the speaker, and her own broke out in a smile.

"Lyonesse! You fought by my side once, and I am honored you would consider joining me again," Valerie said.

Lyonesse had fought with Valerie in her first battle against the Fractus, but she'd chosen to follow Reaper.

"You see? The vivicus holds no grudges, as I told you!" Lyonesse said triumphantly.

"There is no room for grudges against anyone, even Reaper himself," Valerie said, only realizing her words were true as she spoke them.

Reaper had killed her father, had made her an orphan for the second time in her life, but if she let that consume her and drive her, she knew that she'd lose this war. Her motives had to come from a purer place. Inspiring vengeance in her army would be easy, but the lift would be temporary. Fighting for true justice, like King Arthur, was the real answer.

"Join me, and together, we will create a safer, better future not only for our own families, but the families of all Conjurors and humans who face the tyranny of the Fractus. I can't promise you that victory will come easily, but I know it will come."

A loud cheer followed her words, buoying Valerie's spirits.

"Not bad," Mira murmured.

Valerie turned to him. "I think that we convinced some of these Knights to join us tonight. But tell them not to defect

58

from the Fractus yet. I have an idea that could change the tide of the next major battle, if we do it right."

"I am glad that I will be fighting on your side in this war, apprentice," Mira said. "I do it because it is right, but it doesn't hurt that after tonight, I believe it is also the side that will win."

Though Valerie's ever-present worry about what Reaper was up to during the truce didn't go away, she knew that she'd made the right decision to opt for ten days of peace. Without it, she'd never have had the chance to talk to the Knights, and her instincts told her this could change the tide of the war.

Chapter 8

Somewhere in the recesses of her mind, Valerie knew that Cyrus was planning a huge party on the last day of the truce with the Fractus. But she was still surprised when she stepped out of the Capitol building after a long day of negotiating with the Grand Masters to see The Horseshoe elaborately decorated. Music played, though not loudly yet, and glittering lights hung in the air like fairy children, reminding Valerie of her first date with Cyrus.

Cyrus had also permanently lit the multi-colored path around The Horseshoe that usually only glowed when it was stepped on. The result was otherworldly. Which she supposed it literally was.

When Valerie's foot touched the bottom step of the Capitol building, it lit up in a blaze, and all eyes turned to her. She laughed as fireworks shot up around her.

"To the brilliant, pure, beautiful leader of all that is right with the world, Valerie Diaz!" Cyrus's voice was amplified all around her.

In response, the hundreds of Conjurors gathered in the courtyard whooped. Valerie flushed at their response to her entrance, unable to hide her surprise.

After a beat, she burst out laughing. Cyrus had turned her into a rock star worthy of Hollywood.

She caught Cyrus's eye. He was standing to the side of the Capitol building, and he shrugged when he met her gaze. Her smile must have been huge, because his whole face lit up when he returned her smile with one of his own. It hit her then how long it had been since she'd seen him this happy.

A booming base drummed out a beat that everyone began dancing to, turning the spotlight away from Valerie. She launched herself into Cyrus's waiting arms.

"Thank you," she whispered.

"I remember when you wanted to be a rock star," he said. "I think you were eight. And now, a mere ten years later, you kinda are, minus the guitar."

Valerie hadn't thought about that in a long time. Any dreams of standing out from the crowd, dazzling people and attracting attention, had been beaten out of her in foster care. But Cyrus was right. Once upon a time, she hadn't shied away from the spotlight like she did now.

Valerie saw Thai watching her with Cyrus, but the smile on his face was genuine. He joined the throng dancing to the beat thrumming around them, his graceful dance moves melting into the crowd.

Nearby, Dulcea and Jack danced together, their bodies moving like they were one person. With them was a crowd of boys that Valerie didn't recognize at first without the black stitches on their throats. Her heart grew even fuller as she watched them enjoying the music and checking out girls.

"Come on!" Cyrus said, pulling Valerie into the bobbing mass of bodies.

Valerie gave into the music, letting go of her worries for a little while. Even Henry joined in the dancing.

"I've got a surprise for you, too, sis," Henry said a while later, gesturing to a speck in the distance that was flying toward them.

It was Dasan, the leader of Henry's guild, the Empathy Collective. Everyone cheered as he flew above their heads.

Henry's mind was open enough that she could sense that he was lending his power to Dasan. Together, they cast a spell of peace over the crowd in The Horseshoe. As Dasan's magic trickled down, like a soft, warm rain, Valerie let it wash away her worries.

Colors were brighter, and the light in her mind was able to overtake the dark, for once. Dasan settled to the ground beside them.

"Thank you, Dasan," Valerie said. She felt so light, she thought she might float away.

"A slice of peace is no more than we all deserve," Dasan said, but Valerie saw that he was examining Henry with his head cocked to the side.

"If only Kanti were with us," Valerie said to Henry.

Henry's face fell at her words. But her own anxiety had dimmed, and she didn't overanalyze it when he left the party.

Instead, Valerie embraced having her worries temporarily tucked away by Dasan, and danced with her friends.

It was hours later that she collapsed against a tree, her mind empty enough to enjoy a cool breeze for the first time in a long while. She watched the party, which was still in full swing. She'd find a way to make it like this all the time after the war was over.

Someone sat next to her, and she knew without looking that it was Thai.

"Nice moves out there," Valerie said.

"Looking good yourself. Where did you learn to dance? Judging by the seizures that pass for Henry dancing, it isn't genetic."

Valerie paused. Sometimes her life before magic felt like a dream. "I had an older foster sister who let me practice dance moves with her while we watched MTV. I was never as good as her, but at least now I understand rhythm. Unlike my brother."

"What happened to her?" Thai asked.

Valerie swallowed. "She turned eighteen. Was swallowed up by the streets. Last time I saw her, she was dealing drugs under a bridge where I lived for a while. She didn't recognize me."

She turned her head and found Thai's eyes searching her face. "You deserve a happy ending. Maybe once this war is over, you'll finally get it."

"We all deserve that. And we're going to make it happen," Valerie said. She didn't know if it was because of Dasan's magic, but she believed the words as she spoke them.

"I want to kiss you so badly right now," Thai whispered.

Valerie was hyper-aware of the inches of space between them. She knew that if she leaned forward, even by a hair, that he'd close the gap. Having that thought was a betrayal to Cyrus, and Valerie stood up, stepping back to increase the distance between them.

"I shouldn't have said that. I'm sorry," Thai said. "Blame it on that red bird. What's his name?"

His joke cut the tension, and she laughed.

"Dasan," she said. "And I have to get back to the party."

"I'll see you tomorrow, Valerie," Thai said, and headed in the direction of his dorm.

63

Valerie made her way through the grass toward the glowing lights and laughter, but stopped when she saw something glowing on the ground a few yards away. She knelt to pick it up.

It was a flower formed entirely of light, and there was only one person who could have made it.

Valerie's temporary peace vanished. Guilt was the first emotion that flooded back in her mind as she slowly returned to reality.

ℒ   ℒ   ℒ

Valerie couldn't find Cyrus anywhere at the party, so she turned her steps home. She found him there, sitting on her front stoop. The strangest wave of dread passed over her.

Cyrus stood, his face more still than Valerie had ever seen it. "Remember when you, Henry, Kanti, and I all pledged on Pathos to tell the truth to each other?"

"Of course," she said, gripping the hilt of her blade, which hung in its sheath at her side.

"It binds us. Even if you wanted to lie to me, you couldn't," he said.

"But I haven't lied to you. And I never will," Valerie said.

Cyrus's face softened by a fraction. "I know. And I know you're too honorable to cheat on me. That's not what I'm afraid of. I'm afraid that you're going to stay with me for the rest of your life, even though I'm your second choice."

"Cyrus, I love you. I want to be with you," she said, but a mounting fear was growing in her heart.

"Tell me you love me more than you love Thai," Cyrus said. "That I'm your soul mate."

If Valerie could have lied then, she might have. Cyrus had been the only constant in her life, and if she broke his heart and he left her, she might die. But even as she tried to form the words, they turned to ashes in her mouth. She didn't know if it was the spell or her own conscience, but she couldn't mislead him.

"I don't know if I could survive without you," she said, her hands clenched into fists. "I love you. Believe that."

"I do," he said softly. "But you love Thai even more, don't you?"

Valerie stared at him, tears pooling in her eyes. She didn't answer.

"Don't you?" Cyrus said. "Say it!"

"Yes," Valerie whispered.

Cyrus seemed to deflate, to shrink before her eyes.

"We're over," he said. "You're free. Go be with who you really want."

Cyrus turned and left, and Valerie didn't try to follow him.

ళా   ళా   ళా

Henry's soft knock roused Valerie from a restless sleep. She shuffled to her door like a zombie and opened it.

"You're getting better at shutting me out. I didn't know what happened until I found Cyrus," Henry said.

"I learned from the master," she said, and regretted her words when she saw Henry's mouth turn down.

"You have no idea how much I wish I didn't have to do that," he said.

Valerie relented. "Maybe what Cyrus did is for the best. I'm only going to end up hurting everyone I love when my magic destroys my mind. The sooner he distances himself from me the better."

"It doesn't have to be that way. If you hold back from using your vivicus power—"

Valerie shook her head. "I won't watch people die if I can help it. Every battle I'm in, I think about if I can save more lives by fighting or by using my vivicus power. In the end, after the fighting is over, it always makes sense to save someone. I couldn't live with anything else. By the end of this war, I might be no better than Darling. Cyrus deserves more."

"That's his choice to make," Henry argued.

"Maybe it's for a different reason, but he already made it. I'm not going to stop him," Valerie said.

"Just know that you can never send me away. So don't try."

"I think it's the other way around. You're the one pushing me away," Valerie said. "Cyrus made me tell him how I felt about Thai by using the truth spell on Pathos that binds us. I thought about asking you some questions that you wouldn't be able to lie about, too."

"Part of me wishes you would," he said, his voice ragged. "But a bigger part of me might lose it if you did."

She nodded. "I'm not going to force you to tell me anything. I don't like being cornered, and I'm not going to do it to you."

Henry hugged her then, holding on to her like a lifeline.

"Everything sucks so much, you know?" he asked.

"Yeah, I do," Valerie said. "I keep thinking we've hit the bottom, and then it drops out from under us again."

The early morning light stole through her room then, turning everything pink as Henry quickly wiped a tear from his eye. "This night is finally over."

℮   ℮   ℮

For the next few days, Valerie threw herself into planning her battle strategy with more energy than ever. Azra and Gideon spent as much time as they could helping her refine her ideas.

Inevitably, Valerie was thrown together with Cyrus as they planned potential ways to combat the new light-sucking powers of the Fractus, but that was somehow less weird than her interactions with Thai. Cyrus was always watching them, and she could sense that he was waiting for a sign that she'd moved on.

Finally, Thai cornered her at the Lake of Knowledge, where she'd gone for a dip to clear her mind.

"Hard to believe that a few years ago, you didn't know how to swim," he said.

Valerie shook her short hair to get the worst of the water out and wrapped herself in her towel.

"It reminds me that I'm capable of overcoming something that really scares me," she explained, remembering the first time she'd leaped into the ocean. It was the fact that she was so terrified that made her success so thrilling.

"You've come a long way since then."

"I'm more afraid than ever," she said with a shake of her head.

"I don't think so. You used to have your fear hidden away, but now it's out in the open and you're dealing with it. I think that's brave," Thai said.

He'd stepped closer, and Valerie wrapped herself even more tightly in her towel and started walking home.

"Are you going to tell me what's going on between you and Cyrus?" he asked her when they reached The Horseshoe.

Her heart hammered. "He dumped me."

Thai was quiet for a long time. "I'm sorry. I know how much you love him."

"But not as much as I love you, and that's why he's gone," she said.

He stopped her then, taking her arm to turn her to face him.

"What did you say?" Thai's eyes were alive, his entire face lit up.

But she shook her head. "I wanted you to know. But it doesn't change anything. If he saw us together, it would kill him. And I won't do that."

"But later, after he's moved on..." Thai started.

"I can't give you any promises, Thai. I don't know who I'll be if we ever come out the other side of this war. I can't stand to lose anyone else, and that means I'll use my vivicus power a lot. Even if my body survives this war, my mind might be stripped away from using my magic."

"You don't get it, Valerie. Even if your mind was lost and all that's left is your heart, you would still be the only one I want. When this is over, if all you need is a friend to keep you safe, I'll be your friend. If you need an ally to help you recreate this world, I'll be your ally. And if the day comes that you need a man to love you with every cell of his body, I'll be that man for you. But for now, while you're not sure what you need, how about I just be here for you?"

If Thai would have touched her then, there wasn't a force in the universe that could have stopped her from kissing him. But he didn't. He smiled at her, the rare one that made her heart speed up and her mind slow down, and then he turned and continued walking her home.

Chapter 9

Valerie woke up the next morning with the sense that there was somewhere she needed to be, somewhere important, but she couldn't remember where it was. The air hummed with magic in a way that seemed out of sync with the universe.

She found her brother in the kitchen, and his nervous energy flowed from his mind to hers.

"Do you have any idea what's wrong?" she asked.

Henry shook his head. "I checked in with Chisisi, and nothing has happened on Earth that he knows of."

As leader of the Fist, Valerie ought to have done that already, instead of sleeping.

"I'm lucky I have you here to keep us on track. I could never win this war without you," she said.

Henry turned, but not before she saw the anguish on his face.

"I wish you'd tell me whatever it is you're afraid that I'll find out," she said softly.

"I can't. Not yet," he said.

Valerie took a step closer to him. "You can see inside my head. So why don't you see how deep my loyalty to you goes? Trust me."

Henry's hands trembled. "That's just it. I *can* see inside your head. I can see how some days your grief is a weight that you're struggling to hold up so it doesn't crush you. Can't you understand that I feel the same way? If the weight I'm carrying gets any heavier, I'm going to fall apart."

It took all her self-control not to push him further, but at last, she nodded. "I'll wait," she said, and Henry released a breath of relief. "Let's go to The Horseshoe and see if we can sniff out what's wrong."

Their walk was quiet, so they heard the shouting long before they reached their destination. A crowd had gathered around the fountain in the center of The Horseshoe. Valerie saw Gideon and pulled him aside.

"What is it?" she asked.

Gideon was pale, which frightened Valerie. Her mentor wasn't easily shaken. He gestured to the fountain, and Valerie squinted. It had been dry for weeks because of the drought, but now it ran with a thick black liquid that looked like oil. It was spilling over the sides, running in dark rivulets along the ground. It left a dark, inky stain on everything it touched.

"I do not know how they managed this," Gideon said, finding his voice. "The Fractus were observed at every moment while they were in Plymouth, and I saw nothing other than platforms transporting large boxes."

"It must have been a distraction. The whole time, they were doing something below," Valerie murmured, but she wasn't surprised. She knew that there would be a price to pay for their ten days of peace, and now they'd begun paying it.

"I had Knights I trusted on the ground, hiding, but they saw nothing amiss," Gideon said.

"Until we know what this stuff is, let's get people out of here," Henry said.

Gideon nodded, and he, Valerie, and Henry gently urged people to go home. People were reluctant to leave the spectacle, but eventually, they returned to their daily tasks,

71

giving the black liquid a wide berth. Henry was kneeling by a puddle, staring at it intently.

"I don't know what this is," he said as he reached out to touch it.

Valerie snatched his hand back. "It could work like the Fractus's black weapons. Or be related to that new power we saw in the Fractus from Elsinore."

"I don't think so," Henry said, but he backed away.

"The flow is being stemmed," Gideon said, and Valerie saw that the fountain's output was now just a trickle.

But the once-beautiful work of art was stained with black, and the edges were eroded.

"I think the Fractus want to make sure that if they can't get back inside, then neither can we," Valerie said.

"Of course," Gideon agreed. "Why didn't I see it before? But I still cannot fathom how it was achieved."

"This is only the first horrible thing we know of that the Fractus accomplished over the past ten days," Henry said.

Valerie's gut twisted at his words. "I want soldiers tasked with finding a way into Plymouth so we can see what the Fractus are up to down there."

"I'll put a team on it," Gideon said.

Every one of her instincts screamed that something dark was going on under her feet. This was only the first shot across the bow. Something worse was coming.

⁊   ⁊   ⁊

Valerie spent the day with Dulcea at The Society of Imaginary Friends going through tactics to attract new recruits to the Fist. On her way out, she saw Cyrus leaving the Weapons Guild.

She opened her mouth to speak, to apologize somehow for the pain she'd caused him.

"Don't. Even talking about it could kill me right now."

"Do you want me to go?" Valerie asked, her voice small.

"Yes, but what I want doesn't matter right now. We have too much to discuss in terms of next steps for the weapons we use against the Fractus who have the ability to cast darkness."

Valerie nodded, a little ashamed at how relieved she was that she didn't have to face Cyrus's pain right now. He led her into the Weapons Guild to the little lab where he worked on his weapons of light. It was abandoned except for Leo.

"Welcome, Valerie," Leo said, looking up from the dusty volume he was reading. "Cyrus has come up with a new way of working with light that I've never heard of before, even from ancient masters of the craft."

"The other lightweavers and I have a new technique for magically embedding light into the weapons made by the People of the Woods," Cyrus explained, standing a little straighter from Leo's words. "I want to test the theory with Pathos."

"Of course," Valerie said, removing her sword from its sheath and handing it to Cyrus.

He laid it on one of the black tables. Pathos glowed already, because Cyrus had imbued it with light again after her encounter with the Fractus from Elsinore when she visited Reaper's camp.

Cyrus turned a crank on the wall, and the entire ceiling of the little lab opened up to the sky, and sunlight poured in. Valerie's jaw dropped, and Cyrus gave her a little grin that was an echo of his usually mischievous smile.

"How did you manage a major architectural overhaul in here on top of everything else?" Valerie asked.

"That was my doing," Leo said. "A friend in the Architecture Guild owed me favor. It took him several afternoons."

"That's all?"

"Magic, Val, remember?" Cyrus said, and it was like they were best friends again.

But when she smiled, his own vanished, and he turned to her sword.

Concentrating, light collected around Cyrus, and he glowed brightly. His fingers worked the light, and it knit together in ever-brighter strands. Then he touched Pathos, and the strange light pattern became embedded in her sword. There was a bright flash, and Cyrus stepped back, sweating.

Pathos lifted off the table, spinning, the blade flashing so brightly that Valerie had to squint.

"Is that supposed to happen?" she asked.

"I didn't do that," he said, out of breath.

Pathos spun faster and faster, and then abruptly stilled. Valerie started to reach for it when it slammed into the table. The blade sliced through and embedded up to the hilt. At Pathos's touch, the entire table glowed.

Leo and Cyrus nodded in satisfaction.

"Better than we hoped," Leo said.

"What happened?" Valerie asked.

"Leo treated the table with some of the magic from one of the Fractus's black weapons. Our light weapons didn't go out when they were near it, but they did dim. Pathos didn't only resist the power of the magic, it completely reversed it."

"So it transformed the dark magic into light?" Valerie asked.

Cyrus nodded.

"I never dreamed that would be possible," she said.

"It should work against the Fractus's old weapons," Cyrus said. "That's no guarantee it will be immune to whatever these new powers are."

"But it's a start."

"It's a major blow to the Fractus, my boy," Leo said gently.

"But the amount of power I drew...it will take months to create the number of weapons we need with this light treatment," Cyrus said.

Valerie saw now that Cyrus drooped, and his usual glow was almost gone. How much of himself and his magic had he poured into her sword?

"But with the help of the other lightweavers, couldn't you manage it sooner?" Valerie asked.

"They won't be able to draw enough power. I think that my powers changed after you saved me, Val. They were a little above average before, but now, they are untouchable," Cyrus said, but without pride.

"Chern's words are true," a deep voice rang through the room, vaguely familiar.

Valerie yanked Pathos from the table and held it at the ready.

"Will you let her kill us, Cyrus?" a woman's voice spoke now.

"Mom?" Cyrus asked.

Cyrus's parents stepped from the shadows.

"Chern said that you were using magic to create weapons to kill his people, but we didn't believe him," Mr. Burns said.

"You don't understand," Cyrus said, his voice flat.

"Cyrus, sweetheart, you are so much better than this," his mother said, her voice shaking.

"Enough. You're coming home with us," Mr. Burns said.

"Do you really think you can convince me to abandon everything I believe in and the people I love?" Cyrus asked. "Leave. I can't stand to see you right now. You're cowards, hiding behind your values. Can't you see that what's right is protecting innocent people?"

"If you really believe that, then you'll come with us," Mrs. Burns said.

"Chern says that if you come home with us, he will spare our people from this war," Mr. Burns said. "He will bend space so that no one will ever find Messina again, and we will be free of the taint of magic forever."

"He also promised that your father will be the one to lead our people through this time of chaos," Mrs. Burns added.

"You and Cara will come with us. The time for your foolish rebellion has come to an end. I won't let you ruin what I've worked for," Mr. Burns said.

"You're no better than Reaper, grasping for power behind the false idea that you know what's best for everyone," Cyrus said. "Get out of here."

"Now listen here," Mr. Burns began.

"Get out!" Cyrus yelled, and both of his parents drew back in shock.

"If we leave, you'll never see us again," Mr. Burns said.

Cyrus's mother gave her husband a sharp frown, but before she could contradict him, Cyrus spoke.

"I should be so lucky. Leave, and never come back," he said, his voice colder than Valerie had ever heard it.

Cyrus's mother paled. Valerie saw her eyes fill with tears before Mr. Burns yanked her away.

"Cy, no," Valerie whispered. "They're your parents. You only get one set."

"You don't get to tell me what to do anymore, either," Cyrus said, and he left the room, slamming the door behind him.

℠ ℠ ℠

Valerie's headache had been mounting all day, and she stumbled home in a fog of pain. But the closer she got, the more it lifted. She guessed the reason when Clarabelle cantered up to her, exuding the promise of peace and love.

Since Azra and Clarabelle had moved into the forest near her house, Valerie had noticed green returning to the woods, and her little garden was positively lush.

"Were you waiting long, little one?" she asked.

Clarabelle was excited, Valerie could sense when the unicorn touched her mind. Something wonderful was about to happen.

I don't know what's going on with her, either. Azra stepped out of Valerie's house, smiling at the sight of her foal rolling around in the grass.

"Someone's coming?" Valerie asked, trying to interpret the barrage of sweet notes pinging her mind from Clarabelle's.

Indeed. Someone amazing.

The air in Valerie's garden shimmered, and two figures appeared, transported from Earth. She recognized the taller person immediately.

"Dr. Freeman! Is everything okay?" Valerie asked.

Gideon heard her shout and came outside. It was only the third time Dr. Freeman had come to the Globe. He'd said that it was overwhelming to be in a land full of so much magic. He preferred Valerie to visit him.

"Quite excellent, actually," Dr. Freeman said. "Wouldn't you say so, Ming?"

Valerie turned her gaze to the girl standing at Dr. Freeman's side, and her eyes widened. This wasn't the sickly child she remembered from the hospital, or even the thin, pale girl recovering from a long illness. In the months since Darling had cured her of cancer, Ming had flourished. Her short hair shone, and her eyes sparkled with health.

Ming bounded over to her, and Valerie met her halfway.

"Your mom finally let you come!" Valerie said. "I can't wait to show you everything. You've got to see the Guild of The Society of Imaginary Friends."

"Not to be a party pooper, but I'm under strict instructions that Ming's first visit here be a short one," Dr. Freeman said. "And we're actually here for another reason. Long before I knew magic existed, I noticed certain similarities between you and Ming. She would also get weak and her blood pressure would drop for no reason. It wasn't as severe as yours, but it was compounded by her cancer."

"Wait. Are you saying that *Ming* is one of the children you identified who might be suffering from having too much magic?"

Valerie wondered if her smile was as big as the one on Ming's face right now.

"That's what we're here to confirm," Dr. Freeman said.

"Azra? Is it true?" Valerie said, turning to her friend.

Dr. Freeman and Ming wore identical expressions of reverence as Azra and her foal approached, reminding Valerie of the first time she'd met the unicorn. It was a sacred experience.

78

I no longer have any magical gifts. They have been passed to my foal.

Clarabelle approached Ming, who gently touched the little unicorn's iridescent mane as if she were in a trance.

Clarabelle's tiny sounds of pleasure were pure bliss in Valerie's mind. Without using words, Clarabelle communicated her own feeling—certainty. Ming was bursting with magical potential.

"You were right," Valerie said to Dr. Freeman, and he nodded.

"I have magic inside me, like you, Valerie?" Ming asked.

"You do," Valerie said, laughing as Ming twirled in a circle, her arms open wide.

"If only travel between our worlds could stay open forever, Ming could live on the Globe part time and still go home to her family," Dr. Freeman said.

"But as long as there are those with magic and those without it, there is the potential for power to be abused," Gideon said, speaking up for the first time. "We must remove the Fractus from Earth and close travel between the worlds again."

Ming looked up at Valerie with her huge eyes. "It's okay. It's enough to know I'm magical."

"And a princess, don't forget," Valerie said, to make Ming smile, though her own heart squeezed.

As long as this divide between worlds existed, there would always be those who had to live where they didn't quite belong. And from experience, Valerie knew that wasn't a solution at all.

After Ming had left and Azra and Clarabelle retreated into the forest, Valerie made the walk to the spot in the forest where she could access the gardens of Babylon, which were still locked away from the rest of the world by the spell her father had cast.

It was where she went when she wanted to grieve for him in private. Over the past months since he'd been gone, she'd mostly gone to sob where no one would hear her, but today, she went for another reason.

She stepped through the screen of vines into the garden and was overpowered by the sense that in this place, she wasn't an orphan. She wasn't surprised to see a familiar figure at the top of the tiers of flowers.

She hiked up to join Henry, who was staring at the lake on the other side. He came here a lot because it was the one place no one could find him except her.

"I couldn't help thinking about this place—and dad—today," Valerie said. "He locked Babylon away from the rest of the world to make it his special place with Mom. Even though that's romantic, it also robbed all the other Conjurors on the Globe of the opportunity to enjoy its beauty."

"Yeah, he was a piece of work," Henry said, but without the bitterness that had laced his words when Oberon was alive.

"Isn't that also what we're doing with the Globe? Keeping it from humans who belong here, who have every right to be here? How do we stop the Fractus from abusing regular humans without keeping all of the best parts of magic to ourselves?"

"I don't think I'm the right person to talk to about avoiding selfish decisions," Henry said. "But don't stop asking these questions, Val. It's gonna be you who finally finds a better answer. I really believe that."

"Every time I come here, it's like a piece of him is alive, you know?"

Henry regarded her. "I never loved him like you did, but I'm less alone when I come here."

"It's like, if I listen hard enough, I might finally hear him give me the answers I'm looking for."

Henry squeezed her arm, and they listened for a long time. But as always, there was nothing but silence.

Chapter 10

The clashes between the Fractus and humans returned with a new ferocity. For weeks, Valerie's existence was consumed with fight after fight. As soon as her vivicus power had recharged after tapping it to save a life, she'd use it again. Valerie had lost count of the lives, but she never forgot the faces. She became increasingly forgetful, and headaches followed her even into her dreams.

More than once, Chisisi had already identified the next place she was needed by the time she'd returned from her last encounter with the Fractus.

Between keeping the Fractus at bay—barely—on Earth and doing the minimal chores she had to attend to personally to keep the Fist organized on the Globe, Valerie had almost no time to sleep and eat. Sometimes, Henry, Thai, or even Cyrus joined her when she fought the Fractus, but there wasn't time to talk to her friends about anything other than the war.

So it was a bit of a shock to check in with Chisisi and find that he didn't have an assignment for her that day.

"Nowhere you want me to check out?" she asked.

Sanguina and Chrome were both in attendance, and Sanguina spoke up.

"Even the leader of the Fist needs to take the occasional day of rest," Sanguina said.

Chrome flashed an image in her mind of himself, sleeping in the sun, and then rising up with his teeth bared. He'd had enough of wandering around out of the thick of the fighting. He wanted to be a part of the action.

Chrome had followed the magic trail the People of the Woods had found from Armenia all the way to the ocean, where even he couldn't continue to follow it.

"Chrome and I can take on any Fractus who attack humans today," Sanguina said.

"Your friends' offer is a good one, young miss. You would be wise to heed their advice," Chisisi added.

Valerie decided not to argue, for once. She gave them a grateful nod and returned to her home on the Globe.

Her first thought was to go straight to bed. Only pure adrenaline kept her moving most days, and without an immediate threat, her whole body seemed slow and clumsy.

Not the state that she needed to be in when a flickering movement in the trees set off her sixth sense for danger. She raced out of her garden and heard the sound of hooves stomping on the ground.

She passed into the woods and saw Summer up on her hind legs, batting at something in the air before her hooves pounded into the soft dirt. The ancient centaur's teeth were bared.

Valerie followed her gaze and saw Kellen zipping through the trees, his wings fluttering madly.

"Don't let his dust touch you!" Valerie said, which drew the fairy's attention away from Summer, as she'd hoped.

She registered a tiny movement in the bramble behind Summer. Clarabelle was hiding in there with Azra, Valerie knew. Did Kellen notice, too?

"You're here to fight me, so let's do this," Valerie said, hoping she could keep his attention so that Summer could sneak the unicorns away.

"You've grown self-important in addition to being generally useless," Kellen sneered. "I'm here for Clarabelle, not you. She has real power."

Kellen flew closer, black dust falling from his wings. Valerie ducked and rolled, and it didn't touch her. He scrabbled at her mind, trying to control her like he'd done many times before, but that tactic wasn't as effective for him as it had been in the past.

Valerie kept her locus firmly in her mind, her love for her friends, and swatting away Kellen's attempts to wriggle inside was nothing more than an annoyance.

If the fairy was surprised, he didn't show it. He was moving so fast that it was impossible to keep track of him, never mind knock him out of the air.

Little rainbows danced on the ground. Kellen wasn't alone. He'd brought a dozen or more invisible Fractus with him.

"Summer, behind you!" Valerie shouted, and the centaur kicked out with her hind leg, connecting with a breakable Fractus with a loud crunch.

The next few minutes were a blur as four transparent Fractus attacked her at once. But her skills had never been more honed after all of the fighting she'd been doing on Earth. She managed to disable them while still noticing that Kellen was zipping through the trees, looking for Clarabelle.

Clarabelle is shielding our location with her mind. Azra's words rang in Valerie's mind. *I don't know how she is doing it, but somehow, she has created a circle of purity that no one*

84

may enter in anger or hate. Kellen cannot find us as long as his intentions are evil. We are invisible to him.

Valerie let out a relieved breath, punching one of the breakables in the face and then jump-kicking to knock another in the area she guessed was his jaw.

One of the invisible Fractus had leaped on Summer, who bucked, trying to shake him off. Before Valerie could move to assist the centaur, Summer slammed him against a tree, and she heard a yelp of pain.

Kellen flew past Valerie, and she leaped into the air and crashed into him. As they fell, she maneuvered his tiny body so that it was trapped beneath hers.

The energy in the little glade where they fought changed. The air crackled with electricity, and Valerie's fearlessness vanished. The Laurel Circle on her thumb turned to ice when she saw Reaper standing on the other side of a portal he'd created in the air.

Through the opening, she saw him make a strange gesture with his hand, and her world turned on its axis. She lost her balance, falling to the ground and losing her grip on Kellen.

"Get out of there, now," Reaper commanded Kellen.

"Not yet! I've got her now. She's as good as dusted," Kellen said.

"Don't be too sure," Valerie said, gritting her teeth and making another grab for the fairy. She missed by a millimeter.

"I didn't send you to fight the vivicus. She's easy enough to kill when I decide it's time. I sent you for the baby unicorn," Reaper said.

"She's here. I'll find her," Kellen said, sounding almost possessed.

85

"She's nowhere close. I can't sense her presence at all. Your informant must have been wrong," Reaper said, dismissing the fairy.

Valerie was still struggling to find her center. She stilled, gripping Pathos and letting her magic guide her.

But before she could strike out at Kellen again, the fairy screamed, a sound so filled with pain that Valerie wanted to block her ears.

"You will do as I say," Reaper said, his annoyance darkening into something much more dangerous.

Kellen continued to moan.

"Stop! I'm coming, please, no more," Kellen begged.

"You're growing ever more useless," Reaper said, as the fairy flew haphazardly into his portal.

Before it snapped closed, Valerie saw the crazed anguish in Kellen's eyes. It reminded her of someone, and it tickled the back of her brain until she remembered. She'd seen the same look in Rastelli's eyes after Reaper had destroyed his brain and turned him into a single-minded killer.

ഗ   ഗ   ഗ

After making sure that Azra and Clarabelle were safely tucked away, Valerie returned home to relay her news to Gideon.

"Why would they want Clarabelle?" Valerie asked, as much to herself as her mentor.

She paced the kitchen restlessly as she tried to guess Reaper's strategy. It was like playing chess with a master, when she barely understood the game.

"Consider what we know. Clarabelle is the first unicorn born in centuries. Unicorns arguably have more magic than anyone in the universe," Gideon said.

"Including Reaper himself. Do you think he wants to kill her?" Valerie asked, and the thought alone made her sick.

Gideon shook his head. "Not before he would see if he could use that power to his own ends."

"But if he can't, then he might consider her his greatest threat. Azra's successor, with more magic than even he possesses. Someone who would set us on a path of peace, not war."

Gideon's mouth was set in a grim line. "Though I know she craves your presence, Clarabelle must hide. There is nowhere in Arden safe enough for her right now."

"Maybe nowhere on the Globe, even," Valerie said thoughtfully.

Gideon raised his eyebrows. "A brilliant idea or a terrible one, but which it is, I cannot say."

"It's not for us to decide," Valerie said, releasing a breath. "Azra will know what to do."

A knock on the door interrupted their conversation, and Valerie answered it to find Thai waiting for her. He looked especially good in his nicest jeans and a new shirt. She must have been staring a few seconds too long, because Thai started grinning.

"Hey," she said, embarrassed at how tongue-tied she was.

"Hey," he teased, imitating her shy tone, and she laughed. "I came to invite you to my apprentice ceremony. We're allowed to bring one guest, and you're my first choice. I know it's a long shot, and if you're off saving lives, I understand, but if you're free and you could come, it would mean a lot to me and..."

Now it was Thai who was nervous, and it was so endearing that it was all she could do not to pull him into her arms.

Behind her, Gideon stood in the hallway.

"Go," Gideon said, his eyes warm as he watched them.

"As luck would have it, this is a free day. And there's no one I'd rather spend it with," she said, tickled by the excitement on Thai's face.

After changing into a dress that somehow still looked decent with a sword strapped to her, she joined Thai in the garden. This time he was the one who was staring. It was the first time he'd seen her in a dress, but after this reaction, she would have to think about wearing them more often.

"I'm embarrassed. I don't even know what guild you're apprenticing to," Valerie said as they started the trek to The Horseshoe. "I've been in this time warp, fighting enemy after enemy, and have completely missed out on your life."

"You're fighting the battles that no one else can. Don't apologize for that," Thai said. "I'm apprenticing to the Healers' Guild."

Valerie tried to hide her surprise. The Grand Master of the Guild, Nightingale, was a Fractus sympathizer.

"Do they know you fight with the Fist?" Valerie asked.

"Yes. The Guild is supposed to help all Conjurors who need healing, without prejudice. They've strayed from that now, healing only the Fractus, but I hope to bring them back to the right path."

"Be careful. It could be a trap," Valerie said, trying to swallow her sudden fear.

"Maybe, but I don't think so. Many Healers in the Guild are angry about the decision not to remain neutral in the war. If Nightingale doesn't make a change, they may elect a new Grand Master. I'm hoping I can tip the scales for Nightingale and convince him to come back to our guild's mission."

"You will," Valerie said. There was no task she could imagine that Thai wouldn't do well if he put his mind to it.

"If I really believe those values, which I do, it means I'll heal Fractus as well as our own army," Thai said.

Valerie stopped and turned to him. "Of course. Do you think I'd ever want you to do anything else?"

Thai touched her cheek briefly, and the contact made her blush. "Your heart is what I love most about you. It's why you are the only one who can end this struggle with the Fractus for good."

Thai pushed the doors of the Healers' Guild open. The entryway was filled with Conjurors. Despite the crowd, the noise was a low hum. Even during one of their biggest ceremonies, it seemed the Healers didn't want to disturb the patients.

Nightingale was hard to miss as he moved through the crowd, shaking hands. He saw Valerie, and she braced herself to be kicked out. But instead, he nodded to her, and she nodded back.

"Nightingale keeps looking at you, then looking down, like he's feeling guilty about something," Thai said.

"He refused to heal me once, even though I could have died."

Thai's hands balled into fists. "That will never happen again. I'll kick him out of his own guild first."

"It's okay, Thai. It's war. People do awful things that they wouldn't do otherwise. I'd rather have Nightingale as an ally than drive him away because he denied me care once."

"That's the smart choice, but I'd rather give him one good punch first," Thai said, but without heat.

"I think your ceremony is about to start," Valerie said, glad of the distraction.

The apprentices gathered around an etching of an enormous tree in the far wall.

"Today, we welcome our novices, who come to us to devote body and spirit to the art of healing," Nightingale said. "We dedicate our lives to easing suffering and saving lives. There is no nobler calling. Novices, join hands and let your magic well within you."

The eight novices, including Thai, stood in a circle and clasped hands. Magic hummed in the room, deep and low, creating a pleasant warming sensation within Valerie.

Valerie and the other observers of the ceremony gasped as the etching of the tree peeled from the wall, becoming three-dimensional. Gold threaded the dark bark of the trunk and wound through the veins of the leaves on the trees, like the ones in Arden's forests.

Before their eyes, eight new branches grew from the tree, joining hundreds that already existed on it.

"Today, you join a family. We have our roots in knowledge, magic, and intense study. We share the trunk of common values, to save lives and ease pain. Each of you is a branch shooting from this tree, and the leaves are the lives you will save."

The hum of magic grew louder, rattling the structure of the building until an explosion of leaves burst from the tree, showering everyone in the room before vanishing when they hit the floor. When the leaves were gone, so were all of the aches, bruises, and scratches Valerie had sustained during her many battles. She was grateful for the unexpected gift.

"Welcome, apprentices, to the Healers' Guild!" Nightingale said, and the room erupted in cheers.

Thai turned to her then, and she could see even from where she stood the open joy on his face. It reminded her of the thrill of becoming a Knight when she joined her own guild.

The tree faded back into an etching on the wall, and Valerie knew she'd never look at it the same way again.

Thai threaded his way through the crowd until he found her and swept her up in a hug that lifted her off her feet.

"Can you believe how lucky we are?" Thai said when he put her down.

"I can't imagine life before magic," she replied.

She wished that everyone on Earth could have magic humming in their veins and know the thrill of its possibilities.

"The apprentices have some kind of top-secret after-ceremony tradition. I'm sorry for bringing you all this way and then ditching you," he said.

"Don't be! Go embrace your magic. Heal things. Do... whatever you guys do. I'm proud of you, Thai. And so grateful you're here, fighting this battle with me. But tonight, go live it up, apprentice."

He hugged her one last time and took off. The other apprentices whooped when he joined them, and they all ran off into the recesses of the Guild.

Valerie turned to leave, but Nightingale pulled her aside.

"I will turn no one aside who needs healing, as I did to you, again. Fractus and Fist are both welcome here," he said.

She wasn't sure she could trust the offer, but if it was genuine, she also didn't want to offend a Grand Master with the potential to help her army.

"I'll remember your words," she said.

Outside, Valerie didn't head home immediately. Instead, she walked along the path between the guilds, watching the stones glow each time she stepped on one.

"Valerie!" Willa's voice stopped her in her tracks.

Willa was sitting on the steps of her guild. Her long hair was tied up with three pencils in a messy bun, and she had piles of books around her.

"Do you have news? Did Al agree to leave the Fractus?" Valerie asked eagerly.

Willa waved her hand dismissively. "That old fool did little more than whine and give excuses, as I knew he would."

Valerie slumped.

"But I promised you a solution, and I have found one," Willa continued. "Magic is wonderful for many things, but one downside is that we have forgotten the old, non-magical ways of getting things done."

"What are you saying?" Valerie asked.

"I've been studying some scientific texts on farming in areas of low rainfall on Earth," Willa said, gesturing to the books around her. "With the help of the Architecture and Glamour Guilds, which are both allied with the Fist, and the People of the Woods, I believe we can quickly construct some irrigation canals and hide them from the view of the Fractus."

"Irrigation canals..." Valerie's brain tried to wrap itself around what Willa was proposing.

Willa huffed in exasperation, but the hint of a smile hovered on the corners of her mouth. "I'm saying that we can end this drought without Al's help. We can save Silva from falling into the Fractus's hands."

Chapter II

Willa wanted to put her plan into action that very night, but Valerie convinced her to wait until morning to begin knocking on doors. She knew from experience that ideas were rarely well received when people were pulled out of bed.

She raced home, hoping this would be one of the nights that Henry was home. He was the perfect person to manage the project and make sure that Willa didn't ruffle any feathers.

In the kitchen, she found Henry and Gideon talking with Henry's Empath friends, Elle and Will. Their grim expressions stopped her from sharing her news right away.

"We were about to go looking for you," Henry said.

"The Illyrians are announcing a formal alliance with the Fractus," Gideon said.

"We knew that they were leaning that way. Is this a major blow for us?" Valerie asked.

"The Akashic Records have provided key intel in weapons development and strategy, among other things," Gideon said. "The loss of Illyrian contacts will be missed."

"Is there anything we can do?"

Elle and Will glanced at each other, and then Elle spoke up. "We don't tell very many people this, but our parents were Illyrian."

"I didn't know the Illyrians were allowed to have kids. Ignorant of me, I guess," Valerie said.

"No, you were right," Will said. "It's against Illyrian law, and our parents were both cast out forever when the authorities found out. They couldn't survive on land for long."

She remembered Leo saying that when Illyrians who had lived beneath the waves for a long time returned to land, they had trouble remembering how to function with human needs, and many perished.

"You must miss them so much," Valerie said softly. The pain of her own loss overcame her so fast, she didn't see it coming, and she had to bite her cheek to contain her tears.

Elle cleared her throat as if to shake off the painful memories. "Before they were cast out, we lived in Illyria for over a century. It's not very long in the way that Illyrians measure time, but we do know more than anyone else on land about the world beneath the waves."

"We don't think that you should accept the Illyrian alliance with the Fractus without visiting the people yourself and seeing if you can change their minds," Will said.

"Or maybe convince a few to disagree and stall an official agreement," Elle said.

"If a formal alliance with the Fractus is declared, a spell will be placed on the waters so that only Fractus can contact Illyrians," Gideon explained.

"How do I talk to them? It's not like I can swim there and meet them in person," Valerie said.

"In fact, you can," Elle said. "Technically, Will and I couldn't be kicked out of Illyria because we hadn't broken any laws. We chose not to return because of what they did to our parents."

"We can both return whenever we want—and Illyrians are allowed to bring guests under special circumstances," Will said.

"In this case, as the leader of the Fist, we could bring you to Illyria to plead your case," Elle said.

"You want me to swim to Illyria as a merperson?" Valerie asked, simultaneously thrilled and terrified. "I only learned to swim a few years ago."

Elle and Will chuckled.

"It's all different when you have a tail. It's as natural as breathing," Elle said.

"When do we leave?" Valerie asked.

"No time to lose. The alliance could be formalized at any time," Henry said.

"We dive at dawn," Elle said.

೪   ೪   ೪

After filling Henry and Gideon in on her plans with Willa, Valerie tried to sleep. But the idea of being deep underwater, with leagues of ocean pressing on her, led to her old nightmares of confinement.

She awoke in a sweat, and decided not to try to rest any longer. Instead, she jogged to the Lake of Knowledge, where she'd agreed to meet the twins. When she arrived, she saw someone sitting by the shore.

Valerie would recognize the bend of that head anywhere in the universe. At the sound of her approach, Thai jerked awake from what must have been a deep sleep.

"Didn't think you'd be here so early," he said, rubbing his eyes.

"It's a bit of a long story," Valerie said. "How was your night with the Healers?"

"The other apprentices are kind of intense. I think the Healers' Guild attracts that type of person."

"I can see why you'd fit right in," Valerie teased.

Thai tugged her hand, so she sat next to him and leaned into his warmth as she told him where she was headed.

"For some reason, the thought of you so far away makes me nervous," he said, his grip on her tightening. "Dumb, I know, since it wasn't that long ago that we were a universe apart."

"At least, if anything happens, you'll know the best person to heal me," she said, and Thai shuddered.

"Don't even joke. Can you bring someone with you?"

"She'll have me," Elle said, and Valerie turned to see her emerging from the trees.

"Where's Will?" Valerie asked.

"He went ahead of us to scout out the city we'll be visiting," Elle explained. "Getting to Gabriel won't be simple."

"Gabriel?" Valerie asked.

She'd met the Illyrian when he'd visited Arden as an ambassador, and he'd been distant and difficult. Negotiating with him wouldn't be easy.

"Officially, Illyrians don't have Grand Masters or kings or anything, because everyone is considered ethical and in charge of self-policing. But unofficially, Gabriel is one of the oldest Illyrians, and a lot of people listen to him. He's one of the most skilled readers of the Akashic Records."

"The Illyrians value integrity, right?" Thai asked.

"Yes, that's an essential trait to be considered for immortality," Elle confirmed. "Though I don't know if I agree, since they kicked my parents out and basically handed them a death sentence for falling in love and having kids."

"If even just some of them value true integrity, then I know they'll listen to you, Valerie," Thai said. "If they believe in what is good and pure, they'll believe in you."

Thai was giving her the intense stare that she remembered from the first time she'd seen him. His faith in her was a powerful thing.

Elle moved toward the water's edge. "Let's go, Valerie. It's a long swim to Alexandria, the city where we're going."

Valerie joined her in the water after a last look at Thai. Elle placed her palms on the flat surface of the water and began to hum a strange tune. A gold ribbon of light swirled through the water. Valerie watched it in fascination.

A sharp tug pulled her beneath the surface, and Valerie gasped, expecting to pull in a lungful of water. Instead, the water passed through her system as naturally as air, and she didn't choke.

Her eyes adjusted to the underwater world. From above, the water's surface glittered. But once beneath the surface, she could see a complex series of pathways on the floor of the lake.

She saw Elle elegantly slicing through the water with powerful flicks of her tail. Valerie admired her own tail, which shone with green scales. She'd wondered if having a tail would be like trying to walk with her legs tied together, but it was nothing like that. Her tail was a natural extension of her body, and propelling herself forward was as easy as taking a step on land. Easier, even.

"Come," Elle said, her voice sounding a little hollow, but reaching Valerie's ears with no difficulty.

Valerie swam after her into a dark tunnel in the corner of the lake that quickly gave way to open ocean. Her tail was more powerful than she imagined it would be, and as they sped through the water, it strangely reminded Valerie of when she'd flown through a wind tunnel years ago from Elsinore to Dunsinane. She was weightless. Water rushed past her skin, exhilarating her.

The deeper they went, the cooler the water became, but it wasn't dark. The water was lit by thousands of little sparks, like underwater fireflies. The effect was a surreal blue-green world highlighted in gold.

Unless Elle or Valerie spoke, it was also a silent world, and Valerie found it peaceful. She could understand how decades might pass down here without the Illyrians noticing.

The first sign of the city of Alexandria was a giant, spiraling conch shell with light shooting from each of its points. As they swam closer, she saw hundreds of other shells surrounding the main conch, like homes surrounding a palace.

"I can see why people don't want to leave," Valerie said, taking in the ethereal world.

Merpeople jetted between structures and off into the wider ocean. Next to Valerie, Elle surveyed the scene with a strange expression on her face, her hair a gold cloud around her head.

"It still feels like home after so many years away. I wasn't sure if it would," she said.

Elle swam toward one of the shells a good distance away from the giant conch. Up close, it was as big as Valerie's home on land. There was no door, only a small opening where they could swim inside.

Will was waiting for them, turning over strange silver triangles in his hands.

"Mom and Dad's tools are still here. The whole place is exactly like we left it," he said.

"Except everything's covered in algae," Elle said.

"Remember how we'd race to see who could find a bit of trivia in the records the fastest?" Will said, still fingering the triangles.

"The winner would get to choose the story we read that night," Elle said, her voice more childlike than Valerie had ever heard it.

The twins seemed to snap out of their memories at the same time, and they turned to Valerie.

"Gabriel's here for the rest of the day. We made it in time," Will said. "He didn't recognize me, and he definitely won't be expecting Valerie. We should go now and not waste the element of surprise."

"Are you ready?" Elle asked Valerie.

She nodded, and then followed the twins to the conch shell. When they swam in the opening, Valerie immediately noticed a change in the temperature of the water. It was warmer, and filled with bubbles. The extra oxygen when to her head, making her a little dizzy.

The inside of the shell was pearlescent, lit by even more of the underwater lights. It was a giant room with grooves in the walls where Illyrians gathered in pockets. At the very top was a small crowd.

"His majesty is on his throne," Will said, and Valerie couldn't miss the bitterness in his tone.

"The last time we were here was when Gabriel sent Mom and Dad to the surface. He took their immortality right here in this room. They almost drowned before they made it to the surface," Elle explained.

"He sounds like a hard man," Valerie said.

They swam closer to Gabriel's group.

"What if there are pockets of knowledge in the seas on Earth that we don't know about?" Gabriel asked the group, who listened eagerly. "The Fractus will give us the chance to explore those depths. The Fist will shut us off from that knowledge forever."

"Not true," Valerie said, not waiting to be invited to join the conversation. "As leader of the Fist, I don't wish for a future where connection between the worlds is closed. But we need to do it responsibly, in a way that is safe for those without magic."

Gabriel hid his surprise well, but his brows drew down in obvious displeasure at her presence. His quick eyes took in Elle and Will, and his frown deepened.

"The child-leader of the Fist has come to our depths. What an honor," Gabriel said, not bothering to hide his condescension.

Some of the other Illyrians were more excited, muttering to each other and taking the chance to examine her more closely. Valerie could see merpeople from around the conch swimming closer.

She raised her voice so she would be heard. "You were all chosen to guard the knowledge of the universe because you are the best among us. You chose paths of integrity. I ask you, is it right to use violence to force a world order upon the humans?"

"You said nothing of this, Gabriel," an Illyrian woman said with a flick of her tail.

"She exaggerates. There will be conflict, but the Fractus's goal is to save lives, not end them. The humans are irresponsible and need to be reined in," Gabriel explained.

"Is it ethical to decide what's best for them? True, the Fractus may stop some of the evil people on Earth, but how many good people will be quashed in the process, because they do not possess magic?" Valerie said.

"Perhaps the answer to this problem exists in the seas on Earth," Gabriel said. "We'll never know if we don't have the chance to explore them."

"I want to find a safe way for travel between worlds. Someday," Valerie promised.

"The promises of a child who has no idea how she would achieve such a thing. Do you have a plan to unite our worlds?" Gabriel spat.

"Not yet," Valerie said.

"She has been elevated to a position of power because she is a vivicus, but she will never lead us back to Earth. She doesn't even know that her own brother is helping the armies of the Fractus to defeat the Fist!"

Valerie was too shocked to hide her reaction. She didn't doubt Gabriel's words were true, and the revelation almost shut down her mind, making it impossible to find the words she needed to win the hearts of the Illyrians. Next to her, Elle and Will drew back in shock.

"You can see that I'm right. No doubt her heart is in the right place, but she is not special. She is not a true leader, but a vivicus whose mind will soon be stripped of its consciousness by her power. Is it wise to chart a course with her?" Gabriel said, his eyes flashing with triumph as he stared Valerie down.

"We will find a way to stop the Fractus, with or without you. And when we do, there will be time to investigate how to open up relations between the worlds. All those who come in peace will be welcome," she said, but her words were lost in the roar of chatter that followed Gabriel's speech.

She had already been dismissed by the Illyrians. Silently, Elle and Will led her away from the conch.

"You need to hurry to the surface," Elle said. "Gabriel could take away your temporary immortality at any time."

Valerie didn't have to be told twice. She raced to the surface, with Elle and Will right behind her. She burst to the top seconds before her tail vanished. She swam to the shore, which thankfully, was close by. She didn't recognize the beach of the little pond they'd arrived in.

"Where are we?" she asked the twins.

"You're in luck. We're in Arden. You're about as far as you can get from Silva, but there's an entrance to the cities in the trees around here. The People of the Woods will give you quick passage home," Will said.

"He gave you time to make it up without a struggle. It's more than he gave Mom and Dad," Elle said.

"He didn't want anyone to find out you'd been treated badly. It would undermine his case," Will replied.

"I don't think I changed anyone's mind," Valerie said, shaking the water out of her short, wet hair.

"How could Henry..." Elle began, but Valerie cut her off with a short shake of her head.

"I owe it to him to give him a chance to explain," Valerie said. "Maybe there's more going on than we know."

"There has to be," Will said.

Valerie took a breath and changed the subject before the anger that was brewing in her toward her brother showed on her face. "The merpeople will never be our allies."

"Mom used to say that the Illyrians were falling away from their old ideals. They hunger for knowledge and forget what's really important," Elle said.

"I hope that we'll still be able to keep our edge without knowledge from the Akashic Records," Valerie said.

"You'll still get the information you need," Elle said. "Will and I aren't experts, like the Illyrians who were helping you before, but our parents taught us the basics. And the spell that will be placed on the Illyrians won't apply to us, since we never took the vows that everyone else had to when they embraced their immortality."

"That means we'll have to move back," Will said thoughtfully. "But it's time, isn't it?"

Elle nodded, and Valerie wondered if they were also talking telepathically, like she and Henry often did. It was extremely irritating for the person outside the conversation. She'd have to remember that.

Thinking of Henry stirred her anger even more. It was time to go home. Henry owed her answers, and this time, he wasn't going to wriggle out of them.

෨ ෨ ෨

It took Valerie the rest of the day to navigate her way back to Silva. Elle and Will helped her find the tree she needed to climb, and the People of the Woods were happy to escort her to the platform she needed to float back to Silva, but not before taking the time to visit with the wounded and consulting with the council of leaders, who were at loose ends without Elden's solid presence to ground them.

Her responsibilities fulfilled, she finally got on her way and floated down, landing in the woods near The Horseshoe. A day of travel hadn't calmed Valerie down. If anything, it had given her anger time to fester. She didn't bother to close her mind to her brother, so her rage must have been blasting across the Globe.

He was waiting in the garden when she arrived, and he wasn't alone. Gideon, Cyrus, Thai, Dulcea, and Jack were with him, watching her with confusion. Henry must have gathered them there, hoping she wouldn't confront him in their presence. She didn't care. They could all hear what she had to say. She slammed the gate behind her.

"I've racked my mind, trying to think of one good reason that you could be helping the Fractus. But I can't think of a single one! So tell me, Henry, what could be so important that you'd put the lives of thousands of humans and Conjurors at stake, risk the fate of two worlds?"

Henry's eyes were desperate as he answered her. "Kanti."

Chapter 12

Henry opened his mind to her, and all of the secrets that he'd been hiding for the past few months flooded in. Valerie tried to process the information, but it was coming at her so fast that she could only absorb it in flashes.

"Reaper turned her to stone? Is she alive?" Valerie asked when she began to make sense of what she was seeing.

"Yes, or so he says," Henry said.

"Hold up, wonder twins," Cyrus said. "What happened to Kanti?"

"Reaper kidnapped her," Henry said, sinking onto the doorstep.

Valerie could sense his all-consuming panic now. How had she ever missed it?

"*Kidnapped* her? How the hell don't we know about this?" Jack asked. "Haven't you been talking to her? I thought she was one of the four pillars!"

Valerie had known that something was terribly wrong with Henry, but she'd stuck her head in the sand, unable to face his pain while dealing with the loss of her father. But hadn't Henry lost his father, too? Then to have Kanti taken from him, who could blame him for doing anything to save her? Her rage at herself nearly eclipsed her anger at her brother.

Now that Henry's mind was open, his secrets spilled out in rapid succession. The meeting with Reaper where he'd made the deal for Kanti's life. Hours spent imbuing the Fractus army with the power of darkness, draining him until he vomited up bile. Nights awake, tortured by the thought of innocents who would be hurt because of what he'd done. Three, no, four times he'd gone to Reaper, ready to say that he was done helping him, but at the sight of Kanti's beautiful, still stone form, the words would evaporate on his tongue.

Last, she saw the times that he'd gone to Babylon, standing on top of the tiers of flowers. He hadn't visited for peace. He'd been contemplating throwing himself off the ledge and ending his ability to hurt anyone else ever again.

"You'd leave me?" Valerie shouted, and Henry took a step back. "That's a worse betrayal than equipping Reaper's army!"

Thai pulled her away from Henry. "Take a breath. I don't know what's happening, but he's suffering enough."

Valerie shut her eyes and sat down next to Henry. Her arm brushed his, and he was as cold as stone.

"You should have told me. We could have found a better way, together," she snapped.

"As leader of the Fist, you ought to throw me in jail for my betrayal, since I know you don't have it in you to execute me, which is what I deserve. We're going to lose the war because of what I've done, and millions of humans will be enslaved, or die. I'm a coward. I betrayed you, like my prophecy said I would," Henry babbled.

"Someone please tell us what's going on," Thai said, reminding her that she was the only one who could see inside Henry's mind.

106

"Reaper turned Kanti to stone and would only change her back if Henry gave his army the power to create a darkness strong enough to put out the light from our weapons," Valerie said, since Henry was mute.

She watched her friends faces cycling through the emotions that churned through her. Cyrus and Thai were frozen, stunned by her words. Dulcea's lips were pressed with disapproval, and Gideon shook his head. But Jack lay a hand on Henry's shoulder, and Valerie knew that he understood what it was to get caught up with the Fractus.

"So we go get our girl back," Cyrus said, speaking first.

"Right now," Dulcea added.

Henry looked up then and Valerie was flooded with his awe through their connection.

"Don't you hate me?" he asked.

"I'm mad enough to throw you halfway across the Globe, but I could never hate you," Valerie said fiercely, and their friends nodded.

"It's done. We understand why you did what you did," Thai said. "Let's move on and fix it."

"Kanti's in the Black Castle?" Gideon asked.

Henry nodded.

"Then we have an advantage. The orb Valerie activated with Pathos when we rescued Darling will dampen the powers of any Fractus in the castle. They may not even be aware of its effect on them until it's too late," Gideon said.

"Even still, I'm sure he's got a million guards on her at all times, not to mention whatever portion of his army is there right now. We'll have to sneak in," Jack said.

"We should talk to Sanguina. She helped you last time," Cyrus added.

This time, it wasn't up to Valerie to plan the battle. Without asking, her friends were crafting the rescue mission as if they knew that she and Henry were too upset to think straight.

"To think that I once thought I could never forgive Sanguina for terrorizing me and my dad," Henry whispered, as much to himself as to his sister under the chatter of their friends' planning. "I've destroyed lives on a magnitude that she never dreamed of."

"It isn't the same, Henry. Then, when Sanguina was a vampyre, she was driven by hate. You were driven by love," Valerie said.

"And selfishness. You'd never have made that deal," Henry said.

Valerie considered his words. "I don't know what I'd have done if they took the most important person in my life."

"You would have found another way. Or, if you couldn't, you would have let Thai go," Henry said.

"I'm not talking about Thai," Valerie said, her eyes connecting with Henry's. "If Reaper took the most important person in my life, if Reaper took *you*, I might have done the same thing you did."

"No you wouldn't. But thank you," Henry said, so softly that she could barely hear the words.

She thought back over the past weeks, her mind reeling as she adjusted to the fact that Henry had been working for Reaper. "Why did you convince me to accept Reaper's ten-day truce?"

"I overheard him talking to Zunya about transporting things, and I thought that it'd be safe for you and the Fist to have a break from the fighting, even if it was only for a little while. I didn't know there was more to their plan, I swear," he promised.

"Come on now, you two," Dulcea said sternly. "We need your mindshare if we are going to rescue Kanti before Reaper makes Henry do something even worse or takes Kanti's life."

"And we will rescue her," Cyrus said fiercely. "She'll be okay."

"I swear it," Valerie added.

ഛ   ഛ   ഛ

"The Black Castle is locked up tighter than the Justice Guild," Sanguina said when Valerie and Henry visited her on Earth later that day.

"No secret passages that Reaper doesn't use often, or doesn't know about?" Valerie asked hopefully.

"The building was originally constructed to contain anyone who abused magic on Earth or the Globe, before the Fractus took it over," Sanguina said. "The stable part of the castle has one entrance and one exit."

"What about the unstable parts?" Henry asked. "That's how Oberon escaped."

"Very risky. And the farther you go from the center of the castle, the riskier it is. But because the castle is always changing, there are some ways in and out that are less well guarded, since the Fractus are afraid to be in the parts of the castle that aren't stable. But finding them from the outside would be impossible."

"Then we'll have to attack to get in," Valerie said.

Sanguina shook her head. "There are other ways to sneak in. Reaper mines an ore from one of the mountains of Dunsinane for his weapons. It welds to dark magic well,

109

and nearly all of the Fractus's weapons are made from it. One of you could deliver a shipment of ore to the castle."

"But won't we be recognized? Reaper's mind is too powerful to be tricked by a simple glamour disguise," Henry said.

Sanguina nodded. "It would have to be someone he's never seen before."

"That only solves the problem of how to get one of us in. But we'll need more people than that, even if we're careful," Henry said doubtfully.

"I have an idea," Valerie said.

و م   و م   و م

Two hours later, with a rough blueprint that Sanguina sketched and her promise to join them on their mission, Valerie and Henry returned to the Globe. Their house was empty, even of Gideon, who was working with Cyrus and Leo to get weapons ready for their team.

"This plan could get us all killed. Kanti won't thank us for that," Henry said. "I've only got another hundred or so of Reaper's soldiers that I have to give the darkness power to. What difference will it make?"

"Who knows? Maybe none. Or maybe it's the difference between winning and losing. Kanti won't thank us for handing over Earth to the Fractus in her name, either," Valerie said, and then regretted her words as she watched Henry's face crumple.

"She'll never forgive me," he said.

"Give her some credit and some time," Valerie said.

But her words didn't reach Henry. He had the faraway look in his eyes that she'd seen so many times when she'd visited him in Babylon. How could she have left him alone with his grief and pain?

The door opened, and Gideon came in. Before speaking, he made them all a pot of Oberon's tea and sat down.

"We go at daybreak. We dare wait no longer, but we also must be rested before we attempt the rescue. Drink this, so you can find a night's peace," Gideon said.

Henry drank his tea in one long swallow and then left for bed, absently chewing his thumbnail. His mind was shut tight against Valerie's gentle probing, and for now, she let it be.

Valerie gripped her mug and watched her mentor as she sipped the drink. "I hope you know how grateful I am that you're here to lead this. Fighting this war without you would be impossible."

Gideon shook his head. "I am only one of your tools. I know you value me, but even without my help, you would lead the Fist to victory."

"I don't know how you still believe that, after all of the mistakes I've made," Valerie said.

"Your errors were made with pure intent. You have the intelligence, the skills, the magic, and the heart to win. Right is on your side, and it will prevail," Gideon said.

Warm and a little sleepy from her drink, Valerie absently turned the Laurel Circle around and around on her thumb, remembering how he had given it to her to teach her not to be paralyzed by her fear.

"It's gold," she said. "That can't be right."

The ring's color and temperature reflected how much fear ruled her, and after Gideon had first given it to her, it was usually cold and dark. When had it begun to grow warmer?

"It must be broken, because I'm still afraid of so many things."

"The Laurel Circle doesn't change because you no longer have any fear. It is only showing you that you are no longer ruled by it. Your decisions come from somewhere else, somewhere better," Gideon said. "That is how I know you are ready for anything that comes."

"Long as I have you with me," Valerie said, resting her head on her arms, unable to stay awake.

She barely registered Gideon lifting her and carrying her to bed before she fell into a deep and dreamless sleep.

Chapter 13

"I still think I need to be inside the castle on this one," Cyrus argued again the next day. "I'm the only one who can call light to help us on the fly."

"Not much help in a castle with no windows, man," Jack pointed out.

Valerie, Gideon, and Henry were still strapping on their weapons as Dulcea passed out pastries. Thai was stuffing two in his mouth at once, which would have made Valerie smile if she wasn't so tense about the mission.

"Cy's right," Thai agreed, his words a little muffled. "Take us all. Juniper and Claremont, too, maybe."

"All of this is my fault. If anyone should be risking their life, it should be me," Henry said, and from his mind, Valerie could hear the part he left unspoken. He believed his life had the least value, as well.

"It would not be wise for you to return to that place," Gideon said. "The castle affects some more than others, and it has worn away the light within you."

"We talked about this," Valerie said, her patience wearing thin. "Minimal force. Gideon and I are the best fighters, and Dulcea is the only one who Reaper won't recognize, so she'll have to drive the cart in."

"Did I mention I hate that part of the plan?" Jack said, his usual smile completely absent as he gripped Dulcea's hand in his.

Valerie agreed with Jack, but there was no way around it.

"There's no one else he won't recognize," Valerie reminded him.

"You should send me and my boys in," Jack offered, not for the first time. "We know the castle best."

"You'll be thrown into the dungeons, best case scenario," Valerie said. "No way do we want you all to be forced to re-enlist into Reaper's army."

"Fine, boss," Jack grumbled, but Valerie knew that his gang never wanted to see the inside of the Black Castle again, and Jack didn't really want to put them there. He just didn't want to send Dulcea by herself, and Valerie didn't blame him.

The air shimmered, and Sanguina appeared in the kitchen.

"There's still no way to get into Dunsinane except by foot," Sanguina said. "I tried projecting there again this morning with a tuft of weeds that I have from the hills near the castle, but it didn't work. Reaper doesn't want anyone sneaking up on him."

"We'll do it the hard way, like we thought we'd have to," Valerie said. "Time to split up."

ৡ৹ ৡ৹ ৡ৹

Half a day later, Valerie, Gideon, and Sanguina had traveled through the cities to the border closest to Dunsinane. It had been a grueling trip, since they had to carry an enormous callbox with them.

They stopped, and Valerie pulled out some squished sandwiches from her pack that she gave to Sanguina and Gideon.

"We are ready for this," Gideon said, and Valerie saw that he was watching her as she put her uneaten sandwich back in her pack.

"Don't forget, you've got me ready and waiting if something goes wrong," Sanguina added.

"Thank you both," Valerie said.

"There's something else," Sanguina said, and she looked away. "If you do need me, you have to promise not to protect me. Get yourself and your friends out of there."

"You're my friend now, too," Valerie said. "We leave together or not at all."

"If what you say is true, and I am your friend, then respect my wish. I could die today if it is in service to you and Henry, and be happy. But if you die with me, then there is no redemption for what I've done," Sanguina said.

Valerie wanted to argue, but she couldn't. She knew what it was to live with immense guilt. Sanguina was asking not to be buried alive by hers. Valerie nodded once, and Sanguina's face relaxed.

A flash of light darted through the leaves and coalesced into words before their eyes. Cyrus's message was clear.

Dulcea's on her way. Get ready.

Gideon, Valerie, and Sanguina all climbed awkwardly into the callbox. They were uncomfortably close, standing toe-to-toe. It would have been easier to travel from a callbox in Silva, but Valerie wanted to be close to Dunsinane in case the magic didn't work. If she and Gideon ran, they could still make it to the Black Castle in time to extract Dulcea.

"I must admit, I don't think even Reaper would have imagined this method of entry into his land," Sanguina said. "How long do you think we'll—"

Before Sanguina could finish her sentence, Valerie had the sensation of being yanked by the back of her neck. Her entire body was like elastic, bending in ways she didn't know it could. Then there was a jumble of colors and light, and she toppled onto the ground inside the Black Castle.

A relieved Dulcea helped Valerie and Gideon stand.

"They sent me around back. We're in a storeroom underground, I think," Dulcea said.

Next to her was a cart that was filled with a black substance that seemed less like something solid and more like a vacuum that absorbed the light near it. Valerie shuddered at the sight of it.

"Was anyone suspicious of you?" Gideon asked.

Before Dulcea could answer, the door to the storeroom opened, and Tan stormed in.

"Seize them!" he said, and five Fractus poured into the room.

Two had eyes that were entirely black, like the warriors from Elsinore, and the other three were wielding staffs that shot lightning.

"Dulcea, down!" Valerie commanded, and Dulcea dropped to the ground without hesitating.

Valerie's blade connected with a dark weapon wielded by a stout woman in armor from Elsinore. The woman was creepy, her eyes black slits as she directed her power at Valerie. But with Pathos in front of her, Valerie's magic continued to blaze within her, untouched by the darkness pouring from her attacker. Cyrus's light spell was working.

Without the advantage of ripping away Valerie's power, the woman was still a match for her. It took all of Valerie's concentration to ward off the woman's increasingly frantic blows, but at last, Valerie saw her opening.

In a deft move, she flicked Pathos across the woman's wrist, making her drop her weapon. Valerie followed up with a kick to her chest, and then an elbow to her head, and she dropped to the ground.

Next to her, two of the Fractus wielding staffs had been disarmed and dispatched by Gideon. But in the melee, the other Fractus with darkness in his eyes had the presence of mind to yank Dulcea off the ground and lay his weapon against her throat.

"Drop your weapons or she's dead," the man said.

Gideon and Valerie obeyed without hesitation, and the other conscious Fractus yanked Gideon's hands behind him. The Fractus holding Dulcea loosened his grasp on her by a hair, and Dulcea turned and head-butted him.

The man staggered back, and Valerie leapt on top of him, jamming the heel of her hand into a pressure point on his neck. At the same time, Gideon had thrown the Fractus who was tying him up over his back and onto the ground.

Tan had hung back in the shadows, but Valerie grabbed him before he could squirm away.

"Is this who you really want to be?" she asked him.

"Let me go or knock me out, but don't make me listen to your preaching," he spat at her.

Valerie granted him his wish and knocked him unconscious with a blow that she knew would leave him with a nasty headache.

It was quiet. Dulcea, Gideon, and Valerie looked at each other, breathing heavily. Dulcea was scratching a nick on her neck that was bleeding lightly.

"Everyone okay?" Valerie asked, and Gideon and Dulcea nodded.

"Do you think anyone else knows we're here?" Dulcea asked.

"Tan must have recognized you when you drove up. But something tells me if he'd told Reaper we were here that more than six Fractus would have come to take us down," Valerie said, and Gideon nodded at her words.

"It does not matter. The plan doesn't change," Gideon said.

"We don't leave without Kanti," Dulcea agreed.

Valerie wished they could send Dulcea back to the callbox, but only the objects that came from the box could return to it. So they'd all have to find another exit together.

Quietly, they left the storeroom and made their way through the dark, cold hallway beyond. There were several turns, and Valerie hoped that she was remembering Sanguina's blueprint correctly, since she didn't want to take the time to read the map unless she had to.

She sighed with quiet relief when they reached the entryway to the castle. The giant door was sealed shut, except for a sliver of light that fought its way through a chink in the corner of the door.

"The throne room isn't far," Valerie whispered.

They ran now that they were certain of where they were heading. Twice, Gideon yanked Valerie and Dulcea into side passageways so that they wouldn't bump into Fractus guards in the hall. His hearing was so good, Valerie would bet that he could give Chrome a run for his money.

Finally, they were inside the room with the blood-red throne. As soon as Pathos crossed the threshold, a blue glow briefly flashed in the cracks of the stone walls.

"The orb," Valerie said.

"Pathos has ensured that it is still active," Gideon said.

Valerie saw Kanti's statue in a corner, but before she could approach, a fluttering by the throne caught her eye.

"My wish was granted," Kellen said. "I couldn't come to kill you outside, so you came to me."

Valerie dropped and rolled as the fairy fluttered closer so that he could sprinkle her with dust from his wings. With Gideon at her side, they could take on Kellen. They'd still make it out of here.

"I knew you were here as soon as you arrived," Reaper's voice slithered from the shadows, and Valerie's stomach clenched. "The callbox was a loophole I hadn't thought of, I admit."

"We're here for Kanti," Valerie said, refusing to show weakness to her father's and Midnight's murderer, even if inside she knew their mission was doomed. "We'll take her by force if we have to."

Reaper moved closer to her, and the shadows of his face appeared exaggerated in the dim light.

"Henry's debt has not yet been paid, so Kanti will remain here. Or dead, if you prefer?" Reaper made a twisting gesture with his hand, and Kanti's statue began to shake, bits of dust crumbling off of her.

"Stop!" Dulcea screamed, and stood in front of Kanti.

Reaper's magic hit her squarely in the chest, tossing her against the wall like a doll.

The room exploded in motion as Valerie drew her sword and launched herself at Reaper. Oleander burst into the

119

room, and Valerie heard a clatter behind her and guessed that she had brought the invisible Fractus as reinforcements.

Before Valerie could get close to Reaper, her world turned on its axis, and the room seemed to reorient itself around her.

Valerie gritted her teeth and didn't let her frustration stop her. She'd faced this trick of his before. Shutting her eyes, she let her own well of magic spring within her.

This time, when she struck at Reaper with Pathos, it connected with his scythe. It was a good blow, and Pathos was stronger than it had been the last time she'd fought Reaper. His mouth tightened in a hard line, and she knew that he noticed the difference, too.

Pain singed her arms as Reaper tried to dissolve her. But the attack didn't have the power it might have had without the orb dampening Reaper's gifts.

Valerie didn't let herself stop moving, and the next time her sword connected with Reaper's scythe, it sliced cleanly through. Reaper threw the pieces to the ground, scowling.

Next to her, Gideon was fighting the invisible Fractus; Valerie could tell from the crunch as her mentor's blows connected with their breakable bodies. He nimbly ducked and wove, and if the breakables were landing blows on him, Valerie couldn't tell.

"Pile on, you idiots!" Oleander barked. "There's only one of him."

Reaper opened a portal in the air, and Kanti's statue began to move toward it. Valerie tried to throw herself at Reaper to stop him, but he held out a hand, and she was shoved back against a wall. It was like his hand was a magnet, and she was the reverse polarity. She couldn't move closer, and she watched helplessly as Kanti's statue inched closer to the portal.

A small form with a golden head of curls threw herself onto Kanti's statue. Dulcea had somehow gathered enough strength to stand, and with her added weight, Kanti's statue tipped over and fell to the ground, unmoving.

"You're a brave little Conjuror. But you're on the wrong side," Reaper said.

He flicked his hand, and Dulcea began to scream. Valerie was still paralyzed, but Gideon surged toward Reaper. He was moving sluggishly, coughing as his fist connected with an invisible attacker who was in his way. He'd been exposed to Kellen's dark dust, and Valerie saw the fairy hovering above him again.

"Gideon, move!" Valerie screamed.

But it was too late. Gideon stumbled when the dark specks falling from Kellen's wings landed on him. Dulcea continued to writhe in pain. It was time to put the backup plan into motion.

"Sanguina!" Valerie whispered.

The ex-vampyre appeared next to her, delivered from the callbox. She saw Sanguina quickly assess the situation, and then step calmly through the chaos. Reaper saw her, and Dulcea abruptly stopped screaming.

"You came back," Reaper said, his voice softer than Valerie had ever heard it.

"I never truly left. I was confused. Angry for this," Sanguina said, thumping her prosthetic leg on the ground, once.

Sanguina reached Reaper's side, and she laid her hand on his arm. Valerie could move again. Reaper's gaze was unfocused, as if he were hypnotized by Sanguina.

"I had to do it. Justice even for those closest to me. Especially for those closest to me," he said, staring into her eyes.

Valerie shivered, for the first time imagining how it must have been for Sanguina to watch the lower half of her leg dissolve before her eyes. But she couldn't waste the distraction that Sanguina was giving her.

Kanti's statue lay next to her, and Valerie slipped a vial out of her pocket that Cyrus had procured from the Glamour Guild. She dropped its contents onto her friend's head, and the statue shrank small enough to fit in her pocket, which was where Valerie immediately shoved it.

The movement caught Reaper's eye, and Valerie saw his face spasm with something like true grief before it became hard again. He gripped Sanguina by her throat.

"You're one of them now, and I'll slaughter you along with the rest of the cattle."

But Sanguina slugged him in the eye, and he dropped her.

"You forget. I *let* you take my leg. I won't let you do anything this time. Add to that the fact that there is powerful magic at work in this room, weakening your powers. If we fight now, you will win, but not without cost," Sanguina said, twisting out of Reaper's grasp when he grabbed her shoulder. She followed up with a sharp punch to his jaw that snapped his neck backward. "Or we can negotiate."

"I don't negotiate with traitors," Reaper said, but his eyes searched the room, looking for whatever source of magic Sanguina had spoken of that was limiting his flow of magic.

"You'll never be safe in this castle now," Sanguina said, her face drawn and vicious. "I lost my leg, but you've lost your home. Where will you marshal your forces from now?"

At the truth of her words, Reaper's face became red, and electricity sparked off of his body.

122

He was angry, which was Sanguina's intent, Valerie guessed. She was hoping he'd make more mistakes if he wasn't cool-headed. Reaper threw his hand up. Sanguina was launched into the air.

"Run, Valerie!" Sanguina shouted, before she crashed into the wall. In spite of her leg, she was swiftly back on her feet, ready to charge Reaper.

Valerie yanked a moaning Dulcea up and turned to find Gideon. During Sanguina's distraction, her mentor had managed to shake off the effects of Kellen's magic enough to snatch the fairy from the air and throw him onto the ground. Kellen lay, unmoving, but Gideon had also collapsed next to him.

"Can you walk?" she asked Dulcea, who nodded once and began limping as fast as she could to the exit.

Valerie hefted Gideon to his feet and threw him over her shoulder, never more thankful for her strength. She looked back at Sanguina and saw that the ex-vampyre's hair was streaked with white from prolonged contact with Reaper's magic.

She fought with grace that belied the pain she must be in. Sanguina was resistant to the touch of most magic, and maybe she'd escape. But even if she didn't, Valerie had a promise to keep.

Slashing her way through the glass bodies between herself and the door, she struggled to balance Gideon's bulk as invisible fists pounded her.

Once she was out the door, the going was a little easier. She quickly caught up with Dulcea, and they made their way down a long hall that was flickering, an unstable part of the castle. The farther they ran, the more nauseated Valerie became. Next to her, Dulcea was turning green, but she didn't complain.

"We're close," Valerie said, recognizing the landmark Sanguina had told her about a few yards away.

A stone gargoyle was hunched in a nook in the wall. He was a huge dog with wings sprouting from his back. Before Valerie could reach out to touch the beast's head, as Sanguina had instructed, Dulcea shrieked.

Oleander had followed them, and she grinned as Dulcea twitched on the ground. Oleander had shocked her with her touch, and Dulcea shook until her teeth rattled.

Valerie dropped Gideon and tackled Oleander, making sure to stay clear of her hands so that she wouldn't be immobilized like Dulcea. Oleander was scrabbling against Valerie's mind, trying to find a way in, but her power wasn't as potent as Valerie remembered. Had the pulse of electricity that her father had given Oleander's mind the year before still affected her, or was the magic orb that Pathos had unlocked dampening her magic?

With her magic flowing through her, Valerie knocked Oleander to the ground and turned back to the gargoyle. But she must have missed the pressure point, because Valerie turned just in time to see her lunging with a black knife. Oleander only had to nick her with it for Valerie to fall.

Dulcea surged forward to protect Valerie, and Oleander slashed her cleanly through her throat.

After that, everything moved in slow motion. Before the first drop of Dulcea's blood hit the floor, Valerie flipped Oleander over her shoulder. The ex-Guardian landed on her back, her blonde hair splayed around her. The castle flickered, and a wave of nausea made Valerie so sick that she threw up. Then the flickering stopped, but an entire section

124

of the hall was missing, now replaced with a wall. Oleander had vanished. The castle had swallowed her up.

Valerie threw herself on top of Dulcea to use her vivicus power to save her friend. But though her magic surged inside her, there was no one to release it into. Dulcea was gone, and this shell that had once been her beloved friend wouldn't accept her magic.

Valerie released a sound that was somewhere between a scream and a sob. She grabbed Dulcea's body with one arm and Gideon with the other, and then touched the gargoyle's head.

Its eyes glowed blue, and Valerie thought she saw sympathy in his face before she was tumbling through darkness, away from the Black Castle.

Chapter 14

Light was everywhere, blinding Valerie. She had landed, with Dulcea and Gideon, in a lake in the middle of the Oasis.

Thai, Henry, Cyrus, and Jack splashed into the lake to help them get out.

"What happened?" Cyrus demanded, but Valerie couldn't reply through her sobs.

"Sweetie? What's wrong?" Jack asked as he gently took Dulcea from Valerie's arms.

Jack's eyes flicked down Dulcea's body, and her blood spilled all over his shirt. He clutched her close, making a low moaning sound.

Henry huddled on the ground. "No no no no no no no no," he said.

"Get it together, Henry," Thai said sharply. "Your sister needs you."

Thai struggled with Gideon's weight, dragging him ashore. Valerie collapsed next to her mentor on the beach.

"Step back," she said, though her tears still fell.

She wouldn't let her mentor meet the same fate as Dulcea.

She unleashed her vivicus power into Gideon, and this time, nothing stopped her. Her power poured into him, and the intense heat of her magic was a sweet pain that burned away everything else.

But then something changed. Instead of burning bright and clear, her power became sluggish, polluted with something dark—Kellen's dark dust. She fought against it, reaching out to Henry for his help.

Valerie and Henry's combined magic obliterated some of the dust, but its dark magic fought her efforts to expel it. Valerie gritted her teeth and pushed back, pouring more and more of her power, and herself, into Gideon.

"Valerie, stop!" Henry's voice sounded so far away, but then he was in her mind, and his presence had never been more immediate.

He pushed against the flood of her magic, forcing her to stem its tide.

"Stop! I'm not finished!" she said, but her voice sounded weak.

"Yes, you are. Any more and you'd be gone," Henry said.

"That isn't what Gideon would want," Thai added.

"I can't lose him, too. Please, I can't," Valerie said, turning in to Thai's shoulder and burying her face in his shirt.

"Shh, you didn't. He's still breathing. We'll take him to a Master Healer," Thai said.

"It's Kellen's dark dust," Valerie said.

Cyrus was already pumping light into Gideon. For several long minutes they both glowed, then at last, Cyrus fell back.

"I did as much as I could," he said, and Valerie could read the truth of his words in the shadows under his eyes.

"We'll take him to Nightingale. There's still hope for him, Valerie," Thai said.

Valerie nodded numbly, fatigue trying to consume her as it always did after she used her vivicus power. But before she gave in to oblivion, she reached in her pocket to remove Kanti. Henry knelt beside her, and she opened her hand. She

127

saw light return to his eyes before she was overcome by darkness.

❧   ❧   ❧

When Valerie woke up, she was back in her own room, and Cyrus was holding her hand. He seemed fragile, drained of his power. Light wasn't attracted to him, so he lacked his usual glow, and his eyes had never seemed so haunted.

He turned away to shake a sleeping form on the chair by her bed.

"She's awake," Cyrus said. "And I'm sure it's not me she wants by her side right now."

Before Valerie could contradict him, Cyrus left the room and Thai took his place on the bed next to her.

"Henry's asleep in his room. Gideon's in the Healers' Guild, and Nightingale is looking after him personally. Somehow, Sanguina made it to the Healers' Guild, too, and she's in better shape than Gideon," Thai said.

"And...Dulcea?" Her voice cracked as she said her friend's name.

Some part of her hoped that maybe there'd been a spark of life in Dulcea, that she would be okay. Because it couldn't be real. Dulcea wasn't gone forever.

"Jack brought her body to Azra and Clarabelle, to see if they could help," Thai said softly.

"And could they?"

The tears in Thai's eyes were enough of an answer.

"Her soul is in the ether," Thai said.

"She's really gone," Valerie said.

Thai pulled her close, and she cried for a long, long time.

128

It was morning when she awoke again and quietly slipped out from under Thai's arm. A dull sense of unreality pushed down on her. Her magic was a mere spark within her, nearly drained from expending her vivicus power on Gideon.

Her mind was also confused. She couldn't remember the layout of her own home, trying several doors until she discovered which one led to the kitchen. Then, as she tried to write a note to Thai explaining that she was headed to the Healers' Guild, she found she couldn't remember how to form certain letters.

A temporary panic almost blinded her. How much of her mind had deteriorated by using her power over the past few weeks? She refused to face what that might mean and forced the thoughts from her mind. Maybe she wouldn't survive this war, anyway.

Instead, she ran to Silva, the cool morning air waking up her sluggish mind a bit. The Horseshoe was empty in the dawn's first light, and inside the Healers' Guild, all was quiet. She peeked into room after room and finally found Sanguina in one, huddled on one of the cots. Her eyes were open, and her gaze followed Valerie as she crossed the room.

Valerie gripped Sanguina's hand tightly. "In the middle of all this mess, do you know how glad I am that you made it back to us?"

Sanguina's skin was gray, and with her hair streaked white, it was like she'd aged ten years. But she was alive. "After you left and the others left, the throne room began to flicker. That room has never been unstable before. Reaper left so that the castle didn't absorb him into itself. I'd say I was lucky, but really, I think he didn't consider me enough of a threat to risk staying the extra minutes it would have taken to kill me."

"He doesn't think anyone's a true threat to him," Valerie said. "Maybe he's right."

"He's not," Sanguina said, her hand steady in Valerie's.

"Do you know where Gideon is?"

Sanguina shook her head. "But Nightingale will."

Valerie turned and saw Nightingale's green form approaching Sanguina's bed.

"Come," he said.

After surprising Sanguina by giving her a fierce hug, Valerie let Nightingale lead her to a chamber she'd never been in before.

Instead of rows of cots, this room held one bed, where Gideon lay. Her mentor had always seemed so large. He stood a foot taller than her, and his lithe strength gave him a presence that made him seem even bigger. But in the bed, he wasn't invincible. He was human.

"Will he live?" she asked Nightingale, turning so she could examine his face.

She knew from experience that doctors sometimes bent the truth, and she wanted to read his expression for herself.

"He will survive. But it is likely he will never regain consciousness," Nightingale said.

"He has to. I need him," Valerie said, her voice wobbling.

"Oberon would have said that you're made of sterner stuff than that," Henry said.

She hadn't seen him enter, or even felt him through their bond, and she jumped at the sound of his voice.

"Even with the damage I did, even without Gideon and Dulcea, you will lead us out of this," Henry said.

"Yesterday, you told me that your actions had cost me the war. Today, you think I'll pull us all through?" she asked dully.

"Yeah, I do," he said, and he opened his mind to her to let her know the certainty of his words. But along with that certainty came a sense of the volume of pain he was enduring. It would drive him to madness.

"So do I," Nightingale whispered quietly. "And I promise you that Gideon will be cared for, whether his mind returns to us or not, until the end of his days."

Valerie fled the room, away from the still form of her mentor, away from her brother, away from her responsibility, and away from her guilt, which was tearing at the fragile fabric of her soul.

Valerie ran without thinking, and her feet guided her to the best place she could be. In a small grove, Clarabelle was waiting for her. Azra slept next to her in the grass.

Valerie dropped to her knees, but the little unicorn didn't immediately approach.

"Am I tainted now? Is that why you won't touch me?"

Clarabelle trotted closer and nuzzled Valerie's shoulder. Valerie's mind pinged with the sweet sounds of Clarabelle's voice, which was filled with love and tenderness. There was no hint of the disgust she feared she'd find after failing Dulcea and Gideon in the Black Castle.

Azra's eyes opened.

Clarabelle has been inconsolable since you left. The pain surrounding you called to her across the Globe, and it was all I could do to stop her from racing to Dunsinane to be by your side.

"I missed her, too. I missed you both," Valerie said.

131

I must take Clarabelle somewhere safe. I have taken your advice and visited Chisisi. He has told us of a place on Earth where we will be safe, but Clarabelle will not leave you.

Clarabelle clearly sensed the gist of what they were saying, because she stomped her tiny hoof, and Valerie's mind was filled with sounds of her indignation.

"Little friend, the best gift you could give me is to hide. Knowing you are alive and happy will protect a corner of my heart, whatever may come," Valerie said. "When this is all over, we'll find each other again."

And you could visit us.

Valerie shook her head. "Wherever I go, horror seems to follow. They won't stop trying to find Clarabelle. It's better I don't draw any fire in your direction."

It will be the first time that I have not been in the heart of a major battle of my people. It is not in the nature of unicorns to retreat from danger.

"If I fail, you and Clarabelle are the only hope of goodness surviving the Fractus's reign. When she's older, she can take up the mantle if I fall," Valerie said.

Your thoughts echo my own, though they bring me great sorrow.

"Good bye, Azra," Valerie said, and she buried her face in Azra's mane.

She knelt and hugged Clarabelle. The unicorn's blue eyes were clear as the sky, but her grief at their separation filled Valerie's mind with a sweet sadness that was very different from her other losses.

Then the two unicorns vanished from sight, leaving nothing but the scent of lilies in the little grove.

ℑ   ℑ   ℑ

132

Returning home, Valerie still dragged a load with her that was tangible in its weight.

Henry and Thai were kneeling in the dirt of her father's garden, working silently side by side.

"I thought this garden bloomed from some leftover magic of Dad's, but it didn't, did it? You guys were taking care of it the whole time," Valerie said.

Thai wiped his forehead, streaking it with dirt. "It wasn't a secret. I thought you knew. Cyrus and Dulcea helped, too."

Valerie swallowed twice, trying to keep her tears from rising.

"There's a piece of her here, with a piece of Dad," she said.

A flash of Henry's guilt slipped through his mind's defenses, and it hit Valerie like a punch to the gut. But before she could sense anything more, he turned away from her toward a shadowy corner of the garden.

Valerie saw that Kanti's statue was there, life-size again now that the spell from the Glamour Guild had worn off. Henry touched her face. Valerie opened her mind so he could understand that in spite of her anger, she forgave him, since she knew that was what he yearned for.

"I don't deserve forgiveness from any of you," he replied.

There was nothing more to say, so Valerie came and stood next to Henry. Thai stepped behind her and she leaned back into his chest.

"Now we have to bring her back to life," Thai said.

"It seemed like the least of our problems yesterday, when she was trapped in the Black Castle with Reaper. But now that she's here, who else could change her back?"

"Maybe Dulcea...Gideon... Maybe it was all for nothing," Henry said, his tone emotionless, as dead as the look in his eyes.

"Or maybe not. Maybe it's simple," Thai said. "Maybe Valerie can bring her back to life, once her power is back."

Valerie reached for Thai's hand and tentatively brushed her friend's frozen fingers with her own. At her touch, a spark of life pulled at the flicker of magic in Valerie's core. Thai's power leaped out to join hers, amplifying it, and the little spark became a flame. Without even trying, a pulse of magic zinged through her and out her fingertips with no pain or even much effort.

The stone statue melted into the living, breathing, gasping girl. Kanti was back.

Chapter 15

Kanti threw her arms around Henry.

"I told Reaper you'd save me, and you did," she said.

Henry stumbled back a little from the force of her hug, and muttered into her hair. "Valerie saved you. I bit my nails in a corner."

Kanti laughed, and then threw her arms around Valerie. "My hero."

Valerie returned her friend's hug. When she pulled away, she quickly swiped the tears from her eyes, but not before Kanti noticed them.

"What is it? Tell me," Kanti said, all of her laughter gone.

Henry trembled when he met her gaze. "I'll show you what happened."

Henry opened his mind to Kanti, Valerie, and Thai. Flashes of scenes appeared in Valerie's mind of Henry helping Reaper and of preparing for Kanti's rescue. When Henry showed Kanti the part where Jack held Dulcea's broken body, her fingers tightened around Valerie's arm.

The scenes stopped, and Kanti turned away from them, leaning against the tree for support. Her chest heaved, and she took great gulps of air.

"Kanti—" Henry began, but Kanti held out a hand to stop him.

"Don't speak," Kanti said, her voice barely above a whisper.

Valerie thought her friend was crying, but when Kanti turned, her cheeks were flushed and her eyes flashed. She glared at Henry, and her beauty only made her more terrifying. She seemed to grow taller, and a hum of magic filled the little garden. Valerie doubted that Kanti was aware that she was touching her power.

"How could you think that I would want you to value my life above all of the innocent humans and Conjurors who will die now because of what you've done?" Kanti's voice was low at first, but grew louder as she spoke. "I'll carry this stain on my conscience for the rest of my life. You knew what I would have wanted you to do, and you did the exact opposite. What you did was the most selfish act I've ever witnessed, and you've met my parents."

"Kanti, don't do this," Valerie said.

"And you! How could you let this happen?" Kanti said, turning her wrath on Valerie. "Gideon might be dead because you thought you had to rescue me!"

Thai took a step forward, his entire body tense, but Valerie held him back. She knew what Kanti was doing. She'd done it herself, when her friend died of leukemia when she was nine. As long as Kanti was angry, she wouldn't have room for the pain. So Valerie let her rage.

"Henry might be guilty for all of the strangers who will die, but it's your fault that Gideon and...and...Dulcea..." Kanti's voice weakened then, and her face crumpled.

Valerie held Kanti. It was Kanti's turn to sob, and Valerie let her own tears fall quietly into her friend's hair. At some point, Henry had left. Thai finally ushered them inside and made a pot of Oberon's tea.

136

Even with red, puffy eyes, Kanti was still beautiful.

"Where'd Henry go?" Kanti asked, her voice hoarse.

"He's going to stay with Cyrus tonight," Thai said. "He thought you both wanted some space from him."

Kanti slumped. "I know I need to talk to him, but I'm glad he won't be here tonight."

"He couldn't handle losing you. Especially not after Zunya murdered Joe," Valerie said. "He tried to let you go, but he couldn't do that and live."

Kanti nodded, her eyes shadowed. "I know. But right now, I'm furious with him. He should have been stronger. I don't know if I can ever look at him the same now."

The front door crashed open, and Valerie drew Pathos. Skye rushed into the kitchen, his mane wild. He was gigantic in the small space.

"Tell me where to go," Valerie said.

"It's too late. The battle is over," Skye said. "Come with me."

9o   9o   9o

Skye led Valerie, Kanti, and Thai to The Horseshoe. Even though it was the middle of the day, it was missing the regular bustle of Conjurors going about their work. Valerie's eyes were drawn to the Capitol building. An enormous crack split the steps to the structure in half. The building itself looked as if it had been struck by lightning, and an enormous, smoking hole had obliterated the front door.

"Calibro and I saw an opportunity, and we seized it without consulting you. It was a mistake," Skye said.

"That hole in the door looks like it was made from one of those staffs that throws lightning," Kanti observed.

Skye nodded. "I didn't think Reaper would be able to get the Fractus here so fast."

"Back up," Thai said. "What started the battle?"

"The Grand Masters were meeting today, and Oleander didn't appear. Rumor was that she was dead. Several of her fellow Guardians said they felt her power released into the universe," Skye began.

"You're right. She died yesterday," Valerie confirmed.

"Calibro and I decided to try to seize control of the group while we had the chance to force an election. Many more Grand Masters are opposing the Fractus, but quietly. We thought this would be our chance to cast off Reaper for good."

"But he knew, somehow," Thai guessed.

"Reaper descended on us, ranting about doing what was right. But the Grand Masters weren't listening. That's when Calibro and I attacked him."

"What were you thinking? He could have dissolved you," Kanti said.

"Worse. He has scrambled Calibro's mind. She is at the Healers' Guild, but I don't think there is much that can be done," Skye said, his head bowed. "As for the other Grand Masters, some escaped when Reaper's forces blasted through the doors, but Reaper used portals to send many to a prison somewhere I couldn't place. Not the Black Castle. It was underground."

"Will he kill them?" Thai asked.

"Not before he sees if he can use them first," Valerie said.

"It was a strategic error to strike without you to regain control of the Grand Masters," Skye said.

"I told you to think for yourselves and alter plans when it made sense. You did the right thing," Valerie said, but she couldn't repress a shudder as she imagined Calibro struggling for control of her mind like Rastelli and Kellen.

"I'll oversee Calibro's care myself, along with Gideon's," Thai promised.

"Gideon has fallen, as well?" Skye asked.

"Yesterday," Valerie said, her voice cracking.

"The tide of this war is turning. We must take it back," Skye said.

"We will," Kanti said, and everyone turned to face her.

Valerie didn't know what her friend's plan was, but the steely determination in Kanti's eyes gave her hope.

ς ς ς

Valerie and Kanti were in a carriage, heading toward Elsinore. Thai had stayed behind in Arden to watch over Henry.

"You were stone only a couple of hours ago. Don't you need time to recover?" Valerie asked, and in truth, she wouldn't mind some rest herself.

"I've been sleeping for too long. I have to do something to make up for what happened in the name of protecting me," Kanti said.

"Okay, so tell me your plan," Valerie said.

The carriage came to a halt in front of the dorm for The Society of Imaginary Friends.

"Why are we here?" Valerie asked when she saw where they'd stopped.

"We need someone with experience in diplomacy, someone charming," Kanti said.

"Cyrus," Valerie realized.

Why did she always underestimate him? It was a mistake she seemed doomed to repeat.

Cyrus was flying down on a platform as Kanti stepped out of the carriage. Cyrus hugged her fiercely.

"Everyone was a wreck without you," he said. "Even me."

Kanti smiled for the first time since she'd heard what had happened in her absence.

"I'm here now, and we're going to take back control of this war," she said.

Kanti and Cyrus stepped inside the carriage, and Cyrus squeezed Valerie's hand once before taking a seat as far away from her as possible.

"Go!" Kanti shouted, and the horses took off so fast that Valerie nearly had whiplash.

The animals were spelled to travel fast, and the landscape rushed by, making Valerie dizzy.

"So what's the grand plan, princess?" Cyrus asked, a flicker of his old humor in his eyes.

"Valerie told me that soldiers from Elsinore are fighting for the Fractus. That means that my Aunt Ani must be organizing them, because I don't think my parents would encourage that, no matter how shallow they may be."

"Then let's take her out," Cyrus said. "She won't be a match for Valerie."

"No question, Valerie could have her beaten, bound, and carted away with no trouble," Kanti said. "But that might not help our cause. My people need their own leader to believe in, and I think it will have to be me."

Cyrus nodded slowly. "You need to be the one to defeat Ani and rally your people. Then you can publicly announce an alliance with Valerie and the Fist. That's smart."

"We need soldiers for the Fist, or at the very least, no additional soldiers for the Fractus," Kanti said. "I have to challenge Ani to a Test of Power—it's an old tradition in my country. Ani's ruling now because the people think she's the most powerful Conjuror in Elsinore. I have to prove them wrong."

"I don't like this plan. Ani nearly took me out once. No offense, Kanti, but she could kill you," Valerie said.

"That's the other reason I wanted you here. If things go really south, you can step in," Kanti allowed. "But how do we get the word out? We need people to witness the Test."

"Tell all those birds that carry news. They'll do the work for you," Cyrus suggested.

"But how will you beat her? This whole plan falls apart if you fail," Valerie reminded her.

Kanti grinned. "Aside from the training and fighting I've been doing for the past few years with you, there is also this."

The carriage hummed as Kanti concentrated, drawing on her power. A rose grew in Kanti's palm, first the stem, then the petals, and last, sharp thorns. The rose had the faintest glow, as if something inside was lighting the flower up.

"I'm tougher than you think," Kanti said. "And being touched by a vivicus has enhanced my power."

ॐ   ॐ   ॐ

Kanti managed to sneak them all into her ice castle undetected, so Valerie was able to get a night's sleep before they launched their plan. She awoke to the sound of Kanti and Cyrus deep in conversation.

"You've got to provoke Ani to strike first. It will spark everyone's outrage, seeing their princess attacked," Cyrus said.

Kanti nodded slowly. "Good. I know my people will want the person with the most magic to win, but it will help my cause after the fight if I also have their hearts."

"Let's take some time to practice your skills before we challenge her to this Test thing, okay?" Valerie asked, rubbing her eyes.

Kanti and Cyrus both glanced out the window. Valerie followed their gazes and saw a veritable storm of birds outside the castle gates.

"You've already made the challenge? You're being reckless! We just got you back," Valerie said.

"They spotted us coming in," Kanti said. "We've got to strike now before Ani figures out another strategy."

The door opened, and Kanti's mom floated in on a cloud of perfume.

"Darling, we're thrilled to see you, but there's the strangest rumor that you've challenged your aunt to a Test of Power, and that you're turning it into a common street fight," Pauline said, nodding a greeting to Valerie and Cyrus.

Isabella was cowering behind her mother.

"She'll kill you," Isabella said. Kanti's eldest sister was paler than the last time Valerie had seen her.

"And fighting in the streets? It's for the power-deprived," Pauline said with distaste.

Kanti ignored her mother, glaring at Isabella.

"You're the one who helped fool everyone into thinking I was okay when I was locked up by Reaper. Do you hate me so much that you want me dead?" Kanti asked.

"No, Kanti, I swear," Isabella almost whispered. "Ani said she'd kill us all. I didn't understand what she was really like until it was too late."

"I guess that just makes you a selfish coward, instead of a jealous psycho. Congratulations," Kanti snapped.

Valerie touched her friend's arm. "I can see how your sister would be scared of your aunt. War is no time for grudges. You're both alive, and you're on the same side now."

"I'm simply furious with her, Kanti," Pauline interjected. "But think how it would look if it were discovered that two of Elsinore's princesses were not on good terms. And you're all right now, aren't you, darling?"

"You don't know at what cost," Kanti said, and Valerie gripped her friend's hand and fought tears of her own.

"Kanti is here to do what's best for your country, and that means removing Ani from power and taking her position as the rightful leader," Valerie said. "I suggest you both think about how you can support her in doing what's right for your people. It seems like it's been a while since you've thought about that."

Pauline's and Isabella's mouths hung open a little, as if they were dazed by what they'd heard.

"Thank you for stopping by, but Princess Kanti needs complete peace to prepare for the Test," Cyrus said, ushering Kanti's family firmly out the door.

Once they were gone, Valerie turned to her friend. The time for questioning her decision had passed.

"Let's get you a staff. You're practicing as much as you can until you fight that hag," Valerie said, and Kanti grinned, which was what she'd intended.

Chapter 16

By the end of the week, all anyone in Elsinore was talking about was the upcoming Test of Power between Princess Kanti and the Reigning Royal, Ani.

Kanti trained relentlessly with Valerie, and Cyrus put some contingency plans in place to help ensure the outcome they needed.

The morning of the Test, Kanti's father, George, came into her room. His demeanor, along with the rest of the family's, was almost deferential now.

"Henry is at the main mirror again, Kanti dear," he said. "I've begun to feel quite sorry for the young man. And your mother says he is quite a powerful Conjuror."

Kanti rolled her eyes at his comment, but glanced down the hall.

"Say something to him," Valerie said.

Kanti straightened her back and nodded. Valerie followed her down a long hall to an immense mirror. Henry's face filled the glass. His hair was disheveled, and there was a wildness in his eyes. When he saw Kanti, he drank in the sight of her, and from across the Globe Valerie felt his relief.

"You're okay," he said. "Is it true that you're challenging Ani to some kind of battle?"

"It's a Test of Power. Nothing to worry about," Kanti lied.

Valerie knew otherwise, but Kanti showed no outward sign of the risk she was taking. Standing straight with her head high, Kanti was the embodiment of perfect confidence.

"I won't ask you not to do it," Henry said.

"Good, because I wouldn't change my mind, even for you. I'm doing the right thing," Kanti said. "You should try it. You'd be amazed how fearless you are when you've got right on your side."

Henry's eyes were unfocused as he answered, and Valerie's mind was disconnected from his, which scared her more than his grief and guilt.

"There's no one who could stop you, I know that. I'm sorry that I let you down. I love you," he said.

Kanti's rigid posture relaxed a little.

"Me, too," she replied, but Henry's face had already disappeared from the screen.

"After this is over, I'll find Henry, and we'll fix what's broken between us," Kanti said, her eyes a little desperate as they searched Valerie's.

"You will. We're going to make it all right," Valerie said.

ço   ço   ço

The challenge was scheduled for the end of the day. Kanti, Valerie, and Cyrus rode in an enormous silver ice carriage through the town. People crowded the streets the entire way, waving and cheering. Some held flags stitched with white swans in the air, chanting Kanti's name. Ani's Fractus supporters wore black and glared at the carriage.

The horses stopped in a town square that had an elevated platform made of solid ice. Etched into the ice was the image of a crown.

145

Kanti was quiet now, but her voice didn't shake when she turned to Cyrus and Valerie.

"Don't interfere. I know I said Val would be backup if something goes wrong, but it won't. You'll come in too soon, and you have to trust me that I can do this," Kanti said.

"Please don't ask me to watch you die," Valerie begged.

"I'm not. I'm asking you to watch me win."

Kanti exited the carriage, and Cyrus and Valerie tried to melt into the crowd around the platform. But they were swarmed by the tiny birds that were buzzing over everyone's heads.

"What does the princess think her chances are?" one squeaked.

"How is she doing today?" another chirped.

"Is it true that the princess opposes the Fractus?"

After unsuccessfully swatting them away, Valerie saw Cyrus release tiny beams of light into their eyes. The birds were irritated, as much by their lack of response as by the light, but they fluttered a little distance away.

The people of Elsinore gave them a wide berth, which had the advantage of giving Cyrus and Valerie a prime spot by the platform.

Kanti stood in the center. The crowd split apart as Ani approached, a black sword strapped to her side. When she stepped beside Kanti, a hum of magic vibrated from the platform.

"The Test has begun. Now no one can approach until it's complete," one of the birds nearby said.

"What does that mean?" Valerie asked. She tried to touch the platform, and it zapped her. "We can't help her!"

Cyrus cracked his knuckles. "I've heard of this ritual before, so I suspected we might not be able to help her. But when she made you promise not to interfere, I was sure. She didn't want you to stop her."

"I wouldn't. It's her choice," Valerie said.

"I know," Cyrus said, and he gripped her hand. Valerie was grateful for the warmth of his touch.

"You're but a child," Ani said, loudly enough for everyone to hear. "I release you from this Test now, with a promise that your life will be spared."

"I reject your offer," Kanti said.

"Then prove your magic," Ani said.

Kanti nodded, and from the center of the ice grew a rose. The crowd applauded politely as it grew and grew, finally bursting into a bloom the size of a basketball.

Ani smiled indulgently. "Very pretty."

Ani threw back her head and released a sound that clawed at Valerie's mind. She fell to her knees, and in some part of her brain, it registered that everyone in the crowd was on their knees, as well. On stage, Kanti staggered.

Seeing her friend in distress triggered Valerie's locus, and she pushed Ani's siren song from her mind. Around her, everyone in the crowd had shut their eyes, in answer to Ani's magic and in awe of the beauty of her song, so they didn't see Ani unsheathe her sword to cut Kanti down.

Valerie and Cyrus surged toward the platform, but its magic pushed them backward so hard, they fell flat on their backs.

Kanti dropped to one knee, still gripping her staff, white knuckled. Ani raised her sword, but before it fell, Kanti raised her staff and smashed it into the platform once. From where her blow landed, grooves shot through the ice, etching a complicated pattern into its surface. The sound awoke the crowd from their trance, but everyone was silent as they watched the battle progress.

147

Ani lunged forward with her ink-dipped weapon. Kanti twisted away, deflecting the killing blow that Ani aimed at her heart, but the blade sliced through Kanti's side.

"No!" Valerie shouted, and she heard the collective gasp of the people of Elsinore at the sight of their princess being attacked.

It seemed to snap them out of their stupor from Ani's song.

"It's against the rules to draw blood!" someone shouted from the crowd.

Kanti's blood poured down her side onto the platform. It ran into the pattern of grooves that she'd created with her staff, flowing fast and with purpose.

"Letting Ani cut her wasn't an accident," Cyrus said, gripping Valerie's hand even tighter.

The grooves Kanti created with her staff were channeling her blood to the rose at the center of the platform.

Valerie stared in shock as Kanti's blood reached its destination. The rose pulsed once and then struck out at Ani, twisting its stem around her arm. The thorns pierced her skin. The rose throbbed, as if it were pumping something into Ani through the thorns, and Ani began to glow like she'd been given an injection of light.

The light raced through her body, illuminating her, and shot out of her fingers, turning her black sword to plain metal. Ani dropped it as if it were a snake. She opened her mouth to scream, and more light poured out of her, bathing Kanti in its glow. The wound on Kanti's side stopped bleeding, and the cut faded to a scar. That's when Kanti struck Ani in the head with her staff, and Ani fell to the ground, unconscious.

The magic humming from the platform abruptly stopped, and the crowd burst into cheers so loud that Valerie's eardrums hurt. The commotion was intense as people began to rush the platform. No one noticed the way the atmosphere darkened.

"The Fractus are here," Valerie said, drawing Pathos.

Around the edges of the courtyard, creeping out of doorways and alleys were easily thirty Fractus.

"We knew this might happen," Cyrus said.

He made eye contact with Kanti's sister Peach, where she stood with her family on a nearby balcony. Peach nodded and then burst into song.

Like her aunt, Peach was a siren. Valerie, Cyrus, and Kanti stuffed their fingers in their ears so her spell wouldn't distract them, but the rest of the crowd was hypnotized. She wove in a message to leave the square as quickly as they could.

The Fractus were swarmed as the mob hurried to obey the siren song. Whatever they'd been expecting, this wasn't it. They couldn't fight the sheer number of bodies pressing them back, away from the platform.

Kanti ran to the carriage, and Cyrus and Valerie leaped in after her. They raced away from the scene.

Kanti was glowing, high from her success, as Cyrus pumped light into her to drive out any residual magic from Ani's dark weapon.

"I did it. I know there are Fractus among my people I'll have to root out, but now I have a chance. We have a chance," Kanti said.

Cyrus leaned back, grinning even though his glow had diminished from helping Kanti. "I think it's safe to say the ruling princess of Elsinore will live. Make sure the people know who the real hero was today."

149

"This war had its first real victory in a long time today," Valerie said.

ॐ   ॐ   ॐ

When the chaos died down, the square was filled with debris, but no one had been hurt. The only loss was that Ani had escaped.

Valerie and Cyrus couldn't remain in Elsinore any longer, and they all cried a little when Kanti sent them back in one of her carriages.

"It's only been four years since you first came to the Globe, Val, but we've all changed so much," Cyrus mused as they raced back to Arden. "You, most of all."

"I'm sorry I hurt you," Valerie said, reaching for his hand. "Can we find our way back to being best friends again?"

But unlike when they'd watched Kanti fight Ani, Cyrus pulled away.

"I know we're in the middle of a war, and that makes everything else seem petty," Cyrus said. "But I can't help that I'm still in love with you. I was, even before the first time you were with Thai, but back then, I didn't know what it was like to have you love me back. Now I do, and watching you together, knowing what I've lost... It could wreck me if I let it."

Valerie didn't let herself release the little sob in her chest at his words.

"I'm not with Thai," she said.

What she didn't say was that she'd decided that she couldn't be with anyone. With her mind falling apart, there'd be nothing left for anyone by the time the war was over.

150

Maybe it was better that Cyrus blamed Thai. Whatever helped him get distance from her.

"But you will be!" Cyrus said. "I need you to stay away from me. I can't be your best friend right now. Let me go, and promise me you'll be okay if I'm not here for you right now."

"I promise," Valerie said, making her voice strong.

Thankfully, the carriage reached Cyrus's dorm, and he left. Only after she was sure that he couldn't hear her did she let out a sound of pain. Cyrus was gone.

Chapter 17

It was good to be in her own home again, even if it was an empty one. Without Dulcea stopping by to deliver treats and general cheer, Cyrus to break the tension with his humor, Gideon to keep her centered, or Kanti's practical support, the atmosphere was relentlessly grim.

Henry stayed in his room, and from the occasional glimpses into his mind, Valerie knew that he was battling his own demons. Thai spent long hours at the Healers' Guild, as wounded soldiers of the Fist poured in, starting with injured Grand Masters who'd escaped Reaper's attack at the Capitol.

Valerie split her attention between organizing the forces on the Globe with Skye and battling the Fractus on Earth.

After a long, fruitless day chasing down clues about the charm binding magic on Earth, Valerie stopped in Egypt to talk to Chisisi for her daily update.

Using a handful of sand that she carried with her in a little bag, she projected to a patch of land near the safe house where Chisisi was currently based. The safe house door was ajar, as Chisisi usually left it at this time of day so she could enter.

She went inside and spun the wheel on the door so that it locked tightly. Chisisi was eating dinner and reading an old text at the same time, but he put both things down when he saw her.

"I have news of an alarming nature," he said, and Valerie tensed up. "Your young friend Ming was attacked today, but Dr. Freeman arrived with the police in time to save her."

"Then it must not have been Zunya who came for her, or she'd be gone," Valerie said. "But next time it will be."

Chisisi nodded grimly. "Reaper wants to possess something you hold dear."

"Or destroy someone I hold dear," Valerie said. "He knows that I won't turn to his side, so he wants to cripple me with grief. I can't lose anyone else."

Her grief overwhelmed her, hitting her in her chest. She yearned for her father the most in that moment, and almost choked at the knowledge that she'd never see him again.

Chisisi had never hugged her before, but he did then. His own eyes were full of tears when he pulled back.

"We will not let them have her," he said fiercely. "We will assign a bodyguard."

Valerie pulled herself together, stuffing her pain back in the box in her mind where she kept it.

"Yes, a bodyguard. Maybe we can use this to our advantage. If Reaper is determined to take Ming, he'll send Zunya next. We'll be waiting for him. This will be our chance to take out Reaper's most powerful ally."

Chisisi considered her words. "We need someone who can be by her side at all times, but will not alert the Fractus to his presence."

"Chrome," Valerie said. "He won't like the assignment, but he'll do it when I tell him he'll have the chance to fight Zunya. He'll detect Zunya's vampyre magic in time to call for reinforcements."

"Young miss is wise. But it would be best if you asked the wolf yourself. He grows ever wilder," Chisisi said.

"Where can I find him?"

૭ ૭ ૭

Chrome was rolling around like a puppy in the soft green grass of a hill in Ireland, evoking the first genuine smile Valerie had had in a long time. He was nothing like the bloodthirsty picture Chisisi had painted.

The wolf trotted up to her, and Valerie saw that he was leaner than when she'd seen him last, and his coat had even more gray in it.

Chrome sent a reel of images to her mind of the battles he'd fought with Sanguina over the past weeks. Every drop of blood he'd drawn was remembered with relish, and Valerie shivered. For the first time, Chrome's sharp-toothed grin scared her.

A flash of red caught Valerie's attention, and she saw Sanguina approaching.

"I've been looking for you all afternoon," she huffed to Chrome, flashing Valerie a worried glance. Valerie was relieved to see that Sanguina had fully recovered from her encounter with Reaper. Even her hair was red again, thanks, she suspected, to the Glamour Guild.

Valerie saw an image of a wolf pup sneaking out of its cave while its mother slept. The image was tinged red with Chrome's irritation.

"No one's saying you need a babysitter," Sanguina said, in a tone that made Valerie suspect it was an argument they'd had many times before.

"Actually, I'm here to ask you to watch over someone for me," Valerie interrupted before Sanguina and Chrome lost their tempers.

She explained the situation, and Chrome scowled, flashing an image of himself in battle again.

"I know you want to be at the heart of the fighting, but this is your chance to fight Zunya," Valerie said, and Chrome's scowl vanished. He cocked an ear in her direction.

"Reaper failed to capture Ming twice now—once last year and again today. He'll send Zunya next, and you'll be waiting for him," Valerie said.

"I cannot aid him in this without giving away your plan. Zunya will bring an army with him if he sees me near Ming," Sanguina said. "But Chrome needs watching."

Chrome growled low in his throat.

"Ming's a kid. You can't go around slaughtering anyone who looks at her the wrong way. You'll scar her for life," Valerie said.

Chrome stopped growling, but his scowl was back.

"I need you, Chrome. Please trust me," Valerie said, her voice softer. "You'll know Zunya's coming from a mile away, and you can alert us so that we'll all be waiting for him. If we capture him, it could turn the tide of the war."

"Reaper can't be everywhere at once," Sanguina agreed. "Without Zunya, he will struggle to keep the Fractus organized."

Chrome bowed his head, and Valerie saw an image of his murdered mate, Jet. Chrome howled his pain, and the sound echoed the grief in her own heart.

"We will win this, Chrome. We'll destroy Reaper and the Fractus," Valerie promised, and the wolf rubbed his body against her leg.

He'd help her.

ℝ   ℝ   ℝ

Valerie and Chrome found Ming on a swing in the tiny backyard of her apartment complex. Her eyes were wide as she watched Valerie approach with the wolf at her side.

"Ming, meet Chrome," Valerie said, noticing a yellowing bruise on Ming's cheek.

"He's beautiful," Ming said. "Where's his leash?"

Valerie tensed, waiting for Chrome to growl or scowl, but instead, he rolled on his back, exposing his tummy, which Ming obligingly scratched.

An image of Chrome curled up by a warm fire flashed through Valerie's mind, and Ming's face lit up.

"You're magic, too. You're a person," Ming said. "I always wished I could talk to an animal."

Chrome grinned and licked her cheek, making Ming giggle.

"How are you, Ming?" Valerie asked.

Ming shrugged with one shoulder. "The bad men pushed Mom, and she's scared. Another one shoved me, and I banged my head. Still, it wasn't as scary as cancer."

She touched the bruise on her cheek with her little fingers, and Valerie clenched her hands into fists reflexively. Chrome released a little growl for the Fractus who'd done this to Ming.

"No one's going to hurt you ever again. Chrome is one of the best fighters I know, and he's going to watch over you."

"You will?" Ming's smile was pure joy. "We'll have so many adventures together!"

Chrome sent an image of himself running by Ming's side as they raced across an open plain. He was open to all possibilities.

"Are you hungry? Mom's got a steak in the fridge I'll steal for you," Ming said.

Chrome released a bark that sounded like a laugh, and Valerie almost sighed with relief. Ming would be safe under Chrome's protection.

ے۔   ے۔   ے۔

Thai was waiting for Valerie when she returned to her home on the Globe, patiently weeding a flower bed. She watched him for a while before she knelt beside him in the soft earth.

"Long day?" she asked him when he turned to face her. Two grooves had etched themselves between his eyes, like he'd spent the day concentrating, or worrying, or both.

"Yeah," he replied, settling back on his heels.

They sat together in the dirt, turning up their faces to absorb the last rays of light before the day dimmed to twilight. When she opened her eyes, she saw that he was watching her.

"I wish I only had good news for you today," he said, touching her cheek with a dirt-streaked finger.

"That must mean you have some good news, so let's hear it," she said, trying to hold on to her peace for as long as she could.

Thai gave her a half smile. "Willa managed to get water flowing into Silva. I think she had about fifty people helping her on the project, and today the first drops trickled in. That woman has almost as much determination as you do."

"Something about her does inspire confidence—and obedience," Valerie said. "I hope it means that people will settle down."

"I think they will. And maybe having suffered a little deprivation will give these Conjurors some empathy for what humans endure all the time," Thai said.

"What's your bad news?" Valerie asked.

"It'll sound naive, but I thought with magic, there'd be almost no one we couldn't heal. But I was wrong. These black weapons of Reaper's are as bad as weapons on Earth—maybe even worse. You can treat a gunshot wound, but the black weapons eat away at your magic, and your life. And now that Henry's given Reaper's army the ability to cast darkness, the black weapons are more effective than ever."

Valerie gripped Thai's hand, watching him swallow once, then twice.

"I've seen people die from their wounds. And today, Juniper came in with a deep cut on his hand," Thai began.

Valerie stood up. "I have to go to him!"

Thai stood, as well. "He'll live. We stopped the flow of dark magic inside him. But he lost his hand. No magic in the universe will be able to fix him."

Valerie heard a sharp intake of breath, and she whipped around to see Henry standing behind them, one hand on his stomach and the other covering his mouth.

"This is all happening because of me," he said. "I'm the reason Juniper lost his hand."

"No, you're not," Valerie said firmly, pushing down her own horror so that Henry wouldn't find it in her mind. "It's Reaper and the Fractus who are choosing to hurt people."

"Reaper's crazy, and I might as well have given him a nuclear bomb," Henry said. "I have to go. I can't listen to you defend me. I don't deserve it."

Henry left, and Valerie knew she should follow him. But her heart was so heavy, so exhausted, that instead, she leaned into Thai, resting her head on his chest. Gently, he wove his fingers in her hair. She knew she should pull away, but her body wouldn't let her.

"Henry'll find his way back to us," Thai said.

"I don't know how to help him," Valerie said. "He's slipping away from me, as surely as my dad slipped away when he bled out in front of me. But I don't know how to fix him."

"Anyone would crack under the amount of pressure Henry's been under," Thai said. "I know how much you've got going on, and I'll keep an eye on your brother. When he's ready for our help, we'll be waiting."

ço   ço   ço

Valerie sat on the edge of Juniper's cot in the Healers' Guild, waiting for him to wake up. He was very pale, but his breathing was even. He moaned a little in his sleep, and Valerie gripped his hand. His eyes cracked open.

"I'm so sorry, Juniper," Valerie said.

Juniper rubbed his eye with his right hand, and Valerie saw him stare down at the stump of his left hand, which ended at the wrist.

"It's war," he said. "I knew what could happen when I joined the Fist. Look at the bright side. I'm alive."

"Does it hurt a lot?" she asked.

Juniper nodded. "Even the numbing potion Nightingale made only helps a little. But he said it won't be like this forever."

Valerie sucked in a deep breath. "Are you angry?"

"At you? No. At Reaper and the Fractus who did this? Hell, yes. But I'm still going to fight. Maybe not on the battlefield anymore, but I believe in what we're doing. Seeing this darkness the Fractus are wielding firsthand, I know we've got to end this threat. The whole universe could go dark if they aren't stopped."

"If you still want to be a part of this, I could really use someone to organize the training of the Conjurors in the Fist who haven't had a lot of fighting experience," Valerie said.

She'd always hated being treated like she was made of glass when she'd been in the hospital, too weak to be of use. And she suspected that Juniper felt the same. He smiled at her words, and she saw that one of his teeth was chipped, as well.

"As soon as Nightingale releases me, I'll start," he said.

A man who looked like an older version of Juniper stopped at the end of the bed. He glared at Valerie.

"I know who you are, and I don't want you filling my son's head with any more of your poison," he spat.

"Dad, be quiet. I'm a man now, and I can decide for myself what's right," Juniper said. Then his face softened. "You always taught me to work hard and stand up for those who couldn't do it for themselves. That's what I'm doing."

Juniper's dad turned away from Valerie. "I take it all back. I want you safe."

Valerie quietly walked away, letting Juniper talk to his dad, thankful that he was alive to receive his scolding.

Chapter 18

The days blurred into weeks as fighting escalated on Earth. When Valerie heard that a group of Fractus was entering the Pantheon in Rome, she didn't suspect that they would be different from the dozens of Fractus she'd been battling day after day in their search for clues to how to break the rules binding Earth's magic.

Chisisi reported that five Fractus had been seen entering the monument, so Valerie decided not to tackle them alone. She brought Alex and Olwain, Knights of her guild who had stood by her side from her first battle against the Fractus.

They passed through the enormous pillars at the front of the Pantheon and entered through the massive front doors with a crowd of tourists. Valerie scanned the massive, circular room. The ceiling was a dome with a hole in the middle that let light in.

It was quickly apparent that the Fractus were making no attempt to blend in with the crowd. They studied the floor, sometimes bending down to trace the pattern in it.

Valerie recognized Logan, Thai's ex, right away, even though she'd cut her beautiful hair short. Valerie fought the urge to run over and unleash her powers on the girl who'd held Henry's father while Zunya murdered him. Two of the other Fractus looked familiar, as well.

"What are they doing?" Alex asked, sliding her hand into her jacket, where Valerie knew she kept a dagger that Cyrus had imbued with his new light treatment.

"See that woman tapping the circle on the ground over there?" Valerie asked. "I think her name is Toma, and she's got the ability to use electricity to mess with anything electronic."

"That's not going to do her a lot of good in here," Olwain said.

"She can also throw lightning. The other woman is Logan, and her hands and feet can secrete poison, like a frog," Valerie added. "I don't recognize the other three guys. Do you?"

Alex nodded. "I fought them when Zunya attacked us at the playground last year when we were recovering the Byway. They were guarding him."

"I remember them now, too," Olwain said. "They've got the speed and strength of leopards, which is why their magic isn't completely incompatible with Earth's rules. No match for us if we were on the Globe, but here we'll have to watch out."

"Let's wait and capture them somewhere less public so we don't put any humans in danger," Valerie said.

The words were barely out of her mouth when Logan shoved a man who was trying to usher the group away from where they were standing. He fell to the ground, gripping his chest. Security guards came running, and the five Fractus formed a loose circle, ready to fight.

"So much for waiting," Alex said.

"You two fought the leopard guys before, so take them. I'll handle Logan and Toma," Valerie said.

By the time they reached the Fractus, three guards were lying on the ground, and people were starting to back away from the scene.

"I suggest you run," Logan said loudly.

People didn't wait to hear more. They turned and began pushing their way out toward the front doors, the only exit.

Valerie landed a sharp punch to Logan's cheek, which leveled her. But the blow made her stagger, so Toma was able to touch Valerie's arm, sending electricity zinging through her body. Even with her magic flowing as much as Earth's rules would allow, Valerie went down, temporarily paralyzed.

Toma took full advantage, kicking her hard in the temple, but it didn't keep Valerie down for long. As she sprang to her feet, she saw Toma glance toward the exit with longing.

"Too late to run," Valerie said, and swept her foot across the ground to knock Toma off her feet.

But the Fractus nimbly dodged the kick. Something above them caught the woman's attention, and Valerie seized the chance to hit her in a pressure point in her neck. Toma fell. Valerie confirmed that Logan was still down, then saw that Olwain and Alex had taken out their targets, as well, though Olwain was limping.

But Valerie's sixth sense for danger was still going off, and she looked up and saw three faces peering through the circular opening at the top of the Pantheon. She barely had time to register that two of the faces had eyes that were completely black before the room dimmed.

Valerie knew that the third Fractus was Reaper as soon as his feet touched the ground. His eyes met hers, but they held no surprise. He'd been expecting her.

Valerie had never seen Reaper on Earth before, and she suspected it was because his magic was at complete odds with Earth's rules. He bent the laws of physics, which went against the very tenets of how the planet functioned.

Knowing he was vulnerable, she launched herself at him with all of the speed that her magic could lend her, bound as it was.

Instead of flattening him, she passed directly through him. He was only projecting his mind to Earth. But the two Fractus who were with him were not projections, and Valerie's hold on her magic slipped as they both turned their power on her and her Knights.

"Disable them and take what I need," Reaper ordered, ignoring Valerie and the Knights.

Valerie collapsed under the weight of the darkness sucking at her magic, and her very life. Next to her, Alex and Olwain had also fallen, their faces pale. Alex's eyes fluttered back in her head. The Fractus approached, and Valerie couldn't find the strength to lift Pathos from its sheath at her side.

A human couple, who had been hovering at the edges of the crowd that was trying to force its way out of the building, leaned down to help Valerie.

The Fractus turned their magic on the couple, and they both made horrible gasping sounds that ended in choking. They fell to the ground, blood trickling from their mouths. The panic of the crowd surged, and people screamed as they clawed their way to the exit.

"More will die if you interfere," Reaper said, his eyes connecting with Valerie's for the first time since he'd arrived.

Almost hopelessly, Valerie reached out with her mind for Henry. She didn't know if his mind would be open to her

164

across the universe, locked in a prison of his own making, but she knew that many more people would die if only she, Alex, and Olwain were there to protect them.

Her desperation must have reached Henry, because he was by her side in an instant, clutching a lock of her hair as the object that anchored him to Earth, sending him directly to his sister.

"I know how guilty you feel for helping Reaper, but starting now, you can make it right. Help me protect these people," Valerie said to her brother.

His magic flooded her, joining and strengthening her own. Valerie was able to draw Pathos, and the effect of the Fractus's magic weakened. The room brightened, and a beam of light from the opening on the ceiling struck a circle on the ground.

"Strike now, as I told you," Reaper commanded one of the Fractus, who wore his long hair tied back in a ponytail.

The Fractus turned to face Valerie then, and a torrent of darkness poured out of his eyes. She raised Pathos higher, and the light pushed back.

Alex and Olwain had found their footing and drawn their own weapons, which weren't as powerful as Pathos but still helped drive back the darkness, especially when the second Fractus added his power.

Henry's magic pooled with her own, and Valerie didn't think, but struck through the darkness. It shrank away from her sword like a slippery, living thing.

"It is like a living thing," Henry said, catching her thought. "See if you can strike it with Pathos, like the table in Cyrus's lab."

Valerie raised Pathos and drove it through the heart of the darkness, stabbing it directly into the floor.

"Yes," Reaper breathed, and the Fractus wielding the darkness retreated.

Pathos poured its light into the stone floor, and symbols made of light appeared where before there had only been a circle.

Reaper's eyes scanned the symbols as if he could read them, and then he vanished, his mind retreating to the Globe.

The two Fractus who remained standing tried to flee, but Alex and Olwain tackled them before they got far. Alex tore off a piece of cloth from the leg of her pants and blindfolded the Fractus she had pinned beneath her, and Olwain followed suit.

The humans who had witnessed the fight were openly gaping. They had their cell phones and cameras out, but Valerie could see from the dismay on their faces that their electronics weren't working. Toma must have taken care of that before Valerie knocked her out.

Alex and Olwain were tying up the other five Fractus who lay unconscious on the ground.

"The situation is under control now," Alex said to the remaining people crowded in the Pantheon. "Please exit the building in an orderly manner. The authorities will be here soon."

"Seven Fractus captured. We won this battle," Olwain said.

Valerie deliberately didn't look at the two humans who lay dead on the ground. There had been no victory. Just two more lodestones on her heavy heart.

"Reaper wanted me to use Pathos to activate that pattern in the floor. He sacrificed these humans and his people to trick me into doing what he wanted," Valerie said.

"Whatever that information was, it must lead to the charm binding magic on Earth," Henry agreed. "I don't know what those symbols mean, but I memorized them. Someone on the Globe will be able to decode them."

"I'll call Chisisi for a crew to get these Fractus safely locked up," Alex said. "You get this knowledge to the Fist so we can try to decode that pattern before Reaper does."

"Make sure the blonde, Logan, doesn't slip through your fingers," Valerie said. "She's tricky, and if anyone deserves to rot in jail for the rest of her life, it's her."

Alex took a rope she wore coiled at her side and began tying up Logan's hands. "She's not going anywhere." Alex reached over and gripped Valerie's arm in solidarity.

Valerie was thankful that someone else was taking the lead right now. She nodded to Alex, then Olwain, and touched the stone in her pocket to return to the Globe. The last image burned into her eyelids before she left was the human couple lying still, blood on their lips. They were holding hands.

ço   ço   ço

"Those two humans who died... Their end is my fault, not yours. You know that, right?" Henry said when they returned to their garden on the Globe. Blue shadows under his eyes made him look sick.

"Their end is Reaper's fault, and his Fractus minions who obey him," Valerie corrected him, her voice gentle. She changed the subject, hoping to distract him from his guilt. "How were you able to memorize those symbols so fast?"

"The Empathy Collective teaches us how to harness our magic to absorb and remember large amounts of information.

167

People with photographic memories on Earth are tapping into similar magic inside themselves."

"I think that there's a guild that's into puzzles and decoding messages," Valerie said. "Maybe they can help us. Can you—"

Valerie was shoved roughly backward by an invisible force. Her feet dragged in the dirt as she was being pulled back, through the trees that surrounded her house. She scrabbled to hold onto something and regain her footing, but the pull was inexorable. Then, as suddenly as it started, the pull stopped and she fell to the ground.

She stood, and a profound dizziness overtook her. She gripped a nearby tree for support as her entire body shuddered.

"Henry!" she shouted, searching for her brother.

"Val!" his voice responded, though she couldn't see him.

She struggled toward the sound, but every step she took in his direction was like fighting a strong current under water. No matter how hard she tried, she couldn't move closer to him.

Henry cracked his mind open to her, and she knew that he shared her confusion and fear. He was sure that Reaper had done something to them. She had no sooner wondered why Henry suspected Reaper than she saw their enemy walk deliberately through the trees toward her.

Valerie drew Pathos, hoping that whatever happened in the Pantheon hadn't weakened it. This time, would Reaper really fight her?

"I won't have you polluting Henry's mind more than you already have," Reaper said.

Valerie didn't miss the tremor in his hands, even though she was several yards from him. Whatever magic he had expended had been powerful.

"What did you do? You obviously want me to know," Valerie said, in part to distract him as she calculated the best angle to hit him so that she'd render him unconscious—or kill him. This time, she wouldn't leave him alive and free, whatever the cost to herself.

"I made sure that you and Henry will never join forces against me again," he said.

Valerie crossed the space between them in less than a second and raised her sword to cut him down. But before Pathos found its target, Reaper created a small portal and stepped through it.

It took three hours for Valerie to track down Sanguina. She found the ex-vampyre asleep in a hostel on Earth. Valerie shook her awake.

"You have to help us," Valerie said, and her desperation must have shown in her eyes, because Sanguina was instantly awake.

"Anything," she said.

Valerie told her what had happened, and a dawning look of comprehension replaced Sanguina's initial puzzlement.

"He reversed your polarity," Sanguina said. "I've seen him test the theory on small animals on the Globe. He was successful, but it took so much of his magic that it was never practical to try it on a Conjuror."

"What does that mean?"

"Think of it like magnets. In a natural state, you and Henry are drawn together by the force of your blood tie. By reversing your polarity, the very blood that pumps through your veins rejects that connection and will not allow you to be near your twin. Your body is rebelling against your mind, protecting you against what it perceives as an enemy."

"How do I fix it?"

"I don't have an answer for that," Sanguina said, regret making her voice low.

"Surely Henry, with his psychic powers, can find a way to repair this polarity thing inside him," Valerie said.

Sanguina shook her head. "From your description of your symptoms, I think Reaper reversed your polarity, not your brother's. It's you we'll have to find a way to switch back."

"I don't have time to figure this out! I'm trying to plan and fight a war on two fronts!" Valerie said, lowering her voice when she realized she was shouting.

"That's what Reaper's counting on," Sanguina said. "He knows that when you combine your power with Henry's, you are more than a match for him."

"Henry's not a match for anyone right now," Valerie said, sitting on Sanguina's bed. All of her energy had abruptly left her.

"True. But I know you can defeat Reaper on your own. That's your secret weapon, because Reaper doesn't believe that. If he did, you'd be dead. You're alive because he still wants to use Henry's power, and he knows that if he killed you, Henry wouldn't survive it."

"I don't know what to do anymore," Valerie said. "I wish there was someone here to tell me. Midnight, Gideon, my dad..."

"Your mother was always wonderful in these kinds of situations. When things were at their worst, something more powerful than magic rose within her to face it. You have that in you, too," Sanguina said. "Now go find it."

Chapter 19

"Seven of our people have vanished this week alone," Chisisi said when Valerie came in for her daily report. "We don't know if they were captured or killed by the Fractus. But our enemies are no longer simply searching for clues to Earth's magic-binding charm. They are actively seeking out the Fist to engage in battles to weaken us."

Dr. Freeman was also present. He'd become a close adviser to Chisisi since Thai was spending more time at the Healers' Guild, and Valerie was glad that Chisisi had someone he could trust.

"There's another problem. Someone must be following me," Dr. Freeman said. "I've identified three families with a high potential for latent magic, and each of those families was targeted by the Fractus after I met with them."

"Do you think they know what you're doing?" Valerie asked.

"Perhaps," Dr. Freeman said. "At a minimum, they know that I am with the Fist, so they would clearly assume the humans I contact must be Fist supporters, as well."

"Was anyone killed?" Valerie asked, dreading the answer.

"No. They were all told to be on the lookout for the Fractus, and we had teams come to protect them in time," Dr. Freeman assured her.

"But our resources are spread thin," Chisisi said. "We cannot assign bodyguards to every human the Fractus targets."

"Those humans may have to protect themselves sooner than we thought," Valerie said, and then explained the clue that had been uncovered on the floor of the Pantheon.

Chisisi and Dr. Freeman wore identical frowns as they listened to her story.

"What comes next will be a slaughter," Chisisi said. "Right now, humans are at a disadvantage, but they still have weapons and can fight back. But with the Fractus's full magic unleashed, humans will be no threat to them."

"Even humans with magical potential won't have learned how to harness it in a meaningful way yet," Dr. Freeman said.

"We need to start bringing more soldiers of the Fist to Earth," Valerie said.

She knew that Skye was already strapped for soldiers on the Globe, but if more Fractus would be flooding Earth, this was where her forces needed to be.

Cyrus appeared at the doorway. Valerie drank in the sight of him, relieved that he looked healthy and had his usual glow, even if he wasn't wearing his typical grin.

"Henry wanted you to know that the symbols have been deciphered," Cyrus said. "He'd have come himself, but he couldn't travel to Earth anywhere within half a mile of you."

"He solved it already?" Valerie asked. It was about time for some good news.

"It wasn't a code at all. It was ancient Sumerian, and a master in the Language Guild was able to translate it right away," Cyrus explained. "It said that there is an eternal flame burning in the heart of the Atacama Desert in Chile."

"That desert is huge," Dr. Freeman said. "You'll have to narrow the location down. It's not a place you want people wandering around, magic or not."

Chisisi folded his hands. "I will assemble a team to quietly search for this flame. We have local contacts in coastal cities in Chile who can help."

"Good. We're less likely to attract attention if we actually find this flame that way," Valerie said. "Let's not do the Fractus's work for them."

୭ ୭ ୭

When Valerie returned to the Globe, she found Kanti waiting on her front stoop. Her hair, which was pinned back in a complicated pattern, was coming loose. Her clothes were wrinkled and dusty.

Kanti's eyes brightened when she saw Valerie. "Took you long enough. I was scared I'd run into Henry while I was waiting for you."

"We had to agree on which days we'd be home, now that we can't be in the same location at the same time," Valerie said. "It's my day today. But you should see him, Kanti. He needs support, and I literally can't be there for him right now."

"I know," Kanti said. "That's why I'm here. I'm going to make things right with him tonight at the fundraiser."

"Fundraiser?"

"The Glamour Guild is raising magic for the Fist, remember?" Kanti said. She stood up and gripped Valerie's shoulders. "This is a big deal, Val. You have to be there."

"I need to talk to Skye about sending more soldiers to Earth, check in with Willa on the water situation, and if I have any free time after that, sleep," Valerie said.

"The magic that gets raised is the pure kind, currency in Elsinore. There are a lot of ways you could use it—you could hire soldiers who won't fight for free, or give it to

173

Conjurors to shape into potions and charms that humans can use to protect themselves. At the very least, it keeps the magic out of Reaper's hands," Kanti insisted.

"Back up to the part about hiring soldiers," Valerie said.

"I wanted to talk to you about that. Conjurors in Elsinore think differently about magic than Conjurors in Arden. No one is going to sign up to fight to protect a bunch of magic-less humans," Kanti said. "Changing that attitude will take years, decades even. But if we could pay soldiers, it's a different story."

"How much of this currency would you need to hire a few hundred soldiers?" Valerie said.

"More than you'll raise tonight, but it's a start. I'm going to use my family's savings, as well," Kanti said. She held up a hand when she saw that Valerie was about to interrupt. "I'm not asking you for your permission, Val. There's no better use for our fortune than this war."

"Your parents agree?" Valerie asked.

"I'm the Reigning Royal now. They'll do what I say. But they're starting to come around," Kanti said. "I'm trying to make it trendy to live simply and not show off your wealth."

"How's that going for you?" Valerie said with a small smile, trying to imagine Kanti's parents downsizing from their ice palace.

"Not especially well. But you never know," Kanti said, returning her grin.

"We really need more soldiers for the Fist on Earth," Valerie said, thinking of kids like Ming who didn't have a Chrome to protect them.

"So you're coming?"

Valerie nodded.

"Good. Let's start with what you're going to wear."

≫   ≫   ≫

An hour later, Valerie was scrubbed, groomed, and zipped into a blue dress that came to her knees.

"What do you think?" Kanti said, turning Valerie so she could see herself in the mirror.

Valerie slid on her battered sneakers and strapped on Pathos. Kanti rolled her eyes. "Guess you have the accessories covered."

"Last time I wore high heels, someone tried to kill me. I promised myself I'd always wear shoes I could run in and have Pathos at my side," Valerie said.

"So you're saying I should be grateful to have you in a dress at all," Kanti replied.

"Yes. And I love it. Thanks, Kanti."

"There's one more thing," Kanti said.

A low hum of magic came from Kanti's hands. She threaded her fingers through Valerie's hair and pulled gently. As she did, Valerie watched in awe as her hair became longer and longer, until it hung down the middle of her back, like it had two years ago. Its familiar weight felt right, grounding her, and the streak of silver that wound through it was hidden.

"Guess there are some side benefits to the flowers-and-hearts brand of magic," Kanti said. She placed a wreath of flowers in Valerie's hair as a final touch.

"Will Thai be at the party?" Valerie asked, blushing as soon as the words were out of her mouth. "Never mind."

Kanti burst out laughing. "I'll drag him myself if I have to, okay?"

Valerie had yet to confide to Kanti that she wasn't going to date Thai, ever. She hadn't had a memory lapse in a few weeks, but only because she hadn't healed as many soldiers lately. But she decided not to ruin the closest thing to a normal afternoon that she'd had in a long time by telling Kanti that.

"No letting Thai steal you away until you've given a toast to say thank you to the Guild and everyone who donated."

"Yes, Mom," Valerie said.

"Go make your entrance, Cinderella. But don't lose your slipper. It would be cruel to make anyone other than you touch those ratty sneakers."

જ જ જ

In spite of Kanti's instructions, Valerie insisted on sneaking into the party through a side entrance of the Guild. The ballroom was easy to find, because people were pouring into the giant room. It was lit with an enormous, golden chandelier, and the floors were covered in shiny marble.

Kanti peeled off from Valerie to go in search of Henry, so Valerie forced herself to mingle with the Grand Masters and Conjurors of the Fist. She immediately knew that Kanti had been right. Her soldiers needed to see her. She had to be no more than a ghost on the battlefield with them.

The food was incredible, but it reminded her of Dulcea's culinary creations, and turned to dust in her mouth.

The Grand Master of the Glamour Guild, Roza, glided over on eight long tentacles. Her upper body was human, and very beautiful, though Valerie knew that she could choose to look any way she wanted.

"Skye assured us that you wouldn't miss the fundraiser, but I admit I had my concerns," Roza said.

Roza handed Valerie a glass of something bubbly that would temporarily increase the volume of her voice, and she took a sip. She cleared her throat, and the room went quiet.

"Seeing you all here, selflessly giving your time, your lives, your blood, and your power, gives me hope not only for this war, but for what comes after. Thank you all," Valerie said.

Everyone cheered, and Valerie raised her glass. She saw Skye across the room, and he nodded his approval at her words. Then she drained her drink, and relief worked its way through her as lilting music began to play.

As people started to dance, she headed toward the door to make her escape from the party, stopping every few feet to shake hands with soldiers who wanted to meet her.

She'd reached the door and was about to make her getaway when she saw Thai hurrying up the steps of the Guild. He saw her and stopped moving.

"Kanti said...you needed me?" Thai asked, still staring.

"Oh, sorry, did she pull you away from your work? I don't know what she was thinking," Valerie said, vowing to give her friend a good shake when she saw her next.

"I'm really, really glad she did," he said. He'd reached her side then. "I hear music in there. Want to dance?"

Valerie knew that the right answer to give was no. She had a million things to do, and this would only give Thai false hope.

Before she could shape an excuse, Thai pulled her back inside. The ballroom was less overwhelming when he held

177

her hand. Valerie was able to appreciate the fairytale lights, and the fact that everyone was smiling for a change.

A heavy beat melted into a slow tune. The Conjurors began a couples' dance that had moves Valerie didn't recognize. Thai watched for a little while and then pulled her to the dance floor. He effortlessly guided their movements. He was so sure on his feet that she didn't stumble, didn't even have to think about what the right steps were.

She looked up and saw that he was staring down at her, his dark brown eyes intense. Every place their bodies touched tingled. Her hands, her waist, her shoulders... They had never been more sensitized.

Thai fiddled with the ends of her hair, and Valerie remembered the nights in their tent back on Earth when she'd lain next to him and he'd played with her hair.

"You rocked in short hair, don't get me wrong. But I missed it like this," he said.

Valerie let her hair fall forward to hide her blush. Another benefit of having long hair again.

Then he tipped her chin up so she couldn't avoid his eyes. The yearning in them made it almost impossible not to lean forward to see if his kisses were as good as she remembered. But the little part of her mind that was still capable of logic was screaming at her. She couldn't have this, have him, even if she wanted it.

Valerie forced herself to look away from Thai's eyes before she changed her mind. That was when she saw Cyrus watching them, his lip turned in utter disgust. Valerie pulled herself out of Thai's arms. He followed her gaze and saw Cyrus.

"Go ahead and talk to him," Thai said, and Valerie saw only sympathy in his eyes.

Cyrus ran out of the party, and Valerie chased him down the steps of the Guild.

"Cyrus, wait!" Valerie said.

He turned on her, his eyes flashing. "I have actual news about the war we're fighting, the one you're supposed to be leading. But maybe you'd rather play dress up and dance with your boyfriend."

"Of course not, I was—" Valerie began.

"Save it. People are dying, Val. On the Globe, on Earth. I shouldn't have to tell you that. How can you be dancing right now? Don't you have better things to do?"

Part of Valerie was humiliated because there was truth to his words. But the bigger part of her was consumed by an emotion she only recognized as rage when she saw that the Laurel Circle was a warm, bright gold.

"You're my best friend, the person who knows me better than anyone else in the universe. What do you think?" Valerie said. "It's a fundraiser. I had to show up to raise magic for the Fist. And, yeah, I forgot myself and enjoyed a dance. You're the one who said that we had to snatch moments of happiness when we could in the middle of all this horror, remember?"

"But I meant with me! Not with him!" Cyrus said.

Valerie had no reply, and Cyrus sucked in a breath.

"Some days, I wake up and I can't believe that you'll never be mine again," he said. "You're so woven into my heart, cutting you out will kill me."

"Then don't cut me out. We can find our way back to friendship," Valerie said.

Cyrus sagged. "You'll never understand. That's why there's no point talking about this anymore."

He stood a little straighter as if he was consciously trying to cast off his pain.

"I found you to tell you that Elle and Will need to see you," he said. "They're in my room."

∾ ∾ ∾

Valerie and Cyrus went to his room in the dorm of The Society of Imaginary Friends, and she found Elle and Will on the bed Henry slept in sometimes. Their hair was slightly damp.

"How are you both? Are you safe in Illyria?" Valerie asked.

They nodded, but neither twin smiled.

"What is it? Has Illyria fallen completely to the Fractus?" she asked.

"Illyrian politics are complicated. And decisions are never made quickly," Elle said.

"There is an endless amount of information to be gathered and analyzed," Will explained. "I think they forget that just because *they* are immortal does not mean that time moves slowly above the waves."

Valerie let out a breath of relief. "I feared the worst, after my trip there."

"Your trip wasn't a waste. There are Illyrians who agreed with your logic and are supporters of the Fist," Elle said.

"It is those supporters," Will said, "who informed us that the Fractus have tapped into a new source of magic, one that is far more powerful than the black weapons they've been wielding."

Valerie sat down on Cyrus's bed. "Where?"

"Plymouth," Elle said. "Beneath the bedrock is a special kind of dark magic that pooled there during the early wars on the Globe. The records call the magic *Carne*. There is a river of this stuff that Reaper can use to enhance his army's powers."

Valerie remembered her own trip to Dunsinane through the tunnels of Plymouth, and how she'd sensed something evil far below.

"What will happen when Reaper uses this magic?" she asked.

"The Akashic Records hold all of the information in the universe, but they do not predict the future," Will said. "For that information, you must visit Ephesus."

"In the meantime, send some scouts of the Fist into Plymouth to see if you can uncover what they plan to do with the Carne," Elle said. "Their plans are shrouded, and even the most skilled readers have not found that information."

"What about you two? Are you going back to Illyria?" Valerie asked.

"It's our home," Will said. "We belong beneath the waves."

He gave her a shell that buzzed a little in her hand.

"If you need us, toss it into the lake," Will said.

"I hope I'll see you again soon," Valerie said.

"You will. The time for change has come, and that includes Illyria. We are with you, and the Fist," Elle said.

Chapter 20

While Cyrus sent messages about the twins' news to the various leaders in the Fist, Valerie ran to the Empathy Collective, where Sibyl and the other Oracles who had fled the Roaming City in Ephesus were living.

Despite the late hour, Valerie found her friend in the garden behind the Collective. Sibyl fluttered from flower to flower, absorbing each scent. But when she turned and saw Valerie, she appeared unsurprised.

"Is it time?" Sibyl asked.

"I'm not sure what you mean," Valerie said.

Sibyl's little body shook silently, and Valerie realized she was laughing.

"I am still unused to living around anyone other than Oracles. One of our novices said that the time was nigh for us to retake the Roaming City. Is that the news you bear?" Sibyl asked.

Valerie sat down on a bench. "I came to see if any of you were drawn to give me a prophecy about how Reaper will use the magic he's tapped into in Plymouth, but maybe you're right. There are a number of answers that can only be found inside your city."

Valerie knew that Putrefus had given Reaper a prophecy when he'd visited the Roaming City with her when she only knew him as Chern, the bumbling Grand Master of the

History Guild. The words of that prophecy could give them an inside look into his motives, or possibly explain why he so badly wanted Valerie to kill someone by her own hand.

"The tug of our home has grown ever stronger, but we did not wish to draw away resources when you have so few," Sibyl said.

"You can always come to me and tell me what you need," Valerie said. "The Oracles' insights have given us an advantage in many battles. It's our turn to help you."

"Fighting for right is not a favor," Sibyl said sternly. "But I do believe that we are being drawn back to the desert for a reason."

"I'll gather a team to take back the city," Valerie said. "With Cyrus's new light magic in our weapons, and Reaper's forces being funneled to battles on Earth, I think this is a fight we can win."

"So say our prophecies, as well," Sibyl agreed.

"Then let's take your home back," Valerie said.

Valerie allowed herself two nights of rest and a full day of planning before trekking to Ephesus. Thai came with her, and Mira and Claremont would join them at the border of the desert of Ephesus.

"Do you think there are enough of us to take over the Roaming City?" Thai asked as they climbed a tree up to Arbor Aurum.

"Enough or not, it's all the soldiers we can afford," Valerie said. "I'd even leave you in Arden, saving lives, if you'd let me."

"I know you fight the Fractus on your own all the time, but this is different. You don't know who will be waiting for you in the Roaming City, and I want to be there in the event Reaper shows up with an army to support him," Thai said.

Valerie shrugged, but she was glad of his company. The warmth of his presence kept the chill of her guilt and fear at bay.

They pushed their way up the trunk, through the leaves, and found Cerise waiting for them at the top with her son, Emin. Emin's eyes sparkled with delight when he saw her, and he immediately jumped onto her back.

"I missed you, too," Valerie choked out as he gripped her neck with his little hands.

"Lemme come fight with you! Mom says no, but you can make her let me, since you're her boss!" Emin said.

Valerie suppressed a smile as Cerise glared at her, daring her to overrule her decree.

"It doesn't work that way, Emin. Your mom's always the boss of you," Valerie said, and was rewarded with a small nod from Cerise. "But even if I could, I wouldn't bring you. Every good knight knows that he has to train before he can fight in a battle. That training takes a long, long time."

Emin dropped off her back and stamped his foot before scampering away into the trees.

"I hope this war is long over before he would be of an age to fight in it," Cerise said, her voice weary.

"It will be," Thai said with certainty.

Valerie was glad he'd answered, because she didn't have the same faith that he did. Maybe if her father, or even Gideon, were still around to guide her, it would be different.

184

As they hiked through the cities in the trees, Valerie was grateful that her companions were quiet. She reached out with her mind to see if she could sense Henry, but other than a vague sense of his pain and guilt, his thoughts were shrouded from her.

"Is Henry doing okay?" she finally asked Thai, when Cerise was walking ahead, scolding Emin for carelessly leaping from branch to branch.

"Not really," Thai said. "If we were on Earth, I'd say he needs to see a therapist. But since he's in the Empathy Collective, which is the closest thing on the Globe, I'm not sure who else could counsel him."

"I'll talk to Dasan, his Grand Master. The physical distance Reaper put between us when he reversed my polarity is cutting off our mental connection, too," Valerie confessed.

"Exactly what Reaper was hoping for. But don't worry too much about Henry. When I'm not around to keep an eye on him, Cyrus and Ceru watch out for him. He hasn't been going anywhere other than his guild and Cyrus's dorm room," Thai assured her.

"I don't think he'll ever help Reaper again. But the damage is done," Valerie said.

Their conversation ended when they reached the edge of the platform that led down to the border of Ephesus.

"Emin will remain here, but I will join you in this fight," Cerise said, and Valerie noticed that she wasn't asking for permission.

"Is that a risk you want to take?" Valerie asked, casting a meaningful glance at Emin.

For the first time since Valerie had known her, Cerise shifted uncomfortably on her feet.

185

"I seek a prophecy, and likely would not find the city on my own. You would be doing me a service, and I would not forget this favor," Cerise said formally.

"Of course. The thanks is ours," Valerie replied.

Before Valerie stepped off the platform, Emin gripped her in a quick hug before he squirmed out of her grasp. His little gesture reminded her of her visits to Clarabelle, obliterating the cobwebs of pain in her mind with his innocence.

૭૦ ૭૦ ૭૦

Claremont and Mira were waiting when they descended.

"Glad you could make it. Now that you're leader of the Conjurors, the rules of proper punctuality don't apply, I take it," Claremont said, her eyes stormy.

Valerie ignored her, knowing that a good fight would put Claremont back in good spirits.

"The Oracles are returning to Ephesus the way they left—through Illyria, entering the city through the pool," Valerie explained. "Elle and Will are going to guide them back. I want to keep them out of the fighting, so they should emerge only when the city is safe."

"Good. They'd only get in the way," Claremont said, gripping the mace that Cyrus had infused with light for her.

"If things go as planned, this takeover will be bloodless," Valerie reminded her. "Mira, are you ready?"

Mira nodded, and his form shimmered as he shapeshifted, growing taller and human. He was a perfect copy of Putrefus, the most powerful Oracle in the Roaming City, and the leader of the pack that had driven Sibyl and her friends out of their home.

186

Valerie, Claremont, Thai, and Cerise all pulled up the hoods on their plain brown robes. It wasn't much of a disguise, but Valerie hoped being escorted by Putrefus himself would deflect attention from their little group.

"Let's get this done," Valerie said, and they trekked into the desert.

For nearly an hour, they saw nothing but sun and sand. It was disconcerting, because every other time Valerie had sought the Roaming City, she had found it quickly. But at last, the simple brown huts appeared in the distance, shimmering like a mirage.

"Move quickly. Let's blend in before anyone examines us closely," Cerise said.

"Duh," Claremont muttered under her breath, and Valerie shot her a look. No bickering mid-mission.

A novice wearing white greeted them as they neared the pool from which Sibyl and her friends would emerge. The pillars surrounding the pool, which had fallen the last time Valerie had visited the Roaming City, were upright, but crooked.

"Welcome, wanderers," the novice began, but her eyes widened when she saw Mira in his Putrefus disguise.

"Sir, I didn't know it was you," the novice said, and bowed subserviently.

"Of course not. If I wanted you to know, you would have. But novices are not informed of my activities," Mira said in a fair impression of Putrefus.

Valerie was impressed, considering Mira had never met the Oracle. He had copied his looks from a drawing by Sibyl, but his tone and word choice were all his own.

"Be off with you," Mira said, dismissing the novice with a wave of his hand.

187

"But...you told me to stay here, to make sure no one entered who couldn't pay," the novice said, confused.

"Yes. Right. Maintain your post, then," Mira said, and he hurried off with the rest of the group behind him.

"Down this alley," Valerie hissed, and the group followed her as she hustled toward the hut of an ancient Oracle called Mer, who had been all but cast out of the city, forbidden to deliver prophecies. He had helped her once, giving her information that led to her reuniting with her father, and she hoped he'd help her again—as well as answer a question that had been buzzing in her head for over a year.

The huts were all alike, and Valerie began to worry that they were lost. The Oracles they passed stared at the group strangely, and a few raised their hands to hail Putrefus. But Mira stuck his nose in the air and pushed on, and no one forced them to stop.

At last, she came to a hut at the edge of the city that was a little more run down than its neighbors.

"Here," Valerie said with a little breath of relief.

Valerie knocked once before pushing through the fluttering curtain at the entrance, and her team followed her inside.

At the sight of her, Mer dropped the pan he was cooking with, and it clattered on the makeshift stove. His face turned pale, and his eyes were huge as he took her in.

"Mer, it's Valerie. Do you remember me?" she asked him.

Mer regained some of his color. "I thought you were someone else. I did not think to see you again, especially in such company."

Mer glared at Putrefus, but after a minute he squinted. "You are not Putrefus."

"Your mind is strong," Mira said, resuming his true shape. He stretched, cracking his neck once.

The old man's eyes sparkled as he took in the little group. "You're here to take back the city."

"That's right, old man," Claremont said. "And we're commandeering your hut for that purpose."

Mer raised his eyebrows, and Valerie subtly stepped on Claremont's foot, hard enough to make her yelp.

"We ask your permission to hide here while Mira scouts the city in the shape of Putrefus," Valerie explained.

"You're welcome to stay, but the Oracles will not be deceived by his shapeshifting for long. Anyone who takes a good look will not be fooled. Oracles spend years training to steel their minds against magical attacks."

"Much like my own people," Cerise said with a nod of approval.

"We want to see where Putrefus and his key supporters are located. We're going to kidnap them and lock them in a hut," Thai chimed in, removing a charm from his pocket.

The stone, once activated, could turn any room into a prison. Only the bearer of the stone could leave at will.

The curtain on Mer's doorway moved, and Valerie gripped Pathos's hilt, only releasing it when she saw Sibyl walk into the hut, her telltale wings hidden under a novice's white robes.

"We're not ready for you and the other Oracles yet," Claremont said.

"My friends remain beneath the waves in the pool. But I will fight with you," she said. "I know this city and its inhabitants, and that will make all the difference if we're going to resolve this without bloodshed. This is my home, and it is right that I am part of taking it back."

Valerie didn't argue. She'd learned to take soldiers where she could find them, though her heart hurt every time one of her friends was put at risk.

Mira resumed the shape of Putrefus, and he and Sibyl ducked out of Mer's hut.

"I can't wait around in here," Claremont said, pacing the hut restlessly.

"You're the least likely of us to be recognized," Valerie said. "If you want to don your robe and scout the perimeter of the hut for any threats, go ahead."

"Thanks for the reminder that I'm a nobody," Claremont snapped as she left.

"I will watch over the volatile one," Cerise said, following Claremont out.

Mer had resumed his cooking, but his movements were jerky.

"Do you know what I want to ask you?" Valerie asked him.

Thai gave her a questioning look, but he didn't interrupt.

"Last time I was here, you told me that my father was alive. I found him. His name was Oberon, and my mother was Adelita."

"If you are angry that I did not tell you his name, know that your journey to find him shaped you into the leader you are. And I only suspected your heritage," he said.

"It's not about that. My father told me that you interrupted a prophecy being delivered to my mother, stepping into the sacred circles in the middle of a prophecy about the Pillars of Light."

Mer sat down, and his body sagged. "It is an offense that will never be forgiven. They would have cast me from the city if I had anywhere to go."

"Why would you do that? I don't believe that you want the Globe to follow a path of darkness, but I can't think of any other reason why you wouldn't have wanted my mother to get her whole prophecy. And she's dead now. If she'd heard the whole thing, maybe she'd be alive."

Valerie was shaking. She didn't know how important Mer's answers were to her until the words had left her lips. Thai moved to stand by her, his hand warm on her lower back.

Mer's posture straightened, and when he met Valerie's eyes, he stood.

"I did it to save her, to save us all," Mer said. "I saw that I would go from being one of the most powerful and respected Oracles on the Globe to a hated outcast if I entered those circles, for it is sacrilege to stop a prophecy, no matter the reason. But I saw a world enslaved if I didn't, and your mother dead. If she lives now, it is because of me."

Valerie had no words then. The edges of her vision went black.

"Valerie's mother is alive?" Thai asked, his arm the only thing keeping her upright.

"There are no certainties when it comes to prophecy. But it is what I believed when I interfered," Mer said.

The hope was more painful than the certainty that her mother was dead, so Valerie banished it from her mind. Maybe someday, if this war ever ended, she would think about it. But now, she had to put aside even her dearest hopes for the war she was forced to end.

"Tell us what you saw in your vision," Valerie said.

"This woman who was receiving her prophecy—Adelita— would have two children. If she had known they were Pillars of Light, she would have hidden them on the Globe rather

191

than take them to Earth. They would have been found and killed, and two worlds would have been plunged into darkness."

"Then you saved us all," Valerie whispered. "And you have a home with me, Mer, if you want it."

Chapter 21

After an hour of pacing Mer's tiny hut, Valerie finally saw Mira and Sibyl returning with Claremont and Cerise on their heels.

"How many do we have to capture to end Putrefus's rule?" Valerie asked Sibyl.

"Most follow him out of fear. But his core followers are his best friends of many years. There are eleven," Sibyl said.

"We have located nine," Mira added. "They reside in the new hut they call the castle."

Sibyl's face was red with indignation. "That structure was intended as a hospital, so that critically ill Conjurors could come for the healing waters of our pool. But Putrefus has turned it into his headquarters."

"I don't know how they get off calling it a castle," Claremont said. "Looks like a big pile of mud to me."

"What about the other two of Putrefus's friends?" Thai asked.

"We didn't find them, but I know where they live," Sibyl said.

"Let's grab them first," Valerie said.

After conferring with Sibyl, the group headed out. Sibyl directed them to the huts of the two allies of Putrefus who didn't live in his castle. At each stop, Valerie and Cerise snuck in and quickly knocked the target unconscious.

Thai, Mira, and Claremont hauled them back to Mer's hut, where Thai had activated the charm to turn it into a little prison. It would last a few hours, which should be enough time to take Sibyl and her friends back into the city. Mer was gleeful about his role of jailer of Putrefus's gang.

It was only two hours later that they gathered at a back entrance of the Oracle hospital.

"I'm guessing Putrefus and his friends are on the top floor," Sibyl said. "It has a view of the whole city."

Quietly, the group stepped on platforms that whizzed up a ramp that had stops at each floor.

"Mira and Thai, wait a floor below. If we don't come for you, flee back to Arden for reinforcements," Valerie commanded.

Claremont was all but rubbing her hands in anticipation of a fight as she, Cerise, Sibyl, and Valerie took the platform to the top floor.

They stepped onto the landing, and the hall was quiet. A murmur of voices was the only sound, and they followed it.

Valerie stopped at a doorway and saw Putrefus with three of his friends, laughing as they clashed with black weapons obviously given to them by Reaper. But other than that, no signs of Fractus reinforcements were visible.

"This won't even be enough of a fight to be fun," Claremont said before launching herself into the room, her light-imbued mace in her hand.

Putrefus's face was a mask of horror when he saw Valerie, Sibyl, Cerise, and Claremont charge in.

"G-get back! These weapons will suck your magic!" Putrefus said, but he and his friends had backed into a corner.

One of Putrefus's friends, who had close-cropped hair and a snout that reminded Valerie of a pig, threw his dagger at Cerise with more skill than she would have guessed he had.

Valerie's magic surged, and she knocked the knife to the ground before it lodged in Cerise's heart. Then Claremont struck him with a hard punch to his temple, and snout-nose crumpled to the ground.

Claremont laughed then turned and swung her mace, knocking the black weapon of another of Putrefus's cohorts to the ground. Valerie had drawn Pathos, and she struck Putrefus's sword with her own, shattering it.

Cerise delivered a stunning blow to the last of Putrefus's followers, knocking him unconscious with more force than necessary, before Valerie yanked her back.

"I think they surrender," she said.

Cerise's snarl fell away.

"This fool almost killed me," she said, nudging snout-nose's unconscious form with her toe. "I was careless, and Emin would have been an orphan if you had not saved me."

"You're okay," Valerie said softly. "We wouldn't want Emin losing his boss today."

"Thank you, vivicus," Cerise said.

Claremont went to the door, looking out eagerly, as if she was hoping for more attackers to mow down. But no one came, and Putrefus was trembling.

"Don't kill me," he begged. "I'll give you whatever you want."

"The Fist doesn't kill anyone unless we have to," Valerie said.

"Unfortunately," Claremont muttered.

"You will come with us and stand trial for your crimes," Sibyl said.

"You always thought you were so much better than me, because you were Pythia's daughter. Not even her real daughter!" Putrefus said. "Now I suppose you'll rule the Roaming City."

"Keep it up, and I'll take you with me unconscious," Valerie said, and Putrefus shut his mouth.

"This city was not created to be controlled by a single Oracle," Sibyl said. "Pythia guided us, but we all made the rules together. That's what I want to bring back."

ഉ   ഉ   ഉ

Thai and Mira had discovered the rest of Putrefus's gang while Valerie, Cerise, Sibyl, and Claremont captured Putrefus. The entire operation had gone more peacefully than any in Valerie's memory, and she was grateful.

Everyone in the streets stared as Putrefus and his friends were hauled to Mer's house, where they'd stay until they were tried, one at a time.

An enormous crowd had gathered by the time they were shut inside, and Sibyl cast off her novice robes. She fluttered a little above the heads of the Oracles, and an excited murmur rippled through the crowd.

Valerie had sent Thai to let the rest of Sibyl's Oracles know it was safe to return, and she saw them meeting friends and family they hadn't seen in over a year, gripping them in hugs.

"Friends, I hope you welcome back not only me and all of the Oracles who left, but also a return of a democratic Roaming City," Sibyl began.

Her words were met with cheers. It was a pleasant relief to only have to stand and watch as Sibyl outlined her plans for reorganizing the city to be more in line with the values that Pythia, the original Oracle and Founder of the city, had instilled, and explained her hope for an alliance with Valerie and the Fist.

"But no one will force a decision on you, ever. We decide as a group," Sibyl said.

Valerie walked around after Sibyl had finished talking, meeting many of the Oracles and stating her case again and again for why the fight against the Fractus was important. At last, as everyone drifted away, Sibyl turned to Valerie.

"I will take you to the Hall of Prophecies now, if you wish it."

Valerie nodded. Sibyl led her back to the hut where Valerie had received her first prophecy four years ago.

"Down there," Sibyl said, gesturing to a staircase that led underground. "Concentrate on the prophecy you seek, and it will come to you."

Valerie nodded, and started down the stairs alone. She'd only taken a few steps when Thai slid his hand into hers.

"You're not going alone," he said.

Valerie lost count of the number of stairs as they descended down, down, down. Being so deep beneath the ground was oppressive, like being buried alive, and she was even more grateful for Thai's presence. He kept the ghosts of her childhood in foster care at bay. How would she survive without him once she found the strength to send him away?

When they reached the bottom at last, everything was dark, except for the pinprick of light at the top of the staircase.

"What's next?" Thai whispered.

First one light, then another and another, appeared in crevices in the walls. There were hundreds, then thousands, then millions of tiny gold lights in the room, casting a warm, golden glow.

Valerie shut her eyes and concentrated, thinking of Chern and the prophecy he received in the Roaming City. When she opened them again, a single light whizzed from a spot on the wall, darting around the room like it was alive. It shot down and smacked Valerie directly in her forehead, and her vision went dark.

ဗ   ဗ   ဗ

Her sight cleared, and she was looking at a redheaded Oracle sitting on a stool in the center of the room that was above Valerie now.

"I'm lost. I know what I want, but I can't get it! Tell me what to do." Chern's voice sounded younger than it did now, and it cracked with despair. Valerie guessed that she was looking through Chern's eyes, seeing the Oracle from his perspective.

The Oracle swayed in his stool, and when he spoke, his voice was melodic.

From Daughter of Earth and Father of Globe
Twins shall be born.
If you command their power, you will rule,
But in failure, down from your throne you will be torn.

Valerie gasped, and her mind returned to the present. Thai was kneeling next to her.

"It wasn't the prophecy I needed," Valerie said.

Before she could say anything else, another beacon of light zipped through the room and hit her in the forehead, and she fell backward.

There was a flash of a dusty street, and Putrefus's face, red and a little sweaty.

"Tell me, quickly, are you drawn to prophesize for me? Know that if your words help, you will be rewarded," Chern said, speaking quickly.

"Rewarded how?" Putrefus asked, narrowing his eyes.

"I will need regents to help me rule the Globe. Even I cannot be everywhere at once. The Roaming City will be yours to command."

"Yes," Putrefus said, his eyes glazing. "I have words for you."

Two worlds, both alike in uncertainty
In a shifting tide of unrest
From ancient rules sweep new possibility
Of chains on men and the shroud of death.

Seize the power of the psychic twin
To gift your army the power of shadow.
Stain the vivicus with the blood of another
And her power will be yours to force man to bow.

But if the vivicus remains untainted by death,
And brother and sister against you unite,
An amoebiate's power will amplify their gifts
You will fall to the Pillars of Light.

Valerie's vision returned, and she saw Thai's anxious face searching her own until the tiny lights of the prophecies winked out.

"Tell me what you saw," he said.

"There's hope. But only if Henry and I can find our way back to each other."

Chapter 22

Sibyl sent Valerie and her team back to Arden equipped with plenty of supplies, so the trek back wasn't arduous. Valerie and Cerise walked with Claremont and Mira to the edge of Arden, where they would part ways.

"A word, Valerie," Mira said, pulling her a little away from the others. "The Knights in the Fractus who wish to fight for the Fist are growing restless. When will you give your order for them to turn against Reaper?"

"I think about asking those Knights to join us every day," Valerie said. "We are desperate for soldiers. But my instincts are telling me that Reaper is planning something, and with his discovery of Carne in Plymouth, he's already at an advantage. Knowing I have Knights acting as spies, ready to turn if he attacks, is the only weapon in my arsenal that he doesn't know about."

Mira nodded slowly. "I will tell the Knights to be patient, and to listen for whispers of Reaper's plans. They will be willing to wait a little longer, since it is you who asks it."

Then Claremont and Mira returned the way they'd come, through Arden's roller coaster system. Thai went with them because it was the quickest way back to his guild.

Valerie and Cerise returned to the cities in the trees so that Valerie could meet with leaders and visit Elden.

The walk back was quiet for a long time.

"Did you find what you were looking for in the Roaming City?" Valerie finally asked.

She turned to examine Cerise's face, only noticing now how pale and withdrawn she was.

"I found an answer, but it was not the one I sought," Cerise said.

"What do you mean?" Valerie asked, stopping in her tracks.

Cerise stopped walking and turned to face her.

"The People of the Woods have their own prophets, and one has foreseen my end," Cerise said.

Valerie couldn't process what Cerise was saying.

"A prophecy says you're going to die? Those things never mean what you think they do," Valerie said, gripping Cerise's shoulder.

"Our prophets are not like the Oracles. They do not speak in riddles, and they are never wrong. But to be sure, I went to the Roaming City to see if an Oracle could show me another path, but the Oracle who had words for me offered no hope."

"Maybe your prophet thought you'd die by that weapon that Putrefus's friend threw, and now you're safe," Valerie argued.

Cerise shook her head. "Death stalks the People of the Woods differently than other Conjurors. We live many centuries, but when death makes up his mind to come for us, he is relentless. I have lived longer than you could guess from my features. I would not dodge my fate, but for Emin. To be gifted with a child so late in life, and to leave him so soon... My heart cannot bear it."

202

A silver tear fell down Cerise's cheek and onto the ground. A little bud popped out from where it landed. Valerie watched in awe, and Cerise gave her a shaky smile.

"New life can be made so easily, but just as easily it can be taken away. Thrice now death has aimed his arrow at my heart, and thrice he has missed. The next time, he will not fail. I must prepare my son."

"I'll watch over him, Cerise," Valerie said. "I know what it is to be an orphan, and it is true that it can be lonely. But I will make sure Emin always has a family, in ties of love if not blood."

"Thank you, vivicus," Cerise whispered. "Emin is not completely accepted by my people because his father, now dead, was human. I know his uncle would take him in as a true son, but I do not know if Elden will ever recover, much less be able to take on raising a young boy."

For the rest of the walk back to Arbor Aurum, Cerise and Valerie talked of Emin's future, personality, and how to help him through his grief if his mother fell. It was the strangest conversation Valerie ever had.

When they parted, Valerie forced herself to school her emotions, knowing that Cerise would not appreciate her pity.

"I still don't believe this prophecy can't be stopped," Valerie said. "But if it's true, you have the chance to say goodbye to Emin, and that is something. I know from experience."

"There is a rising storm of darkness hurtling toward me even now," Cerise said, her eyes empty.

Whether Cerise liked it or not, Valerie couldn't help hugging her. A bit of warmth returned to Cerise's eyes, and Valerie decided that was how she'd remember her.

The chill of her conversation with Cerise had unsettled Valerie, but when she returned to her garden, the dread that had followed her eased.

"Clarabelle?" she whispered.

The baby unicorn emerged from behind the big tree in the garden. Everywhere her hooves touched, flowers bloomed. Azra and Summer were a few paces behind.

We had to see you. Clarabelle insisted, and her will overrules mine, I'm afraid.

"Children should never rule the home," Summer said with a sniff, but when she looked at Clarabelle, it was clear that she was also in love with the tiny unicorn.

Clarabelle nuzzled Valerie's side until she gave in and dropped to her knees to cuddle her properly.

"It's not that I don't want to see you. But it's more dangerous for you to be near me now than ever," Valerie said.

We will be brief, though not because Clarabelle fears danger. She has found a role for herself in the Fist.

"What? Promise me you're not anywhere near the fighting!" Valerie said, staring into Clarabelle's sky-blue eyes.

"I would never allow it!" Summer said indignantly.

Little pinging sounds of reassurance bounced around in Valerie's mind from Clarabelle, and she relaxed a little.

Some of Reaper's soldiers are leaving the Fractus. They wish to develop their powers, rather than have any more of Reaper's "gifts" of power from your brother. I am coaching Clarabelle on how to help Conjurors call forth their latent magic.

"How did they find you?" Valerie asked.

One of these ex-Fractus, Blake, was searching for me. Clarabelle heard his call and found him. He has brought others that we can trust.

"That makes me nervous. Both times I met Blake, he tried to kill me," Valerie said. But she remembered her encounters with the breakable Fractus, and he had never seemed truly evil.

I defer to my daughter's judgment. Azra's tone was affectionate, and she nuzzled Clarabelle.

"Blake has brought no one who could defeat me in battle. I stand guard at every meeting with these ex-Fractus, I assure you," Summer said, and Valerie gave her a grateful smile.

"Could Clarabelle help humans develop their magic, as well?" Valerie asked, her excitement rising.

Everyone has a spark of magic within them that can be developed with time and effort. It would be more work for humans, but in time, their magic would blossom.

"There's someone I want you all to meet."

৶   ৶   ৶

Valerie brought Dr. Freeman to the Globe, rather than bringing Clarabelle, Azra, and Summer to his home on Earth. Summer was dozing in the sun while Azra and Clarabelle gently grazed in the grass.

Dr. Freeman stared for a long time, drinking in the sight.

"I have no words," he said at last.

"I know what you mean," Valerie said, allowing the sunshine in her garden to warm up her heart.

Clarabelle approached shyly, but soon, she was nuzzling Dr. Freeman like they were old friends as Valerie explained his mission to Azra.

"Do you think you and Clarabelle could help him? If he identifies people with more magic than the average human, wouldn't it be easier for them to develop their powers with Clarabelle's help?"

Clarabelle's excited noises pinged Valerie's mind.

My daughter is saying it would be our honor.

The rest of the day was spent making plans, but it was the sweetest afternoon Valerie had enjoyed in many months. When the day's light disappeared from the Globe, Azra, Clarabelle, and Summer returned to wherever they were hiding on Earth, and Dr. Freeman went home.

Valerie didn't immediately check in with Chisisi, instead falling backward onto the grass to stare up at the pattern of stars now blazing in the sky.

At first, she bathed in the afterglow of peace that Clarabelle had left behind, but then, her heart unaccountably began to pound, and her palms grew sweaty. She barely registered that these sensations weren't her own before she was roughly yanked into Henry's mind.

 و۔   و۔   و۔

Henry's fear and guilt were a storm within him, robbing him of the strength to move. And he had to move, because Reaper was standing next to him.

"If you accept what I know to be true, then you can release all of your guilt. Your help arming the Fractus is creating a better future for humans and Conjurors," Reaper said, his voice hypnotic.

Valerie recognized the perfect reflection of the pool of water Henry was staring at. He was in Babylon. She leaped to her feet and began running in his direction, but the force pushing them apart was too strong.

"Don't listen to him, Henry," she shouted, hoping he could hear her through their connection.

But though his mind was open to her, she didn't think her voice could penetrate the wall of his pain.

"Leave me or kill me," Henry said, still staring out at the lake.

His voice was dull, in contrast to the pain raging within him. Valerie doubted even Reaper guessed at what was inside Henry.

"We had a deal and you broke it," Reaper said, changing tacks. "Your girlfriend lives, unharmed, but your debt remains. I will come to collect."

Valerie saw what was in Henry's mind then. If he was dead, Reaper would have no reason to come after anyone he loved.

"No, Henry! That's an excuse you're telling yourself," Valerie screamed. "You want to escape all that pain, and I understand. But we need you. I need you!"

Valerie was running to the Healers' Guild now. She couldn't get to Henry herself, but Thai would find him. She crashed into trees and shrubs as her vision flickered between the forest she ran through and Babylon, where Henry stood on a precipice with Reaper.

"Henry?" Reaper's tone had changed subtly, as if he knew he might have pushed him too far.

Valerie never thought that her greatest enemy might help her, but now, she hoped he would do anything other than kill Henry, or let Henry kill himself.

"There's nothing more for you here," Henry said tonelessly.

"That's not completely true, is it?" Reaper asked. "There is one thing I still owe you."

Henry turned to Reaper, and Valerie saw his calculating smirk.

"What's that?" Henry asked.

"Zunya. Didn't you wish to kill him yourself?"

A flame ignited in Henry. Valerie almost cried with relief that he was feeling something other than self-loathing.

"It's you I ought to kill! Zunya's your henchman. He was acting on your orders when he killed my dad. And you killed Oberon yourself!"

Magic pulsed out of Henry, and it hit Reaper squarely in his chest. He flew backward, slamming into a loose stone. Reaper touched his forehead, shock replacing his usual smirk at the sight of blood on his fingertips.

Then Reaper's face twisted, and Henry was upside-down, hanging in the air. He screamed as Reaper began to dissolve him, starting with his back.

Valerie shared his pain, but not his reaction to it. She was horrified, but Henry embraced it as what he deserved. He was relieved that he would die in battle, rather than by his own hand.

"Fight back! Henry, you have to fight back!"

Valerie stumbled into the Healers' Guild.

"Thai! Someone find Thai!" she shouted.

Footsteps raced as Valerie collapsed in the entryway.

ço   ço   ço

With a pulse of power, Henry mentally shoved Reaper backward and dropped to the ground as Reaper's magical hold on him released. Now, Henry's rage fueled his magic, and Reaper struggled to move toward him. From where he crouched, Henry raised a pebble in the air, and it shot through the space between him and his attacker. It would have lodged in Reaper's heart if Reaper hadn't reoriented Henry's world at that moment, shifting his perspective by ninety degrees.

But the stone did tear through Reaper's flesh, ripping a hole in his arm.

"I killed the last man who drew my blood," Reaper seethed. "My father couldn't stop me once I embraced my magic, and neither can you."

"Please run, Henry," Valerie said, but she was hopeless. She loved him so much, and she was terrified that she was about to watch as Reaper killed the last blood tie she had in the universe.

Nothing else had reached Henry, but those words did. Maybe it was the love behind them. Henry hesitated, and then ran.

Reaper struggled to follow Henry, as Henry used his magic to create a shield around himself. Occasionally some of Reaper's magic would slip through his defenses, and Henry would stumble as Reaper tried to dissolve him again, but he was gaining distance.

Valerie saw Henry's target. He was running toward the tree that led up to Arbor Aurum.

Henry gained a foothold and hauled himself up. But before he could make it far, Reaper reached the tree, grabbed Henry's ankle, and threw him to the ground. Then Henry's pain started in earnest, and his screams filled the forest.

Valerie tried to tear herself from her brother's consciousness so that she could send someone to help him, but he wouldn't release her.

"Don't let me die alone," he murmured, blood on his lips.

"I won't let you die at all," she said.

There was a flash of green, and Henry's pain abruptly diminished. Someone had dropped down on Reaper, and was tackling him.

"Emin, no! Get away from here!" Henry croaked, recognizing the little form before Valerie did.

Reaper tossed Emin aside like a doll, and he hit the side of a tree with such force that he was instantly unconscious.

Before Reaper could turn back to Henry, vines grew from the ground and wound around Reaper's arms and legs. He yelped as sharp thorns pierced his skin, digging in.

His face contorted as he fought off the vines.

"You hurt my son," Cerise said, her voice calm as she stepped from behind a tree. "You will die for that."

Whatever magic was in Cerise's thorns was turning Reaper green, and he squirmed as the vines tightened.

"Not here, or by you," Reaper said, and stopped moving.

He became still, and then a rumbling shook the ground. Reaper corralled his magic, and when he released it, the vines holding him dissolved, along with everything else within three feet of him, including Cerise.

Henry turned, looking for her.

"Cerise!"

"She's gone," Valerie whispered, unsure if Henry could hear her. It had only been hours since she'd hugged Cerise goodbye, and already the fate she feared had become reality. Death had finally found her, and this time, he did not fail. Valerie pushed down the pain that rose up in her throat.

"She is no more than particles in the air you breathe," Reaper said, but he didn't renew his attack on Henry.

Whether Cerise's vines had weakened him or the effort of releasing his power had drained him, Reaper's gray face reminded Valerie of her own after she expended her vivicus power.

Now would be the perfect time to kill him.

Henry had the thought at the same time Valerie did, but it was too late. Reaper had vanished through one of his portals.

Henry tottered over to Emin, and lifted the boy from the ground. He buried his face in Emin's jacket and began to cry. As his tears fell, he released his hold on Valerie's mind.

Chapter 23

Valerie was in a bed in the Healers' Guild, Thai on one side of her and Nightingale on the other, checking her pulse. She pushed herself up so she was sitting.

"I'll explain everything later, but can you go help Henry?" Valerie said. "He's by the tree that leads to Arbor Aurum."

Thai kissed her forehead and left.

"I'm okay, but thanks for looking out for me," she said awkwardly to Nightingale. Then she thought of something. "I know you can cure almost any disease on the Globe, right?"

"Most of the diseases that a human might face, perhaps. But we are not gods. We cannot stop aging, or death, or terrible wounds like the ones that Reaper's black weapons inflict," Nightingale said. "There are also magical diseases with no cures."

"What about mental diseases?" she asked.

Nightingale examined her narrowly. "What is wrong with your mind?"

"Not mine," she said. "But I think my brother is suffering from depression. Can you help him?"

Nightingale's expression cleared as he considered her question. "I am not the expert on cures of the mind. But there is a Grand Master who may be able to help you."

"Dasan," Valerie said, and Nightingale nodded.

"He is your best hope for helping your brother."

Valerie found Dasan at the Empathy Collective. The giant Feng was teaching a class to novice Empaths, and Valerie waited until he finished before approaching.

He cocked his head to the side, watching her with beady eyes.

"You must know why I'm here," Valerie said.

"Your brother is growing sicker," Dasan replied.

"You told me once that he might lose himself after his dad died. And I'm afraid he is. Can you help him?"

"His is a case I have considered more deeply than any other in this life," Dasan said. "There is nothing I can do to help him."

"What about magic? There has to be some way to save him," Valerie said, not letting herself give into the desperation that made her want to scream and never stop.

"Henry will always struggle with the dark beast that has sunken its fangs into his spirit, no matter what direction his life takes now. However, he could fight its hold on him if he could live a normal life. Up until now, this beast within him has been fed and fed and fed by years of mental torture, losing his father, and now the guilt of aiding an enemy in murder. The beast is strong now, stronger than any I've known in the many minds I've touched in this life."

"But there is nothing normal about our lives. So is Henry doomed?" Valerie asked, and her very soul shrank from Dasan's answer.

The bird's eyes were gentle as he replied. "I am a creature that believes there is always the possibility of new life. Henry is no exception. There is one thing that starves this beast within Henry. Can you guess what it is?"

Valerie thought for a long time. She knew there was a beast like the one Dasan described within her, too, and she knew the only thing that kept it at bay.

"Love," she whispered.

Dasan nodded. "Your love, my love, and the love of all his friends will starve the beast. But until Henry finds love for himself, the beast will never die."

୭   ୭   ୭

Valerie was leaving the Empathy Collective when she saw two figures approaching from a long distance away. She recognized Thai, but it wasn't until they were closer that she identified the boy whose hand he was holding.

Emin looked little and lost, and he broke out in a run when he saw Valerie.

"It isn't true. Mom isn't gone forever!" Emin said, launching himself into her arms.

"I'm sorry, Emin. I saw her die," Valerie said simply, and she held him as he was racked with sobs.

She made eye contact with Thai over Emin's head, and she saw that Thai's eyes were filled with tears of his own. She couldn't break down right now, when Emin needed her, so she forced her own grief into the box inside her.

Emin's sobs turned to sniffles, and he finally lifted his head from Valerie's shoulder.

"Who will make my dinner now? Who will make sure I go to school, and don't skip bedtime, and hug me when I fall?" he asked, his voice desperate.

"I will," Valerie promised. "And your Uncle Elden and all your friends, too."

"Can I live with you?" Emin asked, his enormous eyes pleading.

"Yes," Valerie promised. "You can stay at my house with me and my brother for as long as you want."

"And me, too," Thai said.

Valerie gave his arm a grateful squeeze. There was no way she could take care of Emin by herself in the middle of leading a war, and he knew it.

"I'll stay with you for a while, if that's okay," Thai whispered as they headed to Valerie's home.

"Thank you," she said.

"This is what I want, too," Thai said. "I miss having all my brothers and sisters around to watch out for."

"Taking care of Emin will be good for Henry, too," Valerie said.

They'd reached Valerie's house, and she gave Emin some of her dad's tea and tucked him into her own bed.

"You can stay in my dad's room," Valerie said to Thai as she shut the door to her room quietly behind her.

"Are you sure?" Thai asked. "I'm fine with the couch."

"Take it. Make this your home here on the Globe," Valerie said, turning so he wouldn't see her blush.

She was about to scrounge for something to eat for dinner when the ground began to rumble. She knew what this was.

"Earthquake," she said, and the trembling grew stronger.

"They have earthquakes on the Globe?" Thai asked.

"I don't know," Valerie said, gripping the side of a table.

Books started falling off of shelves, and the teapot clattered to the floor. Valerie made her way back to the door to her room to check on Emin, but the shaking stopped. She peeked into her room, anyway, but he was still asleep.

Valerie's sixth sense was going off.

"This wasn't an ordinary earthquake, if they even have those on the Globe," she said.

Thai nodded. "It's the Fractus."

"I'm going to see what Skye knows about this. Besides, it's Henry's night to be home. I know it's a lot to ask, but can you watch them both? Emin's grieving and Henry is lost. I'm scared he might try to hurt himself, especially after watching Reaper kill Cerise."

"I'll take care of them both," Thai said. "Go save the universe for a while, and I'll see you tomorrow."

Valerie gave him a lopsided smile and left before she started kissing him, because then, she'd never be able to leave.

෨ ෨ ෨

The Horseshoe was alive with Conjurors leaving their guilds to identify the source of the earthquake. Valerie noticed that the grass everyone gathered on was green again. Thanks to Willa, the drought was over. She was distracted from her thoughts at the sight of Skye galloping toward her.

"It's coming from Plymouth," he said, halting when he reached her side. "Tiny rumblings have been coming from below the ground for days, but I did not alert you since we had no news of what was causing the problem. But after today's quake, we must consider that the Fractus have had a major success."

"Or failure," Valerie said. "Maybe something collapsed underground."

Skye snorted in disbelief, and Valerie agreed with him. The very air around them hummed with power. It made her queasy. The magic seemed twisted, somehow.

Valerie stared at the ruined fountain that marked the entrance to the underground world of Plymouth, and saw that giant cracks had appeared in the hardened black substance that had spewed from the fountain after the ceasefire with the Fractus had ended.

"We have been trying every magical means to access Plymouth since the Fractus shut us out, to no avail. But today, the loud Conjuror from the Literary Guild who built the irrigation system found me and announced that she knows of a way that we can enter Plymouth."

"Willa knows a secret entrance?" Valerie asked.

Skye tossed his mane with a huff. "Nothing so dignified. I will let her explain, since the science eludes me, I confess. I'm always suspicious of scientific techniques that work where magic has failed, but I'll let you be the judge."

Valerie suppressed a smile at Skye's prejudice against science and followed him to Willa's Guild. They found her in the library at a table with three other Conjurors. Her eyes lit up when she saw Valerie.

"Being raised human, you'll appreciate that we have a non-magical answer to our Plymouth problem."

"What are you thinking? A drill? Maybe a giant excavator?" Valerie asked, trying to remember what construction equipment on Earth would be used to dig into the ground.

Willa and the Conjurors stared, looking at her as if she'd spoken in another language. Finally, Willa spoke.

"You must tell us about these devices some time. They sound fascinating, but I do not think we have these items on

217

the Globe. However, we do have dynamite," she said with a smile.

"That works, too," Valerie said. "But it's dangerous, and I'm guessing that we don't have any experts on explosives to help us."

The Conjuror sitting next to Willa, a man wearing glasses, spoke up.

"I'm Messina-born, and while we do not mine with dynamite on the island, I am very familiar with the technology. I taught a class at the university on explosives," he said.

"This is Steven," Willa said. "He left Messina five years ago when he found out the Literary Guild existed in Arden."

"The thought of all that knowledge that we don't have access to in Messina... I couldn't die without seeing it," Steven said.

"I don't like this," Skye said. "This man could end up killed if his theories are incorrect."

Steven drew himself up. "I would gladly die for the Fist. The Fractus will destroy us all if we are unwilling to take risks in this war."

Skye appeared taken-aback, and he gave Steven a nod of respect.

"Perhaps you are right," Skye said.

Now everyone looked at Valerie for guidance. She swallowed, wishing that she could talk to her dad, or Gideon, about what to do next. Aside from risking Steven's life, what if creating an opening into Plymouth unleashed all of that evil Carne magic below? It could create havoc in Arden. But leaving the Fractus to their own devices might be even worse.

"Let's blast our way in," Valerie said, and Willa and Steven smiled. "But first, Willa, do you have any maps of

Plymouth in this library? Because we don't want any of the civilians on the ground down there getting hurt."

"Excellent question," Willa said, pulling out a stack of maps from beneath the books on the table. "Yes."

ço   ço   ço

The preparation to break in to Plymouth went through the afternoon and into the night. Finally, they had hammered out a plan that Valerie was satisfied with, and everyone left to get some sleep before they made their attempt. Skye accompanied Valerie on their way out of the Literary Guild.

The centaur was pawing at the ground, a sign of Skye's uncertainty that Valerie had come to recognize.

"What is it? Do you think the plan needs more work?" she asked him.

"Plans always need more work, but there's never time. It's fine as it is. The only part that I don't like is that you'll be going in. It's too risky. We need you," Skye said.

"I wouldn't do this if I didn't think it was important. I don't want to throw my life away," Valerie said, thinking of her brother. "I go wherever the work is the hardest, because that's where the leader of the Fist should be, don't you think?"

Skye bowed his head, a centaur gesture of respect. "I question many things in this war, vivicus, but never that you should lead it. And every day, you give me more reasons to continue following you."

Valerie briefly rested her hand on Skye's flank before turning her steps to the dorm of The Society of Imaginary Friends.

When she reached the tall blue building, she couldn't help thinking about all of the times she'd seen Dulcea flying down the side on a platform. She shook her head to clear it of cobwebs and jumped on a platform that would take her to Kanti's floor.

The room was exactly as Kanti had left it, but without her friend, it was lonely. Valerie brushed her teeth and collapsed in her old bed for a few hours, until the sun hit her face, waking her up.

Even though her sleep had been short, she was running late. Still, she dragged her feet as she faced her next task. She took the platform up to Cyrus's room. Seeing Cyrus would make their lost friendship more real, and knowing that the sight of her brought him misery made her want to crawl into a dark corner and never emerge.

While the average eighteen-year-old might have the luxury of hiding, she didn't, so she knocked on the door and forced herself to stand straighter.

Cyrus answered, rubbing his eyes, but he tensed when he saw her face.

"I need you for a mission. I wouldn't have come if there was anyone else who could help," she said.

"I know, Val," Cyrus said, his tone weary. "Where are we going?"

Chapter 24

By the time Valerie and Cyrus made it to the glade a few miles outside of Silva, Steven and Willa had already set up the dynamite and were ready to blow a hole into Plymouth.

"Ready?" Valerie asked Steven. Steven nodded. "Then light the fuse."

Steven snapped his fingers and a flame appeared. But before she could ponder exactly what Steven's power was, the little flame raced along the cable to the dynamite, which exploded and sent a mist of dirt and rocks everywhere.

Willa jogged over to the hole in the ground.

"It's here, right where the map said!" she exclaimed, tugging at a rusty wheel on the outside of an ancient door beneath the ground.

"It must have been buried when the residents of Plymouth, the Groundlings, decided to cut off ties with the world above. Reminds me a little of Messina," Steven said. "We tried to cut off contact by being on an island."

"Do the Groundlings refuse to use magic, as well?" Cyrus asked.

"The opposite," Willa said. "They are a people who revere magic as a religion."

"Then hopefully, they won't want it to be polluted by the Fractus," Valerie said.

She used her strength to twist the wheel, and the door creaked open. She pulled it wide enough that she and Cyrus could fit through.

"Let's go," she said, and she and Cyrus stepped into the darkness.

"We'll make sure no one follows you in," Willa's voice floated behind them.

Inside, it was completely dark until Valerie felt magic hum from Cyrus. Light spilled from his hands, illuminating a cavern that was studded with gemstones of many different colors.

"Beautiful," Valerie whispered.

Cyrus touched a red gem, and the light from his hands made it glow. Then the light spread, jumping from stone to stone. Now the cavern was filled with multi-colored lights of blue, green, red, and purple. The muted light reminded Valerie of sunlight pouring through stained glass.

"Not a bad trick," Cyrus said with his old, cocky grin. "Not one that every lightweaver would be able to manage, I might add."

"No one but you would dream up such a unique use of your power, even if they could manage the magic," Valerie said, and Cyrus's grin widened. "Now let's get moving before your head grows too big to fit inside here."

Cyrus gave her a playful shove, and Valerie flashed him a surprised smile. It was like old times, until Cyrus's grin vanished.

"It can never be like it was," he said, as if he could read her mind, and then he began jogging down the hall.

For a long time, they walked, not speaking, and Valerie began to worry that they'd taken a wrong turn, or that the maps that Willa had given them were outdated.

But finally, they heard the distant murmur of voices, echoes of people talking or shouting.

"Over here," Cyrus said, waving her over.

Valerie went to his side and saw that he'd found an opening in the wall the size of a window. She peeked through it and saw a city spread below them. There were homes carved out of the bedrock, magnificent stone structures that were elaborately detailed with columns, pillars, winding staircases, and soaring arches.

Despite being underground, the city wasn't dark. Orbs of light were suspended throughout the city in nooks and crannies. They hummed with power, and Valerie suspected they were powered by magic. Blankets of green moss gave the impression of well-trimmed lawns, and instead of real flowers, elaborate blooms cut from gemstones decorated windowsills and gave life to the little parks that dotted the city.

The people were short and pale, but not out-of-the-ordinary. Certainly, in a diverse city like Arden, they wouldn't be out of place, but even on Earth, they could pass for human, as long as they hid their hair, which shone in jewel tones that could never be achieved with human hair dye.

"The Fractus must be close by," Cyrus said. "Everyone's scared."

Valerie had been dazzled by the beauty of the underground city, but now that she examined the people, she saw how quickly they moved through the streets, glancing around as if they were expecting to be jumped.

Her eyes scanned the city, and she saw that there was a river running through the middle. She remembered from her earlier visits to the city that there were beautiful streams in Plymouth that children had splashed in.

But now, the turquoise waters were muddied, and farther upstream, the water was black.

"There," Valerie said, pointing to a group of about a hundred tents. They were set up next to where the stream disappeared into a cave in the bedrock. The water that poured out of the opening was like ink.

"We have to get closer," Cyrus said. "I won't be able to tell anything about the water down here, where it's completely diluted."

Valerie nodded and scanned her map.

"There should be stairs cut into the wall around here where we can descend, but once we're on the ground, we'll have to try to blend in," she said.

"Maybe the Groundlings will assume we're Fractus, and vice versa," Cyrus said hopefully.

Valerie found a rough ladder carved into the wall, and she began descending, testing each groove before putting her weight on it. She reached the ground and looked around to see if anyone has spotted their descent, but they were in shadow. There were no orbs of light to give away their entry into the city.

"I think we should move fast," Valerie said. "Let's not give anyone time to ask questions."

With unspoken agreement, they followed the stream. Cyrus occasionally dipped a finger in. The farther they went, the more Valerie noticed a deep humming that rattled her core.

"That hum is coming from the river, isn't it?" she asked Cyrus.

"Yep. It reminds me of the magic in Reaper's black weapons, but slipperier, somehow," he said.

Before Valerie could ask him what he meant, they passed a house and almost ran into a boy and girl playing with different colored gemstones, tossing them on the ground in some kind of game. They both froze when they saw Cyrus and Valerie.

"Sorry," the little girl said, her pale face turning even paler. "Please let us go. We won't leave our house again."

"It's okay. We won't hurt you. We're not with them," Valerie said, gesturing downstream to the tents.

"We're the good guys," Cyrus added, and both kids grinned when he raised his eyebrows dramatically.

"Then can you help everyone they've taken?" the little boy asked.

"They've got our dad and our aunt," the girl explained.

"Got them where?" Valerie asked, searching the tents for any signs of captives.

"They took them into the cave where the river flows from, and we haven't seen them since," the girl said.

"We'll help," Valerie promised, not missing the sharp look Cyrus gave her.

They continued to follow the river.

"I thought we were here strictly to gather information on what the Fractus are up to," Cyrus said. "Judging by how many tents there are, there are too many Fractus to fight, even for you."

Valerie was distracted, squinting as she tried to make out what the activity was at the mouth of the river.

"Of course, intel only. I remember," she said, and then put her finger to her lips.

They'd reached the tent city, and it was mostly abandoned.

225

"Everyone must be in there," Cyrus said, peering in the cave. "I can check the river water out here, and we'll head out before they're back, if we're lucky."

They hurried to the river, where the water ran the darkest. While Cyrus tested how light reacted to the black Carne staining the water, Valerie moved closer to the cave.

She could make out the sounds of people shouting instructions, and the occasional grunt. Being so far beneath the ground gave her goose bumps if she thought about it too long, and she couldn't imagine how much worse it must be for the people in the cave.

"Val! I'm done!" Cyrus called.

Valerie was peeking in the cave, unable to help herself. That was when she heard a scream of pain. Her reaction then was pure instinct.

She launched herself into the darkness, barely registering Cyrus cursing as he followed her in. He illuminated the darkness, and Valerie saw Fractus everywhere, clearly identifiable by the black weapons they carried. They were standing over a crowd of Groundlings, who were on their hands and knees, scraping a substance off the walls that was dark and sticky, reminding Valerie of blood.

Everyone froze, staring toward the light Cyrus had created, and Valerie took advantage of the pause to start attacking.

The first four Fractus she took down didn't know what had hit them, but after that, weapons were drawn. She unsheathed Pathos in a blaze of light.

"Cyrus, take the Groundlings out of here!" she shouted.

Then she turned back to the Fractus.

"I'm Valerie Diaz. You know who I am. Who wants to drag me back to Reaper as your prisoner?" she taunted.

Her words had the desired effect. The Fractus turned their attention to her, their eyes gleaming in Pathos's light. The Groundlings were quick to take advantage of Valerie's distraction, and they scurried to the exit of the cave, where Cyrus ushered them out.

Valerie gave in to her magic then, and it was a kind of bliss, fighting with pure instinct, moving as fast as she could to deflect attacks. The black weapons of her enemies were a blur of metal, and she couldn't distinguish faces in the dim light.

After a time, part of her brain registered that most, if not all, of the Groundlings had made it out of the cave. She made eye contact with Cyrus.

"Run. I'm right behind you," she lied.

Cyrus left the cave, but instead of following him, Valerie stabbed Pathos into the ground. The entire cave rumbled as Pathos pumped its own magic, intertwined with hers, into the earth.

The shuddering increased, and the exit to the cave became blocked as several boulders broke loose.

Pathos was dimmer after having expended its magic, and Valerie fought her attackers in near darkness. Still, a combination of magic and adrenaline coursed through her full force, and she was a whirlwind of energy. The darkness had the advantage of disorienting her enemies. Valerie wasn't relying on her sense of sight, so her fighting ability wasn't impeded.

The Fractus were tripping over the unconscious bodies of their comrades, but still they kept coming. How many were there? Eventually, even her energy would run out. Before it did, she had to act.

In one swift move, Valerie sheathed Pathos, and the cave became pitch black. She curled into a ball and rolled, and she could hear the Fractus grunting as they bumped into each other, searching for her.

A flash of light in the corner caught her attention. She squinted, and realized that the light formed a message.

This way.

The handwriting was Cyrus's, and Valerie followed the glimmer of light, no more than a speck on the ground. It led her into a side tunnel of the cave. She could tell that she was headed up, away from the Fractus fumbling in the river below.

Finally, she emerged in a cavern that was glowing from light pouring from Cyrus's hands. She expected to see rage on his face, but found only determination and relief.

He was surrounded by the Groundlings they had saved. They were dirty and tired, their jewel-toned hair stained with the Carne they had been scraping from the walls, but alive.

"Listen to me," Valerie said. "The Fractus who have invaded your land do not represent all of the Conjurors in the world above. I lead the Fist, and we will send help to drive the Fractus out of your land."

The Groundlings murmured, absorbing her words.

"Tell your people to look for Conjurors with weapons that have been embedded with light. They will help you. Those wielding the black weapons are the Fractus," Cyrus said.

"Even below, we have heard of you, vivicus," a low voice said. "And you do not disappoint."

The Groundlings had Cyrus and Valerie back in the cavern that led out of Plymouth faster than either of them had anticipated. When they were finally alone, Valerie stole a glance at Cyrus.

"Don't you want to yell at me for not listening to you and getting out of there before we had to fight?"

"No," he said.

"Okay, then don't you want to tell me that we saved a couple dozen Groundlings today, but what was the point, since the Fractus surely have hundreds more working as their slaves, mining Carne somewhere in Plymouth?" Valerie asked.

"No," Cyrus said. He stopped, and so did she. "As a girlfriend, you suck. As leader of the Fist, you did the right thing, and saving those people today was one of the best things I've ever done in my life."

Valerie bit her lip.

"And even though I can't be around you right now, as your best friend, I'm proud of you for doing what was right."

Chapter 25

When Valerie and Cyrus emerged from Plymouth, Chisisi was pacing by the door. It was the first time Valerie had seen him on the Globe.

"Miss lives," Chisisi said, briefly shutting his eyes in relief.

Valerie saw that Skye was also waiting for her. Willa and Steven were watching the scene, eyes wide with curiosity.

Chisisi brushed dirt off of his wrinkled shirt before he spoke. "The attacks on Earth have increased dramatically. The Fractus have switched focus from targeting specific individuals or groups, presumably for information, to attacking major seats of power, such as Washington, D.C., Beijing, London, and Singapore."

"Why the change in strategy?" Cyrus asked.

"Perhaps they found the information they were seeking, and are now beginning their plan to conquer Earth," Chisisi suggested. "The Fractus are occupying all of our forces, and we cannot protect everyone. People are dying by the hundreds."

"I don't think the Fractus attacks on humans are really about taking over their governments, at least not yet. Right now, they're distracting us," Valerie guessed. "They must be close to finding the charm that binds magic on Earth, and they don't want us in their way."

"That may be," Chisisi said. "My sources are scouring the Atacama Desert, but we are no closer to finding the flame."

"We have to send reinforcements," Valerie said.

Skye nodded. "Chisisi and I came to the same understanding. But it will mean weakening our protection of Arden."

"We don't have a choice. We can't let people die," Valerie said, and then turned to Cyrus. "Get Henry and tell him to check in with Sanguina on Earth. The prophecy I read in the Roaming City said that we're at our strongest when we're working together. Even if we can't be next to each other, maybe if we're both on Earth, we'll have a better chance of driving back the Fractus."

"There's another matter," Chisisi said. "One of the battles is raging around the home of young Ming."

Valerie fought the urge to instantly go to Ming's side, but she knew she had to organize everyone before she left to fight. She'd sent Chrome to Ming for a reason, and she had to trust him now.

Valerie and Skye identified which Conjurors would be best utilized on Earth, given the rules binding magic, and Skye left with Chisisi to determine where on Earth the soldiers should be sent.

Valerie turned to Cyrus.

"After you find Henry, I need you to update Thai," she said. "He's watching Emin, and he needs to know what's happening. I'm sorry to ask you this, but–"

Cyrus shook his head. "I get it. First, give me Pathos."

Valerie handed him her weapon, and he concentrated, weaving a light pattern into her blade, which was dim after using it in Plymouth. The pattern embedded itself in her sword, and it glowed brighter than ever.

"Now go," Cyrus said.

Valerie took off as fast as she could, running to the mirror in Kanti's dorm room. Kanti had set it up to call her at the palace whenever Valerie needed her.

As soon as Valerie tapped the mirror, an image of Kanti's ice palace appeared. Peach, Kanti's middle sister, was passing by and saw her.

"Get Kanti, now," Valerie said. "And come back with her. We need all the help we can get."

Peach must have run, because Kanti was in front of the mirror in less than a minute. Valerie filled them in on what was happening.

"How can we help?" Kanti asked.

"Those soldiers in Elsinore, the mercenaries we talked about hiring—are they ready to be deployed?" Valerie asked.

"I've formed a guard of a hundred soldiers I trust, up to a point. I'll work with Chisisi on where to send them," Kanti said.

"Can you do that, Peach?" Valerie asked. "I have another job for Kanti."

Peach paled, but when she spoke her voice was firm. "I can do it."

"Kanti, find Henry. He's not stable, and we need his help on Earth," Valerie said.

"I'll try. But when I tried to talk to him at the fundraiser, he avoided me. He would barely look me in the eye," Kanti said.

"You're still my best hope for getting through to him, since I can't do it myself," Valerie said.

"Consider it done," Kanti replied.

Valerie wasted no time gripping a chipped piece of brick from Ming's home so she could transport to her friend's side.

Ming's apartment complex was a war zone. Valerie counted no fewer than twenty Fractus around the building. They had smashed in all of the windows on the bottom floor, but the thick metal bars in front of the glass must have prevented them from getting inside. Now five of the Fractus were trying to break through the front door. People were screaming inside the building.

Another fifteen or so Fractus were battling with soldiers from the Fist. Valerie recognized two Knights from her guild by sight, but not by name, and Elisabeth, one of Chisisi's guardians on Earth. The three of them were barely fending off the attacks from the Fractus, and Valerie saw the bodies of two of her soldiers on the ground, both bleeding, the light in their weapons extinguished.

There were no police, and Valerie guessed that the Fractus who were skilled at manipulating electronics had taken the precaution of disabling the police cars and phones in the area. Still, it would just be a matter of time before human help came on foot.

Elisabeth saw Valerie first, and gave her a nod. Valerie was impressed by how much better Elisabeth's fighting skills were since she'd seen her last.

Valerie unsheathed Pathos, which blazed brighter than ever, thanks to Cyrus, and it caught the attention of the Fractus who weren't trying to break down the door.

Pathos flashed as she encountered the first weapon, a black staff. She cut it cleanly through, and it shattered from the impact. The Fractus backed up a fraction, glancing at each other in surprise.

233

"Their weapons are stronger than the others we've encountered," one of the Knights gasped as he dodged a blow from another Fractus's black sword. Valerie guessed that the sword was sucking at the Knight's powers.

She turned Pathos on the man's attacker, and her blade met his with a sharp clang. This Fractus was a better fighter than average, and Valerie feinted before twisting her blade so it caught him in his ribcage. With a flick of her wrist, she'd cut the armor protecting his chest.

Valerie waited to see if he would bare his heart to her, asking her to kill him as Reaper had ordered his soldiers in the past, but he didn't.

Instead, he thrust at her arm, almost grazing her skin. He'd leaned in for the blow, and Valerie kicked him squarely in the chest, sending him backward with enough force that he slammed into the wall of the apartment complex and was knocked out.

The Fractus who had been trying to break down the front door succeeded, and the door gave way with a splintering of wood. Valerie was about to leap past three Fractus to make her way to the door when Chrome shot out, his face twisted with rage.

He leaped onto the nearest Fractus and dug his teeth into the man's arm. The man screamed when Chrome yanked his head back with his mouth full of bloody flesh.

"Chrome, no! Protect Ming!" Valerie yelled, but Chrome was blind to everything but his enemies in his bloodlust.

Chrome tore through two more Fractus, slicing the tendon of one and the muscle in the arm of another, maximizing his damage.

Valerie was set upon by three Fractus wielding staffs that she knew could shoot lightning. She blocked the first bolt

234

with Pathos, and the lightning rebounded and hit her attacker. A hole in his leg from the wound was smoking, and the other two Fractus backed away from her.

Around her, Valerie saw that the attack was ebbing. Eleven Fractus were on the ground, unconscious or severely wounded. The rest were looking around them, gauging the best exits.

When there were only five Fractus left, they turned tail and ran. Chrome bolted after them, and he tackled one of the Fractus to the ground. His teeth were on the man's throat, ready to rip it out, when a little form raced out of the doorway and jumped onto Chrome's back. Valerie almost choked with fear when she realized it was Ming.

"Hush, hush now," Ming crooned, stroking Chrome's fur, which was standing on end.

The tension in Chrome's body eased at the sound of her voice.

"Jet wouldn't want this, and neither do you," Valerie said, moving closer to the wolf.

Ming slid off his back and knelt before Chrome.

"He's okay," she said, her eyes staring into his.

Chrome's eyes were wet, and he gave Ming's cheek a little lick. Then he flashed an image of a mother wolf guarding her pups in Valerie's mind. At first, the image was tinged with red, but the haze faded, and the colors of the blue sky, green grass, and purple mountains seemed brighter than ever.

Valerie understood that Chrome was letting go of his hatred. Right now, he was choosing to protect something precious that would grow into something truly great and good. Ming.

"You're right, she's special," Valerie said.

A sensation tickled the back of her mind, and she recognized Henry. He was inviting her into his mind, something he almost never did, even before his dad had died.

"Is there somewhere I can be alone?" Valerie asked. "Henry needs me."

"My room," Ming said, pointing to a window on the bottom floor of the apartment complex.

"I'll get things in order out here," Elisabeth said, her voice ringing with authority as the sound of police sirens became clear.

Chrome gave a little growl at her tone, but it didn't hold any menace. After a quick circuit around the block, Valerie hurried to Ming's room before the cops could stop her, satisfied that all was calm.

ço   ço   ço

As soon as Valerie reached for Henry's mind, it opened for her. He was eager for her to witness what he was seeing. Valerie didn't understand where he was at first. She was expecting to find him fighting on Earth with Kanti at one of the locations Chisisi had identified as needing the most help.

Instead, he was in the throne room of the Black Castle. Valerie understood why Henry wanted her to be with him now. Zunya was unconscious on the floor in front of him, blood trickling from wounds on his forehead and a gash on his arm.

"Henry, what's going on?" Valerie asked.

A jumble of images came to her mind, of Henry finding a portal in his bedroom that led to the throne room. He'd gone through the portal alone, hoping to fight Reaper and maybe even die. Instead, he'd found Zunya, tied up in magical rope and left like a gift.

The wounds Zunya had now were from Henry, Valerie saw with shock. Her brother, who had never raised a weapon in anything other than self-defense, had taken full advantage of Zunya's defenselessness and had beaten him. And now he intended to kill him. Reaper must have been distracting her with the battle at Ming's apartment, hoping to draw out Henry's hatred while she was mentally disconnected from him.

"No! This isn't who you are. We don't execute people," Valerie said.

"You don't execute people. But isn't a part of you glad that I will?" Henry asked.

Valerie cursed her inability to travel to her brother's side. Tan burst into the throne room.

"What are you doing here? Get out, before I have to hurt you," Tan said, and he saw Zunya. "He'll kill you when he wakes up."

"Piss off," Henry said, and gave Tan a mental shove.

Henry used more magic than he'd meant to, and Tan flew across the room, crashing into the throne. Tan screamed and then fell to the ground, silent.

"What are you doing?" Kanti's voice made Henry whip around.

Kanti and Sanguina were both standing at the doorway to the throne room. How had they found him?

"Get out of here, Kanti!" Henry said. "You don't want to see this."

"The hell I don't," she said, coming closer.

"Reaper handed Zunya to you?" Sanguina asked Henry.

"He owed this to me," Henry said through gritted teeth.

237

"Reaper doesn't do anything without a reason. He wants you to murder Zunya because it will change you, make it easier for him to use you," Sanguina said.

Henry snarled, reaching for his machete, which lay next to him on the ground. But as much as he hated Sanguina, Valerie could see that he also didn't dismiss her words.

"Murder," Valerie echoed Sanguina. "That's what this would be."

"Fine," Henry said.

He knelt next to Zunya and shook him. Zunya's yellow eyes opened, and Henry cut the magical rope binding his wrists and ankles with his light-infused machete.

"What are you doing? He'll kill you!" Kanti said.

Zunya sucked in a breath and smiled. Kanti's fear was giving him energy. And if he tapped into Henry's fear, he'd have a feast, Valerie knew.

"You don't want me to murder him. Fine. I'll kill him in a fair fight. Now stand up," Henry ordered Zunya.

"I've been yearning to take your life for years. If I had to listen to you whine one more time, I'd have killed myself and saved Reaper the trouble," Zunya said with a little grin.

Zunya reached for Henry's arm, but Henry dodged his touch. Still, even Zunya's presence was sucking in all of the magic in the room. Zunya produced a little sunflower blossom, an echo of Kanti's magic.

"Useless, like the princess who wields this power," Zunya said.

Henry lashed out with a wild swipe of his machete, and Zunya easily danced out of its path.

Kanti passed out on the floor from the effect of Zunya sucking at her powers.

"Not her, me!" Henry said, and his rage focused on him.

Sanguina moved to enter the fray, but Henry pushed her back with his telekinesis, and she stumbled awkwardly, her prosthetic leg twisting under her.

"Stay out of this, for once!" Henry yelled at her. "I'll slit my own throat if you get in the middle of this fight, I swear it."

Sanguina nodded, her lips white, and stepped back.

Zunya didn't pause during Henry's interaction with Sanguina, and instead, launched himself at Henry, tackling him to the floor.

Valerie was blinded by pain as Zunya made contact with Henry's skin and ripped away his magic. But Henry fought back with a strength that seemed inhuman. He managed to nick Zunya with his machete, and Zunya screamed.

It was the first time Valerie had heard him make a sound of pain, and it was a terrible thing to hear.

જ   જ   જ

Someone yanked open the door of Ming's room, and Valerie came back to her own reality.

Sanguina stood in the doorway.

"How are you here? Don't leave Henry with Zunya!" Valerie said.

"Good, you know what's happening. Come with me," Sanguina said.

She gripped Valerie's shoulder, and they returned to the Globe, inside Henry's room.

"Kanti found me, and together we searched for Henry. We found Reaper's portal here, still open," Sanguina quickly explained.

Hovering at the end of his bed was a rip in the air. Valerie tried to move toward it, but the force that repelled her from Henry stopped her from getting any closer.

"I'm going to force him to go to Earth with me. As soon as he's gone, go through the portal. Once you're inside, he won't be able to return until you're gone," Sanguina said.

Sanguina limped through the portal, and Valerie tried to re-enter Henry's mind, but he was distracted now, and his mind wasn't completely open to her. For an instant, she saw Zunya's face as Henry raised his machete, blazing with light, before slamming it into his chest.

A sudden lessening of the pressure forcing Valerie away from the portal let her know that Sanguina had succeeded in getting Henry out of there. She stepped through the rip in the air and was standing outside of the throne room.

Zunya was twitching on the ground as cracks of light raced from the entry wound the machete had made through his entire body. She put her hand to Zunya's chest and let her vivicus power flow through her.

"No! Don't waste it on him!" Henry's voice was loud in her mind, and she allowed him to witness through her what was happening.

Valerie's magic didn't enter Zunya in time. There was no life to save, and her magic returned to her like she'd called it home. But before his life flickered out, Valerie saw the image of a girl who looked like Midnight—her daughter, Valerie remembered. Midnight's daughter had tried to save Zunya, and she'd come close to drawing him away from the Fractus. With the image came a pang of regret, and Valerie understood that he'd loved her. It had frightened him so much, he'd killed her rather than let her change him. It was the one pulse of goodness in him, the flicker that she could have used to save Zunya's life if she'd been there sooner.

Then Zunya shattered like one of Reaper's black weapons when she struck it with Pathos. His body was no more than dust, except for his right hand. She shuddered. Why did it remain while the rest of him was gone?

"He's dead, but I don't feel better," Henry's voice in her mind was a distant echo, as if most of his thoughts were elsewhere.

"Valerie," Kanti's voice drew Valerie's attention, and she saw her friend next to the throne, with Tan cradled in her lap.

She'd forgotten about Thai's clone in the mayhem.

"Is he okay?" Valerie asked, kneeling beside him.

Kanti shook her head. Valerie reached for Tan's wrist, searching for a pulse, but there wasn't one. She opened herself back up to her vivicus magic, even though she could see it was too late.

Her magic hovered at her fingertips, but there was nowhere to unleash it. Even a vivicus couldn't bring back the dead.

Valerie cried, letting her tears fall on Tan's still face. She'd never really tried to extract him from the Fractus, even though she'd told Thai they would. Now it was too late.

"I really am no better than Reaper," Henry's words in her mind were the last contact she had with her brother before he shut himself off from her completely.

Unbidden, the prophecy that her mother had received from an Oracle in Ephesus came to her mind. One of the Pillars of Light would fall into darkness, and only if that person could be rebuilt would the Balance be restored. But as she held Tan's broken body, she wondered if her brother

241

could ever be brought back from the hell he'd created within himself.

Chapter 26

Kanti left to find Henry on Earth, and Valerie searched the Black Castle to see if any Fractus remained from Reaper's original force, but all she found were bones. Whether they were soldiers of the Fist, or prisoners Reaper had executed, she'd never know. But the castle was abandoned.

She knew that she was delaying the inevitable. Chisisi and Skye would be awaiting her direction, and Thai needed to know what had happened to his brother.

Valerie looked over the throne room one last time and turned when she heard footsteps. Sanguina walked over to Zunya's remains and paused.

"Artificial," Sanguina said, nudging Zunya's hand, which was the only part of him that hadn't disintegrated, with her toe. "Reaper took his real hand as punishment. Later, he gave Zunya a fake hand and animated it with his magic, but Zunya always rubbed it, and I'm sure Reaper made it hurt as a reminder never to betray him."

"Are you sorry he's dead?" Valerie asked. She couldn't summon up any regret in her own heart for the man who'd made her life hell from the time she was a child.

Sanguina's face twisted. "He turned me into a vampyre. My only regret is that he didn't die by my hand."

"And that his death didn't give Henry any peace," Valerie said.

"Kanti is with your brother now, but he is a shell. Even she cannot penetrate the fog of his pain," Sanguina said.

"I don't think anyone can," Valerie said.

"I know something about being lost in your guilt, tortured by decisions made that cannot be undone," Sanguina said. "And I know that it is possible to find your way back to yourself."

Valerie couldn't speak, not wanting to let her emotions escape the tight rein she had on them. But she gripped Sanguina in a brief, tight hug.

"You have my forgiveness, and my friendship," she said.

ço   ço   ço

Chisisi was in a safe house in India when Valerie found him at last, but he wasn't alone. Crammed into the tiny space were at least twenty people, many of them shouting.

"You will be heard, but only if everyone stops talking at once," Chisisi said, and the crowd quieted slightly.

"Why should we show the Fractus mercy when they give us none?" Elisabeth asked, and the murmuring that followed her words sounded like agreement.

"Because we're trying to create a better world than the one the Fractus are forcing upon us," Valerie replied.

All of the heads in the room swiveled to look at her, and now the quiet in the room was complete.

"I know what it is to have the Fractus attack you and kill the people you love. My father was killed by Reaper, as was one of my closest friends only a few months ago. I have the ability to kill my enemies on the battlefield, and even though sometimes I'm so overwhelmed by rage that I could choke, I choose to stay my hand. I do it to make the world a little better,

244

so that one less child loses a parent, or sister loses a brother, or husband loses a wife. And so far, I don't regret that decision."

"Are you asking us to be martyrs?" Elisabeth asked.

"No! I know that some Fractus will die when we fight them, and though we grieve, we have to move on," Valerie said. "But when we can, let's capture them. It will mean that both Earth and the Globe will heal faster when all of this is over."

"I've seen too much death in my line of work." Dr. Freeman's deep voice calmed Valerie's heart, like it always had when he'd taken care of her at the hospital. "I, for one, will follow Valerie's lead in this."

"As will I," Chisisi said, his voice quiet but powerful.

Valerie was reminded that even with her advisers dead or sick or absent, there were always friends who understood her ideals and would stand with her to defend them.

The debate continued, but much of the anger in the room had dissipated. When people drifted away, she made her way to Chisisi's side.

"Did the Fractus retreat? Is that why people have gathered here instead of fighting?" Valerie asked.

"They didn't so much retreat... More like they vanished," Dr. Freeman said.

"My contacts all say that battles were raging, people were falling on both sides, but then the fighting ceased. It was as if the Fractus had received a signal to stop attacking," Chisisi said.

"Somehow, I doubt this is good news," Valerie said.

"Indeed. My guess is that Reaper has located the flame," Chisisi said. "He was drawing away our forces from the Atacama Desert so that he could search without interference."

"But the charm that binds magic on Earth is still in place, right?" Dr. Freeman asked.

"It must be. I'm as weak as a kitten from all the fighting I've done today, but if I was on the Globe, I'd be fine," Valerie affirmed.

"Everyone on the planet will know when the spell is broken," Chisisi said. "It is very powerful."

"We have to get to Reaper before he figures out how to put out the flame," Valerie said.

"I will continue my search in the desert. My contacts had several leads they were following," Chisisi said.

"Good," Valerie agreed. "But I'm going to try another angle. I'm going to go directly to Reaper."

ॐ   ॐ   ॐ

After leaving Chisisi and Dr. Freeman and briefly contacting Skye, Valerie returned home. It was dark out, and she saw Cyrus sitting on her stoop, a slight glow coming off of him as it always did. As she came closer, she saw that he was sitting next to Thai.

Cyrus handed him a curved, double-bladed knife that glowed brightly with his magic embedded in it.

"No weapon is more powerful than this one, except Pathos," Cyrus said. "It's from the People of the Woods, and I've woven as much light as I can into it. It will shatter any black weapon you meet."

"Thank you," Thai said. "But—"

"I didn't make this for you because I want us to be friends, okay? It's for Valerie. She's lost enough people that she loves, and I don't want to see her lose anyone else. Now you can protect yourself when she'd not around."

They both saw her then, and Cyrus stood. Valerie was glad it was dark so that he couldn't see her expression. He brushed past her, but as he did, he squeezed her hand once, and Valerie let a little hope flutter into her heart that maybe they'd be friends again someday. She couldn't bear to believe the alternative.

"Thank God you're back," Thai said as the gate shut after Cyrus. "I've had the strangest feeling that something was wrong, missing somehow, and I thought maybe you'd been hurt."

Thai folded her in a hug, and she breathed in his smell, relishing it before she had to deliver her bombshell.

"Something awful did happen today," Valerie said. She could barely look him in the eye as she gathered the courage to tell him of his loss. "Tan died today."

The rest of her account of what happened came out in a rush, while Thai stared at her, stunned. He sat back down on her front stoop, his head in his hands. He raked his fingers through his hair.

"I'm sorry I couldn't save him," Valerie said, resting her head on his shoulder. "Not just today. I should have tried harder to rescue him, to drag him back to us so we could make him see reason. He wasn't bad, not at his core."

"Maybe not just from Venu's poison. It changed him, but it was after he murdered Venu... Another piece of the good part of him died. Still, I loved him. You don't stop loving a brother, ever."

Thai let her hold him, and they stared up at all the stars from her stoop.

"Maybe it's wrong, but I can't stop thinking that I'm glad that my bad feeling today wasn't that I lost you," Thai said, his voice low in her ear.

Valerie knew that she should tell him that she would be seeking out Reaper soon, and that they could never truly be together, even if they won the war, but it wasn't the time. Instead, she said what was in her heart.

"I love you."

$$\text{\textit{ه} \quad \textit{ه} \quad \textit{ه}}$$

The next morning, Valerie got ready with extra care, making sure to tie her hair back in a long braid so it wouldn't get in her way, and carefully strapping Pathos tightly to her side. But she wasn't afraid of what the day would bring. Before, Reaper had always sought her out, and a part of her was always tense, waiting for their next encounter. This time, it would be on her terms.

Before beginning her search, Valerie headed to The Horseshoe to check in with Skye. She found the centaur in his office in the Relations Guild. He was neighing lightly, and Valerie realized he was asleep. But when she crossed the threshold, he awakened with a snort.

"A bit early for your morning call, aren't you?" he asked.

"Sorry for waking you," she said. "But I have an idea, and I don't think we can wait. We're almost sure that Reaper has the flame. We can wait for him to figure out how to put it out, and then incite war on both worlds, or we can beat him to it."

Skye flicked his tail as he considered her words. "An act of aggression. Not your usual style."

"Humans will be slaughtered if the Fractus can unleash their full magic on Earth. We have to cripple them now, and I think we should wage that battle on the Globe to keep innocent people from getting caught in the crossfire."

"If we attack now, it will be bloody," Skye said. "And we will lose. The Fractus outnumber us, especially with so many of our soldiers on Earth."

"The Fractus are spread all over the Globe. What if we attacked only where we could maximize the damage we cause?"

"Of course. Plymouth," Skye said.

Valerie pulled out the map Willa had given her of Plymouth and traced her finger over the river that she had found with Cyrus. Her gut told her that Reaper would want to be close to his new source of power, exploring how he could exploit it to his own ends.

"If I'm right, these caves will have the greatest concentration of Carne. Let me sneak in and signal you if it turns out I'm right. Then you can burst in with a hundred of our best soldiers, and we'll destroy it all."

"I agree with your logic, but how will we enter Plymouth?" Skye asked.

Valerie grinned. "That's where a little help from Willa comes in."

"Should we call on the Knights in the Fractus to turn to our side for this battle?" Skye asked, pawing at the ground.

Valerie hesitated. "Not yet. If this plan fails, those Knights will be our last chance to stop Reaper if he attacks Earth."

Chapter 27

After firming up the details of her plan with Skye, Valerie left his guild to head to entrance to Plymouth that Willa had found. She was crossing the grass of The Horseshoe when she saw a familiar figure walking up the broken steps of the Capitol Building.

"Jack, wait!" Valerie called.

Jack continued to march up the steps, and Valerie raced to his side, stopping him before he reached the doors.

"The Grand Masters are following Reaper now," she reminded him. "Many don't support him, but some do. They could capture you, or worse."

Jack's eyes met hers then. They were rimmed with red, and his face was pale. He'd lost weight since she'd seen him last. He looked even worse than he had when he escaped the Fractus two years ago.

"Let them do their worst," he said. "I hate them all. Anyone who supports the Fractus should be killed, like they killed Dulcea."

Jack choked on Dulcea's name, but in spite of his haggard appearance, he was lit up by a restless energy.

"This isn't the way to make a difference," Valerie said. "You won't last long against these guys. They're some of the most powerful Conjurors in the universe. Besides, what about your boys? They still need you, and if you get killed, who will take care of them?"

Jack hung his head and nodded. Valerie took his arm, and they started back down the stairs. She'd only gone a few steps when Jack turned and raced back up. He was through the doors before she fully comprehended what had happened.

"Damn it, Jack!" she said, but she ran after him, slipping through the doors before they'd fully closed behind him.

Valerie intended to drag Jack back outside if she had to, but he was running down the hall like he knew where he was going. She heard voices shouting, and then saw the geometric gold design on the door Jack was bursting through. Jack had timed his attack for a gathering of the Grand Masters.

Valerie gritted her teeth and followed him in. The room was a chaotic mess of bubbles floating above, and Jack was temporarily stymied.

He glanced over his shoulder, and when he saw her still following him, plunged himself into the fray. His entrance had attracted some attention in spite of the chaos in the room, and eyes narrowed as they took in Jack and Valerie.

"Your invitation was revoked," the Grand Master of the Illuminators' Guild, a large bear, barked at her.

"I know. I'm here to—" Valerie tried to explain.

Valerie was cut off when Al, the Grand Master of the Stewardship Guild, slammed his bubble into her.

"You talked to Willa? You had no right!" he shouted.

Before Valerie could respond, Jack leaped toward a bubble occupied by a crazy-haired Grand Master. When the man turned, she saw it was Rastelli. He snarled when his gaze met hers and the bubble surrounding him popped. He moved toward her with murder in his eyes. Had Reaper reinstated him as Grand Master of The Society of Imaginary Friends now that Dulcea was out of the way?

Jack intercepted Rastelli before he got close to Valerie. He got in several solid punches to the Grand Master's face before Valerie pulled him off. She gripped him by his wrist, but he fought her with every ounce of strength he had and managed to throw her off.

Rastelli was standing again, and when Jack attacked this time, Valerie could see that Rastelli had tapped into his power. Jack's movements were in slow motion as Rastelli slowed time for his opponent and then hit him in the skull with his staff.

Al shoved Valerie back as Rastelli raised his staff to smash in Jack's skull. She lunged toward Rastelli, to pull him away from Jack, but Al clutched her leg.

Dasan fluttered down then and landed heavily on Rastelli's back so that his blow missed Jack's head.

"Remember, my friend," Dasan said, his voice soothing.

Rastelli stared into Dasan's eyes, and Valerie hoped that whatever magic the Feng was weaving was helping restore Rastelli's mind.

Rastelli's eyes filled with tears, and he laid his hand on Dasan's wing.

"My old friend, however much you try, I fear that I am lost," Rastelli said. "Even now, the veil of darkness in my mind envelops me."

Rastelli groaned, and Valerie shuddered at the pain in the sound. Then he broke his staff over his knee. Valerie thought maybe he'd triumphed over whatever darkness was within him, until she saw him drive the broken staff into his heart.

She raced to Rastelli's side, ready to unleash her vivicus power to save him, but Dasan held her back, pinching her arm gently in his beak.

"I have seen inside his mind, and this is what he wants. He cannot live with the darkness Reaper has created within him, and it cannot be cured," Dasan said.

All of the shouting and movement in the room had ceased. Even though it might be cowardly, Valerie couldn't watch any longer, and she turned away as Rastelli uttered a last, gasping breath.

She leaned down and slung Jack, who was still out cold, over her shoulder.

"I apologize for the interruption," she said in her most authoritative voice, hoping that it didn't wobble. No matter how many people she'd seen die, it never failed to unravel her.

Al stood squarely in her path, his snarl in place.

"If you have a score to settle with me, I welcome the chance to give you the beating you deserve," Valerie said, and when she brushed past him, he didn't move to stop her.

With as must dignity as she could muster, Valerie walked from the room, out of the Capitol building, and down the steps, nearly tripping over the spot where the crack was the widest.

She deposited Jack on the grass in the middle of The Horseshoe. He woke up when Valerie shook him, and shrugged off her touch. Then he stood up and began walking back to the Capitol building, in spite of the limp he was now sporting.

"You want to kill yourself, like Rastelli did?" Valerie shouted after him. "Then go back! But don't kid yourself that you're honoring Dulcea by doing that, because it's the last thing she'd want. She didn't give up on living after both of her parents were murdered when she was a kid. She kept her faith in other people and made the Globe better by helping people. What you want to do is essentially easy, and selfish. Go ahead and give up."

Jack stopped walking, but he didn't turn back. His entire frame trembled, and Valerie moved to stand next to him. He leaned against her, and his hollow eyes found hers.

"I thought I'd finally found where I belonged. That I'd found a home," he said.

"I think life is mostly suffering, but that doesn't mean there aren't little moments of happiness mixed in. You have to believe that there's another moment like that waiting for you," Valerie said. "We both do."

᧧   ᧧   ᧧

Valerie took Jack to Cyrus's dorm room. Cyrus opened the door and assessed both of them.

"Jack needs to channel his rage into something other than taking on a room full of Grand Masters," she said, striving for a light tone.

Cyrus picked up on her intent, like he always did.

"I think you need to shoot something," Cyrus said. He squinted at Jack. "Maybe even make something explode."

Jack didn't smile, but he rolled his eyes, which Valerie took as a sign of life.

Outside the dorm, Valerie hugged Jack and then turned to Cyrus. "Get ahold of his gang. I think they're staying in the Actors' dorm with Jack. They'll make sure he doesn't go looking for trouble again."

Then she squeezed Cyrus a little longer and harder than she ought to, knowing how he felt about her, but she needed to borrow a little of his light before she faced Reaper.

Chapter 28

Valerie returned to the entrance to Plymouth that Willa and Steven had blasted open, hoping that no one would be nearby. She was relieved to see that glade was empty. She walked across the scarred earth, where the dynamite had created a huge hole, and turned the wheel on the ancient door.

It was dark inside, but not completely without light. The gems embedded in the walls of the cave held a faint glow, a remnant of Cyrus's magic. Valerie remembered the tunnel well enough to follow the path back.

She climbed down the ladder and approached the city. It had been quiet the last time she had come, but now it was completely empty. She was relieved that Skye had managed to evacuate the Groundlings who lived here so quickly. It was probably the only city in Plymouth where the people weren't enslaved by the Fractus.

As she followed the river and approached the cave, she saw that the debris from the cave-in she'd created at the mouth had been cleared away.

Inside, Valerie couldn't hear anything. She was forced to unsheathe Pathos to light her path, even though she knew that it would make her a target if there were any Fractus stragglers still in this part of the cave.

The space was empty, and Valerie decided to follow the river. She suspected that the location of the greatest concentration of Carne was somewhere deep in the caves.

The ground beneath her feet was slippery with black slime that gave off a faint hum of power. It smelled like the dank spot underneath an overpass where she'd huddled during the year she'd been homeless in Oakland. It was the scent of desperation and fear.

Valerie sheathed Pathos, only pulling it out occasionally to check that there weren't any obstacles in her path. The sound of the river moving and her own breath made a kind of soundtrack, and Valerie's heartbeat ratcheted up as the closeness of the tunnel bore down on her.

It was an acute relief to make out the distant sound of shouting. The hum of power that surrounded her increased in volume, and she began to jog.

Valerie stopped when the cavern widened into an enormous room that was dimly lit by balls of light suspended in the air. The rock face looked like it had been painted with pitch. An enormous lake was in the middle, and it was pure black, so dark that it seemed to absorb the little light in the room.

Everywhere were Fractus, overseeing the Groundlings as they scraped and scraped the walls of the room. The sludge they gathered was carefully deposited into the lake. They wore magical chains that chafed at their wrists. Reaper must have tightened his grip on his source of slave labor after Valerie had fought the Fractus at the mouth of the cave.

She reached into her pocket and squeezed the little ball that Skye had given her. He had a matching one that would vibrate from her touch, signaling him that she'd found the source of the Carne in Plymouth.

"Beautiful, isn't it? The perfect blackness?"

Reaper's voice in her ear made Valerie want to jump, but she forced herself to hide her reaction.

"This Carne was created from the bodies of hundreds of Conjurors, dumped here during the early wars on the Globe. Time degraded the magic left in their corpses into something pure, something that can be manipulated with the right power."

"I'm glad you're here," Valerie said, drawing Pathos from its sheath. "I think it's time we settle this between us for good."

Reaper grinned. "You shouldn't tease me. I'm beginning to think you've outlived your usefulness, now that I have what I want, and it doesn't look like your brother will be much use to anyone now that he's given up on living."

"Then we agree," Valerie said.

"I think it's a bit arrogant, even for you, to think that in addition to defeating me, you could take down all of the Fractus in this room by yourself, don't you?"

"It would be. But I'm not by myself."

There was a colossal boom as the ceiling of the cavern exploded, and fragments of black rock shot everywhere. Valerie crouched on the ground, protecting her head with her arms.

Light poured into the cavern, and the black lake of Carne shivered. The liquid retreated from the center of the room, sliding down the various tunnels that led into it, as if seeking to escape the light.

Groundlings and Fractus scattered, and chaos erupted. Soldiers of the Fist rappelled down through the giant hole created by Willa and Steven's explosion of dynamite.

Valerie had kept her grip on Pathos, but her target had disappeared. When she heard Reaper's voice shouting instructions, he was already across the cavern.

Two soldiers of the Fist attacked him, but their determined expressions morphed into screams as he unleashed his power on them.

With their leader in charge, the Fractus regrouped. Valerie saw the eyes of eight or more of the Fractus turn black, and the light from the hole in the ceiling dimmed, though it wasn't entirely extinguished.

Magic hummed in the cavern, and Valerie saw the Carne sliding back into the center now that the light was dimmer. But instead of reforming a lake in the center of the room, it was drawn to Reaper the way light was drawn to Cyrus.

The darkness pooled at Reaper's feet and then covered his legs and torso, working its way up his body until it poured itself into his mouth. Valerie stared in revulsion as he gulped the substance greedily.

Around her, Fractus engaged with the soldiers of the Fist, and black weapons met light. But Valerie didn't engage in the fight. There was no one else who could take on Reaper and have a chance of surviving.

Valerie let her full power flood her, until her magic was singing in her veins. She was ready for Reaper's usual tricks—his ability to reorient her sense of direction and the burning pain when he tried to dissolve her body.

But when Reaper embraced his power, instead of a hum of magic, there was a rumble, like an earthquake. He saw her charging toward him with Pathos blazing, and his face lit up with anticipation.

He opened his palm, and a sword grew from it, pure black with edges that glinted like polished metal.

"Let's use your weapon of choice," Reaper said. "I wouldn't want you to claim that you didn't have every advantage."

Valerie gritted her teeth at his condescension, but refused to let it distract her.

When Pathos met Reaper's blade, they clashed with enough force that Valerie's arm ached. Any other weapon she'd hit with that combination of her magic-fueled strength and Pathos would have shattered, but Reaper's sword absorbed the blow.

Valerie's magic surged, and she let it completely own her. Reaper moved fast, but she was faster, dodging his thrusts and parries and managing to land the occasional glancing blow.

The smile had left Reaper's face, and his lip beaded with sweat. But she didn't have his full attention. It reminded her of when she'd fought him before he'd taken her father to the Black Castle to kill him.

The memory of her dad bleeding out in Reaper's throne room made Valerie impossibly faster and stronger, as if she'd tapped into a well of magic within her that she hadn't been aware she was growing.

Rage blasted away any of the fear in her heart, and on her thumb, the Laurel Circle blazed. This was the bastard who'd taken her father's life, who had stolen her brother's peace. He wouldn't take her down today.

Valerie backed Reaper toward a wall of the cavern, and he kept glancing behind him, as if he was searching for an exit. She had the briefest flash of hope that she was winning before a sticky substance clinging to her feet made her insides rumble.

Reaper had maneuvered his way to a black pool of congealed Carne. When it touched him, his sword morphed into his signature weapon, the scythe.

Valerie had to abruptly switch tactics. Reaper's reach with the scythe was longer, and the blade came within a molecule of nicking her skin and pouring its dark magic into her.

Was it her imagination, or was Pathos dimmer? The Carne that formed Reaper's scythe tugged at her magic, leaving her breathless.

Scythe connected with sword in a crushing blow that made Valerie drop to one knee. But before Reaper could follow up with another swipe, a high, keening sound filled the cavern, and Reaper pulled back.

He opened a portal in the air, and through it, Valerie saw the wavering image of a desert. There was no way she would let him go through alone.

ço ço ço

Valerie jumped on Reaper as he stepped through, making him drop his scythe. Contact with him was agony, like touching Zunya. Her body was being shredded while her magic was ripped from her soul.

She released her hold on Reaper and fell into burning sand. It got in her mouth and hair and eyes, and Valerie spit it out. The weight of the rules binding magic on Earth made her limbs like stone.

Reaper kicked her in her stomach.

"Stay down," he said.

He must not know her.

Reaper moved to turn from her, and she grabbed his leg. It wasn't elegant, but it had the desired effect of making him trip.

"If you get in my way, I will make sure you, your brother, and all those you love suffer before they die. I swear it," he said, and then kicked her viciously in the face.

Valerie saw stars as her head snapped back, and she tasted blood. A tooth cracked, but the pain was distant. Something in her took over. Something that wasn't magic. It belonged to a deeper part of her.

She wiped the gritty sand from her eyes. Reaper moved toward a blue flame that flickered silently in a shadowy cloud of darkness, like a sunny day in the middle of winter. It was sundown, the time of day that the rules binding magic on Earth were typically at their weakest, and Valerie had no doubt what he was here to do.

Next to the flame were two Fractus, and both of their eyes were black. Even with their combined power, the light from the flame blazed, in spite of the darkness that hugged it.

"We made the flame visible, master, but we cannot dim it. Spare our lives for this failure, we beg you," one of the Fractus said.

"You've done enough," Reaper said. "I will extinguish it myself."

"Quickly," the other Fractus groaned. "I can't hold so much of this power for much longer."

Valerie staggered toward them.

"Turn your magic on the vivicus," Reaper said.

Pathos lay on the sand next to Valerie, an impossible gift that she couldn't make sense of. She wasn't sure if she reached for her blade or if it leaped into her hand, but its familiar weight was with her again, completing her.

The Fractus turned their gaze on her, but Pathos held the darkness at bay, like the flame in the desert had. Neither man appeared surprised. They drew weapons of their own, a short, sharp dagger, and a bow and arrow.

The man with the dagger attacked first, and Valerie parried with him. He was skilled, but not a match for her, and she kicked him in the head, knocking him unconscious. However, his attack gave the second Fractus the chance to load his bow, and he launched two black arrows at her in quick succession.

Valerie sliced the first one mid-air, and ducked and rolled to avoid the second. By design, her roll brought her closer to Reaper. She raised Pathos to bring down on him, whatever the consequence, when Reaper dropped to his knees.

He vomited the Carne that he had swallowed in Plymouth onto the flame. It poured and poured from his mouth. The flame flickered once, then again and again, rapidly, madly.

Valerie shoved Reaper aside to try to wipe away the disgusting sludge, but it resisted her touch.

The flame collapsed in on itself, and there was a perfect silence. The wind on the sand, Reaper's shouts, even her own ragged breathing was swallowed by the vacuum created when the flame went out.

A spot of red where the flame had been still smoldered, and Valerie hoped it might spark again. Instead, the red spark spread, blanketing the Atacama Desert with a blazing red glow. When it faded, the desert shone like ice. Valerie touched its smooth surface. The sand had turned to glass.

Valerie's magic surged within her, but for the first time, she didn't welcome its presence. The rules binding magic on Earth were broken.

Reaper turned on her, his cheeks flushed. A new scythe grew from his hand to replace the one he'd dropped.

"I thought I was above petty vengeance, but there is poetry to the idea that you will be the first to die now that magic has been unleashed on Earth," Reaper said.

His eyes were a little unfocused, like he was seeing past her.

Valerie raised Pathos as Reaper struck, but fighting him this time was different. The desperation and rage that had fueled her were gone. She'd already lost, even if she beat Reaper in this fight.

Valerie reached into her pocket to grip a chip from the pathway of The Horseshoe that she kept with her for her travels between worlds.

"No you don't," Reaper said.

He gripped her wrist, and as the Atacama Desert faded into the guilds at the heart of Arden, she screamed from the contact with his skin.

Valerie thrust upward with Pathos, and Reaper was forced to release her to block her blow with his scythe. Around her, The Horseshoe was alive with the sounds of battle.

The fighting in Plymouth had spilled into Silva, and now the Fractus and the Fist were present in full force. Arrows of light rained down on Fist and Fractus alike, turning dark weapons back to simple metal.

Valerie saw Skye trampling enemies with his hooves, but before she could make sense of what she was seeing, Reaper was attacking again.

"You wanted this to end today. I'm ready to grant your wish," he said.

Reaper's scythe flashed, and it was all Valerie could do to evade his blows.

"Val, wake up! It's like you're fighting underwater!"

Cyrus's voice was barely loud enough for her to make out over the sounds of the battle, but it brought her back to herself as Reaper raised his scythe and brought it down with the full force of his magic.

Valerie threw her own power into her counter-blow, and when Pathos met the scythe, her entire body rang from the impact. A dark crack appeared in Pathos at the same time as a fissure of light appeared in his scythe, turning it to ash in Reaper's hand.

The dark crack spread down her blade to the hilt, and then Pathos shattered into a billion sparks.

Valerie couldn't fathom that Pathos was gone. She looked from her hand to Reaper, too late to see that he gripped a dagger in his other hand. He slammed it into her heart in one powerful thrust, and Valerie saw Cyrus's face contort before her world narrowed to a point, and then was swallowed by darkness.

Chapter 29

Valerie didn't know what it would be like to be absorbed into the ether, with her parents, but she doubted that it included a shard of ice lodged in her heart. That was how she knew that there was a flicker of life within her.

Her vivicus power rose like a rising tide, spreading from her heart through her veins to every part of her body. Every time she'd saved someone with her power, it had almost consumed her. She thought she'd drown in it, or be swept away by it. And always, there was pain, as if something incalculably precious was being torn from her.

This time, releasing her power was simple and painless. Her magic hummed within her, winding itself around the shard of ice in her heart and melting it bit by bit.

She became aware of the sensation in her fingers first. They were interlaced with Thai's, she knew from the scar on one of his knuckles. He was pumping his own magic into her, amplifying and containing her vivicus power.

Her body ached everywhere, and an acute pain in her chest made her worry that Reaper's dagger was still inside her.

Then she heard sounds, a low bustle that reminded her of the Oakland Children's Hospital. She cracked her eyes open, half expecting to see Dr. Freeman leaning over her, listening to her heart with his stethoscope.

Instead, she saw a large tent set up with neat rows of cots. Thai's grip on her hand relaxed a fraction. His face was gray, and Valerie pulled her hand away, guilty that she had stolen so much of his strength to heal herself. But he grabbed her hand back and gripped it tighter.

"Don't you dare," he whispered.

"Another heroic battlefield rescue that you were unconscious for," Cyrus said, and she turned her head and saw her best friend in the chair next to her. "Why I'm not the guy who gets the girl is beyond me."

Cyrus sounded tired, and his jokes were forced, but he was there, even though Thai was holding her hand. She could guess what it cost him.

"Reaper?" Valerie croaked.

"In Plymouth, we think," Cyrus said. "Sanguina and I attacked him together, and I called forth as much light as I could. I think he would have killed us, but Willa set off a whole bunch of explosions around that fountain that used to lead to Plymouth, and he left to close the hole she created. We took off with you while he was distracted."

Valerie tried to sit up, but the effort made the room spin, and she collapsed back on her pillow. She touched her chest with a gasp, expecting to find a shard of Reaper's dagger still lodged in her heart, but all that was there was the bump of what promised to be a fantastic scar.

Involuntarily, she reached for Pathos, before remembering that it was gone, destroyed by Reaper's scythe. Its loss wasn't anything like losing a person, but it was more than a broken weapon to her. It was her connection to her mother, and a reminder when she doubted herself that this ancient, powerful sword had chosen her to wield it.

Pathos had had dozens of owners over the centuries, and had survived thousands of battles. But she had broken it. An old, horrible feeling clawed at her heart that she was meant to be alone because everything she touched suffered.

There was some truth to it. Hadn't she failed Midnight, her father, Dulcea, and Henry? They were only a few of many more who had been hurt because of choices she'd made, or times when she hadn't been strong enough. Her eyes drifted to Cyrus, whose heart she'd obliterated, and then to Thai. Would he be next?

She pulled her hand from Thai's, and this time, he let her go. She couldn't stand their love, didn't deserve it. She knew that the worst part of herself was surfacing, but she didn't have the energy to fight it. It was time for the Fist to find a new leader. She'd done her best to defeat Reaper and hadn't come close. But she knew no one would let her quit, not now. The thought was so overwhelming that Valerie squeezed her eyes shut.

"I'm really tired," she said. "Can you guys leave me so I can rest for a while?"

"Sure, Val," Cyrus said. "I'll tell Skye and Chisisi that you'll talk to them later, when you've had a chance to recover a little."

"You can do better than this," Thai said, and she heard a thread of anger in his voice.

Even with her eyes shut, she knew that he was still there, as if he hoped that she would get mad at his comment and fight back.

Instead, Valerie found that she could summon unconsciousness and draw its numbness around her like a blanket, so she did.

Valerie's dreams were odd fragments, shards of time that contained memories too painful to touch when she was awake. Her memories were intermingled with Henry's, and she relived with him the loss of his mother and father, and countless nights of terror from Zunya and Sanguina.

Wherever he was, did he see her memories of fending off thugs when she'd lived beneath the overpass in Oakland, foster homes where she'd been beaten or locked up, or each moment when she'd lost someone she'd loved?

The pain kept mounting and mounting, so intense that her head ached. It was more acute than even the stabbing pain in her chest from the wound Reaper had given her. Had Henry seen that, too? Did he know she'd almost died?

Abruptly, her memories and Henry's memories were wiped away, and Valerie knew she was fully in her twin's mind. He was back in Babylon, on the top stone tier of flowers, staring down at the lake, which perfectly reflected the trees around it.

His self-hatred had reached a crescendo, and then it evaporated all at once. She saw his decision. She didn't even have the chance to scream before Henry threw himself off the edge, not into the water, but onto the rocks beside it.

Valerie was falling, falling, falling, and she sat up in bed with a gasp when Henry's body smashed into the rocks, expelled from his mind.

Valerie reached for him, and her certainty that their connection was one that could not be broken so easily obliterated any other possibility. Her mind found his, so faint that it was almost an echo, but completely open to her. His thoughts flowed through her as if they were her own.

He was almost gone, and in his final breaths, he was overpowered by the need to see his sister, his only family, one last time, to look into her eyes when he passed into the ether. If she could be there, she'd see that he was sorry, understand how much he loved her, know that he had to die because he was a plague on the universe.

Valerie had taken a wobbly step out of bed when her body hummed, touched by magic that was within her and around her at the same time. She heaved as she was racked with waves of nausea.

The bed she gripped faded, and she collapsed on the wet sand of the lake in Babylon. For the second time in her life, blood had called blood, and it was a tie that overcame even the magic that Reaper had sewn into the fabric of the molecules in her body.

Henry's broken form was bleeding on soft, green grass, where he'd rolled after crashing on the rocks. He didn't move when he saw her, but the relief in his mind flowed through hers. He couldn't let go without seeing her first. The force of that need had dragged her to his side.

"I won't let you die," Valerie said, kneeling at his side and summoning whatever magic remained in her after using her vivicus power to save her own life.

"You can use your power to fix my body, but I'll always be broken inside," Henry said, his words barely audible. "Please forgive me, and let me leave you."

"I can fix it all," she said, as a strange sensation of weightlessness enveloped her.

Valerie always thought after she used her vivicus power, her magic was gone until she built it back up, but she was wrong. More magic than Valerie imagined could live in the entire universe, much less inside of her, filled her. It was light and love, and she would embrace it even if she lost her connection to the logical part of herself by using too much of her vivicus power, like Darling.

She squeezed Henry's hand and brushed his cheek with a kiss that released her power into his body, joining with his. Their combined magic collided with a low boom that rippled out around them.

Valerie gasped as her magic tore through her in a torrent. Without Thai there to help control it, the pain was intense, but it worked its way through Henry's system. Her connection with Henry's mind let her see her power at work more intimately than she ever had before. It stitched together broken bones, healed torn places within him that were internally bleeding from the impact of the rocks.

But the magic didn't stop there. It traveled through the circuits of Henry's brain, rerouting, rewiring. She saw broken connections and healed them. Places where the flow of chemicals in Henry's brain had been choked off opened back up.

Finally, even her newly discovered store of magic was used up, and she collapsed backward on the grass next to Henry, entirely depleted. She managed to turn her head to look at him, and the sight was familiar. When she'd been initiated into her guild, she'd had a vision of the future where she'd seen Henry from exactly this angle before he vanished from her mind, gone forever.

But little things were different from her vision. Instead of smiling at her in resignation, Henry's eyes were watery. And her connection with his mind was intact, though it felt like an entirely new thing. His self-loathing and fear were muted, and in their place was a tentative peace. It coexisted with grief and pain, but in an entirely new way.

271

Henry was telling her something, but Valerie couldn't hear the words. She watched his mouth and finally realized that he was reciting the words of the prophecy he'd received from an Oracle three years ago.

Over mountains, across seas,
Through despair, into bliss,
Though pain will bring you to your knees,
You'll find the answer you seek in a kiss.

"You're the answer, Val. You can heal more than me. You're going to make the whole universe better somehow," he said. "And I'm going to help you."

Henry's words should have added to the burden of responsibility she always carried with her, but right now, she was weightless, and she let Henry's hope flow from his mind into hers, buoying her up.

❧ ❧ ❧

When Valerie awoke, she was back in her cot in the long tent. Before she could question if she'd dreamed her entire encounter with Henry, she saw her brother sleeping in the chair next to her, still wearing the bloody, torn clothes he'd been in when she saved him.

She thought she'd been drained before, but she'd been stronger than she knew. Now, she couldn't summon the strength to even let Henry know she'd awakened.

Her mind was as sluggish as her body, and she struggled to remember little details, like when her hair had grown long again, or why Nightingale was nearby, obviously caring for her when he'd made it clear that he wouldn't heal her, the last she remembered.

In place of her memories was a connection to something or someone else. At first, she couldn't place what it was, but after a minute, she figured it out. She could sense Darling, the only other vivicus in the universe, as if he lived in a piece of her heart. She hadn't seen him all year, and it was a relief to know that he was okay. She didn't understand what had triggered their sudden connection, but before she could think about it more closely, Henry's eyes opened and he saw her.

"Nightingale! She's awake!" Henry called, moving to her side.

Nightingale's cool green hand was on her back, helping her sit. He brought a drink to her lips and helped her sip it. She coughed at the taste, but he kept pouring it down her throat.

The potion hummed as it made its way down, and a little of her energy returned. She searched the room for Thai, and saw him assisting another Master Healer with a patient.

He looked over his shoulder at her and briefly shut his eyes in relief. But before he turned back to his patient, she saw him shake his head once, his lips compressed tightly. Henry followed her gaze.

"He's mad at me because of Tan," Henry said, staring at his shoes.

"Not you. Me. Because I was giving up, and he knew it," Valerie said.

Getting the words out required about as much effort as running a marathon, but Nightingale's potion was helping. It was like being hit by a bus instead of a train.

A giant red bird entered the room and came to rest beside her. She stared at him. Why was he so familiar?

"You have brought Henry back to us," he said, his black eyes alight.

Valerie turned a questioning gaze to Henry.

"Who?" she managed to ask.

Henry began biting his thumbnail.

"What's wrong with her, Dasan?" he asked the bird. "Why doesn't she know you?"

Dasan passed a wing over Valerie's head, and from the buzzing between her ears, she guessed that he was using some kind of magic on her. She trusted that Henry wouldn't let him near her if he was dangerous, so she remained still.

As the buzzing continued, little memories flickered across her mind. Dasan dropping Henry into a fountain, Dasan giving her a gift of peace, Dasan counseling her on how to help Henry.

"Yes, I remember," she croaked. "Why did I forget?"

Thai joined them at her bedside now, his forehead creased as he listened.

"Your mind has begun to fray a little, only at the edges, little vivicus," Dasan said, his head cocked to the side as he examined her with beady eyes. "The vivicus power will take its toll, and tapping into it twice in one day sped up the process. Rest your power, and your mind will recover this time. But every time that you unleash it, your mind will unravel a little faster."

Valerie wanted to tell him that the unraveling of her mind had started months ago, but she didn't have the energy to form the words. Anyway, she didn't regret any of the lives she saved, in spite of the price, especially today. Henry was whole.

"Thank you for helping her," Henry said.

"It is my honor," Dasan said, and then moved to another patient's bed.

"Why didn't you take me with you to find Henry?" Thai asked, gripping her hand so tightly, it almost hurt. "Were you trying to kill yourself?"

"She didn't have a choice, man," Henry said, when Valerie struggled to find the strength to answer. "I didn't mean to, but I basically snatched her from thin air to my side."

"Before she left, she'd given up. She didn't say so, but I knew. It didn't matter that she had friends who loved her, that she had *me*. She wanted us all to leave her."

"Even Valerie can't be strong all the time," Henry said.

Why were they talking like she wasn't lying right there? Then she noticed that her eyes were shut, too heavy to stay open. Before she slid back into unconsciousness, a warm pulse in the part of her mind that was now connected to Darling soothed her to sleep.

Chapter 30

Valerie didn't know if it was Nightingale's potion or her own exhaustion, but for a long time, everything was fuzzy. There were a few times when she was almost conscious, and she remembered Kanti braiding her hair, Cara urging her to come back to them, and Emin singing softly in her ear. Once, she could have sworn she felt the cool touch of Dr. Freeman's stethoscope while Chisisi murmured softly at his side.

More than once, she recognized Cyrus's touch as he rested his hand on her forehead, and she knew that he was sending pulses of light through her body, because afterward, the shard of ice from Reaper's dagger melted a little more.

Thai was never far, and his touch against her throat and hand were reminders of the world she wanted to return to. Once, she cracked her eyes open and found him sleeping next to her on her narrow cot, his forehead pressed against hers.

And always, Henry was at her side, leaving a permanent impression in the seat of the chair. His mind stayed open to her, and it was like a lullaby to know that it didn't have dark threads of self-loathing choking it.

Pathos was gone, but her locus remained true. Nothing could shake her love for her friends, alive and dead, and what she understood now was that nothing would shake their love for her, either. It was time to consider the possibility that she deserved that love.

ℒ   ℒ   ℒ

The morning Valerie was finally able to sit up on her own, the makeshift hospital was quiet. Thai was collapsed on an empty cot next to her, and Henry snored quietly in his chair.

As she surveyed the room, she saw that there wasn't a soul awake. Even Nightingale was asleep standing up, leaning against the wall of the tent.

Before Valerie could question the oddness of it all, a little light peeked into the tent as a tiny hoof stepped through the opening. Then Clarabelle walked over to her, and Valerie buried her face in the unicorn's soft, iridescent mane.

I love you. Never leave me.

It was the first time Valerie had heard Clarabelle speak in her mind, and the sweetness of it was almost unbearable.

Azra had entered the tent behind Clarabelle, and Valerie's heart was full. *We came as soon as it was safe. Dasan lulled the minds in this room into sleep for a time to ensure Clarabelle's safety, or Summer would never have let us come.*

"Where is Summer?"

Standing guard outside. Azra's words came with a hint of her amusement at the centaur's protectiveness, and Clarabelle whickered beside her, like a chuckle.

Clarabelle made little noises in Valerie's mind, and though Valerie couldn't discern the words this time, the unicorn's excitement was palpable.

"What's this about Clarabelle meeting lots of people?" Valerie asked Azra.

*My little foal has been finding more and more humans
and Conjurors who want help developing their powers. She is
more skilled at it than I ever was, and she considers everyone
she helps as another soldier for the Fist. She hopes you'll be
proud.*

Valerie laughed.

"As if I could be anything else, little one. But are you
finding time to search for daisies and roll in the sunshine?"

Now Clarabelle's babbling began in earnest, and Valerie
understood only part of her story about the drama she'd
witnessed between a dragonfly and a butterfly, and how
they'd become friends.

Summer entered at the end of the story, and her eyes
flicked over Valerie, as if she was assessing the damage.

"I've survived worse, and so will you," Summer said. "But
I wish you did not have to encounter so much pain while you
are barely more than a foal."

"I haven't thought of myself as a foal since long before I
ever came to the Globe," Valerie said.

"That is good. Because it is a leader we need, not a child,"
Summer said. "Now we must leave."

Clarabelle gave a stomp of her silver hoof. *Not without my
gift!*

"Indeed," Summer said.

Summer braided a small part of Clarabelle's mane, and
then reached to her side for a dagger she kept there. In one
smooth slice, she cut the braid off.

Valerie gasped. "What are you thinking?"

"It is what she wishes," Summer said with a gentle pat of
Clarabelle's flank.

It will grow back. Azra watched Clarabelle toss her mane,
which was now a few strands lighter. *Wear it, and you will*

heal much faster. Clarabelle is not yet ready to share waters from her horn, but this will help.

Summer tied the iridescent braid around Valerie's wrist. Azra nudged Henry with her nose, but he didn't stir.

Each day, I have hoped that he would find peace, and I think perhaps my wish has come true.

"It seems like he's finding his way back to himself. To us," Valerie said. "I wish you were here to guide me."

Your heart needs no guidance. Follow it freely and see where it leads.

As the three left the tent, Valerie considered the fact that Pathos wasn't the only thing that had chosen her. Clarabelle had, too.

Ꭸ Ꭸ Ꭸ

Henry helped Valerie walk out of the tent that afternoon, and she didn't know if it was the cool breeze or Clarabelle's gift, but she was fully alive again.

"Am I remembering right that Kanti was here?" Valerie asked her brother.

Henry turned away when he replied so she couldn't see his face. "Yeah. She had to go back to organize more soldiers from Elsinore, but she'll be back soon."

"Did you two finally talk?" Valerie asked.

"We tried. It was weird," he said.

"Try again. This is your soul mate we're talking about, right?"

"There are so many people I can't imagine will ever forgive me, and Kanti's one of them. What I did in her name... Who knows how many people will die because of the powers I gave Reaper's army?"

279

"I think it's time to take your magic back from Reaper," Valerie said.

"What are you talking about?"

"Use your power for the Fist, on your own terms. I've seen the inside of your mind. I think you have a much better imagination than Reaper does. Explore your ability to gift Conjurors with new powers and help me turn the tide of this war," Valerie said.

Henry's mouth hung slightly open at her words.

"I've always thought of my power as the opposite of your vivicus magic, something evil inside me," Henry said. "But you're right, it doesn't have to be."

"There's nothing evil in you, Henry," Valerie said.

Even if Henry's mind hadn't been open to her, she would have known from the tears he was holding back that, for the first time, he believed those words.

∽   ∽   ∽

That afternoon, Skye burst into the hospital tent, nostrils flaring. Valerie worried that he might trample the cots.

"Are you aware one of the Healers here has been forbidding me to enter this tent ever since you were stabbed by Reaper? And your brother supported this!" Skye said, tossing his mane.

Valerie glanced at Henry, and he shrugged, not even a little sheepish. And she had a pretty good guess which Healer had forbidden Skye to enter. Thai was still barely talking to her, but she knew he was near, trying to make her more comfortable, though she could tell he didn't want her to know he was doing it.

"I apologize for them, Skye," she said.

"You are the leader of the Fist! Injury or no, you can't be unreachable for eight days. Eight days!"

Valerie was a little dazed at his words. Had she been out of it that long?

"You're right. I won't make excuses. Starting today, I'm back and ready to resume my responsibilities as leader of the Fist," Valerie said.

Skye flicked his tail, but some of the tension had left his stance.

"I'm sure your friends told you that the battle in Arden was a crippling defeat," Skye said.

The weight of the war settled fully back on her shoulders, and she pulled her blanket around her, suddenly cold.

"Tell me," she said.

"We lost more than two hundred soldiers, and Arden is in the hands of the Fractus," Skye said.

"Two hundred..."

"And another score of Conjurors lost their lives on Earth. That doesn't address the human toll," Skye said.

Valerie rubbed the goose bumps on her arms, as she thought about how many humans had been hit by lightning, slaughtered with black weapons, or torn apart by Reaper's powers. All while she'd embraced oblivion to avoid it all. She should have been out there, fighting.

Something of what she was feeling must have shown on her face, because Skye's tone softened.

"The losses are not on your shoulders alone, vivicus," he said. "It is a weight we will all carry together to our graves. But now, we must focus on the battles at hand. We must help those on Earth while also retaking control of Arden. We must use our grief as our strength to move forward. We must use it to crush the enemy."

"Is Reaper creeping into other parts of the Globe, or are his forces localized in Arden now?" Valerie asked.

"Arden and Plymouth are infested with Fractus. But Reaper has not yet tried to retake the Roaming City. The People of the Woods have experienced occasional attacks, but not a full assault. He has made no forays into Elsinore outside of recruiting new soldiers. Even in Dunsinane, we only have occasional skirmishes."

"Then we need to take back Arden first. Reaper's going to find out that holding a city that's hostile to your presence is much harder than conquering it. He once told us that he had people in every guild that supported him. Now that's going to work against him, because we have people everywhere, even in his own army, who will turn on him. The Knights Mira helped me recruit are waiting for my order to turn on Reaper. It's time to use that to our advantage."

After hashing out plans with Skye, Valerie went to the safe house on Earth where she usually met with Chisisi, but he wasn't there. Henry had come with her, and she turned to him.

"I think I know where he is, and I want to visit him alone," Valerie said.

"Keep your mind wide open to me," Henry said. "I'm coming if you sense even a whiff of Fractus trouble."

"I will, but I don't think I'll find them where I'm going."

℘   ℘   ℘

Chisisi sat with his back against his brother's gravestone, staring up at the night sky. Valerie sat next to him, gazing up at the familiar constellations that she'd studied before her adventures on the Globe ever began.

"Though I've known the legends of magic since I was a boy, at times, it is unbelievable to me that Conjurors are crossing the universe to enslave humanity," Chisisi said.

"Every day, I wonder if I'll wake up and find myself back in foster care, and all of this will have been the best dream and worst nightmare of my entire life," Valerie confessed.

"Zaki should be marshaling the forces on Earth, not I. I am ill-suited to leadership," Chisisi said.

"I'm beginning to think that the more you hate being the one with power, the better-suited you really are," Valerie said. "That's what I hope, anyway. Because I can't wait for the day when no one is looking to me for direction."

"I am thankful you guide us today," Chisisi said.

"How bad is it here?" Valerie asked.

"When the flame went out, a series of coordinated attacks were carried out that appear to have been planned in advance. Leaders in twenty-four countries were assassinated, and countless others died in the attacks."

Valerie swallowed, hoping she'd be able to save her tears for so many lost for when she was alone.

"But if the Fractus thought that they would simply step into the power vacuum they created, they were wrong. New leaders have already been elected by humans in nearly every country, and they are resisting the Fractus with all of the fight they can muster," Chisisi said. "People will not bend easily to the Fractus's will."

"Then Reaper will break them," Valerie said.

"He will try," Chisisi replied.

"How do we fight a war that's all over the world? I don't know where to start," Valerie admitted.

"One battle at a time," Chisisi said. "Beginning, I think, back at the Atacama Desert in Chile."

"Why?" Valerie asked.

"When the flame went out, it released a phenomenal amount of power. The sand that melted into glass is woven with pure magic," Chisisi said.

"Kind of like the Carne Reaper is dredging up in Plymouth," Valerie said.

"Perhaps, but that magic had degraded over years. This is new magic, and not released from a person, but a flame born of thousands of Conjurors who donated their magic to create it," Chisisi said.

"I never knew that was how it was made," Valerie said. "Reaper will want to take it and use it to his own advantage."

"A large number of his army reside in the desert, so miss's speculation rings true to me," Chisisi said.

"This time, we'll stop him before he can seize more power," Valerie said, but she was faking her confidence.

Valerie's heart was beginning to beat faster as she began making and rejecting plans in her mind.

"Before we take back the world, stare at the stars with me now," Chisisi said, and his words brought her back to Earth. "You never know if it will be the last time you examine them."

ço   ço   ço

It was nighttime on the Globe, as well, when Valerie returned to the hospital tent.

"What the hell, man? Are you following me?" Cyrus's voice was near, and Valerie peered around a tree and saw his familiar glow.

Thai was standing nearby with his hands shoved in his pockets.

"I don't know who else to talk to about this," Thai said. "Henry doesn't see what a big deal it is that Valerie almost gave up on herself, and abandoned all of us."

"It's not her leaving *all of us* that's bothering you. You just can't stand the fact that you couldn't fix her. That you couldn't be the hero," Cyrus said.

"That isn't it! She can do better than giving in to all her self-loathing. She isn't Henry!"

"You know what I think you need?" Cyrus said.

"What?"

Cyrus slugged Thai in the eye with enough power that Thai banged into the tree behind him. He returned with a punch of his own that skated across Cyrus's cheek, and soon they were grappling on the ground.

Valerie briefly considered interrupting them, but decided that if they wanted to waste their energy fighting each other instead of the Fractus, that was their business. But she wouldn't watch, either.

She quietly walked past them, to the entrance of the tent, and Cyrus spoke again, out of breath. Valerie paused, unable to stop herself from listening.

"You and I can't fathom what it's like in her head," he said. "Our parents, our families, they're all alive. We've never lived on the streets, been beaten up or mentally tortured. She can't be a hero every single second. Every once in a while, she's going to fall down, and you get to be the one to pick her up. She considers you her soul mate. You, not me, are that lucky. So never complain to me about her again."

285

Thai came by her bed that night as she was carefully spreading the ointment that Nightingale had given her on the scar on her chest.

"I saw you pass by when I was talking with Cy," he said.

"Talking seems like a weak word for what I saw," she said.

"So you heard what he said?"

"About cutting me slack since my life has sucked? Yes," she said.

"Well, I completely disagree. It's not that it doesn't make my heart hurt to think of all the ways you've been bruised, but he doesn't know you as well as I do if he doesn't see that in spite of that—or maybe even because of it—you aren't someone who gives up, who takes a nap while the world burns."

"And that's how I want you to see me. It's part of why I love you. You force me to be the best version of myself, and you don't tolerate anything less. But sometimes, it scares me to think that someday, you'll find out the truth about who I am and be disappointed."

"I don't think so. Because Cyrus is right. The day you finally let me be yours, *I'll* be the one who's lucky to be with *you*, not the other way around."

"Ew," Henry mumbled from the cot next to hers, where he'd been napping. But before he rolled over, she could swear she saw him grin.

Chapter 31

With her body functional again, Valerie threw herself back into the middle of battles, only taking breaks to check in on Emin and sleep. Her magic was depleted, but now she knew how much she was capable of tapping into if needed.

The months of fighting she'd engaged in before Reaper had put the flame out hadn't prepared her for the ferocity of the battles now. Her enemies had their full magical potential unleashed, and many relished the opportunity to exercise powers that had been stifled.

She found herself not following Dasan's advice to rest her vivicus power. Again and again, she poured herself into the wounded and dying, and though she didn't regret it, her mind was like a balloon on a string that she had to consciously reel in sometimes in order to access information. The more she used her power, the stronger her connection with Darling became. She could sense every time he saved a life, and she began to yearn to see him again.

Valerie was grateful that Gideon had always made sure that she practiced fighting without the aid of her magic, because now, she had very little of her power to draw on. But she was less sluggish than she'd been when the flame had bound her powers on Earth.

She spent part of each day strategizing with her generals about when and how they would attack Reaper in Arden and the Atacama Desert, but she was pulled away with growing frequency due to emergencies on Earth where every soldier of the Fist was needed. She refused to excuse herself, even if Skye shook his head disapprovingly and Chisisi watched her with worried eyes.

Valerie had successfully led a team of about thirty soldiers to protect the Prime Minister of France and was organizing ongoing protection when a strange, unpleasant buzzing filled her mind. At first, she thought it was an attack from a Fractus with psychic powers, but when she focused on her locus, the sensation remained, and with it a sense that a balance was on the verge of being upset. Then her wrist burned.

The iridescent bracelet made from Clarabelle's mane was humming. A streak of gray wound its way through one of the locks of the unicorn's hair.

Terror filled her, and the Laurel Circle was ice. Kanti had been fighting at her side, and she clutched her stomach.

"Do you feel it, too?" Valerie asked her.

"Something's wrong," Kanti said. "It's like I'm about to fall off the edge of a cliff."

"Clarabelle's in danger," Valerie said. "And I don't even know where she's been hiding."

"Neither do I. But I know someone who does," Kanti said.

They returned to the Globe, to a gigantic field on the snowy plains of Elsinore, where Kanti's new recruits were training. Everyone went silent at their princess's arrival and dropped to a knee.

Valerie turned to her friend with wide eyes, but Kanti took it in stride, as if she was getting used to her new role.

"Send me Blake," Kanti shouted.

Someone pushed through the neat lines of soldiers and came to a stop in front of Kanti.

"What is it, my princess?" he asked.

Valerie barely recognized the man before her. When she'd seen him last, he'd been one of the nearly invisible, breakable Fractus. Now, he was fully visible, and she could see that he was very young, not more than a year or two older than she.

"You told me that Clarabelle helped you develop your power to fly," Kanti said.

"And my speed," he added, standing straighter.

"How did you meet her? We need to find her right away. Something's wrong," she said.

"Every day at high noon, she came to a site on Earth called Machu Picchu. Those of us whose hearts were true could find her," Blake said.

"I know that place," Valerie said. "There's no easy way to get there."

"Unless you have a rock from the site," Blake said, reaching into his pocket. "Azra said I could give it to someone I trust who needed their help."

"Your princess thanks you," Kanti said, taking the rock from Blake.

Valerie and Kanti gripped hands and traveled to Earth. They were transported to a place so ancient that the land had the echo of magic's hum from before Conjurors had ever left the Globe.

"This place is huge," Valerie said, her eyes scanning the ruins.

"And we don't even know if Clarabelle is here," Kanti said.

A crackle of electricity was all the warning that Valerie had that Reaper was near before pain licked her back.

She tackled Kanti to the ground, covering her body with her own.

Kanti plunged her fist into the ground, and the magic Valerie sensed earlier responded to her friend's touch. Green shoots wriggled out of the ground.

"Distract him," Kanti whispered.

Valerie pulled herself up and assessed her surroundings, but Reaper wasn't visible. She reached inside herself for the dregs of her magic and let her power search for her enemy.

Reaper was leaning against a tree, and he was bending light so that she couldn't see him unless she squinted. Her sixth sense for danger wasn't blaring like it usually did when he was near, and she could see why. He was clutching his head.

Valerie erased the distance between them, and hit him with all of her strength right in his nose, which snapped with a satisfying crack. Touching his skin was agony, and she cradled her hand, hoping it wasn't broken.

Reaper reoriented her perspective, so it was like looking at the world upside down, and Valerie stumbled.

But before Reaper could attack her, the green shoots Kanti had called out of the ground surrounded Reaper, growing exponentially faster. They wound around the air near him, and hardened into thick, thorny branches.

Reaper was able to dissolve the branches nearest him so the thorns didn't prick his skin, but dissolving all of them would require more of his power, and Valerie guessed that he didn't have as much as usual.

Abruptly, Valerie's world reoriented itself, and Reaper left through a portal with a growl of frustration.

"You did it!" Valerie said to Kanti, brushing dirt off of herself.

"Flowers and hearts magic has its benefits," Kanti said. But despite her sarcasm, she looked a little dazed that she had forced Reaper to retreat.

"Clarabelle!" Valerie cooed softly. "Please, little one, I'm so scared that you're hurt."

"Valerie, here," Kanti said.

A smear of a silvery liquid was on the side of a tree, and a few drops flecked the ground.

"She's hurt," Valerie said, and she didn't recognize the sound of her own voice. "This way."

Valerie followed the call of her own heart and pulled Kanti with her. They crossed a low wall of rocks and were a short distance from the ruins when Valerie saw Clarabelle lying in the grass, curled into Azra like she'd been the day that Valerie had first met her.

"Go get Thai," Valerie commanded Kanti, handing her the rock. "Now!"

Kanti didn't hesitate, and she vanished.

You're in time.

Azra's words were followed by a little whimper. Clarabelle was still alive.

"Summer?" Valerie asked.

Azra shook her head, her silver mane shining in the light that broke through the clouds.

She died defending Clarabelle. But not in vain. She pummeled Reaper, nearly blinding him, I think. Clarabelle and I made it far enough that he could not immediately find us.

"I'm here," Thai said, appearing beside her.

Kanti stood behind him.

"I need you to lend me your strength," she said.

Thai laced his fingers through hers.

291

Valerie rested her hand on Clarabelle's flank and reached for her vivicus power, and then thanked everything good in the universe that enough was there to save the baby unicorn.

With Thai's help, releasing her magic into Clarabelle was gentle, and the unicorn blazed with light, reminding Valerie of when she'd healed Cyrus.

Joyful little notes pinged Valerie's mind, and she drew her power back into herself. Clarabelle licked Valerie's cheek and made little snuffling sounds in her ear.

I was scared.

"I'm sorry, Clarabelle," Valerie said.

But you saved me. I knew you would.

If Valerie released a few tears into the foal's mane, she didn't think anyone noticed. For the second time in the span of a few weeks, she'd been in time to save someone precious to her.

Reaper considers Clarabelle your successor. He wants you both dead, and even with the wound he received today, he will not rest until it is done.

Valerie had never sensed fear from Azra, until now.

We must disappear until this war is over. I am sorry, Valerie.

"Of course. But where?" Kanti said. "Maybe I can hide you in Elsinore. I've been weeding out the Fractus."

Azra shook her head.

There is a glade on Earth that I know from times of old. But if we go, we may not emerge until The Balance is restored or Clarabelle is full grown, which will not be for several centuries.

Clarabelle was stomping her hoof and poking her mother with her horn, but Azra ignored her.

"You're right to go. It's best for Clarabelle, and it's what's right for the world. As long as she's alive, there's hope," Valerie said.

That is what I think every time I look at you, Valerie. My heart rides with you, though I may not.

The unicorns left, and Clarabelle's piteous complaints echoed in Valerie's mind until they were out of sight.

Without Midnight, her father, and Gideon, Valerie had yearned for advisers to tell her what to do. She hadn't realized how much she relied on Azra's strength and her moral compass, as well, until she was gone.

Valerie was so adrift, she thought she'd float away until Thai put his hand on the small of her back, anchoring her.

"Thank you for letting me help you today. I know you must have wanted to heal her right away," Thai said.

"My life is precious, too," Valerie said absently, remembering something Azra had told her once.

"What new ability do you think Clarabelle will gain since you healed her, Valerie?" Kanti said, grinning.

"What do you mean?" Thai asked.

"When she healed Sanguina, she brought back her humanity in addition to her life. Azra became pregnant after she was healed. Cyrus's powers exploded, and so did mine. And now Henry..." Kanti trailed off, her eyes a little shiny. She cleared her throat. "Now Henry has not only been brought back to life, but I think Valerie cured his depression. Because he's able to be his true self now."

Valerie stared at Kanti for a long time, absorbing her words.

"He's still guilty, insecure, and scared. I know. I've been inside his mind," Valerie said.

293

Kanti shrugged. "Then he's like the rest of us. But we live with it, and find joy in life. Now, so can he."

ço   ço   ço

When Valerie visited Chisisi's safe house that night, it was surrounded by three Fractus with the power to hurtle lightning from their hands.

She crept up behind one and hit him with a swift uppercut that sent him reeling, and followed up with a hard elbow to his head.

Chisisi had deflected the lightning thrown at him with a metal rod he'd stabbed into the ground in front of him, diverting the electricity from its target.

While the Fractus recharged, Chisisi took on two of them at once, and wasn't even out of breath when they lay in front of him, unconscious. He then pulled out his cell phone to call for a team to cart the Fractus off to the magically secure prison they'd created on Earth.

"We'll need a new space to house all these prisoners," Chisisi said, scrubbing at his eyes with his hand.

"The holding cells on the Globe are filling up, too, and the Grand Master of the Justice Guild is still recovering from an attack by Reaper," Valerie said.

"Perhaps some of the Fractus can be convinced to turn against their cause and return home," Chisisi suggested.

"If you think we can trust them, I'm all for it," Valerie said.

"One of the Conjurors from the Empathy Collective offered to search the minds of the prisoners to ascertain if they were telling the truth," Chisisi said.

"I didn't know they could do that," Valerie said. "That skill could come in handy in many ways."

"Indeed. But I am told only a handful of the Empaths have mastered the ability," he said.

"I'll talk to Henry," Valerie said. "He'll help you organize."

"Even though there are many Fractus who would abandon Reaper, given the chance to do so safely, many believe in his plans for Earth," Chisisi said. "I do not know how humans will ever be safe unless we reestablish a boundary between our worlds and make sure those with magic are on the Globe."

Valerie turned the problem over in her mind. "Even if Reaper is killed, there will always be those who want to use magic to control others. Humans are at such a huge disadvantage. How can we protect them in the long run?"

"Your words ring true. The boundary will be broken again in time, and this war will begin again," Chisisi said. "But I can see no other way."

"How could we amass enough power to bind magic on Earth, even if we wanted to?" she asked. "And who would know how to do such a thing?"

With a pang, she knew that Azra would have the answer. But that avenue was shut to her now.

"I will scour my sources," Chisisi assured her.

"I can't help thinking that there must be a better answer than making things like they were before. There are a lot of problems with binding magic on Earth and keeping our worlds separate," Valerie said.

"If that answer exists, then I believe it lives in you," Chisisi said.

Chapter 32

That night, back on the Globe, Valerie dipped a toe in the Lake of Knowledge, and the water sparkled in response to her touch. She flicked the shell that she'd dug out of a drawer in her room into the lake, hoping that it worked the way that Will said it would.

It had felt like ages since she'd gone for a swim in these waters, and she plunged in now, turning over in her head the problem she'd discussed with Chisisi. Was it possible to find a better solution to protecting humans than separating them from Conjurors?

Her swim was interrupted when a tail flicked against her legs, startling her. On the shore, Valerie found Elle waiting for her, wringing out her hair as she dug her toes into the sand.

"I can't stay long. I know what's been happening above the waves, and Will and I guessed what you'd want to know now," Elle said. "Binding magic on Earth requires an incredible amount of magic, but luckily, a lot of it you can mine from the Atacama Desert. All of the magic that ignited the flame isn't lost, it's just in a different form."

"What do I need to fix it?" Valerie asked.

"You'll need a Conjuror with the ability to bind magic, and an object that can contain all that power. When the binding spell was put in place last time, a flame was chosen to

296

contain it because it would never grow weak or tarnish with age. But any object strong enough will work."

"What should I look for?"

"Talk to the People of the Woods," Elle said. "I haven't found more detail than that in the records yet."

"There's something else," Valerie said. "Is there another way to stop humans from being exploited by those with more magic, other than separating them on different worlds? It seems like a temporary, flawed solution."

"Now you leave the realm of facts and enter the realm of possibility. It is a matter of great debate beneath the waves, but we have found no magical solutions to this problem so far," Elle said.

The lake began bubbling, and Valerie, who was in up to her ankles, yelped as it became hot. She hurried to the sand, where she had left the sheath that held the makeshift sword she'd been carrying since she lost Pathos.

"Not yet!" Elle shouted.

Elle dove into the water, but emerged seconds later, covered in blisters.

"Will's below the surface!" she shouted.

"What's happening?" Valerie asked.

"They're sealing Illyria off from outside contact. There's been debate about cutting ties with the surface, but things move so slowly down there that I thought it would be decades before drastic action would be taken," Elle said.

"Maybe this isn't coming from beneath the waves. Maybe someone on the surface doesn't want Illyrians to have contact with Conjurors any longer," Valerie said.

"But that makes no sense! Fractus and Fist alike will be cut off from the Akashic Records this way," Elle said.

"Reaper must know of knowledge down there that he doesn't want to leak out," Valerie said.

"What if everything is boiling down there? What if Will's hurt?" Elle asked, pacing the shore.

"You're both Empaths. Reach out with your mind and find his. Your bond as twins is stronger than you know," Valerie said.

Elle knelt on the sand and squeezed her eyes shut. Her hands, which were clenched by her sides, gradually relaxed.

"He's okay," Elle said. "I can't see anything, but I can touch his mind. He's alive, and he's not in pain."

Elle had relaxed a fraction, but Valerie's fear was ratcheting up. Reaper was systematically cutting her off from any ties to people or knowledge that could help her. There was no one whose advice she could seek, no research she could do that would give her the answers she needed.

She could only rely on herself, and that thought turned the Laurel Circle cold on her thumb.

A loud banging had Valerie out of bed, weapon in hand, before she was fully awake. She almost collided with Henry in the hall as they raced to their front door.

ɉ ɉ ɉ

"Ready?" she asked him, hand on the knob. She doubted the Fractus would bother to knock, but who knew?

Henry nodded once, and Valerie opened the door.

Standing in the moonlight was Cyrus with his father, mother, and Cara.

"You're home," Cyrus said, the relief in his voice unmistakable.

"What happened?" Valerie asked, ushering them in.

As she did, she saw that Mrs. Burns had a gash on her forehead that had been stitched, but there was still blood on her face.

"This Chern fellow—" Mr. Burns began.

"Reaper, Dad," Cara insisted.

"Reaper then, he seemed so reasonable when we saw him last. But he came today, demanding to see Cyrus, and when we explained that our stubborn son didn't care about the well-being of our family, he proceeded to…to…"

Valerie had never seen Cyrus's father upset, but he was gripping his wife's hand so hard, his knuckles were white.

"He attacked Mom, slicing her forehead with his scythe," Cara said. "I think he meant to kill her."

"How did you stop him?" Henry asked, bringing in a cup of tea for Mrs. Burns.

Cara ducked her head. "I was home, trying to reason with my parents when he showed up. I diverted the beam from the lighthouse by our house straight into the living room. It didn't hurt him or anything, but that black scythe he carries started to sizzle, like it was burning."

"Good to know that weapons treated with Carne from Plymouth are weakened by light," Cyrus mused.

"When Reaper saw what was happening to his weapon, he opened a portal and left," Cara said. "I think he'd been hurt recently, because there was scar tissue around his eyes, and his gaze was unfocused."

"He thought we'd be easy targets, and when he found out we weren't, he left," Mr. Burns said, patting Cara on her shoulder.

"We were lucky our daughter used her lightweaver power to administer pulses of light into my system, or the wound from that horrible weapon would have killed me before I reached a healer in Arden," Mrs. Burns said, watching her husband as she spoke.

Mr. Burns shifted his weight, not returning her eye contact.

"If Cyrus had come home with us, like we told him to—" Mr. Burns began, but his voice didn't hold any heat.

Mrs. Burns dropped her husband's hand. "Don't blame the actions of that madman on our son. We should never have been talking to him to begin with."

Mr. Burns released a breath. "Perhaps you're right."

Cyrus and Cara looked at each other like they'd witnessed a miracle. Henry coughed to cover his laughter.

"We're here to ask you a favor, Val," Cyrus said.

"Anything."

"Reaper could come back to Messina for Mom and Dad at any time. Can they stay here with you? It's the safest place I can think of, with you and Henry to protect them. I know Emin's already here, so it'll be crowded. If you can't, it's fine."

"Cy, of course they can stay," Valerie said. "Mr. and Mrs. Burns, you're welcome to live in our house for as long as you need it. You can stay in my dad's old room."

"Thai can bunk with me, and Emin can stay in your room," Henry said.

Valerie closed her eyes, cursing her brother for mentioning Thai. When she opened them, she saw that Cyrus had clenched his jaw, but he met her gaze. Henry sent her a mental apology.

"Thank you, my dear," Mrs. Burns said. "It won't be for long. And perhaps you'd welcome some help in the kitchen. Cyrus says you like Earth food."

Henry's face lightened at the mention of food. "We love it."

Henry showed Cyrus's parents where they would stay while Cara snoozed on the couch. Valerie followed Cyrus to the doorway.

"As long as they're here, I'll protect them with my life, like they're my own parents," Valerie said.

"I know you will. It's selfish, asking you to watch over them, but I knew you'd understand," he said.

"I wouldn't want them to be anywhere else. And I don't think Reaper will attack a place where he thinks Henry and I are together because of the prophecy he received."

Cyrus stared into the darkness, brooding. "Who do you think he'll attack next? Kanti's parents? Thai's? Does he want to make orphans of us all?"

"He hasn't managed to kill us yet, so he's trying to get to us through people we love. I think he wants to cut us off from as much help and support as he can," Valerie said.

In the darkness, the glow coming off of Cyrus pulsed, and Valerie thought she saw sparks. "Does he know that instead of scaring me, he's only making me want to win more?"

His words woke something up in Valerie. What if she let her terror about everything and everyone Reaper could destroy be burned away by her certainty that destroying the Fractus was the right path? Every time he attacked someone she loved or slaughtered the innocent, it was more proof that right was on her side. And Gideon had been right when he told her that right was a powerful ally.

Chapter 33

The next morning, there was more bustle in the little house than ever, but Valerie loved it this way—bumping into a grumpy Cara while she made her tea, assisting a smiling Mrs. Burns while she made eggs and bacon, watching a pink thread of magic wind its way through the halls when Emin hummed a tune. When his magic touched her, she knew the song, and she sang along.

Through her bond with Henry, she could tell that he was enjoying their crowded home, as well, though rooming with Thai was a little awkward.

Valerie was thankful that Cyrus had returned to his dorm room so that he wouldn't have to see how comfortable Thai was in her house.

"Emin, want to come to Arbor Aurum with me today and see some of your old friends?" Valerie asked, peeking into her bedroom, where Emin was reading a book, eggs untouched.

"Maybe Uncle Elden woke up?" Emin asked.

"I don't think so," Valerie said, hating to put out the light in his eyes. "But there are lots of people who miss you."

Valerie hoped her words were true. She couldn't imagine anyone not wanting to see Emin, even if he was half-human. But the People's culture wasn't one she knew well.

"Okay," he said.

They started out, but Emin stopped when they were only a couple of minutes from her house.

"There's an entrance the other way that's a lot closer," he said.

"Really? You're helping me already," Valerie said, and was rewarded with a little smile.

"Mom says I'm the best boy for helping," Emin said, marching off the path and into a part of the woods Valerie had never been in before.

They'd been walking for a half an hour when Valerie began to think Emin was lost. But before she could craft a way to ask him without stomping on his pride, he stopped before a spindly tree.

"Do we climb it?" Valerie asked, uncertain that the skinny branches would hold even Emin's slight weight.

"No," scoffed Emin. "Don't you know?"

He hummed a tune that reminded Valerie of things growing in the sun. The leaves of the tree rustled in response to Emin's magic, and an enormous gold leaf fluttered to the ground.

"Come on," he said, holding out his little hand.

Valerie gripped his sticky fingers, and together, they stepped on the leaf. It rose, swiftly enough that she gripped Emin to her side tightly so he wouldn't fall. Emin laughed, and the sound was as sweet as Clarabelle pinging in her mind.

"You can't fall!" he said, still giggling.

"Magic, right," she said. "What would I do without you?"

"Get lost, probably," Emin said, serious now.

They burst through a clump of leaves and were deposited on the wooden platform that connected all of the trees in Arden. The spot where they landed was devoid of the bustle in Arbor Aurum, but Emin turned as if he knew where he was headed, and Valerie followed.

"That's where Mom and I stayed when we were caught in a rainstorm once," Emin said, pointing to a nook in one of the trees. "She sang to me until I fell asleep, and then I woke her up in the morning with a song. It was an even trade."

"She was lucky to have you as her partner, and now I'm the lucky one," Valerie said.

"That's where I stepped off the platform and got lost," Emin said, not listening to Valerie. "Mom was so mad when she found me. She made me weed gardens for three years."

Valerie turned to him, about to question the term of his punishment, and then remembered that he was older than she was in years, if not in maturity, because of how the People of the Woods aged.

"Even if it was only so she could yell at me again, I wish I could see her one more time," Emin said. "I'm never going to stop missing her."

"You're right," she said. "I miss my dad every day, sometimes so much that it's hard to think about anything else. But knowing that I'm fighting for what's right and keeping on living and loving would make him happy."

Emin was quiet for so long, Valerie wasn't sure if he'd been listening. "I think Mom would want the same thing."

ఞ   ఞ   ఞ

When they arrived in Arbor Aurum, their first stop was the hospital. It was as full as ever, a reminder that the People of the Woods were on the front lines of the war with the Fractus on Earth and the Globe.

Elden lay silent in his bed, and Emin sat next to him, squeezing his hand.

"He's got more color in his cheeks," Valerie said.

"Uncle, wake up," Emin said, giving Elden a good shake.

Valerie pulled him back.

"Let's be gentle with your uncle. He's still healing," Valerie said.

"Emin will not hurt him," a low voice made Valerie turn.

The woman who'd spoken was ancient, as gnarled as the trees that made up Arbor Aurum. But she stood straight, and something about her understated grace made Valerie suspect she was powerful.

"Grandmother North," Emin said, and bowed. The woman touched his little head once, like a blessing, but she didn't enfold him in a hug, as Valerie expected.

"You're Cerise's mother?" Valerie asked.

"And Elden's. These are dark days for my family since you came among us, vivicus."

Valerie was surprised that something stronger than guilt rose in her at the words. "I did not create the darkness that we fight against. I only offer an alternative for those that want one."

North held up a hand that was gilded with gold, like Elden's. "You didn't make this war, you inherited it. The seeds were planted before you were born. But you are not here for a philosophical discussion."

"Emin wanted to see his uncle," Valerie said.

"And you are seeking something from my people."

Valerie explained her mission to find an object strong enough to hold a spell that would bind Earth's magic, and North's face was still as she listened.

"My people will create what you seek. But you must find a Conjuror with the ability to bind magic. None among my people hold this power."

"How long will it take you to make it?" Valerie asked.

North stared up at the sky, as if she was calculating the time in her head. "A moonspan. We will need to use Earth's soil to grow what we need."

"A month is too long," Valerie said. "Reaper might have found a way to use the magic left over from the flame by then."

"Even magic cannot change the tides, or the waxing and waning of the moon."

Valerie swallowed her impatience and turned to Emin who was sitting on Elden's bed, quietly playing with polished stones and whispering to his uncle all the while.

"Do you want to say anything to him?" Valerie asked the woman.

North watched her grandson, but her face gave away nothing. "Perhaps I'm growing softer, for I once swore that Cerise and her abomination would never be welcome in my nest."

"Then leave," Valerie said, stepping in front of Emin as if she could shield him with her body from his grandmother's words.

But North pushed her aside and moved to stand next to Emin. Emin looked up at her, mouth open.

"Your only home isn't with that vivicus. You have one with me, too, if you wish it," she said.

Valerie let out a breath, relieved.

"But Mom said you're very busy, and that's why we never see you," Emin said. "You have time now?"

The furrow in North's brow deepened, and when she spoke, her voice was softer. "Yes, Emin, I have time now."

"Do I have to decide now?" he asked.

"No, little sapling. It is my turn to wait for you," she said.

North swished out of the room, but not before Valerie saw the tears she was struggling to hide.

و   و   و

Emin bounded home with more energy than Valerie had seen in him since he'd come to live with her. Thai greeted them at the door, Emin leaping into his arms with enough force that Thai almost toppled over.

"Good trip?" he asked, laughing.

"You promised to let me try your dagger today!" Emin said, racing to Thai's room to grab the weapon.

Thai saw Valerie's look. "I'll be careful. But he needs to know how to defend himself. We don't know what's coming."

Valerie sighed. "I guess you know how to heal him if anything goes wrong."

Henry joined them in the hall, wiping his hands on his pants.

"Val, can you let us talk alone?" Henry asked.

Valerie looked at Thai and he just shrugged. "Sure," she said, then went into the kitchen.

She was aware that she should visit Chisisi or Skye, but instead, she wanted to hear what Henry had to say.

"I've been avoiding you," Henry said, his voice muffled by the door.

"I could tell. I figured you'd tell me why when you were ready. Is it because I got mad at your sister?"

Henry let out a surprised laugh. "No, I'm sure you've got good reasons. It's because I couldn't face you without guilt swallowing me up. I killed Tan."

Thai's voice sounded farther away when he replied. "I know in a way it wasn't really you. You were lost."

Valerie peeked around the corner and saw that they'd moved to the bench by the front window. Thai stared outside.

Henry's voice shook. "I wake up at night dreaming about the sound his body made when it hit the ground. I didn't even know I killed him. I didn't tell him I was sorry, or try to save him."

"Kanti said he was probably dead as soon as he hit his head. Even Valerie couldn't save him."

Valerie hadn't known that Thai had talked to Kanti about what had happened to Tan. Since she'd told him about what happened to his brother, they hadn't spoken of it again. She'd been a coward, afraid that talking about Thai's grief would unlock her own, and they'd both drown. So she'd let him wade through it on his own.

"I'm sorry. I know what it is to hate the person who killed someone you love, your family. After this war is over, if you and Val want a life that doesn't involve me, I'll honor that."

"Henry, you've got it wrong. I don't think of you as the person who killed Tan. Venu, Reaper, fate, maybe. But the best part of him was long gone before he died."

"But now, we'll never know if we could have brought him back." Henry's voice was a whisper.

"I know. That's the thought that keeps me awake at night. Maybe we all should have tried harder to tear him away from the Fractus. But we were fighting a war, saving lives. I can't think of a moment when we were just sitting around watching soap operas when we could have gone to the Black Castle to

308

save Tan. So I'm trying to forgive myself. And for what it's worth, I forgave you already, Henry."

"How?" Henry's voice cracked on the word.

"Because you're my brother, too."

Valerie was sitting on the floor in the kitchen, her head resting against the wall. In the next room, it was quiet.

"Val, I know you're there. Your mind is wide open," Henry said.

His words broke the tension, and she heard Thai chuckle. "She's been an eavesdropper since the first week I knew her."

Valerie burst into the room. "Real nice, Thai."

She grinned at him and wished that her mind were whole. If it had been, she'd have kissed him right then.

"Mind's still open, Val," Henry said, and she blushed.

"So is yours. Why are you going to Elsinore? To make up with Kanti, finally?"

Henry fidgeted with the cushion of the bench he was sitting on. "I hope so, but the main reason is that I think I'm ready to use my power for the Fist."

"Why use the soldiers in Elsinore for that?" Thai asked.

"My power works best on Conjurors who haven't tapped into their magic. Kanti says there are a lot of Conjurors in her army who hadn't had the chance to work with Clarabelle to develop their powers. They'll dedicate their lives to the Fist if I give them a cool power."

Valerie shamelessly searched Henry's mind to assess if he was really ready to tap into the power that Reaper had wrested from him for so many years. She could see his fear and guilt, but underneath was a vein of pure certainty that this was the right thing, that it would help him atone for his mistakes.

309

Her eyes connected with his, and she gave him a little nod of approval. "What were you thinking of gifting them with?"

"It doesn't work that way, exactly," Henry said. "I'll show you in person when it's time."

"I'm glad you're ready to do this now. Summer bought us some time by wounding Reaper, but he could seize the power left over from the flame burning out at any time."

"If he does, he's going to have a bigger fight on his hands than he thought he would," Thai said.

A little of Henry and Thai's hope rubbed off on Valerie. "And we're only getting started."

Chapter 34

Skye had moved the soldiers of the Fist who remained on the Globe to the foothills of Dunsinane. It was strange to visit the barren purple mountains that she associated with Reaper and find her own people.

The camp was unlike any that Valerie had seen on Earth. There were houseplants that grew into luxurious beds, and the aromas of food cooking smelled like what you'd find in a fancy restaurant instead of the stew you might expect when roughing it outside.

There were even some solid buildings that had popped up, courtesy of the Architecture Guild. They were simple, but elegant, with lots of light.

The organized bustle of the camp slowed when she approached. Soldiers paused to shake her hand or stare at her. It didn't make her uncomfortable anymore. These people were her extended family, and they'd all die for each other.

Skye trotted out of one of the buildings, and under his stern glare, Conjurors returned to their activities.

"We weren't expecting you today."

"I'm here to talk to Juniper, but you should listen, too," Valerie said.

Skye nodded in the direction of a group of soldiers practicing blocks with their weapons. Juniper was among them, correcting stances and giving instructions. He didn't hide the stump where his hand had been, or wear any kind of prosthesis. Valerie couldn't help staring at the physical reminder of the toll this war was taking on them all.

But Juniper was entirely at ease with himself and his role. "Remember that the light in your weapon is the only thing that keeps the Fractus's black weapons from absorbing your magic. Keep your weapon in front of you, blazing, at all times."

"What if those black-eyed Fractus are around? Our weapons are useless then," said a woman who was no taller than Valerie's waist and had a pair of wings sprouting from her back.

"Wyld is right," Juniper said to the group. "Not all of the Fist's weapons are imbued with the new magic that protects you from the darkness. But more of these weapons arrive every day, so call out the code word, and someone will come to help you. We don't send any team into battle without at least a few of the new light weapons."

Juniper saw Valerie and gave her a nod.

"Continue sparring with each other until the lunch bell," he said before walking over to join her.

"Let's talk inside," Skye said, and the three went into one of the buildings.

Inside, it was a workshop of some kind, and it was empty.

Skye noticed Valerie scanning the room. "The lightweavers from the People of the Woods work here, creating more powerful weapons. Cyrus himself visits regularly to oversee their progress. But it will be months before we have all the weapons we need."

"We won't have that long before our next key battle," Valerie said.

She explained what she'd learned about binding magic on Earth, and how Reaper would try to use the magic from the flame for his own ends.

"Before that happens, we need to attack, on Earth and the Globe. I'm hoping that by challenging Reaper here, it will divert some of the Fractus from Earth and minimize human casualties."

"We'll have our soldiers as ready as they can be when it's time to fight Reaper," Skye said. "We all yearn to take back Arden. Living in our enemy's abandoned home is a blasphemy."

Valerie turned to Juniper. "That's not the only reason I'm here."

Her friend cocked his head. "What? You're looking at me like you're about to throw me into a volcano, and you feel really bad about it."

He'd been joking, but he wasn't far from the truth.

"Putting the rules limiting magic on Earth back in place requires a Conjuror with the ability to bind magic," Valerie said.

Juniper was shaking his head, and he took a step backward. "You can't mean me."

"You're the only Conjuror I know with that power. Is there anyone else?"

"My brothers...but they're all younger than me. We inherited our power from my mom, but her powers were much weaker."

Skye pawed at the ground. "It is an unusual power. And, like your mother, most with binding magic have only a weak manifestation of it."

Juniper sat down on a stool, his gaze faraway. "I don't know if this is terrifying or amazing."

Valerie watched him closely. "Maybe it's both."

"When I became a Knight, I wanted to be a hero. But even then, I never dreamed I'd be doing something this big. I'm not even sure I know how."

"I'm hoping the People of the Woods can help you. They're creating the object that will contain the spell when it's time," Valerie said.

Skye flicked his tail. "I do not doubt that Juniper can do this. But is it the best solution? An object that binds magic on Earth has failed us once. What if Reaper destroys it again?"

"It's the only idea we have for now, but I share your worry. I want more for Earth and the Globe than for things to go back to the way they were," Valerie said.

Skye nodded. "We all do."

"For now, I'm glad we have you, Juniper. Are you up for saving the universe?"

Juniper grinned, which was her goal, but he was tapping the fingers of his good hand against the table with nervous energy. "I'm in."

ഗ ഗ ഗ

Valerie was walking through the cities in the trees when she was hit by a wave of joy from Henry. She had a brief flash of Kanti's shining face before Henry leaned in and started kissing her like the sun would stop shining if he didn't.

"Oh, ew. Please block me, Henry," she said. "Not that I'm not happy for you and all."

There was another flash of Henry's happiness, and an echo of his laughter, before he shut her out of his mind and she didn't have to listen to any more wandering thoughts about how good Kanti's dress looked on her.

Despite not wanting a front-row seat to their reunion, a pang of deep joy filled her at the thought that Henry and Kanti had finally made up. It was sweet to revel in an emotion other than pain or grief or guilt, and it also made her think of Thai.

Was she really pushing him away because her mind was fraying, or did she think she didn't deserve the bliss that would come from being with him? She didn't know, but she decided to be selfish for once, and give into the urge that lived inside of her at all times.

That was when she started running, and she knew that the magic that had been all but stripped from her was returning. She didn't stop until she made it home and found Thai in the garden with Emin, carefully planting seeds in the soft dirt.

"Cara is going to show me her power today," Emin said to Thai. "Do you think she'll let me borrow it?"

Thai laughed. "If she can, buddy, I'm sure she will."

Emin turned and gave Valerie a hug before going back inside. Thai turned to her, and his eyes were expectant.

"I've been waiting for you to come home," he said, and she couldn't help sensing that his words held two meanings.

"I'm sorry. I'm sorry I gave up, sorry I didn't help you through your grief like you helped me, sorry—"

Thai interrupted her by pulling her into his arms.

"Me, too."

"For what?"

"For forgetting that you're more than a hero, you're a person. One I love," he whispered into her hair.

"I'm going to face Reaper again and again until I defeat him or he kills me. Even if I survive, I think I won't be in charge of my mind for long. But right now, I want to pretend none of those problems exist."

315

"Okay. Then there's somewhere I want to take you."

❧   ❧   ❧

Valerie's first official date with Thai was different from any other first date in the universe. He went to his room and pulled out a stone.

"Since travel between the worlds has been possible, I've taken walks in places on Earth I never thought I'd see, places that are remote or beautiful or famous. And every single time, all I could think about was how much I wished you were with me."

Valerie's heart thumped as he moved closer to her, standing so her head was level with his heart.

"But there was one spot I swore you had to see. Neither of us is allowed to die before going there together. Let me take you now."

Valerie nodded, wordless, and Thai gripped her hand and held it to his heart. The world melted around them, morphing into the ruins of a once-great castle. Grass had grown in between the stones. Valerie's gaze swept past the ruins. They were on a cliff, and there was a dramatic view of a raging blue-green ocean.

But it wasn't the beauty of the site that struck her most. It was the hum of ancient power that was threaded through the land, through the stones of the ruined castle, and even poured from the stormy sea. Breathing it in was intoxicating. Her own magic surged in response.

The wind whipped Valerie's hair out of its braid as she tilted her head back to breathe in the power of the place. "It's out of a fairy tale."

Thai's face was alight with mischief. "You're right. It's Tintagel Castle, where King Arthur was rumored to have been born."

The legend of King Arthur was one that Valerie had held close to her heart since she was a child, and ever since she'd discovered that her mother had left her a copy of the story, it had become even more tightly knit in her heart. Only Thai would think of bringing her here, and she let the magic and meaning of the place settle into her bones.

Valerie sucked in a breath, and the hum of power from the land around them synchronized with the hum of her own magic. She turned to look at Thai, half-drunk with the sensation, and he put his hand behind her neck and pulled her to him. Then his lips were on her neck, her cheeks, her eyelids, and finally her mouth.

He kissed her with all of the pent up passion of two and a half years apart. Every nerve ending in her body responded. Thai pressed her back against a tree, and she raked her fingers through his hair like she'd been aching to.

For once, her conscience was mute. Just this once, she'd let herself be with Thai. She'd face all the reasons why she couldn't be with him tomorrow. She wanted every part of them to be intertwined, and his magic responded to her wish, leaping to flow into her, amplifying her own until she was almost dizzy. Or maybe it was his kisses that were doing that.

When Thai pulled back, his eyes were dark and shining and beautiful. "When you kiss me like that, I swear I see a world remade."

"When you kiss me, I can almost see it myself."

Valerie woke the next morning, her body humming with something other than magic. Something better, she decided. She had never been more awake, more ready for what was coming.

She had to do something with the energy that was bursting from her, so she tied her shoes and quietly slipped out the window, so that Mr. and Mrs. Burns wouldn't catch her coming from Thai's room.

Then she ran, letting her magic power her legs. Trees sped by in a raucous gold blur. She had reached the Lake of Knowledge when Henry invited her into his mind.

She tucked herself into a nook of one of the trees nearby and concentrated on her brother. He was on a training field in Elsinore with Kanti, who gripped his hand in hers.

Henry's mind skipped between excitement and terror as a Conjuror approached him. She was tall and thin, and her body was tense, wary.

The woman's eyes flicked to Kanti. "You said he would help me find my magic, but I've heard that sometimes his gifts end up being more trouble than they're worth."

"You can trust Henry, Gertrude," Kanti said.

Henry took a breath. "I know you mean people like Blake, who I gave the power of invisibility."

Gertrude nodded. "He was invisible, but breakable. Even now that he has expunged that power from his system, his bones creak in wet weather."

"Reaper made me give specific powers to his soldiers, forcing them all into the same molds. When it ran contrary to the natural direction of that person's magic, the power weakened, or became fractured. I won't force your magic to do anything it doesn't want to."

318

The lines in Gertrude's forehead eased at Henry's words. "I weary of being at the heel of those whose magic is more evolved. I want to protect myself and my family."

"And your country," Kanti added.

Gertrude raised an eyebrow. "If I must. It is not a cheap price to pay, risking my life, but I will do it for the chance that my spark of magic will become a flame."

Henry placed his hands on Gertrude's shoulders. He bent forward, touching his forehead to hers. It was an intimate stance, but Henry's discomfort quickly dissolved as he reached for his power.

Until now, Valerie had never thought much about her brother's power to gift others with magic. It was a part of his mind that was always cordoned off, untouchable. When Henry opened the door that unleashed his power, it was as unstoppable as when her vivicus power raged through her, but somehow more delicate.

His magic tiptoed to the root of Gertrude's power. Instead of being like a spark, as she described, to Henry, it was like a lump of clay, something malleable that could be shaped into different forms. Henry kneaded it, testing its texture for possibilities. What shape would make it strongest?

A power associated with water would weaken it, air would crumble it, he decided. But fire would harden it into something strong and beautiful. Henry's imagination raced through the possibilities of what gift could be made that would enhance Gertrude's natural aptitude.

Lightweaver. She would revel in the warmth of her gift, and the Fist needed as many lightweavers as they could get. Henry encouraged the clay, molding it, his magic manipulating it more and more rapidly as his confidence grew.

319

Then the power within Henry stilled. It was not depleted, but finished. The masterpiece was complete. Henry drew his magic back into himself and stepped back from Gertrude.

Henry opened his eyes, and saw that Gertrude's were still shut, a small smile playing on her lips. She wiggled her fingers, and light danced between them.

When she finally opened her eyes, they were shining. "Thank you."

Henry was dazed, a little in awe of what he'd done. The curse that had made him Reaper's pawn was now his own tool against the darkness of the Fractus, the world, the mostly closed pit inside him. "You're welcome."

"Next!" Kanti shouted, and another eager Conjuror stepped forward.

Chapter 35

Valerie stayed in Henry's mind for a long time as he gifted Conjuror after Conjuror with different powers. There were two more lightweavers, more than a dozen with enhanced fighting reflexes, and many more with powers that Valerie had never heard of. They'd been dreamed up by Henry's imagination.

He was weary, but ecstatic. Valerie guessed that he'd keep working until he dropped from exhaustion or Kanti forced him to stop. But she had to pull away and return to the world and responsibilities that were waiting for her.

She had chosen today to visit Reaper's strongholds on Earth and the Globe as surreptitiously as possible. She doubted that Skye or Chisisi would approve of her putting herself in so much danger, but Valerie needed to see for herself what she would be up against.

At home, she wound her braid around her head and pulled on a sweatshirt with a deep hood. She looked in the mirror, shaking her head at her flimsy disguise, when she realized that she was thinking like a human. If she wanted a good disguise, there was an easy way to get one.

The Grand Master of the Glamour Guild, Roza, had set up a base on Earth in Italy. She'd told Valerie that if she was going to help fight this filthy war, then she'd live somewhere beautiful. From there, she and the members of her guild worked with soldiers of the Fist on various disguises, as well as hiding key safe houses around the world.

Valerie went to Roza's villa and found the Grand Master talking to some of the Masters in her guild. She'd exchanged her tentacles for legs, but she was still striking in an alien way in her human form. Roza dismissed her companions when she saw Valerie.

"If you are here for a cloaking spell for another hundred soldiers, I will need time," Roza said.

"It's nothing like that. I need a disguise for myself. A good one."

Roza examined her. "Who are you trying to fool?"

"Everyone. I'm going into the Fractus's camp, and I can't be recognized."

"I can't disguise you from a mind as well-trained as Reaper's. Even some of his generals would see through any disguise I could manufacture."

Valerie shifted uncomfortably. "I'm going whether you help me or not. Without you, I'm pulling this hoodie over my head and hoping for the best."

Roza snorted, the sound completely incongruous with her beautiful face. "Well, I can certainly do better than that. Come."

Roza led Valerie into a chamber off of the main hallway that was covered with mirrors.

Valerie was a little nervous as Roza examined her. "What will you do? Turn my hair blonde? Or make me into an animal, maybe?"

Roza chuckled. "Subtle disguises are the ones that work best. The magic is often overlooked, even by masters of the craft."

A gentle hum surrounded Valerie, and she watched as a touch of silver threaded her hair. The wrinkles by her eyes and in her brows deepened, and her skin was looser. As a final touch, Valerie's light brown eyes darkened until they were nearly black.

She could still recognize herself inside the disguise, she saw with relief. Her reflection reminded her of someone, but she couldn't put her finger on who.

"Now for your weapon," Roza said.

Valerie handed over the daggers she carried, and under Roza's touch, they dimmed. They weren't as perfectly black as the weapons wielded by the Fractus, but they wouldn't draw attention, like a weapon forged of light would.

"Will they still work like this?"

"Not as well. I worked with Cyrus to see if we could hide the light coming from the weapons, but altering them in any way corrupts the magic. So if you are attacked today, you will have little protection."

"Is this the part where you tell me not to do this?"

Roza's lips twitched. "I wouldn't dream of it, Commander. At it happens, I have a fondness for bold moves, and I suspect you could handle yourself with your bare hands against most enemies."

"Thank you," Valerie said, gesturing to her disguise, but she hoped Roza understood that she was thanking her for more than that.

Roza shook her hand. "Whisper your full name when your mission is complete, and the spell will fall away."

Valerie sheathed her daggers "If only all magic could be dismissed so simply."

Valerie had retained a handful of sand from the Atacama Desert in a vial that she'd brought with her, so travel to Chile was simple.

The sight of the transformed desert took Valerie's breath away. When she'd fought Reaper there, she hadn't had the chance to register the magnitude of the impact the unleashed flame had on the landscape.

Dunes of glass stretched for miles, reflecting the relentless sun. Beneath her feet, the glass was like ice, slippery and smooth.

There were a handful of tents set up about half a mile from where Valerie stood. In spite of the heat, part of her was tempted to pull up the hood on her sweatshirt, disguised or not.

As she approached the camp, the glass beneath her feet subtly changed color from pale brown to a bluish hue.

"What's your business?"

Valerie snapped her head toward the voice and saw an enormous bear who was vaguely familiar standing at the entrance to one of the tents, his black sword held loosely in his hand.

He approached her, and Valerie recognized him. He was the Grand Master of the Illuminators' Guild.

"Reaper sent me for a status report."

The bear's chest rumbled at her words. He raised his sword, and his ink-dipped weapon tugged at her magic. "Lies."

Valerie had less than a second before the bear charged. She braced herself, her strength rushing through her body. When he hit her, it was like a bus smashing into a boulder. She angled her shoulder, and he flew over her back, falling heavily on the ground behind her.

More Fractus were emerging from the tent, two with black eyes. The brilliant desert sun dimmed as the air around her hummed with twisted magic. She threw a dagger at one, slicing his leg, and had knocked a second unconscious by the time he'd registered that his comrade had fallen.

The Fractus's eyes were on her, assessing her weaknesses. She could stand and fight, but to what end? There were between thirty and fifty Fractus in the camp. She didn't want to find out if she could take them all on by herself.

Valerie turned to the Grand Master, who was snarling, about to charge her again. "You're right. I lied. Reaper didn't send me, but I am Fractus. I came because I follow no one blindly. I wanted to see if what he says about this place is true."

The Fractus glanced at each other, uncertain, and Valerie searched for words that would reach them. "Are we human puppets, or are we Conjurors, gifted with magic to wield as we will?"

The bear stood, glaring at her as he rubbed his back, but he didn't attack. "Do you know who you're talking to? I am a Grand Master."

"Illuminators' Guild," Valerie said, and the bear stopped bearing his teeth in aggression. "So I assumed you'd understand."

"Very well. You will only see that Reaper's words are true. We hide no secrets here," the bear growled. "But he will hear of your impertinence."

"That one woman kicked three of you to the ground? Go ahead, maybe he'll let me lead a bigger team," Valerie said with a forced swagger.

She followed the bear to a tent that was larger than the others. She stepped inside, and her gut twisted.

They were in the spot where the flame had once burned. But instead of its light, there was a pit that was bubbling with black Carne that had come from the bowels of Plymouth. A Fractus stood over it, holding a long staff that he occasionally dipped in the substance.

Valerie kept her face blank, for the first time thankful for her years in foster care, where showing any emotions would only be used against her.

"You see? More arrives every day," the bear growled.

Valerie nodded, hoping she looked like she knew what he was talking about. "There's not as much as I thought there would be."

"There is more here than you realize. The pool is half a mile deep. Any deeper, and we will hit water. But perhaps you do not believe me and would like to dive in and check for yourself?"

The bear grinned at his own joke, and Valerie took an involuntary step back. "So we really are close to harnessing the power in the glass desert."

"Soon. After it has served Reaper's purpose, we will push this Carne deeper, so it meets the ocean and can begin to spread all over the world. Then the humans will be safely under our control, as we planned."

"For their own good," Valerie said, but her stomach roiled.

The bear stared into the black pool as if he was hypnotized by its darkness. "I, for one, will be here the day Reaper activates the desert and we begin remaking the world."

"I'll be here, too," Valerie said.

"You think he'll let you, recruit? Because you tossed me over your shoulder once? You have much to learn."

"He won't have a choice."

Chapter 36

Valerie hadn't given the Fractus in the Atacama Desert any warning before she gripped the rock from her garden in her pocket and left. Her sudden exit would be strange, but she hoped that they wouldn't be suspicious enough to report the incident to Reaper.

She saw movement in her house and slipped out of her garden before anyone called her inside. It wasn't time to release her disguise yet, and she didn't want Thai to see her looking like she'd aged thirty years in a day.

Instead, she turned her steps toward Silva, running at first, but slowing as she came closer. She reminded herself that she was another Fractus supporter going about life as usual.

But she couldn't hide her immediate reaction when she reached The Horseshoe. A handful of the buildings were rubble, including The Society of Imaginary Friends. Others were streaked with black, either from lightning cast by the Fractus or the black substance dredged up from Plymouth.

The Horseshoe was eerily empty for the middle of the day, except for a few Fractus who were patrolling the grounds.

Without warning, a storm of fire ballooned out from the windows of the Weapons Guild, engulfing two of the Fractus hovering nearby. They were incinerated. A high whistle filled the air, and Valerie heard thudding footsteps rumbling closer.

Fractus began charging the Weapons Guild, battering the front door and sending lightning again and again into the stone walls. There was a rhythm to it, as if the Fractus had rehearsed. This had happened before.

It dawned on Valerie that the citizens of Silva were fighting back against the Fractus even now. The scorched state of The Horseshoe was a testament to the ongoing battles. Reaper's hands were fuller than she'd guessed.

Valerie took advantage of the mayhem to pass through The Horseshoe and head toward the spot that Willa and Steven had blown open into Plymouth.

The closer she got, the more Fractus she ran into. At first, she ducked her head, afraid of being recognized. But everyone was busy with their tasks, and she welcomed the bustle. Being one face in a crowd was a better disguise than even the one Roza had given her.

At the edge of the pit, she peered in and saw that the vast lake of Carne had diminished significantly. Had it all been sent to the pool in the Atacama Desert, or did Reaper have other uses for it, as well?

She followed a group of Fractus down into the pit and saw that many of the tunnels were filled with workers, both Fractus and Groundlings who had been forced into slavery.

"They've found another well of Carne," one of the Fractus whispered to a friend.

The woman who had spoken was one of the Knights who wanted to leave the Fractus to join the Fist and was remaining only on Valerie's command. They would finally have a role fighting for the Fist in the upcoming battle.

The Knight continued, "We tried to hide its discovery from Reaper, but one of his new generals found it with us. Don't think the vivicus would have liked it if we killed the general and kept this magic from Reaper, but it's probably what we should have done."

Valerie considered revealing who she was, but decided against drawing attention to herself. And their opinions weren't unique among the members of the Fist. The longer the war raged, the more unreasonable her desire to capture instead of kill enemies seemed to many.

Valerie caught sight of Reaper in one of the tunnels, rubbing Carne between his thumb and forefinger as if he could tell more about its properties by touch.

He turned, and his gaze froze when it stopped on her. His face went white. Valerie was certain he recognized her, but he immediately created a portal and stepped through, cutting off the Fractus who was speaking to him midsentence.

Had she seen Reaper frightened before? She didn't think so. But rather than wait to see if he returned, Valerie scrambled up one of the ladders that led out of the pit and back into Silva.

She took her first deep breath when she reached the trees, but it was a breath she took too soon. Reaper was waiting for her, his hair a little damp. His face had regained its color, and his old confidence had returned to his posture. Panic flooded through her so forcefully that she heard a buzzing in her ears. His narrow-eyed gaze left her with no doubt that he recognized her through her disguise.

Valerie reached for her daggers, and Reaper let out a snort. "I defeated you when you wielded Pathos. Will you now try to kill me with those dim little daggers, or can we talk like grown-ups?"

"I'm surprised you can see me, given the beating Summer gave you," Valerie said, hoping to throw him off balance.

A snarl flashed across Reaper's face. "Nothing I couldn't fix."

"What do you want?" Valerie asked, summoning her magic.

Reaper eyed her as if she was a puzzle piece and he was figuring out where to put her. "What if we made a deal?"

"No."

Reaper took a step closer. "What if you didn't have to be an orphan any longer?"

Valerie's mind had been racing with possibilities, and nervous energy made her jittery. But at Reaper's words, she stilled.

Reaper took a step forward. "Oberon is in the ether, where even I may not call him back. But your mother lives, in a way."

Valerie wouldn't give him the satisfaction of asking what he meant, but her feet wouldn't move, so she could attack or run, either.

"I knew she might be a useful tool to control you or Henry or Oberon, so I have kept her in stone these eighteen years. When I saw you, disguised to look older, in Plymouth today, I thought you were a ghost, or that she'd gotten free. But I checked the place where I stashed her, and she stands there still. That's when I knew it must be you."

Valerie's heart pounded, her elation and horror so mixed together that she had trouble focusing on anything else. Then she remembered who she was talking to. "No deal."

"I'm not asking you to join me. Only that you tell your people that you are stepping down as their leader, and then

330

you disappear. Surely, you don't think you're so important that the Fist will fall apart without you?"

The chance to live away from this war with her mother? The dream was so sweet that Valerie's heart ached at the thought.

"No." She'd meant to shout the word, but it came out a whisper.

"I keep my promises. If you refuse, I won't destroy her statue. I will leave her in it forever, so she is unable to join your father in the ether. There will be no peace for either of their souls."

The emotion that crashed through Valerie reminded her of her vivicus power in its intensity, and the pain it brought. Her face was numb, frozen, as if her lips refused to speak the words that would leave her mother buried alive forever. So she shook her head instead.

Reaper's face remained neutral, but Valerie saw the tree near him dissolving, and guessed that he was angrier than he let on.

She drew her daggers, ready to fight him, though it seemed cruel that she would die and join her father while her mother remained entombed in a prison of stone, alone.

Reaper's lip curled in distaste. "I will not make a martyr of you today. Run, little vivicus."

And she did.

ༀ ༀ ༀ

At first Valerie raced blindly, trees snapping in her face as she crashed through the woods. Henry was in her mind, trying to sort out what was happening, but her thoughts were too disheveled to put into any kind of order for him, so she let him know she was unhurt and then shut him out.

Thai was visiting his family today, introducing them to Emin, and Valerie was glad. Sometimes, it seemed that all she had to share was misery, and she'd rather keep it all to herself.

As her burst of energy subsided, she made her way back to The Horseshoe, not really caring if anyone else saw through her disguise. She yearned for a fight. Her steps took her to the Healers' Guild, and the doors opened at her touch.

She made her way down the hall to the little room where Gideon still lay, as distant from her as the moon. When she opened the door, he was thrashing in his bed. Before she could call for help, she saw that Nightingale was at his side, pressing wet cloths to his friend's forehead.

Nightingale eyed her warily, and Valerie remembered her disguise.

"It's Valerie. I'm wearing a glamour. Are you trying some new kind of magic treatment?"

Nightingale wrung out a cloth. "It's water. I'm cooling his fever down. Sometimes, we have no more tools than humans."

A cowardly part of Valerie wanted to turn around and leave, but instead, she made her way to Gideon's bed. "What's happening to him?"

"I don't have answers. No one has ever had so much of the dark fairy dust in their system and survived. But thanks to your vivicus power, he has a fighting chance. And right now, he's fighting hard."

Gideon began groaning, his head thrashing back and forth.

Valerie smoothed back the sweaty hair on his forehead. "How long has he been like this?"

"It began two days ago. I was hopeful, because his pulse was stronger. Your friend Dr. Freeman came by and suggested some treatments that we tried. But if his fever doesn't come down, it will weaken his body, and he will be unable to expel the rest of the dark dust."

Valerie leaned down and whispered in his ear. "I won't ask you to fight, because I know that you're incapable of doing anything else."

Valerie took over sponging Gideon's forehead, and Nightingale quietly slipped out the door.

Valerie gripped Gideon's hand. "Something awful happened today. If you knew, you might not forgive me. I don't know what the right thing to do is. I need you here to help me, to lead with me. I was never meant to do this alone."

Gideon's eyes opened, but he didn't see her. His gaze was searching until it paused on her face.

"Adelita. My love, you came back for me," Gideon said, lifting his head a bit.

Then he fell back on his pillow, still. Panicked, Valerie searched for his pulse and rested her ear on his chest. She almost cried when she heard his heart beating strongly. But when she shook him, he didn't move.

Valerie called softly for Nightingale in the hall, and he hurried into the room to check on Gideon.

"Is he any better?" she asked him.

"His fever has broken. I still don't know if he will wake, but now he has a chance."

Chapter 37

Valerie whispered her full name as she returned home, and her body relaxed, relieved to be in its natural form. As she got closer, she saw someone practicing basic blocks and punches in the shadowy twilight.

As she approached to see who it was, Thai's hand touched her shoulder.

"Emin's been out there all day practicing the moves I showed him. He's determined to get it perfect. Reminds me of you."

Valerie couldn't think of a better compliment, and she almost leaned back so that her head rested on Thai's chest. But she couldn't let herself keep slipping into Thai's arms. It was too selfish.

"I missed you today," he whispered in her ear, and she couldn't stop herself from blushing. "Where were you? With Chisisi and Skye?"

Valerie tensed, knowing that telling Thai the truth would turn into a fight.

Thai surprised her by chuckling in her ear. "Don't tell me. I can feel how rigid you are, and I'm guessing you were doing something more dangerous than you should have been. Tell me you weren't confronting Reaper."

If it was possible, Valerie went even stiffer, and Thai turned her to face him. All of his laughter was gone now.

"Why? If you don't care for your own life, do you at least care what it would do to me, Henry, Emin, and Cyrus if you got yourself killed?"

"Thai, I'm fine. I took a risk, I'll admit, by not bringing support, but I knew I'd attract less attention if I went by myself. I couldn't live with myself if someone got hurt because of my decision when I was capable of executing this mission by myself."

"You may not be committing suicide, like Henry, but there is a part of you that thinks you don't deserve to live, to be happy. Every time I think you've changed, that you see how precious you are, you prove me wrong."

"I wouldn't—"

"How can I forgive you for putting the life of the person I love the most in the universe in unnecessary danger over and over again?"

"I'm sorry," Valerie said, but Thai was already striding away from her.

He didn't understand. Her life had less value every time she used her vivicus power. Some mornings after she saved someone, she struggled to tie her shoes. She wouldn't be whole for long. Maybe it was better if she died in the war, rather than torturing everyone by slowly dissolving afterward.

Valerie was empty, and she sagged where she stood, tempted to curl up right at the base of the tree she was resting against.

Her gaze turned back to Emin, who was still practicing, even though only the stars provided any light for him now. His focus and intensity took her out of her own mind, and she walked toward him.

"I think you're ready for your next lesson," she said.

Emin ran up to her, and she could see how sweaty he was in the starlight. "I was waiting till we were back in Silva, at the Guild of the Knights of Light, to start, but then I decided that with you here to train me, I could start now. Is that okay?"

"Yeah, that's okay," she replied, pushing his hair off his forehead. "But what's your rush? Is it because you're worried that you'll have to fight the Fractus?"

The thought of Emin being afraid made her wish that she could wrap him up in her arms, but he surprised her by shaking his head.

"No, I'm not afraid. But seeing you leading the Fist makes me sure that I want to be a Knight. I'm going to be strong and help everyone, like you."

His gaze was adoring, and Valerie couldn't help smiling at his hero worship. If he only knew.

"I have something for you," she said, tugging the Laurel Circle off of her thumb. "This ring is special. My mentor gave it to me to help me be a good Knight."

Emin examined it, and his voice was filled with awe when he answered. "It's really for me? Don't you need it anymore?"

"This ring tells you when fear is holding you back, and I think that's one lesson I've learned. I'm still afraid lots of times, but I'm able to push through it when I have to."

Emin pulled a chain that he wore around his neck out from under his shirt and unfastened it so he could slip the ring on. It hung next to a delicately crafted silver leaf.

"From Mom," he said when he saw her looking at it.

"It's beautiful. I know you're going to be an excellent Knight, Sir Emin."

"Can Knights still get hugs?" he asked.

Valerie swept him up in her arms, hugging him and tickling him until he giggled. Then she put him back on his feet and held his hand as they made their way back to the house.

"You might want to be like me, Emin, but I'm trying to be as strong as you. So keep training and trying and fighting, and so will I."

~ ~ ~

Valerie awoke the next morning to the sun streaming in. A leaf blew into her room through her cracked window, and settled on her pillow. She picked it up, and Grandmother North's voice filled the room.

"We found a way to prepare the object you requested sooner than expected. Come to Arbor Aurum immediately."

There was a little pause.

"And bring my grandson."

Emin was awake now, and he sat up, rubbing his eyes. "Are we going on an adventure?"

It had been a long time since Valerie had considered her life an adventure, and she smiled at Emin.

They chased each other through the forest and ascended the leaf to the cities in the trees. On their walk to Arbor Aurum, they played *I Spy*, and Valerie embraced being eight again.

But as soon as they entered the bustling city, they both became solemn.

"Grandmother North might change her mind about wanting to see me if I'm too loud," Emin said, his tone very serious.

"Then we'll tickle her until she screams," Valerie said, making Emin giggle.

Valerie saw North's stately gait as they made their way across the winding branches.

Her eyes were bright when she saw Emin, and she placed her hand on his head. He threw his arms around her waist, and after a charged moment, North's face relaxed and she hugged him back.

Three boys around Emin's age approached, bouncing a little on the balls of their feet with excitement.

"You're back! Where've you been?" a boy with long hair threaded with gold asked.

"Is it true that you're training to be a Knight?" the second asked.

Valerie smiled. "Go ahead and play with your friends. I'll find you when it's time to go."

Valerie waited until he scampered off before she spoke to North. "Not that I'm complaining, but how did you get the object to bind Earth's rules so quickly?"

"Come with me," North said, and began walking.

Valerie followed, and North led her up steps in the side of a tree. She remembered the path from her last visit to the Sky Garden. It was alive with colors that contrasted the blue, cloudless sky.

Three other People of the Woods were waiting, and Valerie's steps slowed. "What's going on?"

North turned to her. "We conceived of a new way to create an everlasting object that will contain the spell that binds magic on Earth."

"Not we, you, North," one of the People, a woman with slightly pointed ears, said.

North inclined her head in acknowledgment. "The object must come from you, vivicus. You have the ability to renew

338

life, and if we can create it from the essence of your magic, it can always heal itself from any harm that might befall it."

Valerie wondered how much it would hurt, but didn't say so. "What do I have to do?"

Another of the People came forward and put a crown of flowers on her head.

"Rest," he said.

Valerie breathed in the scent of the flowers around her head, and she became weak-kneed. She barely had time to consider that it might be a trap before she collapsed. The People of the Woods laid her on the table.

"This will hurt," North said. There was no emotion on her face as she spoke. "But it must be done if we are to have a chance of driving back the Fractus. I couldn't risk that you would fail us again, like you did when you let the Byway be destroyed."

Valerie would have undergone any pain to achieve the same goal. But being forced into this made her strain against the paralysis the flowers had given her. She couldn't so much as wiggle her fingers, and her helplessness made her frantic. The edges of her vision went black as memories of being locked up in foster care flashed through her mind.

Her breath came in little gasps, but North's face held no pity. She turned to the other People standing around Valerie. "I was right not to ask for her permission. Look how she quakes, and we have not yet begun."

The other three People frowned, obviously uncomfortable with Valerie's distress, but they only watched her uneasily.

North began chanting, low words in a language that Valerie had never heard before. The others joined her, and Valerie squeezed her eyes shut, going to the little hole inside herself where she could crawl when things got really bad.

Some part of her mind registered that her hand unclenched itself from the tight fist she had made, and magic poured from her spirit through her body like fire, shooting out of the palm of her hand.

The pain was intense, but no more than she had faced so many times before. Being unable to move, or even moan, was a kind of horrifying claustrophobia that made her want to crawl out of her own skin.

The pain ratcheted up in intensity, making her arch her back involuntarily. She managed to turn her head, and she saw light pouring from her hand, reminding her of Cyrus when he used his power. The thought steadied her. Anything that reminded her of Cyrus couldn't be bad, even if it came from her.

The light was coalescing into a stem with its roots in the center of her palm. Each inch it grew made the pain blaze up in intensity, but she watched, fascinated, at the perfect bud that formed.

The pain went higher, higher, and then stopped, flooding her body with sudden sweetness at its absence. The flow of her magic ceased after the bud on her hand bloomed. It was a poppy.

℘   ℘   ℘

Valerie didn't remember blacking out. She blinked, and when she opened her eyes, it was night.

North stood next to her in silent vigil, but the other People who had assisted her were gone. Valerie registered Emin's soft, warm body. His head was resting on her belly. Had North cared to see her grandson at all, or did she only know that his presence would prevent Valerie from unleashing her rage to its full extent? Had every moment she'd shown tenderness to Emin been an act?

Valerie's eyes connected with North's. "Coward. I was defenseless."

"I saw the fear in your eyes, vivicus. You don't have the right to call anyone a coward."

"You don't know anything. Valerie's the bravest person in the world," Emin said.

North took a sharp breath and turned on her heel.

"Wait." Valerie's voice was flat. "Give me the flower. It's mine, born of my magic. You have no right to it."

"I called it forth. You may have it on my terms," North said.

Valerie rose, ignoring the pain beating behind her eyes. "Emin, go downstairs and wait."

Emin obeyed immediately. North turned to face her.

Valerie's magic hummed strangely in her veins. "You'll give me what's mine. Or I'll take it."

"Will you beat it out of me?" North said, her back never straighter. "Kill me? Do what you will."

As she stood before North, facing her challenge, Valerie noticed for the first time that she was taller than the old woman, giving her a feeling of control. The sense of power that emanated from North was simply an illusion. With that, Valerie realized that the woman was just another Conjuror wielding her power as a weapon against those with less, like Reaper did. Valerie had been on the losing side of a power imbalance more times in her life than she could count, but this wasn't one of them. This time, North was on the losing side.

The thought dialed her anger down until it only simmered. She would not abuse her power like so many had with her, even if North deserved it.

341

"I will only put you under arrest. But if you use your magic on someone again without their consent, I will subject you to one of Reaper's black weapons until you are stripped of your magic."

North took a small step back, as if her confidence had slipped. "My people will never allow me to be arrested. We have our own justice here."

"They have no say in this."

Valerie leaned forward and pinched a nerve in North's neck. She caught the Conjuror before she fell to the ground, and hauled her unconscious body easily over her shoulder. She sensed the hum of magic coming from North's robe, and retrieved a cylinder that must hold the poppy she'd made with her magic.

Valerie was surprised to find a crowd waiting for her on the platform when she descended from the Sky Garden. Her eyes scanned the crowd, but she didn't see signs of an impending fight.

Valerie recognized Elden's wife when she stepped forward. "Emin saw what happened to you and told us, vivicus. Do what you wish to North and the People who helped her. We formally expel them from the cities of the trees to wander among the Conjurors below for the rest of their days."

After a long pause, Valerie nodded. She would accept no more pain others wrought upon her as if she deserved it.

♋   ♋   ♋

Valerie couldn't cast North on the steps of the entrance to the Justice Guild, as she would have before the Fractus had taken the city. But the Justice Guild existed in a different form outside of Arden.

She dropped Emin off at home with Thai and Henry and took North to the outskirts of Dunsinane, where the largest of the Fist's jails on the Globe was now located. She wasn't surprised to see Skye dropping off another dozen prisoners in magic-infused shackles, but the sight of a slight form with blonde curls made her break into a jog.

"Calibro," Valerie breathed when she was close enough to confirm the identity of the Grand Master of the Justice Guild.

She unceremoniously dropped a still-unconscious North on the ground and shook hands with Calibro. A hug would be beneath the Grand Master's dignity.

"You're back," Valerie said, surprised by the depth of her relief.

"Is this my welcome back gift?" she asked, nodding to North's form.

"No, this is an abuser of magic who should have been locked away long ago. Let's not waste words on her."

Calibro nodded to a guard, who came over and took North into the underground structure that housed the courts and jail.

Skye had a strange expression on his face, and it took Valerie a while to realize that she hadn't seen him smile in so long that she didn't recognize it. She grinned, too. Calibro released a grunt of disapproval that belied the smile playing at the corners of her mouth.

"How did you recover?" Valerie asked.

"Dasan and a promising young Healer, Thai, worked together to heal my mind. Thai amplified the Grand Master's gift and nursed me back to health, and here I stand."

Calibro was blushing now, and Valerie calculated that the youngest Grand Master in Arden was now the age she herself had been when magic had first entered her life. And when she'd first met Thai. He'd made her blush, too.

"Now that you're well, we can get back to winning this war," Skye said, and Valerie couldn't tell if he was joking or not.

"Starting with this," Valerie said, and unscrewed the cylinder holding the poppy. "With the help of Juniper, it will bind magic on Earth again."

Skye cracked his knuckles; his eyes were eager. "It's time to fight."

Valerie wished the same energy infused her at the thought, but instead, all she could summon was the familiar thread of duty that she was bound to follow. "If this is going to work, we need many more soldiers for the Fist."

Skye flicked his tail. "That is ever the problem."

Valerie turned to Calibro, remembering a conversation she'd had with Chisisi. "Some of these Fractus must only be following Reaper out of fear. Maybe they would join us, if we knew who among them was telling the truth about their willingness to leave Reaper's cause."

Calibro bowed her head. "My power is that I can detect the truth in words spoken. But it is a complex magic that is not as useful as it seems, for often intentions and reality are not the same, and words can be twisted."

"What if you had help?" Valerie asked. "We could bring Oracles to look into the future and Empaths to help navigate the complexities of the mind."

Calibro stared at her, her intelligent eyes alight. "We have worked with Empaths in the past, but the doors of Ephesus were closed."

"I think Sibyl will help us if we ask," Valerie said.

"It will not show us the truth within every mind, but with these tools, I think I can promise you more soldiers for the Fist."

Skye clapped Calibro on her little back, and her smile flashed, brief but bright. "It will be a good fight."

Good fight or not, it would come soon.

Chapter 38

For the next three days, Valerie's house became the headquarters of the Fist, as she planned her attack on Silva and the Fractus's camp in the Atacama Desert. It reminded her of planning for the battle against the Fractus a year ago, until she saw the empty places at her kitchen table that her father and Gideon had occupied.

Valerie never missed them more, as everyone looked to her for final approval on battle plans. Henry, Thai, and her friends advised as best they could, but it wasn't the same as having a wiser head to rely on.

And always, in the back of her mind, was the thought of her mother encased in stone, waiting for eternity for a freedom that would never come. It was a steep price to pay for the possibility that her leadership was necessary to expel the Fractus from Earth.

Emin enjoyed the bustle of planning and the constant stream of visitors, and seeing some of his grief lift was one of the few comforts Valerie had.

Valerie had just finished talking with Kanti through a hand mirror when a strange, almost irresistible impulse came over her to leave her house. It reminded her of when Sanguina or Kellen had controlled her mind, except that she wasn't afraid.

Valerie moved to his side. "I'm here. I'll use my power to—"

Darling rested a paw on her hand. "No, please. I am grateful that my time to be absorbed into the ether has come at last. I did not call you for that."

"I'm glad you let me be with you."

"You are the only person I know. All of the other interactions I've had, even before my powers stripped my mind, have been burned away, save yours. For a few months now, my mind has slowly returned to me, and I hoped it meant that I'd fulfilled my duty as vivicus at last."

"Is that why we've been connected?" she asked.

"Indeed. Vivicus are always linked heart-to-heart and mind-to-mind. But while my mind was a blank, there could be no connection."

Valerie rapidly blinked back her tears, but they were less bitter than the ones she'd shed for Dulcea, or her father. It was different when someone went peacefully, ready for the ether, rather than ripped from life too soon.

Darling briefly touched Valerie's heart, which still glowed. "The tug that draws you to people in pain, urging you to ease their distress, will only go stronger until it consumes you. So cherish these days with the ones you love."

Valerie shuddered at his words. Was it a character flaw that she didn't want to be stripped of her consciousness, even if it meant helping people? "I want a life. I know it can't be a normal one, but I want to know it's happening."

"There is a way," Darling said. "But I was never able to discover it. The vivicus who called me to his passing said that I must burn out my power, rather than let it burn through me. Perhaps you will manage it."

The last of the shine in Darling's fur dulled, and with it, the light in his eyes.

"Darling?" she asked, but he only whimpered in return.

Valerie gathered him into her arms, and he snuggled into her chest. His glowing heart beat in sync with hers, until the pulses grew slower, and stopped.

A burst of power was released into the universe at his passing, but it was small, as if all of Darling's magic and essence had already been used up.

She cried for a long time, unable to let go of him. Her tears were for everyone she'd lost, and she didn't think they'd ever stop. At Henry's soft steps behind her, she gently put Darling on the ground.

"I came as soon as I knew," he said, sitting next to her. "You're not alone. You never are."

She rested her head on her brother's shoulder. "He helped thousands of people in his lifetime. But I was the only person he knew to call when his time came to die. He didn't even remember who his friends used to be."

"That won't be you."

"You can't promise that," Valerie said. "I'd rather be dead than alone."

"Is that why you've got everyone worried that you have a death wish?" he asked.

"Anyone who gets close to me is eventually going to get hurt when who I am is stripped away and nothing exists except my power."

"And your heart. Lots of people loved Darling because he was more than the sum of his magic. He was warm and funny. Remember how he'd make kids laugh when he cured them? He could have healed them and moved on to the next person in need, but he didn't. There was a piece of him there. And as long as there's a piece of you left, Valerie, there will be people who love you."

ɷ ɷ ɷ

Henry and Valerie buried Darling together and returned home. They approached the gate to their garden, and inside, Valerie heard Emin talking with someone whose voice was familiar.

She gave Henry a questioning look, and he smiled. "It's about time you had some good news. Go see who's in our kitchen."

Valerie hurried inside. Sitting at her table, drinking tea with Emin on his knee, was Elden. His dark skin hadn't completely regained its gold accents, and his eyes were shadowed, but he was awake. Valerie couldn't stop herself from throwing her arms around him.

Emin giggled. "Why are you turning red, Uncle Elden?"

Valerie released him, to his obvious relief.

"I have come to thank you for your care of Emin," Elden said in his grave way. "And to learn what has happened while I slept."

After Emin was tucked into bed, Valerie told Elden what had happened over the past year, and what was ahead of them.

"My wife told me of how my mother used you," he said. "I trust it has not shaken your faith in my people."

"No. Though I'm glad you're back at the helm," she admitted.

"I will navigate the politics and strategy with the People of the Woods, but my skill in battle has waned. My magic is all but stripped from my soul. I have no more power than a human."

350

"It's your mind and support that I need the most. Thank you, Elden. I know your family must wish you could be done with this war."

"Mine are a warrior people, and we do not flinch from what must be done. My daughter will fight to regain Arden, and though I fear it, I am proud of her."

"There's something else." Valerie took the cylinder with her poppy from its hiding place under a floorboard in the kitchen. "Can you help Juniper learn how to use this to bind Earth's magic?"

Elden unscrewed the container and removed the poppy from inside. At his touch, it glowed more brightly, and Valerie felt a responding flicker within herself.

"I cannot guide him in this. My mother is the keeper of that knowledge. But I will go with Juniper to her jail cell myself so he may learn what he must."

"About Emin—"

"The choice of where he wishes to live will be his. But as skilled as you are at leading the Fist, are you ready to be a parent? I already think of him as a son."

Valerie thought of the sweet boy in the next room. The idea of taking care of him forever filled her with warmth. "With my vivicus power destroying my mind, I don't know how long I'll be capable of watching out for someone else."

Elden cocked his head to the side, examining her. "Not all vivicus have followed Darling's path."

"But most do, right?" Elden wouldn't meet her eyes, and Valerie knew his answer. "I'm not giving up. But I want Emin to have his best chance, and I think it's with you."

"Thank you," Elden said.

Elden left, and Valerie watched him as he made his way out of her garden and into the woods. She experienced a flicker of panic when she could no longer make out his form in the trees, as if he might disappear back into unconsciousness, unreachable.

$$\text{\Large ℘ \quad ℘ \quad ℘}$$

In the middle of the night, Henry woke her. "Elle sent me a message through the Empathy Collective. We have to meet her right away."

Valerie rubbed her eyes and tied her hair back. After quickly dressing, they slipped out of the house without waking anyone inside.

"Lake of Knowledge?" she asked, and Henry nodded.

They jogged in silence, but with minds open to each other. As long as she had Henry to anchor her, could her mind really slip away?

They found Elle pacing the shores of the lake, chewing her lip. Her words tumbled out without her usual poise. "Will and I have never communicated mind-to-mind like you and Henry, but I think—I'm almost sure—of what he's trying to tell me."

Henry's voice was soothing as he moved closer to Elle. "It's okay. You don't have to be sure. Tell us what you think you're getting from Will."

"We have to attack the Fractus soon, or it will be too late. Reaper somehow got word from Gabriel of knowledge in the Akashic Records on how to harness the dormant power that the flame released when it went out. He's going to use it to remake how magic functions."

"That's possible?" Valerie couldn't fathom what Elle was saying.

Elle took a breath. "Reaper's power is to manipulate the very physics of how elements work. Magic is another element. With the help of all this additional power, he can make sure that magic is only passed to those he deems worthy. Essentially, he can snuff out the spark of magic that lives in us all, human and Conjuror alike, and amplify it in those he thinks are worthy."

"We knew we'd have to attack Reaper soon. This doesn't change our plans," Henry said.

"How much time do we have?" Valerie asked.

"He'll seize the power tomorrow as soon as darkness falls. At least, that's what I think Will is trying to tell me."

Henry sucked in a breath. "Less than a day."

Valerie's heart, which had been racing, slowed, and her mind sharpened into focus. "Thank you, Elle. You've given us a chance."

Elle's grin was fierce. "I'll see you on the battlefield."

ᔦ   ᔦ   ᔦ

The rest of the night was a blur, as Valerie and Henry spread the word to the generals of the Fist about the new timeline for the attack on Silva and the Atacama Desert.

Valerie had to redraw many of her plans because she didn't have the additional days she'd planned on to prepare. She'd never been less sure of victory, but the Fist would give the universe a chance.

By dawn, Valerie was alone in her kitchen with Chisisi. Everyone else had scattered to execute their assignments as she finalized the details on the Atacama front.

"I will keep the human soldiers Dr. Freeman has recruited away from the front lines, but their numbers will be an asset," Chisisi said.

Valerie forced herself not to rub her temples. "I wish we could spare them from this fight, but we must throw everything we have at the Fractus now. I'm starting to believe there won't be another fight if we don't have at least a partial victory tomorrow."

"We will slay Reaper, and the rest will follow," Chisisi said with confidence.

Ordering Reaper's execution wasn't as hard as she thought it would be, but it seemed wrong that the act wouldn't be performed by her own hand. If she wanted to avoid fulfilling Reaper's prophecy, it couldn't be.

"Maybe I'm fulfilling the prophecy in spirit, if not in fact, by ordering his death," she said.

"Your heart has not guided you in the wrong direction yet," Chisisi said. "Will young Juniper be ready to bind Earth's magic?"

"I hope so. He's with Elden and North now. He's nervous, but my instincts tell me he can do it."

"Then he will. I'll leave you now," Chisisi said, his attention caught by something over Valerie's shoulder.

Valerie followed his gaze and saw Cyrus standing in the doorframe. Cyrus's eyes were alive with a little of his old mischief. She hadn't seen that much warmth in them in a year.

"Come on," Cyrus said. "I've got a present for the battle tomorrow."

She followed him outside, into her garden. In the corner, she saw that a big boulder that was part of one of Oberon's old wards was glowing.

Cyrus shrugged. "Your destiny awaits."

Instead, she was drawn toward something sweet that tugged at the part of her that was connected with Darling. He needed her. She walked and then ran deeper and deeper into the woods. The path wound by the Lake of Knowledge, and she found herself on the hidden path that she had last walked with Henry to find Azra when Clarabelle had been born.

Her heart was warm in her chest, and she saw a faint red glow under her shirt. She'd seen something like it before—Darling's heart pulsed red when he healed someone with his vivicus power.

She'd been so connected to him since she'd saved Henry that she hadn't realized that she hadn't actually seen him in over a year. Guilt followed the realization, and she swallowed it down.

As she continued to run, the gold faded from the bark of the trees, and she knew she was in the remote reaches of Messina. She recognized the grove where Clarabelle was born. She slowed her steps and nearly tripped over a ball of fur on the ground.

"Darling?" she asked.

The little creature barely resembled the Darling she knew. His gold fur had lost its shine, but his eyes were more aware than she'd ever seen. They sparked with something like intelligence.

"You heard my call." Darling's voice was nothing like the little squeaks that she'd been used to. It was deep and powerful, and utterly shocking.

"I didn't know you could talk," Valerie blurted.

"I think it's because this is the end," he said. "My life has been a hazy dream to me for so long, and now I am awake."

Valerie approached the boulder and grinned when she saw the hilt of a golden sword sticking out from it.

"What are you waiting for? Don't you want to see if you're the one who can pull it out?" Cyrus teased.

Valerie grasped the hilt, and her hand was bathed in warm light. Gently, she pulled, and it slid effortlessly from the stone. She gasped as she examined the blade.

"Pathos! Cyrus, how did you repair it?"

Even the words of the prophecy binding her to Henry, Cyrus, and Kanti were elegantly etched into the blade.

"Pathos is gone. This is a new blade, made entirely of light. I tried to keep it in the spirit of Pathos, but with some tweaks that make it way better."

Valerie didn't laugh at Cyrus's swagger. Instead, she took some practice swings. It was lighter than Pathos, but had the same even balance. It fit in her hand like an extension of herself.

"It will glow for a thousand years, even in a place entirely devoid of light. Out in the world, it can continually recharge itself. It's unstoppable."

"How did you manage it?" she asked.

"All of the lightweavers lent me their power to make this a reality."

But Valerie examined him closely and saw that a little of his usual glow was absent. "There was a price, wasn't there?"

"If you're going to get all guilt-tripped about it, I'm not going to tell you."

"Okay."

"Fine, you convinced me. I had to sever a piece of my power in order to form this weapon," he admitted. When Valerie gasped at his words, he hurried to continue. "It's not like I don't have my magic or anything. When you saved me with your vivicus power, you enhanced my powers. I'm just giving you back what was yours to begin with."

Valerie swallowed twice to keep her tears from rising. "Thank you."

Cyrus shrugged. "There's nothing I wouldn't do for you."

Valerie hugged him, wishing she could pour everything she felt into his heart and fill the hole that she had put there. A hole that she was afraid would always be there.

"I love you," she said, even though she knew that for Cyrus, it would never be enough.

"I'm your best friend. I always will be. I won't leave you, Val," Cyrus said.

Valerie couldn't trust herself to speak without her voice breaking.

Cyrus reached out to brush her cheek, and then he cleared his throat. "Elle thinks this sword will gain me an invitation to Illyria if it helps end this war. I think I might like it down there, bringing light to the ocean's depths."

"Then I wouldn't see you anymore."

"That's kind of the idea. I'd visit, but I want you to live without feeling guilty every time we bump into each other. And that far away from you, maybe I'd find someone else. Miracles happen."

And they did. Valerie knew, because Cyrus had given her proof.

Chapter 39

Valerie hadn't slept in twenty-four hours, but she'd never been more awake. She carefully re-braided her hair and wrapped it around her head so it wouldn't get in her way while she was fighting. Her new sword was strapped to her side, so weightless that she kept checking to make sure her sheath wasn't empty.

"I thought a key part of the plan was for you to not be too recognizable so you don't get targeted," Thai said, startling her.

She whipped around to face him, and then looked down at her blue jeans, T-shirt, and sneakers. "What do you mean?"

Thai stepped closer. "You're beautiful. Anyone who sees you is going to recognize you. Why not get a glamour disguise from Roza?"

Valerie blushed. "My soldiers will want to see me, to know I'm fighting at their sides."

"Lucky soldiers," Thai said, and he stepped even closer. "I know we have things to discuss, but right now, I'm going to kiss you like it's the end of the world, because maybe it is."

Valerie knew there were about a million other things she should be doing, but the force drawing her to him was a kind of magic she couldn't resist.

As their lips met, the burden she carried dropped from her shoulders. In another universe, maybe they'd be kissing at prom or at the end of a date. For now, she'd pretend they were.

Henry's mind touched hers, and then recoiled. But it was too late. The weight of reality was back, and she pulled away.

"Not yet," Thai said, and his fingers were back in her hair. "What if this is the last one?"

Their lips connected again, and the kiss lost its sweetness and became desperate. When Valerie pulled away again, there were tears in both of their eyes.

She took his weapon out of the sheath at his side and checked to make sure it was sharpened and fully charged with light, and he tucked a lock of her hair that escaped her braid behind her ear.

With a breath that steadied the shuddering inside her, Valerie mentally reviewed her plan. She was ready to fight.

ℒℴ   ℒℴ   ℒℴ

Valerie strode into The Horseshoe like she owned it, holding her blazing sword in her hand. Her army was striking here first not only to retake Silva, but also to divert Reaper's attention and forces from Earth. It was a distraction, so she had to make it a good one.

"Morning, Fractus! We've brought the fight to your doorstep this time. Who wants to come out and claim the title of the Fractus who slayed the vivicus leader of the Fist?"

Her words had the desired effect of drawing Fractus from the guilds and the winding streets of Silva. A crowd was gathering, but no one came within reach of Valerie's blade.

Kellen zoomed from the window of the crumbling Weapons Guild. His eyes were manic when he saw her.

"Is the vivicus finally ready to shed blood? We relish it!" he cried. "Kill her!"

There was a ripple in the crowd as a bear charged through. The Grand Master of the Illuminators' Guild roared as he approached. Over his giant paws was a pair of black mitts that exuded power.

As soon as the light from her sword touched his gloves, they disintegrated on his hands. The bear hid his surprise well, but he was off kilter. Valerie met his charge with a fist to his face, holding back her full force so she didn't kill him in a single blow.

She unleashed enough of her magic to knock him unconscious, and the crowd erupted. Kellen's screech of dismay was close enough that she knew he'd try to shower her with his dark dust soon. Before Kellen reached her side or the crowd of Fractus mobbed her, Valerie made eye contact with Mira, who pumped his fist in the air once.

"At last, Knights, our hour has come!"

"What's this?" Kellen asked, stopping midflight.

A shower of golden arrows of light shot into the crowd from the sky. Cyrus had made them more powerful than any that had been used before, and everywhere dark weapons turned back to metal.

In the resulting chaos, all of the Knights who had patiently remained embedded in the Fractus for months now unsheathed their blades of light, to the dismay of their ex-comrades. Cyrus had equipped all of the Knights with basic light weapons, and a few, including Mira, with weapons that had more complex light patterns woven into them.

"My Knights! What are you doing? Stop this now!" Kellen cried to no avail. His tiny hands were tearing at the hair on his head, reminding Valerie of Rastelli when he'd descended into madness.

Lyonesse reached up and swatted him out of the air.

He buzzed toward her face. "You are loyal to me, to the Fractus. I know you are!"

"Not anymore," Lyonesse said.

They were the last words Valerie could make out as screams of rage filled the air and weapons clashed. The fighting was fierce and bloody as Knights unleashed the rage they had kept on a tether for so long, and betrayed Fractus lashed out against those they had trusted.

Valerie reined in her own horror at the ferocity of the fighting, which she had not anticipated. The death toll would be immense. But she didn't have time to analyze her miscalculation as she dodged the blows of the multiple attackers who surrounded her. They were no match for her blade, which made short work of their black weapons.

The sound of a loud caw reached Valerie's ears over the fighting, and she saw Dasan's great red wings beating as he flew over the battle. From his wings drifted something that looked like snow. It fell on the fighters below. A bit landed on Valerie, and a measure of peace came over her.

Dasan was using his power to calm the crowd, and she was grateful. Maybe it would ease the intense bloodlust that was making this battle so bitter. He landed on the roof of the Empathy Collective, his signal to her that the Empaths were inside, using their power to confuse the Fractus. Valerie hoped that Elle would be safe.

Henry's mind touched hers. He'd spotted Reaper in one of the towers of the Weapons Guild, observing the mayhem. That was her cue.

Valerie gripped her vial of sand and was transported to the Atacama Desert. She raised her sword above her and sent a bolt of pure light into the air, her signal to Chisisi that she was on Earth. She soon made out Sanguina, Chisisi, and Cyrus on the horizon, in front of a crowd of human and Conjuror soldiers.

There was no way to sneak up on the Fractus on Earth, so all they could do was charge. The Fractus in the camp attacked before Valerie could even make out their forms in the distance, sending bolts of lightning into the rushing body of soldiers.

Most bounced off the shields that Leo had specially designed to deflect the lightning that the Fractus wielded, but a few met their mark, and the smell of blood and charred flesh was released into the air, choking Valerie.

By the time they reached the camp, Valerie could see that it was crawling with hundreds of Fractus, far more than when she'd been there last time. With the benefit of even a few minutes of preparation, the Fractus were more organized than those on the Globe had been.

But Valerie had placed her most skilled fighters in the contingent of the Fist on Earth, and the Fractus would be overpowered in under an hour, by her estimate, unless Reaper diverted forces from the Globe.

Sanguina moved through the Fractus with a grim, lethal grace, in spite of her leg. She disabled one, two, three Fractus, her muscles straining as her light weapon met dark. The fourth Fractus she encountered was gored by her sword when she narrowly dodged a dagger to her side. Valerie saw

361

the ex-vampyre's face tighten at the sight of her kill, but she didn't pause.

Cyrus had maneuvered to the tent with the pool of black Carne, but before he could enter, a Fractus yanked him by his collar, sending him reeling. Cyrus fell, and he scrabbled in the sand before he was able to stand. He barely had time to raise his shield of light before the Fractus pounded it with a black club, which shattered on impact.

By then, Chisisi had come up behind the Fractus and hit him over the head with the flat of his blade.

The air crackled with the peculiar energy that surrounded Reaper when he was angry, and Valerie spotted him at the edge of the camp, snarling instructions to his soldiers.

He was red with rage, but not worried, and Valerie saw why. More Fractus were popping into the camp to defend it, eating away at the slight edge the Fist had gained when they first arrived.

A cool breeze kissed Valerie's cheek, and she recognized Kanti's signal. The Fist's reinforcements from Elsinore were close, with Kanti leading the soldiers.

After Cyrus went inside the tent, she gripped a piece of bark from a tree in Arden, and the world dissolved into the trees that surrounded Silva.

ye   ye   ye

Skye was pawing the ground, as if he could barely contain himself to wait for her signal. Alex and Olwain were pacing nearby, but they stopped moving when they saw her.

Only Jack, who already has his blade unsheathed and held at the ready, spoke when he saw her. "Finally! Me and

362

my boys were about to go ahead without waiting for your signal."

"I'm here now. And it's time to take back our home," she said.

She didn't speak loudly, but somehow her soldiers heard her. Their battle cries were joyful as they rushed into the streets of Silva. Soldiers pounded on the doors of known Fist sympathizers to see if more people could be rallied to join the fight.

Her people flooded the streets, pouring toward The Horseshoe, where the bitterest part of the battle still raged. The Fractus had spotted the Fist's reinforcements, and Valerie saw them all glancing up, toward a window of the History Guild.

Something was up there that they were waiting for, she knew with sudden clarity. Reaper had to know she might try to retake Silva, and he was ready.

She raced to the History Guild, touching Henry's mind to let him know what she'd seen. An image of Thai flashed from his mind to hers.

No! She couldn't let Thai get in the middle of this. He was meant to stay with the Healers. He and Cara were supposed to team up to deliver light treatments to those who were touched by the black blades. But Henry had already left the Globe to fight by Kanti's side, and her only chance to keep Thai out of the worst of the fighting had vanished.

Valerie barely saw the steps of the History Guild as she ascended them, and she nearly smacked into least ten Fractus with black eyes.

She'd never encountered so many, and even her sword of light seemed less bright in their presence. Valerie swept her blade around her, and inside the circle of its light, she was safe.

But two sprung at once, and her weapon slipped from her grasp as she moved it so she didn't accidentally kill one of them.

"It's like I told you, she won't kill us. Attack without fear," the Fractus nearest her said. The black eyes threw her for an instant, but Valerie recognized Ani, even with her new power blazing.

This was not magic forced into existence by Henry's power. Valerie suspected that Reaper was testing his ability to manipulate the Carne from Plymouth in new ways, and Ani had been one of the first to benefit. The thought terrified her, but she didn't have time to consider all of the implications.

Valerie ducked and rolled, sweeping up her blade in the process. She parried the blows of her attackers and deliberately positioned herself so that she was closer to the stairwell that led to the top of the History Guild's tower.

She had one foot on the bottom step when she heard Thai's shouts. Ani and the other Fractus were divided now, as several turned to combat the new threat. She could tell that Thai hadn't come alone, and soon, she was only battling two Fractus by herself. She jabbed one in the neck with an elbow and sent the second one stumbling backward with a powerful kick to his shoulder.

The way up the stairs was clear, but she couldn't wrench her gaze from Thai, who was fighting a Fractus with two dark knives. Her self-control almost crumbled, when she remembered the look on the faces of the Fractus who were glancing up at the tower of the History Guild. Even Reaper's own soldiers were afraid of what was up there.

She hurried up the stairs and stopped at a large, heavy wooden door. Kicking her way in, even with her magic blasting through her veins, was no easy feat, but she managed it after a few tries. The shelves of the room were lined with books, and a giant desk was next to the window.

It could have been the ordinary office of the History Guild's Grand Master, if the Grand Master wasn't Reaper, and there wasn't an orb hovering in the air in the middle of the room.

The ball was made of glass. A hollow place inside held a gas that had a faint grayish color to it, like trapped cigarette smoke.

Valerie plucked it out of the air at the same moment that Reaper stepped through a portal that immediately collapsed behind him.

His motions were unhurried as he examined his scythe. "I thought my plans for Earth could not be achieved without your brother's power, and that killing you would destroy him. But last night, I fully harnessed the power of the Carne, and I have another option. You and Henry are now disposable, and now I can do what's best for everyone, for the greater good of two worlds."

Valerie was gripping her vial of sand from the Atacama Desert in her hand so that she could escape with the orb, but nothing happened.

There was a faint buzzing around her, and Valerie knew that Reaper was manipulating the rules of magic, not letting her leave. She tucked the orb under her left arm and raised her sword with the other.

"No more theatrics. You want what's contained in that orb? You can have it," he said, his tone vicious.

The orb dissolved, and the gas inside spread through the air. One breath was enough to know that it was more than smoke. The bitter taste of ashes filled her lungs, making her cough and her eyes water.

"These particles of Carne will eat away at your power, and then your life," Reaper said. "If you'd waited another day, I'd have perfected it to work quickly. But since you sought to surprise me, you will suffer for hours before the gas is finished with you."

Reaper threw open a window, and the rest of the particles flew through it, poisoning the world.

"You'll kill them all!" she said.

"Only those who do not bear one of my weapons. And a culling must take place so there is room for a new order."

Was it her imagination, or did her magic already have holes in it? Still, she packed enough power into her punch to crack Reaper's cheekbone when her fist connected with it.

Despite knowing that she had likely lost the war in this tower, the blow gave a deep, angry part of her complete satisfaction, even when Reaper retaliated with a burst of magic that singed her arms, dissolving the top layer of her skin.

Thai burst into the room with four soldiers of the Fist, including Mira and Claremont.

At the sight of the Knights who had betrayed him, Reaper's expression turned into a snarl. "Take a deep breath. Your punishment for your betrayal is already in place."

Reaper paused, as if he was listening to something that she couldn't hear. Then his eyes assessed the four soldiers of the Fist before him, as if he were gauging how much time he'd need to kill them. Valerie's heart beat fast, but steady, ready to fight him. She didn't have the chance. Reaper stepped through a portal back to the Atacama Desert.

"If he returned to the desert, then I need to follow," Valerie said, but Claremont yanked her by the arm so she was forced to stop.

"What'd he mean about us already being punished for betraying him?" Claremont demanded. She was a little pale, and her eyes were dilated.

Valerie knew she couldn't let her soldiers lose focus with panic. "He released a poison into the air made from that black sludge in Plymouth. If we survive this battle, we'll find a cure."

"Some part of me knew following you would kill me!" Claremont spat, though Valerie knew her former enemy had joined the Fist because she'd thought it would give her a better chance at survival.

"No one's dead yet," Thai said.

Mira nodded his agreement. "What's next?"

Valerie's mind worked fast, assessing her options. "Reaper considers his victory in Silva assured now, and maybe he's right. He'll send his forces to the Atacama Desert. I'll rally as many of our soldiers as I can to follow him, starting with the People of the Woods."

Claremont stuck out her lower lip, and Valerie was glad to see her fear transforming into her usual resentment. "So much for the element of surprise keeping us a step ahead."

Valerie met her gaze. "Now we'll have to rely on skill, passion, and knowing that right is on our side. Now get back down there and direct your rage where it belongs—at the Fractus."

ؼ   ؼ   ؼ

Thai followed Valerie to Arbor Aurum as she snuck out of the History Guild and raced to the woods. In preparation for the battle, another entrance to the cities in the trees had been created closer to The Horseshoe, so they didn't have to run far. When they ascended the tree, Elden and his People were in their armor, awaiting her signal. A nervous Juniper was present, as well, screwing and unscrewing the canister with Valerie's poppy.

"Whither wander we?" Elden asked, his extra-formal speech the only sign of his own anxiety.

Valerie saw his daughter unsheathing her blade so that Leo could check it one last time. He ran his finger along its edge and nodded. How many more would fall today?

Valerie called Leo over and quickly explained Reaper's poison to him and Elden. They listened without changing expression, and she was grateful for their calmness, as her own heart beat in double time.

"Do you think this trick of Reaper's is as powerful as he says?" Thai asked.

Leo pricked Valerie and then Thai with a sharp needle and took some of their blood. "I cannot say. I will work with the lightweavers on an antidote, but you must send Cyrus as soon as he can get away. No one uses light magic as creatively as he does."

"Cara is in the People's hospital, and her lightweaver powers have grown since you saw her last," Elden said, and dispatched a messenger to find her. "What of the rest of the People's soldiers?"

"We all go to Earth," Valerie said. "We have to accept that Silva is lost. I don't know how far Reaper's poison will spread, but the People of the Woods are safer on Earth, and we must seize that victory if we still can."

Elden left to deliver Valerie's orders to the People, and Valerie shut her eyes, allowing herself a minute of escape.

"I'm not leaving your side," Thai said, gently gripping her arms. "I know you're thinking that I belong with Cara and the Healers, but I don't. If you're going to use your vivicus power, or Cyrus wants to blast people with fireballs, or Henry launches some kind of mental attack, you need me to amplify your powers."

"I'm not going to fight you on this. Selfish or not, I want you at my side. Even if we win, we might end up dead, anyway. Might as well be together."

Thai laced his fingers with hers, and she gripped her vial of sand.

Chapter 40

Grunts of effort, shouts of triumph, and screams of pain made a gruesome soundtrack to the battle that raged in the Atacama Desert. Valerie's eyes scanned the scene, and the horror of it all overcame her. She threw up on her shoes.

Thai held her hair, and she was grateful when he didn't say anything about it. There were no words of comfort for what was happening now, all under her direction. She could tell herself there was no other way, that this was all in the name of keeping Earth free, but a part of her couldn't justify the carnage.

Henry's mind touched hers, and her gaze flew to a glassy dune to the north of where she stood. She saw Kanti's swan flag first, a rallying point for her soldiers. Nearby, Henry and Kanti were fighting back-to-back. Kanti held her staff, but it was more of an accessory than a weapon, since she was using magic to conjure up thorny branches that pricked her enemies with light.

Henry wasn't using his light-infused machete much, either. Valerie peeked in his mind and saw that he was using his psychic powers to confuse the Fractus's minds, like his fellow Empaths were on the Globe. Valerie wished that she'd had the foresight to have a contingent of Empaths on Earth.

"To Henry," she said to Thai, and together, they entered the fray.

With their hands clasped, Thai and Valerie became a powerful force. If Reaper's dark particles were chipping away at the magic within her, she couldn't tell while touching Thai.

Even fighting one-handed, she had to rein herself in so that she didn't cause fatal damage to the Fractus she encountered. Thai's hand was tense in hers, and she knew that he was also struggling to wield the immense power they created together.

Though they were holding back, they slammed through the fighting like a freight train, leaving a path of unconscious bodies littered on either side of them. In her peripheral vision, Valerie thought she saw Reaper's dark scythe cutting through her soldiers, but when she turned to verify it, he was gone.

They were still a distance away from Henry and Kanti when Valerie saw Ani walking through the crowd. Valerie's guess as to Reaper's tactic was apparently correct—he was sending his best soldiers to Earth.

Ani's sweet voice worked its magic. The soldiers it touched dropped to one knee, heads bowed, creating a path for her to walk down unhindered. Her gaze was sharp and focused on one thing—Kanti.

"Look out!" Valerie shouted, her voice lost in the battle sounds.

But Henry's mind was connected with hers, and he spotted Ani when she was a few yards away. Ani's eyes went black, and Kanti's staff and Henry's daggers flickered as darkness descended around them like a fog.

Both of their weapons had been embedded with Cyrus's new light treatment, but it was no match for the power Ani was wielding.

Ani spared a glance at Valerie and then shouted an order that Valerie couldn't hear. Quickly, she and Thai were ringed by a dozen black-eyed Fractus.

Valerie was forced to focus on the battle in front of her, and she only saw snatches of Henry and Kanti's vicious fight with Ani. She saw Ani strike Kanti, sending her reeling, and Henry's ineffective swipe with his dim weapon. She made out the screech of frustration when Ani sprang on Kanti, and Kanti's vines wound around her arms and threw her off.

Valerie didn't see the blow that killed Ani. She and Thai broke through the circle of Fractus and saw Kanti's white face and bloody staff. Ani lay still, her skull dented, at Kanti's feet. Henry's arm was around Kanti's waist, but he was concentrating on diverting the attention of any Fractus near them so they didn't attack while Kanti was stunned.

Kanti's eyes connected with Valerie's. "I killed her. I've never killed anyone before."

"You were defending your life, and making the world safe for people with no magic," Valerie said.

Kanti nodded once, and she seemed to shake off her stupor. "I knew one of us had to die, and I'm glad it wasn't me. But she was my friend, once."

Thai squeezed Valerie's hand, and she jump-kicked an approaching Fractus. She hit him in the chest, and he flew twenty-five feet.

"We have to get to the tent with the Carne," Henry said. "I saw Cyrus and Sanguina go in there a while ago, and I don't know how many Fractus they had to battle once they were inside."

Kanti sucked in a breath and dashed away a stray tear. "I hope my soldiers didn't see that. Not good for morale to see your princess crying like a teenage girl."

"We are teenage girls," Valerie said. "Ones who save the universe."

Her words had the desired effect of eliciting a little smile from Kanti, and the four of them began making their way to the tent with the pool of Carne inside.

Valerie didn't know if the Fractus were actively avoiding the four of them, or if they simply fought together efficiently, but battling their way to the tent only took minutes.

Valerie pushed her way into the tent, which was partially shredded on one side. Inside, she heard a strangled scream and saw Sanguina writhing on the ground. Reaper stood over her, his eyes glazed and his body humming with power.

Cyrus had his arm in the black pool up to his elbow, and all of the light that usually surrounded him was gone. He was pale, and his face was covered in sweat.

"I couldn't alter it," he said, his voice weak.

Valerie yanked Cyrus out of the pool, and Henry threw himself on top of Sanguina. He moaned as his body took the brunt of Reaper's punishing magic.

"No," Sanguina said, and she heaved Henry off of her. "Do what you came to do. Follow the plan."

Juniper and Elden stumbled through the tent, a half a dozen Fractus on their heels. Valerie saw Reaper's eyes flicker over the group of them and land on the glowing poppy in Elden's hands.

Reaper raised a hand in the air, and Sanguina's scream reached a higher pitch, and then ceased. Her body dissolved before Valerie could reach her side. She didn't have time to react to what had happened to her friend before the Carne crawled out of the pool and surrounded Reaper. This time, it covered his entire body and disappeared into his pores.

As Valerie stared at the space where Sanguina had been, her grief choking her, one of Reaper's Fractus landed a blow to her skull. She fell, releasing Thai's hand.

Before the Fractus could follow up with another attack, Kanti smashed him in the chest with her staff. Henry gave Valerie a hand to stand up, and their power joined, giving her a jolt of energy.

Valerie examined Reaper, and even wreathed in Carne, she could read the fear in his eyes. All four of the pillars were in one room, and Thai was there to amplify their powers. Somehow, they'd all made it to this spot, alive, as she'd planned.

She stood, gripping Henry's hand, and Henry reached for Kanti, who reached for Cyrus. Valerie staggered to Cyrus and grasped his other hand, creating a circle with Juniper, Elden, and the poppy in the middle. Their shared magic flowed between them, and Valerie shuddered at the sweet burn of it within her. Then Thai laid a hand on her shoulder, and the sensation peaked as it ignited the power embedded in the glass dunes that surrounded them.

Her friends all gasped at the same time she did, and their heads snapped backward. Valerie was blinded by the light pouring out of them all, lighting up the circle they formed like a star. The tent surrounding them crumbled, and the Fractus near them were blown back like they were at the epicenter of an explosion.

Even Reaper staggered backward. He struggled to come closer to them, but it was like he was fighting a strong wind. Inside the circle, though, everything was warm and calm. The dark particles of Carne had been eviscerated by the light.

Their combined magic settled in her core, and her friends' trust poured into her mind. It was hers to wield, to steer, as she willed.

She turned their magic on the remaining Carne in the pool, and it started to bubble. As it boiled, the color changed to something molten, and when it flowed toward Reaper, he grunted at its touch. With all this power, they could end his life, turn the Carne in his pores to lava that would burn him alive.

"It's not enough," she whispered, knowing that her friends could hear her. "We end this for now, but for how long? We have to use this magic for something greater than a victory today."

The solution she had searched for had been behind a door in her mind that now sprang open. Her friends' magic surged in response to her own at the realization of what had to be done.

They sent their magic out, out into the world in an ecstatic burst of power, exploding like a nuclear bomb. But instead of ending the world, they would save it. Their magic rippled out, igniting the spark of magic within the first human it touched.

Soon hundreds, thousands, millions of people were touched by the burst of power, their magic awakened, and it continued to spread until it encased the planet in a glow.

As quick as a thought, they were in Arden, in the middle of The Horseshoe, and their combined light detonated again. The pulse was less powerful than the one on Earth, but Valerie knew that it was enough to drive out the poisonous particles of Carne that Reaper had released into the Globe's atmosphere. She caught a glimpse of Skye and Jack's twin expressions of surprise before they flicked back to Earth.

In its sheath at her side, her sword trembled, as if the soul of Pathos was sending her a message. Without reading the words on its hilt, Valerie knew that its promise had come true today. The Balance was restored. Humans would never be under the thumb of Fractus or Conjurors, because now, they were all united by magic.

Juniper gripped the poppy, ready to bind Earth's magic. She smiled. They didn't need it now.

"It's okay. Don't—" Valerie began, when a movement at the edge of her vision distracted her.

Before she could turn to face Reaper's raised scythe, Cyrus shoved her, hard, and she fell to the ground. Abruptly, the light, the connection, the pool of magic within her vanished.

The absence of her link with Henry, Cyrus, and Kanti was so disorienting that her brain didn't process what happened.

She touched something warm and wet and red. Reaper had cut through Cyrus with his scythe, slicing him cleanly through his torso. He'd been aiming for her, and Cyrus had saved her. Again. Without pausing, even to gloat, Reaper stomped on the flower that Juniper dropped when he raised his blade.

Valerie hardly noticed. She could think of nothing except saving her best friend. But when she gripped Cyrus's hand, she couldn't release her power into his still form. He was gone.

Valerie opened her mouth to scream, but she wasn't sure if she made a sound, because for a few seconds, she couldn't hear anything. She almost gave in to the darkness at the edges of her vision, but then her mind became clear, more focused than she'd ever been before.

No. She would not allow Cyrus to be dead.

Thai hauled her to her feet as Reaper turned to her. She was his next target. Her emotions were curiously absent, even when his face was inches from hers. In one swift move, she knew that she could unsheathe her sword of light and plunge it through Reaper. It might kill him, and there was a kind of poetic justice that the sword Cyrus had crafted with a piece of himself would be the weapon that killed his murderer.

But she couldn't summon any hate, staring into the eyes of the man who had tortured her brother, murdered her father, imprisoned her mother for eternity, and now slayed Cyrus. Instead, something more powerful rose in her. She didn't want any more blood and ugliness in the world.

She'd heal Reaper. If she saved him, she'd save Cyrus. Together, they'd bring her best friend back, use Reaper's magic to turn back time or activate his cells or something. They'd find a way.

Valerie's vivicus power leaped to the surface, and with Thai's hand gripping hers, its flow was hers to control. She'd find whatever darkness lived in Reaper and snuff it out, like she'd done with Henry's depression.

Whatever Reaper had been expecting, it wasn't this. She poured her power into him, chasing out the darkness inside him. The Carne oozed back out of his pores, pushed out by her magic. But the darkness was still there, embedded in the fabric of his being.

Reaper's mouth was open, and his hands opened and shut helplessly at his sides. Valerie attacked the evil inside of him with every drop of her magic, knowing that she was going farther than she ever had before. She was fearless as she

377

poured herself into him, driving out the evil that was intertwined with his soul.

A part of her mind heard Henry screaming at her to stop, to let go of her power, but it continued to pulse out of her. It wasn't that she couldn't stop its flow—she didn't want to. She'd take the evil that had killed Cyrus and banish it from existence, even if she sacrificed her mind in the process. If she poured enough of herself, enough of her magic, into Reaper, she'd bring back Cyrus. The alternative couldn't be borne.

Her power blew through Reaper, dissolving all of the darkness it found, until there was no more, but whether it was no more darkness or no more of her own magic to fight it, she wasn't sure.

She was limp, but remained standing, only swaying slightly. Reaper's gaze was puzzled, as if he was staring at something inside her that he couldn't understand. His pulse beat erratically in his throat, and then he moaned, gripping his chest, and collapsed to the ground.

Thai knelt beside Reaper and gripped his wrist. "He's dead."

Valerie started shaking all over. "No, that's not right."

Henry's mind touched hers as he held her hand. "It's okay. You didn't kill him. If you did, you'd be dead, too. Remember?"

"I healed him. I saved him," she said, knowing she was babbling, but unable to stop. "He's alive, and good, and now we're going to save Cyrus."

She got on her knees and tried to pour more of her vivicus magic into Reaper, but it met a wall.

"It was a heart attack," Thai said, his tone gentle.

"I killed him," Valerie said. "And Cyrus...Cyrus..."

If the ground beneath her feet dropped out from under her, it would make more sense than Cyrus being gone. The pain went too deep for tears.

"Oh, please, don't let it be true," Valerie whispered, as Thai pulled her to him.

Henry rested his hand on her shoulder. "You can't fold yet. Stay with me. We're not done."

The raw pain of losing Cyrus threatened to swallow her, but she pushed it back. Not yet. She sucked in a steadying breath and turned to meet Henry's eyes, allowing him into her mind so he could see that she'd hold it together, for now.

She took a step forward and almost tripped over Reaper's corpse. She'd almost forgotten about him, even as she'd tried to heal him. She was surprised that she felt nothing toward Reaper anymore. No rage for what he'd done, or guilt over causing his death. Only a little relief that her greatest enemy—the world's greatest enemy—was dead.

Chapter 41

Valerie felt detached from herself, as if her body could go on working and fighting, even though her heart was broken. The part of her mind that wasn't reliving Cyrus's death considered the battle still raging around her. The Fractus were shaken, their weapons slipping as they cast glances at Reaper's body lying behind her. With the reinforcements from the People of the Woods, the Fist had the advantage.

Henry gave her a mint that would amplify her voice. "End this. They need to know Reaper's gone."

Valerie sucked on the mint before speaking. "Your leader has fallen. I know many of you fought at Reaper's side out of fear, and I ask you to cast down your weapons. I cannot promise that you will all be pardoned, but I do swear that you will all receive justice."

The Grand Master of the Illuminators' Guild was the first to throw down his weapon. The bear loped toward her, and Valerie tensed.

He stopped in front of her and spoke. "The vivicus could have killed me more than once, or ordered someone to do it, but she never did. I know she held back her magic so she didn't do more damage than she had to. I will surrender to her and abide by the decision of the Justice Guild."

After hearing his words, more Fractus dropped their weapons, and those left gripping theirs were outnumbered. They followed suit grudgingly.

Chisisi wound his way through the crowd to stand by her side. "Per your orders, my people are prepared to take the Fractus prisoners."

"Per your suggestion, you mean," Valerie said with a slight smile. "I never thought we'd make it to the point where we'd be the ones in a position to organize the surrender."

Chisisi smiled, a real one that made his eyes crinkle. "My suggestion, then. I had faith in you when I first met you at Mena House. Today, you lived up to my highest hopes. I thank you for your service."

Chisisi hugged her, and her body sagged. His kindness nearly unraveled her, right there on the battlefield, but she couldn't let herself feel yet. She pushed her friend away and took a deep, shaky breath.

"Go home, young miss."

"Soon," she promised.

ళ   ళ   ళ

In Silva, the fighting continued to rage, fierce and brutal. When word spread that Reaper was dead and Valerie was offering to protect anyone who surrendered, the effect wasn't as powerful as it had been on Earth.

It was a civil war—Knights fighting Knights, guilds turning against each other. So Valerie raised her sword and entered the fray with Thai and Henry. She tried not to think about how Cyrus should have been there, too, meeting with the Healers and helping with light treatments.

381

Explosions rocked The Horseshoe as Steven and Willa used dynamite to keep the Fractus constantly moving. It was effective in preventing them from rallying into cohesive groups, but it was devastating to the buildings. The guilds, which were already pock-marked with chips from the battle, crumbled further.

Kanti brought her soldiers back from Earth to help with the battle in Silva, and even though they were weary, sheer numbers had the effect that Valerie's words hadn't. The Fractus who didn't retreat were captured, and the fighting ended as the light from the day disappeared.

"What's next?" she asked, after she and Skye finalized the details of the surrender inside the heavily damaged Capitol Building.

The centaur bowed his head and swayed a little on his hooves. "We rest."

Valerie patted his flank. "You're right. Let's get some sleep."

Henry had left with Kanti hours ago, but Thai had waited for her. He was asleep on a bench in the hall, his head tipped back against the wall. His face was gray, and for the first time, Valerie thought about the toll the day had taken on him. If it wouldn't completely humiliate him, she'd scoop him up and carry him home like a baby. She was strong enough.

The idea almost made her grin, but she thought of who would laugh the hardest at that idea and her mirth vanished. Had she forgotten, even for a second, that her best friend was dead? An image of Cyrus's blood, still slick on her hands, passed through her mind with perfect clarity, and all of her self-control crumbled.

She heard the echoes of Sanguina's cries before Reaper killed her, and images of the bodies that littered the desert and The Horseshoe kept coming and coming, a kind of mental torture that made what Zunya and Sanguina had done to her as a child pale in comparison. Flecks of Cyrus's blood were still on her hands, which began to shake uncontrollably.

One of her tears hit Thai's cheek, and he woke up.

"How am I supposed to survive this?" she asked him.

Even tired and battered, he didn't miss a beat. "With me. This is only the first night. It won't always hurt this much."

ം ം ം

Valerie couldn't remember walking home and going to bed. When she woke up, it was dark outside, and she guessed that she'd slept through the entire day. Her grief was a weight on her chest, like a living thing that wouldn't budge, but the sharp edge of her pain had dulled a little.

She cracked an eye open and saw Clarabelle sleeping with her nose on Valerie's windowsill. Even asleep, the little unicorn lent her a measure of peace.

Welcome back. Azra joined her foal at Valerie's window, her mane shining silver in the starlight. *Clarabelle told me of your change. How do you feel?*

"My change?" Valerie rubbed her eyes, trying to focus.

Your vivicus powers are but an ember inside of you after expending them so completely on Reaper. They are not completely gone, but no longer yours to wield.

Valerie turned her gaze inward, frantic at first, searching for the power that was always at her core, a kind of fuel that was as fundamental to who she was as her DNA. It was still there, but now, it was like looking at it from behind bulletproof glass, untouchable.

383

"I'll never be able to save anyone again?" she asked, not sure whether she was relieved or terrified.

Not with your vivicus power. But now, it cannot strip your mind.

"I'm free," Valerie said, and even with all of the horror she had yet to process, the idea was exhilarating.

She wouldn't mentally abandon Henry and Thai and everyone she loved. She wouldn't ever forget Midnight, Dulcea, Sanguina, her dad, Cyrus. The relief that they'd always be with her was profound.

You have created a new possibility for a future that has never been conceived of before. There is work ahead, but it doesn't have to be your work if you don't want it to be. The war is over. You could truly be free now.

Valerie combed her fingers through Clarabelle's mane, and the unicorn's sounds of contentment pinged her mind. She didn't know if she'd ever be free of her memories, but she'd learn to be happy some times in spite of them, she hoped.

"Will I see more of you and Clarabelle now that the war is over? Will the Grand Masters elect you as their Grand Chair now that Reaper's gone?"

You will see me, though not as Grand Chair. Clarabelle and I have a new calling.

Valerie was puzzled. "What do you mean?"

Azra's smile was so warm that her eyes seemed to glow. *A new race of unicorns is rising. Clarabelle will not be alone. Together, we will usher in a new generation.*

Valerie didn't breathe, afraid she'd break the magic of the moment. "How is that possible?"

The legends say unicorns arose from Arctic snows laced with the purest magic. Vivicus magic could be the only thing that would have made such a thing happen again. When you saved Clarabelle's life, you awakened the possibility of future generations of unicorns within her. Then, when you and your friends awakened the magic within everyone, you also awakened long-dormant magic within the Earth. That combination of power has allowed our race to arise again.

It was a legacy that even Cyrus would have deemed worthy of him.

Thank you, Valerie.

❧ ❧ ❧

Valerie couldn't sleep after talking with Azra, so she decided to visit the hospital in Arbor Aurum to meet with her wounded soldiers. Azra might say her responsibility as leader of the Fist had ended, but she knew better. She owed her soldiers a debt that couldn't be repaid, but for the ones who still lived, she could acknowledge it.

The sounds within the People's hospital made Valerie's stomach clench. Would this war ever truly be over, or would the sounds of it, the wounds from it, live with her forever? She moved from bed to bed, clutching hands and murmuring words that she hoped were comforting.

She saw Kanti's dad, George, quietly singing to a soldier who was missing an arm and moaning in pain. The healing power of George's song put the soldier to sleep. Valerie knew that, somewhere, Kanti's sisters Isabella and Amaryllis, along with their mother, Pauline, were also helping the sick for a few days before they returned to Elsinore. Peach was working with Kanti to get the soldiers from Elsinore paid and returned home. Valerie avoided them all, not up to the task of small talk in the face of so much suffering.

385

She almost tripped over Cara, who was bent over the bed of a moaning soldier. Light pulsed from her, and the moaning stopped. Cara turned and saw Valerie, and her face seized up, as if she were in intense pain.

"I'm sorry—" Valerie began, but Cara stopped her with a fierce hug.

"Don't. Everything you could say I already know. If my brother had to die, then he went the way he would have wanted, as a hero, saving the person he loved the most. I could never blame you. The only person to blame is dead, right?"

Valerie nodded, hardly able to speak without crying. "Your parents?"

Cara had moved her parents into a home in the trees a few days before the battle, and a cowardly part of Valerie had been grateful that she hadn't had to face them when she returned to her home.

Cara wiped a stray tear from her cheek. "They want to go home, to Messina, and to take me with them."

Ceru approached them, and his expression as he watched Cara was tender. "I hope you will not leave us. Or me."

Cara's ears turned pink, and she had trouble meeting Ceru's gaze. "Why?"

"Because we need you here."

Valerie quietly slipped away, leaving them to their moment. In spite of his protectiveness, Cyrus would have been glad that his sister found solace in her love for someone that he had trusted, too.

She saw a glow coming from someone sitting on a cot nearby. The light was so warm, like Cyrus's, that she almost thought he'd found a way back to her, after all. But a second look showed her a form that she was much more familiar with seeing at a hospital bedside.

"Dr. Freeman?" she asked.

His face was lit up when he saw her. "I have magic now. I can work with light."

"That is—was—my best friend's power," she said softly, so she didn't choke on the words.

"Whatever you and your friends did today, it woke up my power inside me. There are so many more people I can help now that you've made magic possible on both worlds," Dr. Freeman said.

The way the light in the room clung to him reminded her so much of Cyrus that she had to shut her eyes to get her bearings. "You're here to help with light treatments for the Conjurors who were touched by the dark blades?"

"Yes. That's where I'm most needed today. But I am eager to talk with the Healers to see what we can do to help humans. Think of the thousands, millions of lives we can save."

Dr. Freeman's awe was a brilliant thing, and it made Valerie smile when she didn't think the muscles in her face would ever remember how to do such a thing again.

"Thank you," she said, and he gripped her in a hug.

"I could not be more proud of you for what you accomplished today if you were my own daughter."

Years later, when Valerie remembered that conversation, she knew that it was his words that kept her heart from going into a deep freeze of guilt and grief.

༄ ༄ ༄

Thai was waiting for her on the doorstep, sketching on his drawing pad, when she returned home. She hadn't seen him do that since before the war had started, and it made her smile, especially when she saw that he was drawing the curve of a neck that looked a lot like her own. When he saw her, he quickly put it away.

"Emin?" she asked, deciding not to embarrass him by demanding to see what he'd been working on.

"Still at Elden's. I think he might decide to stay there," Thai said. "I'm going to miss that little guy. He was a bright spot in this house."

"I can see how Henry and I might not be the most lighthearted of roommates. I can't imagine how bleak it would have been around here without Emin...and you."

Thai stood, and she came closer so she could peer up at his shadowed face.

"You brought me joy, too," he said, his voice low. "Every day, even when I was scared of the risks you were taking or mad at how you didn't take care of yourself. I know you can't think about us being together right now, with losing Cyrus and figuring out your vivicus powers. But can I hold you?"

She leaned forward and pressed her cheek against his heart. His arms around her were warm and tight. At last, she didn't have to fight what she wanted any longer. Her mind had survived the war, and now her vivicus power was tucked away from her, where it couldn't hurt her anymore.

"I can think about it. I don't want to go another day without you, Thai."

He pulled away then so he could look into her face. Her conversation with Azra tumbled out, and Thai listened to every word.

He kissed her forehead. "This doesn't change much for me. I want what I've always wanted—to be with you. But I'm glad that now you can let yourself be with me, too."

"That's all I want right now," she said. "Everything hurts except being with you."

"Here. I saw you peeking," Thai said, handing her his drawing pad.

Valerie opened it, and flipping through, found sketch after sketch of herself. The way he saw her... She was powerful and beautiful in his eyes.

"Check out the date of the first sketch," he said, smiling as he watched her reaction to what he'd created.

It was dated the day after they'd met at her hospital.

"I think I knew, even then, that you were in my heart to stay."

"Me, too," she said, remembering how she'd felt when she spotted him out of the window in her room at the Oakland Children's Hospital.

"I'm not going to think about anything else other than us for a while, and neither are you," he said, and he brushed his lips against hers.

He was right. She didn't think about Cyrus or war or loss or anything other than Thai for a long time.

Chapter 42

Weeks passed, and Valerie busied herself with days of dealing with the messy business of the aftermath of war and wrestling with her grief, and nights spent lying outside, staring up at the stars and catching up on a lifetime of conversation with Thai. It was a combination of acute pain and utter sweetness, a swing of an emotional pendulum that almost made her dizzy.

The Grand Masters had named her Grand Chair Elect, studying under Skye, who was the Acting Grand Chair. The responsibilities were immense, but in her heart, Valerie knew that she wouldn't run from her new role, as tempting as complete freedom would be. Earth and the Globe were in a state of merry chaos now, and she wanted to be a part of helping to mold it into something stronger and better than it had been before.

Still, it was an intense relief when the prisoners were organized enough that Calibro and Sibyl could take over and she wouldn't have to split her attention between her duties at the Capitol and her role as the leader of the Fist.

"You're sure you don't need me to help with trials or anything?" Valerie asked the golden-haired Grand Master, who was consulting with Sibyl.

Calibro turned and gave Valerie a level stare. "The business of justice is not your area. My guild has handled these matters for centuries. The Justice Council has already tried eleven prisoners today. We'll have swift justice delivered to all within these walls."

Valerie ducked her head so that Calibro didn't see her smile. "Of course."

"I predict things will go smoothly," Sibyl said, a trace of a smile letting Valerie know she shared Valerie's amusement. "The other Oracles and I will travel between here and the Roaming City until the trials are complete."

"If you're sure you don't need me, then I'll leave you to your work, my friends," Valerie said.

"You may be called on to provide testimony in certain trials, but for now, I thank you for your service," Calibro said.

Dismissed, Valerie couldn't help giving first Sibyl and then the serious Calibro one quick hug before turning away.

ɕ   ɕ   ɕ

That night, long after Thai had fallen asleep, Valerie remained awake. It wasn't unusual for her to toss and turn these days. She remembered how Cyrus used to visit her in her dreams when she still lived on Earth, unaware that magic existed in the universe. He'd never abandoned her. But now, she couldn't find Cyrus anywhere, even in her dreams, and his absence created a vacuum in her that threatened to consume her if she let it.

Valerie involuntarily reached for Henry through their mental connection. He was in Elsinore with Kanti, who was getting a constitution in place that would replace the monarchy with an elected democracy. She and Henry wanted to return to Arden, Henry to continue his training at the

Empathy Guild, and Kanti to explore apprenticing at the Guardians of the Boundary.

Henry's peace flowed through their twin bond. It was comforting to know that he was happier than he ever thought he could be, and sometimes, she was glad that she had time to be alone with Thai. Other times, she missed him. Blood will call blood, and he was her only family.

She couldn't bring herself to disturb his peace by calling him or waking Thai, but she couldn't stay still. Quietly, she slipped on her jeans and left to visit Gideon in the Healers' Guild.

Since the night that he had almost awoken, there had been no change in his condition. She liked to sit by his bed and have one-sided conversations with him. She slipped down the quiet, dark halls of the Guild to Gideon's room.

She pushed open the door and immediately reached for her blade, but she wasn't carrying it. Stupid. Kellen was fluttering above Gideon's bed, dust drifting from his wings. The war would never be over.

Valerie's magic gushed through her. She jumped into the air and tackled Kellen to the ground in one smooth move. The fairy spluttered, trying to wrench himself from her grip, but she didn't budge.

"Stop—" Kellen tried to choke out, but Valerie didn't listen.

She was about to strip a piece of cloth from her T-shirt to gag him when she heard the soft rustle of Gideon's sheets.

"Perhaps we should let him explain himself," Gideon said, his voice hoarse.

Valerie dropped Kellen and whipped around to see her mentor sitting up in his bed. She tried to speak, but nothing except a strangled sound came out, so she hugged him instead.

When she pulled back, she saw that he was pale, but his eyes were alert.

Kellen dusted himself off. "I was using the light dust, which I hoped would drive away the last remnants of the dark dust within him."

Gideon was testing his limbs, and he winced as he attempted to stand.

Valerie was at his side in an instant, supporting him. "What's wrong?"

"Too many months of inactivity, I believe," Gideon said, gently pushing her aside to stand on his own.

Kellen fluttered close to Gideon's face, and Valerie fought the urge to swat him away. Kellen stared into his eyes and nodded after his examination was complete.

"The dark dust is gone," he said.

"Why are you helping now?" Valerie asked, making sure to angle herself between the fairy and Gideon.

Kellen reddened. "I was not myself when I attacked both of you. I admit that when Chern—Reaper—approached me three years ago, I was considering putting our guild's support behind his plan in return for a promise that we would have a central role when we returned to Earth. But after he kidnapped me, my mind was not entirely my own again until Dasan healed me. An excruciatingly painful process, rewiring my mind, if it comforts you."

It never comforted Valerie to imagine anyone in pain, but it also didn't sit right with her to think that Kellen would go on with his life like nothing had happened.

"So you go back to being Grand Master of the Knights?" she asked.

393

The fairy huffed. "You think Calibro would agree to that?"

"You're not in jail," she countered.

"I suggested my own punishment, and she and the Justice Council agreed to my terms. I will serve as Silva's groundskeeper for the next one hundred years."

Valerie swallowed, so that the emotion that rose in her wouldn't pool in her eyes. Kellen met her gaze, and she knew he'd chosen the same punishment her father had accepted many years ago to atone for his work with the Fractus as a way to make amends with her.

She cleared her throat. "That seems fair."

Kellen bowed his head, his usual bluster gone. "I hope to train with you both at our guild someday. My esteem for you is more than you can know, and I hope you may return some portion of it in time."

"You have already begun," Gideon said in his usual grave tone.

Valerie couldn't echo his words, but some piece of her was able to begin to forgive Kellen, and forgiveness sparked something within her that she didn't know had had been snuffed out. Peace.

ço   ço   ço

Nightingale made Gideon stay at the Healers' Guild for two more nights before he let Valerie take him home. When they stepped outside, her mentor took a deep breath of the fresh air.

"It was as though I fell asleep in a nightmare and awoke to a dream," he said. "I had faith you would prevail in time, but you exceeded all my hopes."

Valerie stood straighter at his words. It was something her dad might have said, and hearing it from Gideon was like having a piece of her father back.

She caught him looking around The Horseshoe. "As bad as it is now, it was even worse a few weeks ago."

The Architecture Guild was busy with repairs, and in spite of their rapid progress, much remained to be done. The Justice Guild was still in shambles, which was why Calibro and the rest of the Conjurors in her guild were working out of the magical prison that had been created in Dunsinane, but the Capitol Building was rebuilt, and even the crack in the stairs had been fixed.

"This cost is merely property," Gideon said. "It can be rebuilt."

"So can society, I hope," Valerie said.

Gideon glanced over at her in surprise and nodded once at her words. They began to walk down the steps of the Healers' Guild, and her breath caught when she saw the Society of Imaginary Friends building.

It had been rebuilt, and water flowed down all of the slides into the moat. The happy squeals of children filled the air as they splashed in the water. Former imaginary friends now brought their human charges to the Guild in person, and it was busier than ever.

She stepped on the path that led between the buildings on The Horseshoe, and it lit up beneath her feet. She stared down at it, and tears dripped down her face onto the glowing stones. Cyrus's spell had been disturbed during the worst of the fighting here, and no one had been sure if they could recreate the effect. Which lightweaver had managed it? She'd have to ask Dr. Freeman.

Gideon laid a hand on her shoulder, and she could have sworn that some of his strength flowed from him to her.

She wiped her cheeks when she saw Skye trotting toward her with Jack by his side. Skye's mane glowed with health. The centaur was enjoying the details of managing the rebuilding on the Globe, which baffled Valerie, who found the politics and minutiae excruciating.

Jack had become his right hand, managing his old gang as they took on the unending tasks of rebuilding Silva. Valerie could still see traces of his grief in the hollows beneath his eyes, but he didn't have the same desperate restlessness that made her fear for his life.

"Welcome back, Gideon," Skye said with a flick of his tail. "The waters of Illyria will be reopened today. Are you both coming to the Lake of Knowledge?"

"I'm taking Gideon home to rest," she said.

Gideon shook his head, and Valerie saw him hiding a smile. "I have been still for too long. I welcome the chance for movement."

"Sure the boss lady here will let you?" Jack teased, and Valerie gave him a surprised smile. It was the first joke she'd heard him make since Dulcea's death.

Valerie gave Jack a playful shove. "I may not be able to take Gideon in a fight, but I could still take you."

Skye and Gideon shook their heads as Valerie messed up Jack's hair, and he retaliated by jumping on her back.

"I'm not getting off till you take me where I need to go," he announced.

Valerie hauled him halfway through Silva, until he hopped off and returned to his daily tasks. Valerie continued to the Lake of Knowledge with Skye and Gideon. They found Elle impatiently pacing on the shores, splashing the water occasionally, as if she was testing it. On her third try, a smile flashed across her face. "At last!"

She raised her hands to dive into the water when someone pushed his way up through the surface. A drenched Will gave his sister a hug, and they gripped each other tightly.

"You look older," Will teased.

"You look the same," Elle said, punching him on the shoulder.

"What of the traitor, Gabriel?" Skye asked.

"Our people will send him above the waves for justice," Will reported. "Elle and I are tasked with escorting him to Calibro, since we're the only ones comfortable with being on the surface."

"I can't wait to drag him back to face his mortality," Elle said, her hands fisted at her sides. "It's about time Mom and Dad got some justice."

"There's something else," Will said, turning to Valerie. "I tried to find your mom, Valerie."

Gideon had been kneeling in the water, letting it run through his fingers as he examined it, but he froze at Will's words. Valerie's gaze snapped to Elle.

"I didn't want to get your hopes up, but the knowledge exists somewhere in the Akashic Records. All we have to do is find it," Elle said.

"Adelita lives?" Gideon's words were barely a whisper, and his eyes had a frantic, hopeful gleam.

"Reaper turned her to stone and hid her somewhere," Valerie explained, and then turned to Will. "Did you find where?"

"I couldn't find her location, but there was one strange piece of information that I unearthed. You and Henry have both seen her very recently."

"That can't be right. I think I'd remember seeing a stone statue of my mom," Valerie said, but then she fell to her knees. Through her connection, she knew that her brother grasped what she'd learned.

Gideon pulled her back up, and gripped her shoulders tightly. "What do you know?"

There was only one possibility. If she was right, then she could find her mother.

ço ço ço

Valerie waited with Gideon and Thai on the steps of the Society of Imaginary Friends for Henry to make his way to Arden. Gideon's usually endless patience had vanished, and he fastened and unfastened the sheath that was belted to his side. She thought he would drag her away to awaken her mother if she made him wait another minute longer.

But Valerie wasn't as eager. What if she was wrong, and the statue wasn't her mother? Or what if she couldn't awaken her, now that her vivicus powers only slept within her? The hope was so sweet, it was terrifying to imagine the void that would be left if she was wrong.

Henry and Kanti emerged from the newly restored entrance to Plymouth in the center of The Horseshoe. Gideon was already walking to meet them, and Valerie gripped Thai's hand and followed. Henry's nerves amplified her own as he jogged toward her.

"Whatever comes, we're going to find a happy ending for your mom," Thai said.

His dark eyes met hers, and a little of her fear eased.

"To Babylon?" Henry asked, and Valerie nodded.

It was a quiet walk through Arden's woods. Gideon walked a little ahead of them, occasionally stopping to wait for the rest of the group to catch up. When they stepped through the screen of vines, everything was quiet and still.

"She's behind the waterfall," Valerie said. "If it's her, I mean."

Even Gideon's steps had slowed now, so Valerie took the lead, first climbing the tiers overflowing with flowers, and then making her way carefully down to the cave behind the waterfall.

They filed in, and the muted light in the cave clearly illuminated that statue of the warrior reaching for the sword that wasn't in its sheath.

"You found her," Gideon said, gently touching the statue's face with his fingertips. Valerie saw tears in his eyes.

"She's reaching for Pathos," Valerie said. "She must have forgotten that she left it on Earth for us. When Reaper attacked, she was defenseless."

"Adelita is never defenseless," Gideon said. "She didn't win every battle, like she must have lost this one with Reaper, but she's lethal with nothing but her fists."

"Like her daughter," Kanti said, flashing Valerie a grin.

"I can sense her mind in there, like she's in a deep sleep," Henry said.

Valerie wiped her sweaty palms on her jeans. "I don't know for sure if I can wake her."

"Let's try," Thai said, and he laced his fingers with hers and let his power amplify her own.

She reached within herself for the ember of her vivicus power. Channeling it was like trying to light a fire with a wet match. She touched her mother and reached within herself, but her vivicus power wouldn't leap to her command.

Henry's mind touched hers, and his steady certainty that she could do this calmed her nerves. She reached again for her vivicus power, and it sparked. The spark was all that was needed to wake up her mother.

Stone melted into flesh, and Adelita sucked in a breath of air, like she'd been underwater for too long. Her mother was alive. Valerie's heart pounded in her chest, and her hands trembled. Henry's joy echoed her own through their mental connection. But neither of them stirred, as if a sudden movement might pop this dream like a bubble, and their mother would disappear.

Adelita's gaze was disoriented. What was it like, one moment to be facing Reaper and possible death, the next to be surrounded by a group of strange kids?

"Gid?" Adelita said when her eyes met Gideon's.

Gideon was crying now. She'd never seen her mentor's face so expressive. How much had grief numbed him? Who would he be now that Adelita was back?

Gideon hugged her. "You've been gone for eighteen years. We only found you now."

Valerie saw her mother scanning the group for the second time as the weight of Gideon's words sank in, and tears filled her eyes that she quickly blinked away. There were faces that should have been there, and her mother must know what it meant that they weren't. But her mother didn't say anything, and neither did Valerie. She and Henry would have to be enough.

"It'll be okay, Mom," Valerie said.

At her words, her mother's gaze settled on her and Henry, and her expression changed. Her eyes shone.

"My babies," she said, and she smiled. It lit up her whole face, and Valerie knew then why her dad had fallen in love with her so quickly. "I love you. And I'm so very grateful that you found me, so I can know you both."

Adelita crushed Valerie and Henry in her arms, and Valerie felt very small and safe as the biggest, most hopeless wish of her life came true.

Adelita pulled back, staring at both of them as if she couldn't look enough. "Now, tell me everything."

Epilogue

Chrome couldn't get used to the lack of space in Ming's crowded neighborhood, but that one complaint was a speck of dirt on a meaty bone. Guarding the human pup called to him like a full moon on a cloudless night.

Even now, when he was sitting by her feet while she ate dinner with her family, the restlessness in his heart was quiet. He hadn't thought it ever would be again. He listened to Ming chattering with her family about the new powers that everyone was trying to come to grips with.

"It's like I can sense the minds of everyone around me," Ming's mother said.

Ming was pouting, her bottom lip sticking out a little. "Everyone's got magic but me."

She was wrong. Chrome sent her an image of a flame bursting into a fire. It was hard to tell what was happening to his little charge, but the scent of the magic within her was unmistakable, and vaguely familiar.

After dinner, Chrome slipped outside for a run while Ming got ready for bed with her mother. When he returned, she was sleeping. He rested his front paws on her windowsill and watched her breathe until the sun came back over the horizon and Ming's eyes cracked open.

She grinned when she saw Chrome watching her. "Hi, puppy."

He sent her a vision of himself tackling her on the grass outside as playful punishment for her teasing, and was rewarded with her giggle.

She tumbled outside, and as promised, he tackled her. Shrieking with joy, she ran across the small lawn, and he let her get away, only to chase her again when her back was turned.

He surprised her, and Ming released a burst of magic, opening a portal to her bedroom. Chrome was so stunned that he stumbled, and they both went through.

The smell of her magic was unmistakable, like burning leaves in the forest. The last time he'd smelled that magic trail was when he'd followed Reaper. Ming had inherited the powers of his greatest enemy.

Ming was on her knees, eyes wide. "What happened?"

He'd heard of such a thing, of course. It wasn't uncommon when powerful Conjurors died that their powers were released into the universe and ignited in someone else.

"Chrome?" Ming's uncertainty came off her in waves as she gently patted his back. "Did I do something wrong?"

Chrome sent her a vision of a wolf pack surrounding a fire, hoping she understood that he was telling her that she was safe. Her face smoothed. No one had understood him as well as Ming since Jet.

He sent her an image of Azra, and the girl's eyes sparkled.

"Yes! Can we see Azra and Clarabelle? Now that Mom has met her, she says I'm allowed to see her any time I want to."

Clarabelle's scent was the only one that was easy for Chrome to detect through the cloud of magic hanging in the air, burning his nose like gunpowder since the battle two months ago. Clarabelle was in the woods of Arden. Chrome was thinking of the spot as Ming continued to stroke him, and another little burst of power came from her.

A portal opened, and through it he could make out the hazy image of two unicorns.

"I did that," she whispered, and Chrome nudged her with his nose so she could walk through.

You must be the guests Clarabelle said were coming today.

It was strange to see Azra now that she had no scent, having given her magic to her daughter. Chrome had to rely on his other senses to communicate with her, and it put him a little off-kilter.

Clarabelle was nuzzling Ming already, and the unicorn was pinging messages into the minds of everyone in the little grove. Ming could create portals, manipulate matter at a cellular level, defy laws of physics, like gravity, and even the laws of magic.

"I don't understand, what is she saying?" Ming asked.

Chrome's and Azra's eyes connected. Ming's magic had been awakened, and it was fully as powerful as Reaper's had ever been.

The magic that lives within you is awake. You are a powerful Conjuror now, little Ming.

"Me?" Ming's voice squeaked with glee. "Will I be able to help heal people, like Dr. Freeman? Or protect people, like Valerie?"

You can do both, and more. We look forward to seeing what you will do with this magic of yours.

Ming began dancing around the grove, and Clarabelle frolicked with her.

Azra's next message was to his mind alone. *The power is the same as Reaper's, but it is hers to wield, and I think it is in good hands.*

Chrome did, too. In his own mind, a vision unfurled of running through the open grasses he had been raised in as a pup, and he knew that his adventure, which he thought was winding to a close, had only begun now, at Ming's side.

THE END

Acknowledgements

It wasn't only me who spent many hours bringing this series to life. I am lucky to have incredible support from my friends and family, and this series would be a sorry sight indeed without their love and expertise.

My books are so much stronger thanks to my editor, Shelley Holloway, who helped me take my prose to the next level. Glendon Haddix of Streetlight Graphics designed my covers, and managed to capture the spirit of each book with more artistry than I could ever dream up.

A big thank you to my beta readers, who are skilled editors with a keen eye for detail. Ladonna Watkins, Theppong Sae-Low, and Kathy Schmidt, all of your input has been invaluable.

To my brothers, Keith and Davey, thank you for your advice and cheerleading. I never would have begun my self-publishing journey if Keith hadn't urged me to.

Dad, your big picture advice has changed the way I think about writing. You keep my cup half full.

Mom, your unconditional love has made me who I am, and I know that any other kid who says they have the best mom in the world hasn't met mine. I love you.

My husband, Tom, has tolerated many nights of rambling about plot points, and made me laugh even through my first 3-star review. Knowing someone as smart in you believes in my series me helps me believe in it myself.

Last, my sister Cheryl has been my biggest fan. I am so grateful for your moral support, brilliant mind, and the many hours you put into reading, editing, and providing feedback on everything from cover art to website copy to blurbs. You inspire me.

There are many more friends and fans who have read my stories and provided their encouragement and insight, and each of you has touched my life and writing.

Thank you to all of you! I am blessed to have you in my life, and so grateful for your years of help, encouragement and love.

Afterword

Thank you for reading *Edge of Pathos*. I appreciate feedback and welcome your reviews on the site where you purchased this book. If you'd like to learn more about *The Conjurors Series*, please check out www.kristenpham.com, where you can sign up for my newsletter and be the first to hear about giveaways, contests, and new releases.

About the Author

Kristen Pham lives for really great fudge, rollercoasters, and exploring new worlds via fiction. She lives in San Jose, CA with her family, where she eagerly waits for her kids to turn eleven and receive their invitations to Hogwarts. Her childhood memories of adventures with her imaginary friends inspired *The Conjurors Series*.

You can reach her on Twitter (www.twitter.com/theconjurors), Facebook, and her website (www.kristenpham.com).